Deep Blue Saloon

A Novel

Thomas Courtney Click

ISBN: 0692459286

ISBN 13:9780692459287

Library of Congress Control Number: 2015908838

Dastardly Books

Santa Fe, New Mexico

For German – For Pamela – For Ralph
Thank you JM, MW, JP, from the beginning.
Thank you KD for your creative insight on this 2nd edition.

They call it rapture of the deep. Be you not afraid,
You're too far down by now to be scared.
Two hundred eighty-seven feet,
I saw Jesus, and it made sense that he was there.
Stephen Stills

Chapter One

Branch

It was only in the Deep Blue Saloon that Branch Kilgore felt good. But right at the moment—three o'clock in the morning—he was picking the lock on the door of Caribbean Argonauts Dive Shop, and he felt lousy about it.

He shrugged off the lousy feeling. If everything went right, he'd have Victor's boat back before anyone noticed. Locking the door behind him, he slipped into the darkness of the shop, grabbed his gear and carried it out to the skiff. Then he untied the little inflatable, pushed off from the dock, and rowed quietly away.

Once he was out in the empty cruise ship lanes, he fired up the outboard motor and crossed the flat waters between Chinchamos, a large limestone island several miles off Mexico's Caribbean coast, and the mainland. Then he skirted the shoreline and made his way into the swampy channels that permeated the shore. The morning light over the open sea was blushing behind him, reflecting off the channels and illuminating the mangroves with a rosy tint.

Branch hid the little boat, slung his scuba unit over his shoulder then sloshed off into the mangroves until he came to a narrow, round opening in the jungle floor. The Manhole, he called it, a secret access point to the watery caves that meandered below. He tied a length of rope to a stout sandbox tree and tossed the line down into the abyss. With his gear in place and his waterproof tool bag strapped to his side, he looked down into the darkness and felt the cool subterranean air gusting against his face. He jumped.

He dropped through a ten-foot air pocket, splashed into the hidden underground river, then quickly descended into the cold, fresh water. After orienting himself, he tied the loose end of the rope to a boulder and finned away into the blackness of the cave. He switched on his light, admiring the long shadows that flickered behind the ancient stalactites.

Branch looked at the solid stone ceiling over his head. He felt safe and hidden, but then the thought of the job waiting at the end of this commute pressed on him and he heard the tiny whispers of panic. He ignored them and continued his journey.

He hovered around giant boulders that cluttered the passage, past the dark openings to his left that led into the really deep passages, the caves that snaked inland before flowing back out to the ocean. Those passages beckoned him. He felt the urge to ditch the job and just kick down into their tranquil depths. But all habits had to be paid for, and today he was working. So he glided on past and continued in the shallow chamber until he came to a metal gate held shut by an oversized padlock.

A sign on the gate showed a ghastly illustration of a skull and crossbones, with a message printed in large bold letters below it: "Prevent Your Death—Go No Farther."

Branch smiled at the sign. He couldn't prevent it, but he would sure try to delay it. He took a small shaped charge from his tool bag, zip-tied it to the lock, pressed the timer and then scooted back on his fins several yards. There was a flash of white light, and then a metallic twang ricocheted through the chamber. Silt from the bottom filled the tunnel with a milky fog, and Branch nestled motionless on the floor for a few moments, waiting for the silt to settle.

Lying in the murk, Branch again felt the ripples of panic. If the silt never settled, he was blind, he was stuck, he was dead in there. But the laws of physics demanded that the silt would settle, as long as he stayed still. Anyway, he'd made a deal with panic long ago.

When the water cleared, he pushed the gate open and hovered past the warning of the gawking skull into a narrow shaft. He glided another three hundred feet, then ascended into a vertical tube. A tiny point of light appeared above him. Flicking his fins, he floated up, as the pinhole of light gradually expanded into a blue sphere. He merged with the sphere, out of the cave, and then was born into the dim light of a small cenote, a jungle pond that lay within the grounds of a gated villa.

Like a crocodile at the bottom of the cenote, Branch lay silent, scanning the morning sky above him. He watched the spiral leaves of gumbo trees through the prism of the clear water and he waited. Tiny freshwater cichlids darted around him, nibbling on little plants growing in the shallows, but nothing else moved. Branch checked his console and watch. He hovered to the surface, and then, without a splash, he was out of the water.

All was quiet. He slipped out of his gear, secured it to some overhanging branches and crept over the bank onto the landscaped grounds. His underwater journey had been less than a mile, but it might as well have been a trip to another galaxy because it had landed him in forbidden territory—a complex of gated, highly secured estates owned by members of a Mexican drug cartel. They were aware of these caves, had used them as escape routes years ago, but Branch guessed they hadn't been using them lately. They'd become too successful, and too fat, he figured, and the only escape routes they used now were in their bulletproof SUVs.

Branch waited on the grass, taking a breath of the heavy jungle air and a moment to size up the massive stone villa. He could've done this job with a rifle, maybe not as cleanly as Carlsbad could've, but the job would be done. But he loathed using a rifle.

In his navy training—before he was kicked out—he'd been paired with Carlsbad, and Carlsbad was everything the navy wanted from a killer. Professional, unsympathetic, dispassionate for life, able to take commands, and a crack shot. Carlsbad could've done this job from a thousand meters, but that was Carlsbad, and Carlsbad had something that Branch didn't have. But then, Branch had something Carlsbad didn't have, something that no navy sniper was allowed to have. Something the navy didn't want. And that's what had brought Branch to Chinchamos. To do these dirty little jobs that no one else would do. But now he was tired of doing them.

Stone steps curved up through an arched trellis of orange flowers, past hand-carved stone columns, and then Branch was crouching on the villa's marbled terrace. The information he had was that a redheaded man, whose picture he'd studied, would be sleeping alone in the villa. Branch took his lock pick from the tool bag, opened the terrace door, and slipped in.

Inside the home, still dark in the early morning hours, there was the fragrance of a lifestyle Branch had once known. He stopped for a moment to breathe it in and remember. The fragrance was of Cuban cigars, of cream, of expensive bourbon. Fruits and flowers, patchouli. Money. Cocaine. He thought of Melanie, and he smiled at the thought of how impressed she'd be with it all. Then he thought of how trapped he was by Mel's own luxuries. His smile faded and he focused again. There was only the job to do. He couldn't think of her now. He made his way toward the master suite.

He swung the massive teak door open and saw red hair and the huddled shape in the bed beneath an ornate carved wooden headboard. The information was correct: The man was alone. Branch sat on the bed next to the shape, looked at his watch and waited.

The man was too startled to speak, but he kicked at the fine woven linens at the foot of the bed. Branch pushed down hard on the redheaded man's chest with his elbow.

"Omar sent me here to give you a gift," he said calmly, and with his free hand he dangled the gift in front of him.

The tiny souvenir—a plastic dolphin hanging from a silver chain—was one of the cheap baubles from Omar's Swim With the Dolphins Park on Chinchamos. Worth about ten cents, Branch figured, but Omar got twenty-five bucks for them from the cruise ship passengers who'd already paid more than a hundred to swim around in a pen with captive dolphins.

The redhead squirmed, mumbled, and looked up at the plastic dolphin with clouded brown eyes.

"You hear me? It's from Omar."

The man nodded. In one quick motion, Branch took a pillow and pressed down hard over the man's face. He watched as his arms and legs flailed against the silk linens.

Branch pushed down harder on the pillow and fought off the sickness. He tried to remind himself that he was doing the redhead a favor. He'd obviously lived a good life, a strong life. And now he'd been given a break—a clean, quick death in his own bed. If the redhead lived much longer, Branch knew, his life wouldn't be so good, so strong. So he pressed down harder on the pillow and tried to ignore the sickness.

When it was done, he put the pillow back in place, tidied up the blankets and draped the dolphin pendant around the man's neck. Then he took the digital camera from his waterproof pouch, snapped a picture and backed out of the bedroom.

The blue light of the morning filtered through the trees and into the home, and Branch found himself in the living room, decorated with a combination of modern art, ancient Roman statues, and Mayan wood carvings. The motif was a bit scattered, he thought, but the guy had good taste.

Branch ventured into the den. A bookcase made of thick cedar shelves bulged with first-edition collectibles and books on reef coral and fish identification. A framed photo on the wall showed the man with his arms around two other redheads, probably a brother and a son, Branch figured, and then he felt really lousy. He knew he should be getting the hell out, but he lingered, looking for anything that might help him justify the horrible thing he'd done. He wandered into the kitchen and opened the fridge—clean shelves holding fruits and vegetables, bagels, and beer. He peered into the spacious garage. Rather than the large SUVs and luxury sedans he expected, there were two small vehicles—a Nissan Leaf and a Toyota Prius—parked alongside a collection of bicycles and sporting equipment.

He closed the door to the garage and walked back into the den. A heavy wooden armoire housed a stack of audiophile stereo components, and on the turntable rested a vinyl LP—Burl Ives, *The Vegas Years*. Branch opened the drawer underneath. Bundles of US hundreds were neatly stacked inside. He picked up a bundle, flipped through the bills, and shook his head. It would go a long way toward getting him away from the life. But he wasn't a thief, and it wasn't what he was being paid to do.

So, he put the money back and closed the drawer. He slipped out the terrace door and made his way down the stone steps, hoping for a quiet retreat through the underwater cave. But then a radio squawked and a burst of automatic weapon fire sent leaves tumbling around his shoulders. He took his M9 sidearm from his pouch and sprinted for the cenote.

As he flung himself over a hedge, another burst fractured the air and Branch felt the hot rush of a bullet hissing by his face. He knelt behind the bushes and scanned the estate for any sign of his pursuer, the M9 at his ready. But he saw nothing, so he ran for the pond.

Shots rang out wildly through the trees, but not close enough that he'd need to abandon his underwater escape. Entering the water silently, he slid into his unit and fins, then kicked down, and down, annoyed that he'd raised a bit of silt, but welcoming the shadows and the darkness and the cave that would take him to the Manhole and the boat and then home.

Stroking fiercely down the tube, the pressure built in Branch's ears and behind his mask. And then there was the familiar numbness of the nitrogen, already countering the adrenaline from his escape and the nausea from the job.

At the bottom of the tube he glided out into the shaft that would take him back toward the Manhole, and then it was one hundred ... two hundred ... three hundred feet into the system before he took a moment to calm himself. He noted the pristine, watery silence and its stark contrast to the metallic violence he'd felt at the villa. Descending into a cave dive while being shot at was not the preferred method. But it was not so different from the work he'd done for much of his life.

He kicked through the fractured metal gate, into the main chamber, and back on top of his lines to the artery to the tight boulder pass. Hovering through the stalactite area, only a few hundred feet now from his exit, he began to feel relief that this job was done, and that he was one step closer to leaving the life.

Branch surfaced into the air pocket some thirty feet from the Manhole. What he saw there put an abrupt end to his retirement dreams. The rope—the climbing rope—had yanked loose from the boulder and slithered like a snake toward the surface. He watched in disbelief as the end of it rose up into the air pocket and then disappeared over the edge of the jungle floor.

Chapter Two

The Current

Omar Rasgado gazed out the rear passenger window of the white Land Rover as it rumbled away from his mansion in Chinchamos North Country Club. He tapped nervously on the leather upholstery as the vehicle passed several "For Sale—Price Reduced!" signs, all posted neatly in front of lavish, empty villas that lined the greens and fairways of Chinchamos's newest oceanfront golf course. As the Land Rover left the country club, Omar looked at the large sign posted outside the ornate metal gates, his stiff black beard scratching his puffy lips as he mouthed the words to himself: Rasgado Estates, Fairway and Beachfront Homes, $900K to 9 million USD.

"Got any paint, Dorian? Better get out and change the nines to sixes, no?"

The burly bodyguard driver behind the wheel glanced into the rearview mirror, started to speak, then just grunted in agreement.

"The fucking redheads," Omar continued. "And now the bank. Fucking ocean views, too, right on the fairway."

The passenger in the front seat turned around and grinned at him, a white cowboy hat pulled down close over his tan, wrinkled face. "I tell you what, I'd buy one from you if I could, Mr. Rasgado. Maybe I can use my first paycheck as a down payment?"

"Cash only, Len," Omar told him. "Not your style, no? No double-wides. You just do your job on the pier. You do it right."

The cowboy's grin faded. "You can bet I will. What about your jewelry store, though? Gonzago told me you're makin' damn good money with it."

"The money goes fast."

"Overheads, huh?"

"*Policía*. Boats. War. And now you, too, no?"

"Yes, sir," Len said. He pushed his hat down farther on his head and turned back around to face the road. As they merged with the early morning traffic on Ocean Road, he saw it was all taxis and beer trucks.

A swarm of taxis passed the Land Rover, and Omar tapped harder on the leather armrest. The taxis were in a rush to line up at the municipal pier for the day's cruise ship passengers, all of them disembarking with pockets full of cash to spend on the island. Except for the ones who made it into his jewelry store, he wouldn't be seeing any of that money. His nostrils flared again in frustration. As he looked out at the turquoise waters of the Chinchamos channel, he could see the first of the day's ships—the *D'Allure of the Seas*—smoking in.

"Frenchies, they coming in on the *Allure*," he said to Dorian and Len. "Plenty of money, no? Four ships come today."

Omar's cell phone buzzed, disrupting his vexation as he looked at the incoming call. He'd been avoiding the call for some days, but he relented and answered.

"Hola, Gonzago," Omar said into the phone, rasping and nervously petting his close-cropped black hair. "You back in Houston, no?"

"I *am* back," came Gonzago's smooth voice. "Back from an art buying trip. India. Tell me something good."

"Your guy got in last night," Omar said. Len turned around and grinned at him once more.

"Len's got a ton of experience in underwater demolitions," Gonzago said. "Among other things. But he's not cheap. Get him started right away."

"We start the blasting already," Omar replied into the phone. "With Len here, we get the piers up above the waterline in a hurry."

"And the mangroves at Paradise Reef?"

"*Tranquilo,*" Omar said. A slight edge of contempt slipped out and he was immediately sorry for it. He had to keep Gonzago happy, at least for now. "Fucking worthless mangroves, no? The limey bitch, Pamela," he said, pronouncing it like *Pam-Ella.*

"That's a lot of money I sent you, Omar. Time to close the deal."

"She want to sit there in the hotel and look out on the swamp. We get her for one but maybe we up it to two, no? Then we send her back to London or Finland or wherever she come from. In a year we take the cash from every *crucero* that board a ship from Aruba to Miami. They come here for the *paraíso,* we take the cash."

There was only silence on the other end of the line and Omar worried why his sales pitch didn't receive the usual exuberance from Gonzago. All of the cruise lines wanted to stop in Chinchamos, a natural deepwater port with virtually no environmental or maritime restrictions, but there were no piers big enough to dock a cruise ship. And when the passengers were ferried in from the ships to the island, they disembarked on the municipal pier and all of their money scattered like smoke in the ocean breeze.

But with the new pier—Omar's gigantic cruise ship pier—each and every cruiser would be forced to pay him an entry tax. And then they'd be funneled right into his new mall and he'd have first shot at a piece of everything they bought, from trinkets to tacos to taxi rides. And with the ships bringing in more than two thousand passengers each trip, and with more than fifteen ships stopping each week, he'd be raking in around three million a week from the entry tax alone. He could live on that. And he would settle up with Gonzago, one way or the other, when the time came.

"The pier's useless to us without that shoreline, Omar," Gonzago told him. "A fine thing, owning a pier with no place to unload the passengers. No place to take their money. And all of my ten million just pouring into the sea."

"*Tranquilo,*" Omar said again. "Big payday coming for Pamela. Then we get ours, no?"

"And what about the other problem? Branch helped you out with that thing on the mainland?"

"*No se*," Omar said. He looked out across the channel. "The fucking redhead, he pinch off the coca flow. He back the protestors. They tweet about another protest today. That shit cost me plenty when I open the dolphin park last month."

"Branch is good. I'm guessing your redheaded adversary won't continue to engage in his nonprofit behavior. I never understood that sort of thing."

"Still early, no? Branch, he check in with me at the restaurant, later today."

"I didn't tell you this earlier, but Branch and Len are related," Gonzago said. "I've been working with this family for years. Len's the daddy. Branch won't be happy about a reunion."

Omar looked again at Len in the front seat. "The apple, it fall far from the tree, no?"

"That apple got eaten by a bear and shit out five miles up the mountain."

"No worries, Gonzago. We all get along."

"When you get to the restaurant, tell Yvonne I'll be flying in next week. Can't get any decent Italian in Houston at all. Have some good news for me."

Omar pressed the button and threw the phone down. "Skip the jewelry store, Dorian," he told the driver. "Call Sheriff Fibbi. We go straight to the pier, no?"

They passed the municipal dock where a mile of yellow taxis had queued up on the side of the road, waiting for the little ferries to bring in passengers from the *Allure*. Omar smiled, his dark, inflamed nostrils twitched, and the calculator in his head clicked off the money he'd be making when his new cruise ship pier was operational.

"Put on the *música*," Omar told Dorian as the white Land Rover trolled down Ocean Road.

"Yes, Uncle Omar."

"You like the *música*, Len?"

"Only Mexican song I know is 'Guantanamera.'"

"That's Cuban," Omar said, laughing, then firing up a cigarette and pushing the button to lower the power window. "But we get that one on for you later."

Heavy ocean air and exhaust from the cruise ship swirled in, cigarette smoke swirled out, and thunderous bass from the subwoofers blasted. Omar noted that the sun was well up now. That thing on the mainland should have happened already, he knew, it must have, and his smile broadened. The bastard redhead wouldn't be protesting today.

"If ya hangin' around, ya change your mind," Omar crooned along with the song, and Dorian gave him an amused glance in the rearview mirror. "It's a bad influence, but yo! It's my rhyme."

Two miles farther down the oceanfront the Land Rover cruised by a long, low-slung building, its facade adorned with giant plaster seashells. A huge neon sign hanging over the wide glass doors spelled out that this was Omar's Swim With the Dolphins Park. Looking behind the building, Omar could see the perimeter of the chain-link fence that rose out of the sea. A dolphin jumped along the edge of the fence, its dorsal fin glistening silver in the sun as it splashed back down inside its pen.

A few taxis were dropping off cruisers already, and Omar smiled. The money he was making on the dolphin park wasn't dope money, but along with the jewelry store and the taxi protection cash, it would keep things going until the new pier was operational.

As they drove southward, Omar looked to his left at the wild, low-growth mangroves that skirted the shoreline. A channel poured out of the mangroves and flowed through a large conduit under the road and out into the ocean. He looked to his right where the fresh water from the mangroves met the warm, salty sea, turning brown, then orange, then yellow, and finally a deep blue where it flowed out toward the stretch of coral reef known as Paradise Deep.

"Ugly water, no?" Omar said to Len, and now he was scowling. "Murky water from the swamp? *Muy feo.*"

The Land Rover pulled up at the new pier site at Paradise Shallows. Orange mesh fences blocked the beach, warning buoys and ropes bobbed in the water, and a construction crane towered over it all from a floating platform that was anchored into the seabed.

"Looks like a real nice setup, Mr. Rasgado," Len said, causing Omar to smile again. But his smile faded as he surveyed the throng of protestors marching on the beach outside the mesh fence, holding signs and chanting.

"Stop Reef Destruction" and "Hell No I'm Not With the Cruise Ships," two of the signs read. "Don't Pave Paradise," read another. A tall Mexican man with curly gray-brown hair, wearing a shorty wetsuit, carried a sign that stated, "Cruise Ships Slime the Earth."

"That Victor motherfucker, he here," Omar cursed from the back seat, but he was pleased to see that none of the redhead's contingent was present. "I offer him a job, manage the water sports when my pier go in. But look at him prance out there."

"I'd be happy to help you out, Mr. Rasgado," Len said, his voice twanging from the front seat. "I got some experience dealing with this type of boy. I'll kick his ass right off the beach. Then I'll get your pier built for you."

"I pay my *policía* to do that, to kick the ass. They coming already. Dorian, turn on the celly jammer. The fucking social media, they killing me. You and Len get all the cameras and phones. I go talk to the old lady."

Pamela Linton stood on the beach next to Victor. Her bleached white hair reflected the morning sun, and her blue-gray eyes, set deep in her pale, wrinkled face, sparkled behind wire-rimmed spectacles. "Stop the environmental debacle now," she spoke into a megaphone, in a stiff Sussex accent. "Stop destroying Paradise Reef!"

Dorian rolled out of the front seat and walked around to the sidewalk, veins bulging in his swollen forearms as he opened the rear door. Omar flicked his cigarette butt onto the street, squashing it with his crocodile-skin shoe as he stepped from the back seat of the Land Rover.

Through the open door the stereo blasted, "It's dirty and it's stinkin'. It's dirty and it's stinkin', baby. It's dirty and it's stinkin', yes!"

"Million dollars," Omar told Pamela, an hour later. He was standing with her in the lobby of The Blue Angel Inn, after Sheriff Fibbi and the deputies had busted up the protest on the beach. "For the mangroves. You keep the hotel. Pretty big money. Then you make *big* money off the *cruceros*, no?"

"You really should have done your homework before you started building," Pamela said firmly. "My mangroves are not for sale. So if you build it, I'm afraid you'll have to snatch your pier out of Paradise Shallows and move it somewhere else."

Omar smacked his dry lips.

"Feeling the pressure, are you?" she asked.

"We go out. We take a look at your swamp land."

They walked out the hotel's side door and down the rocky path that led to the edge of the mangroves. "Worthless swamp," Omar said, lighting another cigarette. He pointed to the mangroves and blew out a burst of smoke. "We dredge it, we dry it up, we build the mall. To unload the *cruceros*. A new golf course. You like golf. You English, no? People stay at your hotel, play golf. Good business."

"Oh, yes. I know my business. And I know a little about yours. It's controlling the current that pushes the cruise ship passengers all the way along the waterfront and into your gem shops. It's somewhat like the current that whisks divers along the offshore reefs. Where the current flows, the coral prospers. Where the current falters, the coral dies. The same is true topside, Omar. If you control the flow of cruisers, you control Chinchamos. But I'm here to tell you, you won't control *this* part of it."

"No? Good money, Pamela. Big money."

"Turtles and birds and crocodiles live in there. Manatees, too. It's their home."
Pamela pointed her frail, blue-veined hand toward the canopy of manchineel trees
rising up out of the gray water. "Look, there's one now."

Omar, a dull expression on his face, looked out at the dark shape that floated
just below the surface.

"I can't tell if that's Emmitt or if that's Dixie taking their morning nap," she
said. "So you see, Omar, even if these mangroves weren't so vital to the health of
the reefs, I couldn't possibly sell. For sentimental reasons. These are my pets."

"Pets?" Omar asked, anger flashing across his face. He pulled a chromed revolver from his jacket and blasted a shot into the water, narrowly missing the
impassive manatee.

"Not pets," Omar said, grinning at Pamela as she fell back in horror. "Hazards.
They get in the canals, they fucking get hit by the boats. I got a permit say I kill
your pets."

As he fired again casually toward the manatee, Dorian came sprinting across
the street. A portly man in a tan sheriff's uniform lumbered along behind him.
"Dorian! Sheriff Fibbi!" Omar yelled at them. "We get started. We clean up the
swamp, now!"

Fibbi pulled his revolver and joined Omar in firing into the mangroves while
Dorian watched. Gray water splashed as bullets drilled down below the surface of
the swamp.

"Stop shooting!" Pam screamed, but Omar and Fibbi blasted away into the
water until their guns were empty.

"We work now. On the pier," Omar said, and he pushed his gun back into
his jacket. Smoke floated across the water, and the comfortable, familiar scent of
gunpowder made him smile. The dead manatee floated on the surface, and the
gray-green water of the mangrove channel was turning red as it flowed under the
road toward the sea.

"Oh, my poor Dixie!"

"Poor Dixie," Omar said, and then he laughed. "And the current you speaking of? It flows my way now, and it gets stronger. You no can stop it, no?"

Chapter Three

Deep Blue Saloon

The rope dropped into the water and slithered back down to the silty floor. Someone was waiting outside the Manhole. Might just be some kids, Branch thought. Or some divers. But he knew better.

The relief from finishing the job reverted to nausea. He could wait in the air pocket for a few hours, but he was cold, and they'd be coming in to look for him soon.

Branch descended and crawled along the bottom until he was directly underneath the Manhole. He looked up at the magnified, distorted shapes of two men—one of them was a redhead, he thought—standing on the edge, peering down at the water, seeing only their own reflections.

He could stay and fight, or he could return to the deep chambers behind him. That would be a long kick through the cold. If he made all the right turns, he'd end up in the warm, salty shallows and then the ocean—if he had enough air to make it.

Branch closed his eyes and visualized the first option: He pulls his M9, presses his fins into the silt below him and bursts to the surface. Two metallic snaps from his gun, and he plunges back to the bottom. Two big splashes on the surface above him, the water all bloody around him. And then the sickness comes again.

Moving on quickly to option two, he glanced at his console and figured he could make it. So he left his M9 where it was, descended without a sound, and swam away into the watery darkness.

Finning through the boulder pass, Branch turned left and kicked into the tunnel. He followed the cave down and down, and then the pressure was crushing him, pleasantly, and the air from the tank was thick and sweet in his lungs. And in an instant he no longer felt lousy—about what he'd done back at the villa, about what he'd done with his life—and he wasn't afraid of dying. Because with every breath now he was closer to that place where he could be alive *and* dead at the same time. He allowed the narcosis to come over him, and then he could almost hear a piano plinking out some sweet turtle-jazz music. His regulator squealed at the depth, but to Branch it was just the singing of some aquatic vocalist on stage in a dark and dingy bar. The bar he knew as the Deep Blue Saloon.

Open mic night, he guessed. Maybe one day he'd work up his own act. He drifted along, his regret going up with his bubbles, and then at three hundred feet below sea level he hallucinated the watery outline of a girl, wearing a blue one-piece woven from the silkiest sargasso.

"Hi, Branch," he could almost hear the girl say to him, and as she leaned forward, her cleavage bulged out of its watery costume. "Haven't seen you in a while. The usual?"

His name sounded strange to him. For a moment, he'd forgotten it, was hopeful others had forgotten it, too. He had some important business up above, but the awful urgency was replaced by foggy numbness. "Got to get, to go—"

"To go where, Branch?" he could almost hear the girl ask, and then she was whisking a silver platter in front of him, tempting him with shimmering highballs of amber analgesia. Branch felt himself pouring a glass of the tonic down his throat, and then quickly he was so intoxicated he'd forgotten all about the villa.

"There's nothing for you up there, Branch. Stay with me. There is surely nothing more than the single purpose of the present moment. You're always rushing off, rushing away, up there," the girl almost pleaded, nodding upward.

Branch looked up at the limestone ceiling. The stalactites looked like some intricate, sparkling chandelier. "Pretty lights," he said to someone, almost, and he struggled to remember what business was above, like a dream he had just awoken from.

He poured down another drink and wondered which was the dream? Here, with this almost-waitress? Or up there? And whatever was waiting for him?

"Got to get going," he said. "Got an appointment. Up there. Just not sure what it is."

The girl quieted his excuses with more shots of the almost-tonic, and then she told him, "You should stay. Who knows? You might even see a Maltese bikini fish!"

This was both encouraging and hilarious to Branch. He smiled, and with the smile he found the regulator in his mouth to be a nuisance. Why should he be bothered with such a thing? He wanted to spit it out, and then at last his life would have meaning. He'd spend what was left of it researching the mating habits of the Maltese bikini fish. A real job at last. It was all he'd ever wanted.

Branch's dive console beeped and buzzed at him, informing him that both drowning and decompression sickness were imminent. He tried to look at the console but the girl held his gaze with her beautiful green eyes and her bright smile.

"Got to find the pay phone," he said, and as he did, he forced himself to look at the dive computer. The digits and lights gave no meaning. He was too nitrogen-stoned to understand them, but he was dazzled by their backlit, fluorescent beauty. He floated off, heard the girl telling him almost-goodbye, and then the tunnel began its ascent. The bleached bones of a hawksbill turtle lay on the floor of the tunnel, and then he wondered if, like the turtle, he'd lingered too long below.

The water warmed as the cave turned toward the sea. Fresh and salt water mingled in a halocline, a transparent liquid fog. Branch flew into the fog, felt safe there.

A twinkle of light ahead became a blurry patch and then it became the ocean. He exited the cave at a depth of about two fifty, alongside a sheer wall of orange-yellow coral. A turtle gliding by looked at Branch with annoyance then flapped away.

The wall of reef spelled out glowing hieroglyphics, and as he drifted upward, he imagined he was floating by an ancient, submerged Egyptian ruin. Swarming white-tip sharks were below him, layers of jacks were above, and masses of barracudas circled around him.

Too low on gas to stay down and decompress, but remembering now the danger that waited at the surface, Branch topped the coral wall and crawled along the sand as it sloped up to the shore. As he ascended, memories of the job came and memories of his time in the Deep Blue Saloon faded. *What the hell is a Maltese bikini fish? Ain't no such thing.* It had *almost* been all right. He squeezed every last breath out of the tank and surfaced on empty just outside the mangroves on the mainland coast.

His GPS indicated he was north of the boat. He sloshed drunkenly along, found the skiff and threw himself in. Blinded and squeezed by the nitrogen bubbles in his blood, he roared without caution from the channel. Then he headed due east toward the southern tip of Chinchamos and twisted the throttle full bore.

The sun was well up and he was hours late. He looked back at the mainland, plenty worried they'd be coming after him, and then he could see the skiff's distinct, dark shadow chasing him on the sandy bottom of the clear water. *What kind of fish was that again?* The abrupt shift from *that*, his time down deep, to *this*, what'd happened at the villa, staggered him. And he knew no one had forgotten his name.

He could see dive boats heading south from the Chinchamos port to the deep reefs, and on the northern horizon there was a plume of dark smoke from an approaching cruise ship. It was too late to go back to the dive shop. Victor would be pissed and he'd have to explain himself, but there was no choice. He'd have to beat the dive boats around the point and lay up on the beaches of the windward side.

Then he was on Chinchamos's wild side shore, sprawled on the beach at the edge of the jungle. The nitrogen bubbles were hurting his body and he knew he was bent. If he could just get enough money stashed, he promised himself, no more of this. And then he thought about that girl, down in the depths. She was right out there, almost waiting for him beneath the waves.

The dizziness from the decompression sickness subsided a little, so he left the boat and the scuba unit stashed in the mangroves, walked to the blacktop road and hitched a ride on a beer truck that had just made a delivery to the Iguana Rio beach bar. On the ride back to the leeward shore he analyzed the morning as he sobered up, finding no flaw in his planning. There had been no figuring they'd know about the Manhole. It had been a bad break. And one man by himself couldn't plan for every bad break.

Chapter Four

The Familiar Curves and Unique Proportions You Desire

M elanie Lamy pushed aside her crossword puzzle and looked out the window of Diamonds de la Caribe jewelry store as passengers from the day's first cruise ship, the *Great Sea Truth*, began to swarm on the sidewalk, shopping for T-shirts, trinkets, baubles, and bottles. She hoped some of them would be buying jewelry, too.

"OK, then, Mel," Fernando said, standing beside her and gazing out the window. "How about this one? The *Great Sea Truth*?"

Melanie looked out at the huge cruise ship anchored in the channel. Her clever crossword mind worked quickly, jumbling and rearranging the letters on the side of the ship without effort.

"*Huge Rat Treats*," she said, and then Fernando laughed, showing his crooked yellow teeth.

"That's perfect," he said. "The dessert buffet, get it? How do you do that? You should go on a game show or something."

Melanie laughed with him but she was worried. Things had been slow and she had to have a sale today, of one kind or the other. She remembered her time in New York, and she wished she could go back there. Seven hundred bucks an hour, and on a Monday, she could have them lined up all day long if she'd wanted. Which she never did.

"And that one?" Fernando asked, pointing to another cruise ship smoking into view. "Is that a new one? Give your answer in the form of a question."

"Hmm. What is 'A French liner that doesn't make port here very often'? *D'Allure of the Seas.*"

She closed her eyes for a moment, her mind did its trick, the letters rearranged, and she stifled a giggle.

"*Le Fat Rude Asshole.*"

"Good one! Fat and rude, no problem, as long as they buy diamonds. Two other ships coming."

Out in the channel another column of black exhaust rose up from a smokestack.

"That's *Icon of the Seas,*" Fernando said. "Biggest ship in the world. All kinds of all-you-can-eat buffets. Lots of water slides and rides on deck."

"Water slides. Buffets. How wonderful. *Fat Noises Echo.*"

"Could be a big day."

"Haven't had a big day in weeks," Melanie said. "At least *you* get a salary. I'm commission only. I'm not making it."

She watched a group of cruisers from the *Great Sea Truth* waddle by on the sidewalk. "Some kind of great truth out there. Potbellies, short pants, knee-high socks and sandals. The only great truth I see is that cruise ships slime the earth. Trinket buyers. The ships are packed but no big spenders anymore."

"*Cabin* class may be packed," Fernando said. "But the diamond buyers, the big spenders? They come in the first-class suites. Those tickets aren't selling like they used to. They pack them in those lower berths like cattle. The cattle want the buffet and the cattle want the cheap booze. Look at them. They don't even know what island they're on."

"Yeah," said Melanie. "That's what they want. Food and booze. Of course it is."

"It's a good deal if you don't care about quality. Not too many coming in from first class. Now me, Mel, I care about quality, and as assistant manager here, I do draw a small salary. But I couldn't afford first class either. So it makes sense we're not selling any expensive diamonds right now."

Melanie walked away from the window and onto the sprawling, marbled sales floor, where twelve large display kiosks sported loose stones, watches, rings, necklaces, and bracelets.

She took her place behind a counter of diamond solitaires and loose rubies and emeralds. Fernando walked to the kiosk and took an uninhibited look at her, from her painted pink toenails and wedge sandals to her baby blue sundress showing plump, pale cleavage, up to her perfect, waxed brow.

"Either that," he said, "or there must be some flaw in your sales technique. One thing I know for sure, though, Mel. It has nothing to do with the quality of the merchandise."

She looked through the glass window at the turquoise waters and the ships floating there, then unconsciously focused on the shop's insignia printed on the glass in bold black letters: *Diamonds De La Caribe.* Even in reverse, the letters reordered themselves and pronounced to her, *I am blind, coarse, dead.* She shuddered.

"Of course, Fernando," she said. "You're so sweet."

They were interrupted by the loud booming of subwoofers out on Ocean Road. Melanie looked out the window again, saw Omar's white SUV rumbling by, heading south, rap music from the vehicle blasting off the pavement.

"Looks like he's heading straight down to the dolphin park," Fernando said. "And you think *you've* got money problems. He's bleeding cash on that new pier project. And all those unsold villas at the golf course."

Melanie was relieved by the news that she wouldn't have to deal with Omar this early in the morning. There was something *so* creepy about him.

It was Vinnie who'd introduced her to Omar. It was Vinnie—one of her best clients in New York, a connected guy, a generous guy—who'd told her to leave the country until things cooled down. She'd been keeping the books for a high-roller, had seen they were cooked. Vinnie did all he could, but she was in danger, he'd said, and there was nothing else that could be done.

Just cool out in Mexico for a while, Vinnie had told her. The guy won't be in office forever, and when he's gone they'll forget about you. But for now, go talk to Omar, Vinnie had said.

So Melanie had flown to Chinchamos to meet Omar, who greased the wheels of her visa application and put her quickly to work in his jewelry store. Though brazenly flirtatious, he'd never really hit on her. Out of respect for Vinnie, she figured. Whatever the reason for his disinterest, she'd always been glad, because she found Omar frightening. She'd been with plenty of mob types before, but Omar was too perverse, too diabolical.

And now here she was, stuck in Chinchamos, working for commission only, and starving. Hanging out with Branch was the only fun she ever seemed to have. Dopey, narced out Branch. He was just a deadbeat divemaster, but he was always kind to her, and somehow she found him comforting. She would drop in on him later. It had been a week. But for now, she had to make a sale, of one sort or the other.

Anita, the general manager, came in at a quarter 'til, and at nine Fernando unlocked the door. Customers flowed from the sultry sidewalk into the cool, polished showroom, and then Melanie was showing a gold and pearl necklace, priced at nine thousand dollars, to a vacationing middle-aged couple from Dallas.

"This torsade necklace," she told them, "absolutely revolutionizes the usually sedate row of uniform gems into a jumble of glossy glass pearls!"

The man hesitated, and Melanie draped the necklace around his wife's neck. "Wearing a piece of jewelry like this is *such* an evidence of happiness. And on you, it is simply irresistible."

"It seems a little high," the man said. "We're off the *Grand Nautical Angel*. Is there a discount?"

"*Grand Nautical Angel*?" Melanie's mind clicked away furiously. She didn't need the calculator but she pounded the keys on it without looking anyway, and by the time she showed them their four-hundred-and-fifty-dollar discount she'd come up with it. "*Gargantuan Land Lice.*"

"I'm sorry, miss?"

Melanie could barely suppress a laugh. "I said, I've got you a nice price. That's a new one, isn't it? The ship?"

"Oh, yes, this is the maiden voyage," the woman said. "It's wonderful. We did have to evacuate the ship at Grand Cayman because of a small amount of that norovirus they found. Or was it E. coli, honey? Something they found in the ship. But they've given us extra coupons for the burrito bar and now we're having a wonderful time."

Next came the doctor from Atlanta, from the *Great Sea Truth*, who used his limited time on Chinchamos to try on every Cartier watch in the store.

"It's between the classical and futuristic," Melanie told him, laying the gold watch over his tanned, oily wrist. She leaned over the counter a little farther and stroked the watch, and his wrist, with her own hand. "It's got the familiar curves and unique proportions that you desire. And deserve, too!"

But still she couldn't close a deal.

Then she showed solitaires to two young couples from Provo planning a group wedding. "One single diamond accenting the elegance of the platinum band," she told them, but they were unmoved.

A Japanese man with two young American women looked closely at an expensive ring—"The pure simplicity of three magically intertwined circles of pink, yellow, and white gold"—but again, nothing. There were no sales. It was like Fernando had said. Coach class was packed full, and they were all gorging themselves and shopping for T-shirts. But the high rollers, the men who could appreciate quality and were willing to pay for it, where had they gone?

She took her break at noon, putting her financial panic aside and splurging on a salad at Yvonne's Restaurant, her favorite on the island.

26

Back at the store after lunch it was slower than before. The cruisers' enthusiasm had finally been beaten back by the midday heat, and the street crowd had thinned out. Fernando took off for his break at two, and Melanie began to feel the panic. Rent was due, everything was due. And nothing to do but endure it. She couldn't go home until things got straightened out in New York. And that could take years.

Anita sent the security guard off on his lunch break, and then moments later her office phone rang.

"Mel," Anita shouted. "That was Omar. He needs me to bring some cash to him at Yvonne's. Probably planning a party with some cruise ship girls. Will you be all right in the store alone until Fernando gets back? Well, the guard should be back in less than an hour. And Fibbi should be making his rounds soon, so you'll be safe. If any customers show up, just buzz them in. Clean the baseplates, will you?"

After Anita left, Melanie scanned the sparse parade of tourists on the street, then looked up at the video cameras mounted on every wall. *It could be done.* She slung her Burberry purse-pack over her shoulder, took a small hand towel from the janitorial closet and started cleaning around the shiny stainless silver base of each display case, polishing her way to the office door, crouching in the very narrow corridor where she was out of view of the cameras. She took a final glance at the front of the store. Still empty.

It was Vinnie who'd taught her how to pick a lock, and it was Vinnie, just for fun, who'd shown her how to crack a safe. She wasn't a thief, she told herself, as she took her pick set from her purse and easily opened the lock on the office door. She was just in need of a very quiet loan.

The safe was a low-end Assa Abloy, and the same model as one she'd opened once before on a yacht off Martha's Vineyard, when a client had passed out before she'd been paid. She smiled as she remembered how she'd jumped off the yacht and swam back to shore, the money dripping wet but secure in her bikini top.

She had the door of the Assa Abloy open and had her delicate hand on a bundle of hundreds when she heard his voice.

"Your talents truly amaze me," Fernando said, leaning against the Cartier kiosk, outside the office, looking down on her and smiling. "I mean, you decipher anagrams like a computer and you can pick locks and crack a safe, too? Very impressive. A game show's not right for you. Some kind of reality-survival series, I think."

Melanie lay prone on the office floor and said nothing. He'd come in at exactly the wrong time and somehow she hadn't heard him. Just thirty seconds more and she would've been out, invisible, with ten grand to get her straight.

Fernando looked up at the cameras, then back down on Melanie. "Seems like you, too, have been analyzing the flaws in our eye in the sky. Guess there's no proof at all you were ever at the office door. But you know, if anything turns up missing I'll be the one to blame. And Omar doesn't fuck around, Mel. He'll just kill me."

"We can work something out," Melanie said from the floor. "Fire me but please don't tell Omar about this."

Fernando took out his cell phone and pointed it casually at Melanie and the open Assa Abloy safe. "Some photos, I think."

He looked out the store window at the sidewalk then glanced sideways down at her, grinning. "How long has Anita been gone?"

"Fifteen minutes," Melanie said.

"And the guard?"

"Twenty."

"I'm not going to fire you," he said, snapping a photo. "That one's for Omar."

Melanie looked out at the showroom, saw her own distorted reflection in the shiny silver baseplate at the foot of the kiosk.

"Take the straps on your dress down. Yeah, good," Fernando said snapping another shot. "And that one's just for me. How many likes do you think these will get on my Instagram account? Do what I say or I *will* throw you to Omar. You'll be in a Mexican prison or you'll be dead. Better to be dead. Now close your eyes."

Melanie could hear the clicking as Fernando snapped several more shots of her on the floor.

"I'll enjoy these pics later. Omar, too, if you don't do what I say."

The clicking stopped. Melanie opened her eyes and looked up. Fernando was gone from the doorway.

She slammed the safe shut, spun the dial, straightened her dress. Then she scooted back out to the threshold of the office door. She stood up, closed the office door behind her, and slid down low again along the base of the kiosks. Then she heard Fernando's voice from across the showroom.

"I could use someone with your talents. But the office safe? Small-time."

Anita came back into the store a few minutes later. Melanie spent the rest of the afternoon behind the watch counter, sedated from the humiliating incident, worried about the leverage Fernando had on her, annoyed at the way he was leering at her, and pondering how she could get that phone away from him. She was so deep in thought that she almost didn't see Branch out on the sidewalk, walking hurriedly by the shop.

"There goes your boyfriend," Fernando said quietly to her. "Another of your many assets. Guess he didn't have time to pop in and say hello."

"How do you know—"

"About you and Branch? Come on, Mel. I'm taking off now. Meet me after work, your place, six sharp," he commanded, shaking his phone at her. "Or else, very bad things."

29

Chapter Five

The Underwater Blacksmith's Shop

Victor Mendez sat at the table in his dive shop, Caribbean Argonauts, waiting for Bali and Manny and the divers to arrive, drinking coffee and watching the channel. The water was still and flat, turning a million different shades of blue as the morning sun hit it.

Then he looked to the north at the construction platform, dreading the thought of a cruise ship pier materializing there. He rubbed the sore spot on his chest where Fibbi had whacked him with his blackjack at the protest.

The street was starting to buzz with taxis and he didn't hear the door creak. When he turned around to get more coffee, Dorian was standing there, along with the tall man in the cowboy hat he'd seen at the protest. The tall man walked to the window and gazed up the shoreline toward the pier construction site.

"You come to return my cell phone, Dorian?" Victor asked. "Who's your friend?"

"That's Len. He'll be helping with the pier project. You're lucky you only lost your phone."

Dorian's huge arms twitched menacingly, and Victor looked him up and down. Must weigh close to three hundred, he thought, no fat at all, and the divemaster in him couldn't help assessing that this goon wouldn't need an ounce of lead to get him down on a dive. But he knew Dorian wasn't there to sign up for a dive.

"I can't make this scene anymore," Dorian said quietly, almost whispering. "Get me out of here. They're killing me." But then Len turned away from the window and Dorian blustered again. "Uncle Omar sent me to see if you're with us. The job offer."

"I *am* going broke," Victor said. "Just trying to replace all the phones and cameras you've ripped off from me. But I'm not looking for a job. Got my hands full here with this shop. And I got no control over what Pam does."

"It'd be good for your business."

"Business, yeah. At the expense of life on earth. What really inspires me is these reefs." Victor pointed with his coffee cup out to where the water shifted from turquoise to dark blue. "See that dark water? That's Paradise Deep. Ever been under out there?"

Dorian looked lazily at the cup and then out at the blue water.

"Great diving," Victor said. "But just the other day I found an old toilet from one of the ships lying on top of the reef. Beer cans, plastic bags, bottles. And now Omar wants to pave the mangroves and build a big pier and a mall. Good business? When those reefs are all dead, what's the reason for carting folks in here in the first place?"

"I don't know," Dorian said, and he shrugged. "He wanted me to tell you that what has to happen now, if you won't take the job, is just business."

Victor looked back out at the water, and there was a column of brown exhaust. The day's fourth ship, the *Grand Nautical Angel*, was swelling over the horizon to the north, preparing to anchor.

"Business," he said. "And I've got a dive shop to run. So get the hell out."

Dorian fidgeted with the key hanging from a silver chain around his massive neck. He started to speak, stammered, looked at Len, who just tipped his hat. As Len and Dorian walked out the door, Bali and Manny walked in.

Manny, the captain, carried the gas cans out to the dock, and Bali dumped her dive bag by the lockers. She wore tight shorts and a sleeveless shirt over her bikini top, all in colorful contrast to her dark chocolate skin and her long black hair.

"What was that all about?" she asked in her East Indian accent. Her round face was perky, buoyant, and feminine, and Victor noted the intriguing contrast it made with her toned, strong physique. "The Hulk and the Cowboy? Out trick-or-treating kind of early in the year?"

"Yeah. We treat them to Paradise Reef. Or they're going to do some kind of trick on me and Pam. It got kind of rough."

"Sorry I missed the protest," Bali said. "I camped all night on the wild side. Maybe it's too late to stop Omar here. But over there we still have a chance."

"It's *not* too late. Any turtles yet?"

"No. Any night now. If I can get this research grant maybe we can stop him from developing over there. How many divers today?"

"Party of six. From the ship. Branch took the Zodiac out early. Don't know what the hell that guy's up to. Went fishing, I guess. He's never shown any interest in helping us with this thing, but it's funny. At the protest today we were getting pushed around and I couldn't stop thinking about him. How he could've helped us. But he wasn't there. And he's not here. So I'll be out on the boat with you today."

"Branch is a stoner. You've seen how deep he goes. That's all he cares about."

"Maybe so," Victor said. "But he's tough. He could help us. Maybe you can talk to him."

"Maybe," Bali said. She had stripped down to her bikini top, and her brown, muscular shoulders glistened in the sun. "He goes his own way. But, maybe."

"I remember Chinchamos, only ten years ago," Victor said, the lines around his eyes crinkling as he squinted out at the water. "Running the boat down south, when the coastline was still undeveloped, to some spot I'd never dived before and rolling back into an untouched garden of coral. Then on the way back, Bali, every day we'd see dolphins on the surface, plowing the water, moving slow and heavy, not afraid. Now, the reefs are dying. And the dolphins. They got kidnapped. You can pay Omar to splash around with them at the park and get your picture taken."

Victor looked out the front window of the shop at the tour van that had pulled up. "And now this."

They got the divers from the van on board and Manny eased the dive boat past the pier construction site, out into the channel, and then they zoomed south. Later, in the water at a shallow site, Bali took her four divers out in the direction of the coral wall while Victor lingered in the aquamarine shallows with his two beginners. They were doing pretty well, he noted, so he took them on a nice tour, edging into the darker waters.

The grinding of the cruise ship propellers, covert and constant, gave a perpetual soundtrack to the dive. Construction noises from the new pier site clanged and banged through the shallows, and to Victor it sounded as if they were in some underwater blacksmith's shop.

They drifted by some pillars of coral rising up from the depths. Victor could see the dark shapes of Bali and her four divers down current. Four divers flapping, and then there was Bali, hovering motionless like a Buddha. Even in dark, distant silhouette, her shape was graceful and beguiling.

Soon they were back on the boat and buzzing toward the shop. At the dock they tied up and put the divers in taxis, sent them off to the municipal pier and their ferry back to the cruise ship. Then Victor was at the table once again, drinking coffee, logging his dive and watching Bali rinse out the gear, the bright afternoon sunshine glowing on her mocha-colored skin.

"We diving tomorrow?" she asked him.

"Yeah. More from the ships." Victor had a bad feeling when he said it. The only business he got anymore was from the cruise ships, but the ships took such a big commission that there was very little left for him. If he took the job with Omar, managing the dive concession, he'd make a nice salary but he knew there might be no reef left.

"There's another meeting tonight," he told her. "Here at the shop around ten. The protests aren't working, so we've got to rethink our strategy. Our benefactor from the mainland didn't show today. Maybe he will tonight."

"You know I'm with you. But I'll be camping on the wild side again tonight. I'll make the next meeting. As far as Branch goes, I'll see if I can't persuade him."

She took a slim paperback book from her bag and handed it to Victor as she headed out the door. "Maybe this will help. Give it to him."

Later, Victor was checking the weather on his laptop when he heard the door creak open behind him. He was hoping it was customers, not cruisers, but some real divers, like the old days, wanting to do some real dives down on the south point. When he turned around it was Branch, his eyes puffy and looking all beat to hell as he slumped into the shop. He raised his hand to wave at Victor and then he collapsed onto the floor.

Chapter Six

The Range War

B ranch's legs felt like rubber when he hopped out of the beer truck. He staggered in, saw Victor at the table, and waved at him. Then his feet went totally numb from the bubbles in his bloodstream and he collapsed onto the floor.

Victor leaned him up against a pile of wetsuits and draped a green blanket around him. "You break into the shop, you take my boat, and now you come back on foot. Looking all messed up, too. Where the hell is the Zodiac?"

"Capsized it on the windward side. I was going after lobster. Sorry. Had to swim in, got all scratched up in the mangroves."

"Capsized?" Victor asked in disbelief, and he took a breath to calm himself. "So you're not just fucked-up?" His weathered face wrinkled even further with worry as he looked at Branch.

"I'll replace it."

"How?"

When Gonzago had sent Branch to Chinchamos a year earlier, he'd told him to create a nice cover for himself, and that cover was as a starving divemaster at Caribbean Argonauts Dive Shop. No one would guess he had a little stash of cash in his room, and a big stash in the safe down at Yvonne's Restaurant. And Branch wanted to keep it that way. Until he had enough.

"Got a little bit saved up."

"Shut up. This is for you." Victor pressed a gold key into Branch's palm. "Been meaning to give this to you. You don't have to break in here anymore, damn it. You're part of the team. Got this celly for you, too."

Branch took the cell phone from Victor and looked at it with trepidation. He remembered what Gonzago had told him—*no Internet, no cell phones.*

"I need to get a new phone for *me* now. I know you don't like those things. But if I ever need to get hold of you."

"Thanks," Branch said. After showing up without the boat, he didn't want to refuse the gifts, so he stuffed the phone and the key in his pack. "Sorry I missed work."

"We did OK without you. Held that group of cruisers together pretty good, I guess. Could have used you earlier, though. At the protest."

Branch looked into Victor's face. Dark eyes, a face wrinkled beyond his years, but strong and uncomplicated. A face that knew what it wanted.

"You can count on me tomorrow. For work. Thanks for the key. And the phone. But I can't get mixed up in any kind of range war right now."

"Range war. That's good. We got the cattle boats coming in seven days a week, too. There's room for you here at the shop as a partner. Think about it. She left this for you."

Victor handed him the book Bali had left.

"*Life of the Hawksbill Turtle*," Branch said, mindlessly reading the cover. He shivered and pulled the blanket tighter on his shoulders. "A phone. A key. Now a book. Not even my birthday."

He was stoned and sluggish from the bubbles in his bloodstream. The deco sickness might go away over time, he knew, or a nitrogen bubble might lodge in his brain and kill him. But right at the moment he didn't care one way or the other. He just enjoyed the numbness and the cool of the marble floor on his back.

"You're clammy," Victor said, touching his hand to Branch's forehead. "Are you bent? Better get you down to the hyperbaric chamber."

"I'm not bent. Help me up."

After a quick rinse under the shop's outdoor shower, Branch toweled off and put on the dry clothes Victor had loaned him. He combed back his thick brown hair and took a critical look at himself in the mirror while Victor talked.

"We got bounced off the beach this morning," Victor said. He poured a big shot of rum into a coffee cup and handed it to Branch. "We were supposed to have some reporters there. They never showed. Omar brought his nephew Dorian and Fibbi and the deputies. There was some new guy, tall, Texas accent, in a cowboy hat, too. Came by the shop with Dorian when it was all over. Said he was here to help blow up Paradise Shallows for the pier. He was asking about you."

"Tall guy?" Branch asked, and he turned quickly away from the mirror. "Cowboy hat? Demolitions? You catch his name?"

"Dorian said his name was ... Len? Yeah, Len."

Branch threw down the slug of rum, felt the heat from it surge through his chest. Then he slumped back down onto the pile of wetsuits and remembered Len.

Chapter Seven

A Good Life, A Strong Life

"So this is the new superstar," Gonzago said, sitting behind a massive redwood desk in the office of the Penthouse All-Nude All-the-Time Club, BYOB of Houston, Texas. He flashed a brilliant white smile, stood up and smoothed his tan tailored suit, then extended a soft, manicured hand to Len. It was twenty-five years earlier.

Buddhas, bronzes, statues of horses and other animals Len didn't even recognize perched on stands and pillars around the office, Tibetan thangkas hung from the walls, and the fragrant smoke from a cube of burning champa incense filled the air.

"This is the son of a gun that gets my last nine loads over the border with zero losses? Who eliminates the rotten border agents that are never satisfied with their cuts?"

"Just tryin' to do the job right, Mr. Obeto," said Len, engulfing Gonzago's outstretched hand with his own huge, hard paw.

Gonzago chuckled as he sized up Len. "Awesome. Please sit," he said, motioning toward a brightly colored chaise lounge.

"Don't fret it," Gonzago said, noting Len's hesitation. "It looks delicate, but it's covered with Afghan Kazak wool. You can't hurt it. Synthetic fabrics? I can't tolerate that modern, mass-produced shit. Doesn't last. I only go for the genuine articles. You agree with me?"

"Absolutely," Len said. He sat down humbly.

"All of this treasure," Gonzago said, spreading his hands around the office, "and all of the pieces in my gallery? It's my true love. But I can't make a profit on it anymore. Damned customs officials, here in the States, in India, they all got their hands out. It's the cargo *you've* been carrying that pays the bills, Len. The bastards you've been eliminating. That allows me to spread this kind of beauty to the Western world."

"Well, I 'preciate the extra work. You know, I work on the oil rigs most of the time, but when I'm in the city—"

"When you're in the city, you work for me," Gonzago said, lighting a cigar and blowing more smoke into the office space. "And that's what I called you in here to talk about. How we can make more money."

"Yes, sir."

"*I want it all!*" Gonzago bellowed, then he smiled and resumed his tranquil tone. "My guys tell me that you're quite the wizard with diving, underwater demolitions, technical stuff. How'd you end up in Houston?"

"Picking tomatoes on Daddy's farm wasn't much fun. Up near Nac. I guess I was barely seventeen when they busted me in Laredo with a trunk full of mini-bricks. Just a juvenile, the judge said, so it was either trade school or the military. I had my certs in underwater welding, ROV tech, mixed gas, saturation diving before I was nineteen. I been working the rigs the last two years, using the submersible diamond wire saw, high-pressure jetting equipment, like that. The downtime in Houston gets a little boring."

Len looked toward the window that overlooked the club floor, where ten naked girls danced on ten round stages, strobe lights flashing across their toned, bare bodies. "I was spending too much time and too much money down there trying to get your girls to talk to me. Then I had the good fortune to meet up with some of your crew in the club. The extra money's been nice. But I guess it was really the adrenaline I been missing."

"Adrenaline," Gonzago said. "Yeah. They tell me you've done exceptional work. Ten jobs. They tell me you like it. And then, when it's done, you're tucked away back on the platforms out in the Gulf. Nice. What's it going to take to get you to work for me on an exclusive basis when you're on shore leave?"

Len stood and looked out the window and pointed down onto the club floor. "That one. Ginger."

It was in the summer of his twenty-third year when Len received the emergency call on the rig. Gonzago, wondering why Ginger, his most popular dancer, hadn't shown up at the club for three days, went to the apartment and found her dead, a needle in her arm on the bathroom floor. Branch, only two years old, hungry and dehydrated, but alive, was taken to Gonzago's River Oaks mansion and nurtured there until Len was off the rigs. Ginger was buried and then Branch was quickly dumped off at the Kilgore family farm, north of Nacogdoches.

When he was only a toddler, Branch's daily life consisted of farm chores, Bible studies, and regular ramblings with Grandpa Kilgore through the piney wilds. As soon as he was able to walk, he was expected to spend all his time doing what Len had run from only a few years earlier: picking tomatoes and studying homeschool lessons.

Grandpa Kilgore took Branch deer hunting when he was six years old. Deep in the thickets of East Texas, the junior Kilgore shouldered a rifle for the first time, a Winchester 94, and to his grandfather's amazement, he brought down a twelve point buck from two hundred yards. After Branch picked himself up and knocked the pine needles from his bottom, he jogged with his grandpa to where the buck lay stone-dead, the shot having pierced its brain.

"Don't be sad," Grandpa had told him. "This buck had him a good life, a strong life. But if he lived any longer, his life wouldn't be so good, so strong. That's the way it is to live in the wild. Sometimes that's the way it is for humans, too. You helped this buck to end its life in a good way, with no suffering."

Branch knelt down and placed his hand on the buck's massive rack, wishing he could give it back its life. He tugged on the antlers, felt the buck's velvety head move, heavy and lifeless. "Like the way Mama died?"

"Ginger, your mama, she didn't suffer. She couldn't tolerate no suffering. But she died for no good purpose, from drugs. You're here with me now. You live your life with purpose. Someday, a long time from now, you'll give it up, for a purpose. You killed this here buck cleanly, instantly. It served a purpose. We'll eat the meat. He won't be running through these woods no longer, but he done his purpose, he sired plenty of young bucks that will."

"Seems like cheating," Branch said. Serves a purpose, maybe, he thought, but he knew there was nothing clean about it. "To have killed him from so far away. Using the rifle."

"You listen to me good, boy. *Do not conform any longer to the pattern of this world, but be transformed by the renewing of your mind. Then you will be able to test and approve what God's will is—his good, pleasing and perfect will.* Remember that. A good life, a strong life. It don't matter how long it is, if it got purpose."

Branch caressed the soft fur on the underside of the buck's neck. He felt lousy about the kill, but he was comforted by Grandpa's words.

"A good life, a strong life," he heard Grandpa say again.

A few months passed, and then he was eight. On a fine summer's day, he followed one of the farm dogs, a bristly terrier in pursuit of a beaver, into a fifteen-inch-wide irrigation conduit that led into the depths of an abandoned stock pond, hidden away back in the tall pines of Grandpa's farm. The dog and the beaver made it through the obstructions in the pipe and out into the water on the other end. Branch, enthusiastic to follow, became stuck ten feet into the conduit. He was snagged and couldn't back out, and ahead of him in the narrow pipe was an unknown, constrictive tube of black water.

Then the rains came. As the water level encroached, Branch discovered a companion with him there in the pipe, and the companion's name was Panic. Panic was there to whisper in his ear of imminent agony and endless suffering. Branch squirmed to get away from Panic, and he begged Panic to stop the whispering. But he only became more trapped and more breathless.

Panic wouldn't budge. Panic wouldn't be quiet. Panic became stronger. There was no way to beat Panic, Branch discovered, as the water level rose, only a few inches from his mouth. There was only to surrender to it, to be fully permeated by it, in the hope that Panic would lose interest and retreat.

So he stopped his screaming and squirming and he explored the terror of his imprisonment. Muddy pond water was in his mouth and he struggled to breathe the stagnant, rusty-smelling air in through his nose. He thrust his face up against the corrugated metal at the top of the conduit. Panic was there, too, but now he did nothing to acknowledge it. Slowly Panic became quiet, and after a few hours of remaining still and breathing slowly through his nose, Branch found that he could turn off Panic as if he was turning off a light switch.

The hours dragged by. He was dehydrated and hungry and his well-rounded young shoulders began to wither a bit. Each time Panic made a charge at him—and each time Branch ignored it—he felt his body becoming suppler inside the pipe. He could become smaller, he told himself, just by using his mind. He remembered what he'd learned in one of Grandpa's homeschool lessons: A molecule was the smallest physical unit of an element. He could make himself smaller than a molecule if he needed to. Each time Panic lost interest in him he felt himself become a little smaller, and then at last he was able to slither ahead into the submerged tube. At the end of the air pocket, he filled his lungs with an uneasy breath of musty air and then he pushed forward into the dark water.

Branch squirmed along in the pipe, the underwater algae lining its sides slimy against his body. He was quickly starved for air. The darkness of the pond water was unrelenting, and it seemed the pipe would never end. Panic came at him with all its fury. Just as he was ready to give in, ready to flail against the pipe and suck in water, he saw a tiny pinhole of light ahead of him. He exhaled the last of his air and pushed toward the light. The pinhole became a murky blur and then he was out.

He floated to the surface, took a huge gulp of air and thrashed his way across the surface and collapsed onto the shore. The red mud at the edge of the stock pond was warm against his body, and each breath of the East Texas air was heavy and sweet in his lungs as he passed out.

When the terrier led Grandpa to the pond the next day, Branch was breathing and conscious, but he seemed unattached to either life or death. Grandpa was relieved to find him alive, but angrily demanded to know why Branch had done it.

"*To test and approve what God's will is,*" he answered Grandpa. From that point on, it seemed, he was interested only in continuing the duel with Panic. As soon as he was rested, he was back out in the wild woods, finding more extreme ways to fence with his formidable new foe. After a few weeks of playing matador with the bulls on the farm, capturing pit vipers, plunging from high cliffs into shallow streams, and training himself to hold his breath for more than four minutes under the surface of the pond, Branch was loaded in the truck and driven by Grandpa back to Houston. He couldn't handle him. And so it was that Branch's brief childhood on the farm in the tall pines, back by the power lines, was over. And then he was living full-time within the extravagant confines of Gonzago's villa in River Oaks.

Chapter Eight

You Goin' On This Deep One with Me?

B ranch was only nine years old when Len brought him along on one of Gonzago's business trips to the Mexican Caribbean—scouting out locations for landing strips—and it was there that Branch learned to scuba dive. He was always happy for an opportunity to spar with his nemesis Panic, but he was surprisingly apprehensive before his first time underwater.

"You goin' on this deep one with me?" Len had asked Branch before that first dive from the boat. *"Or you gonna be a pussy and I'll have to tell ever'body?"*

Branch went on the deep one with him. After that trip, Branch wanted to do more diving, but as an unaccompanied minor he had to sneak tanks to the lake or the beach, waiting until no one was watching to slip into the water. Traveling with Gonzago on an antiquities-and-opium-buying trip to Indonesia, Branch got his first taste of super-deep diving, in the clear waters off Sipadan Island. It was there he first explored the stoned delights of the Deep Blue Saloon.

When he dived below two hundred feet on plain air, the buildup of nitrogen in his body had an extreme anesthetic effect on him. The pure, soporific hallucinations of the depths, combined with the vivid beauty of the reefs, made the cocaine and pot highs he'd sneaked from Gonzago's stash seem trivial. Branch was hooked. The numbness, comfort, and color he found in the depths helped him forget he was a lonely, motherless child.

By the time Branch was twelve, Len was doing fewer commercial dives but was still busy supervising underwater demolitions. And in his off-time he was busier than ever doing jobs for Gonzago, so Gonzago himself took on more of a role in mentoring Branch, not in any ethical or moral capacity, but in the areas of arts and fashion. Len was helplessly committed to looking and acting the part of the cowboy, but Branch had been born with a natural affinity for the finer things. So Gonzago taught him to appreciate good food, clothes, theater, and music.

In September of that year Branch went with Gonzago and Len to New York, where Gonzago was receiving a container of smuggled antiquities from Nepal. The three attended a performance of Puccini's *Turandot* at the Met. Branch sat between the two men, Len to his left, slumbering and snoring in his cowboy hat, Gonzago to his right, intent on the drama and the music. Branch was interested but unmoved, until the strains of the great aria "Nessun dorma" saturated and thrilled him. He was sitting third row, orchestra center, but at that moment, he felt as if he was again immersed in the subaquatic, sun-drenched grottoes of the deep reefs of the Deep Blue Saloon.

As Branch grew into a young man he finally learned to appreciate the independence that Len's poor parenting afforded him. He went diving every chance he could, and any underwater cave he could find beckoned to him. He learned about cave navigation and the rule of thirds—using one-third of the air supply for going into the cave, then promptly turning around to exit, using another one-third for coming out. The final third was strictly backup. But for Branch, the rule of thirds became the rule of halves plus one minute. Branch would use slightly more than half his air supply going into the cave, setting up a nice duel with Panic on the way out.

He read everything he could find in Len's technical bulletins on underwater charges, and he became proficient with Gonzago's custom gas blending system, where tanks of nitrox or tri-mix could be dialed up to help mules stay underwater for hours at a time. As interesting as the exotic gas mixes were, there was nothing like deep diving on plain air, and nothing was more refreshing than the resulting nitrogen narcosis he found in the depths.

It was the promise of deep underwater caves on Mexico's Yucatán Peninsula near Akumal that lured Branch, now fifteen, to go on a business trip with Len and Gonzago. What could be more perfect? The thrill of narcosis and the delight of fending off claustrophobic Panic was too big a temptation for him to pass on, so he agreed to Len's terms: help out with the job first, then enjoy a week of diving the deep virgin caves.

Len had heard the stories from the family farm about Branch's natural prowess with a rifle, so he gave him the task of holding high ground above the site where he and Gonzago were exchanging cash for two hundred kilos of heroin.

When the deal went bad—Gonzago had brought the cash, but the two Mexicans had failed to bring the heroin—Len gave him the sign, and Branch drilled two perfect holes into the heads of the Mexicans with the Polish Tantal rifle he'd been given.

It was just business, he tried to remind himself, but again he felt bad about killing from a distance. It seemed like cheating.

Even the cave dives to extreme depths in super-tight restrictions didn't make him feel any better. Gonzago began to understand that Branch had an unusual preference for danger, for close-in work, so he allowed him to take care of the *jefe* of the two Mexicans. Branch slipped into the *jefe*'s mansion and killed him close up with Len's .44 Automag. When the remorse came, Grandpa's words came back to him ... "*He lived a good and strong life,*" Branch realized, looking around the Mexican's beautiful mansion. And that would be forever, because he'd helped him to end it quickly.

Impressed with Branch's natural fearlessness, Gonzago put him to work on a number of hits and border crossings that produced immediate cash flow. But the price for working was that the teenager missed classes. So Gonzago arranged for private tutoring at the villa, and he insisted that Branch take his GED when he was still only sixteen.

"You don't need all of that high school nonsense, but you're gonna have your diploma," Gonzago had told him. "Don't be like me. I've got all of this, but I really regret I didn't get to finish high school and go to college."

So, over the next couple of years, Branch took online courses in physics and math, earning his college degree when most kids his age were just graduating from high school.

Though his accomplishments were impressive to Len and Gonzago—a degree in physics, hundreds of cave and ocean dives logged, and now double-digit credentials as a retainer—Branch was dissatisfied. He was weary of the drunken and stoned behavior of Len and other members of the crew. What was the big deal with coke, smack, and booze? What could they do for you, when you had a psychedelic nightclub down below the waves, offering such invigorating tonic?

Their final trip together was Cuba, during the *período especial*, where Gonzago had smuggled in cash to buy pre-Columbian artifacts. Branch came up from a deep dive, elated and meditative from nitrogen narcosis as he waded ashore to their rented beachfront villa in Guanabo. Len and Gonzago, wasted on rum and black hash, danced chaotically in the courtyard to a classic folk melody blasting from the outdoor speakers.

"*Guantanamera*," the speakers blared. "*Guajira Guantanamera! Guantanameeera! Guajira Guantanamera ...*"

"This is a damn good song," Len stammered, his toneless grunts synching along with the tune. "One ton tomato," he chimed off-key. "*Chiquita*, one ton tomato. One ton tomaaato!"

"Yeah, damn good song," Gonzago agreed, laughing. "I normally listen to classical. Mahler, Danzi. Brahm's the best. But this tune is kind of catchy. That goddamn one ton tomato! Branch, you're back. Come join us!"

Branch dropped his fins, slipped out of his scuba unit and gazed at the two men as they hopped and cavorted together in their drunken hoedown. Len, he could understand. But Gonzago, with all of his wealth and style, acting that way?

He couldn't believe this was the same man who had sat next to him listening to Puccini at the Met.

Branch joined them on the patio for a drink. It was only the bliss from his narcosis high that allowed him to hide his contempt for their raucous insobriety.

So it really should have come as no surprise to Len when, on his eighteenth birthday, Branch announced he was leaving home and joining the military. The navy, he'd decided, in the hopes he'd get a chance to try for the SEAL teams.

"Leavin'? For the navy? Hell, you cain't do that," Len said, his voice strangely unsteady. "Why you wanna go and do sumpin' like that?"

Branch paused. He craved a real challenge, and he was resentful that Len hadn't been there for him. But it would never do to tell him.

"It's a job, Len. Get to travel a bit. Do some military diving. Might actually learn something."

"Now, Branch, you know I can teach you ever'thing you need to know about divin'. Maybe I've been spendin' too much time in old Mexico. Now that you're done with school, I thought that, well—"

"Come on, Len. You've always been too busy for me. And now we don't have anything in common. Except diving, of course. So if you're really gonna miss me, you're still young enough to enlist. I checked into it. You can leave all of your dope and booze behind and come with me."

"Yeah, I'd like to take some time off. Go off with you somewhere. Be good. But the navy? Shee-it. That's some kind of plunge. I mean, that's really overboard, son. Why would you do that? You've gone too deep this time!"

For the first time, ever, Branch saw remorse on Len's face. He smiled, and he couldn't hold back.

"Too deep? Come on, Dad. *You goin' on this deep one with me? Or you gonna be a pussy and I'll have to tell ever'body?*"

Chapter Nine

Lasagna to Go

Branch poured another shot of Victor's rum into the coffee cup. The narcosis from the morning's deep dive had faded, he was pretty sure he was bent, and if the trouble on the mainland wasn't enough, now he had Len to worry about, too. But he had to keep his meeting with Omar, and he wanted to get paid, so he threw down the rum and stood up. He left the shop and hurried across the street, merging in with a herd of tourists on the sidewalk. Then he darted up the narrow avenue alongside the Blue Angel, leading him away from Ocean Road.

He walked as quickly as he was able to past the shops and the markets and the hidden restaurants, the ones that only the locals ate at, and the really good ones that couldn't afford the rent of the oceanfront, and the small homes with cast-iron gates and courtyards within. Dive shops and deep-sea fishing outfitters, with their brightly painted stucco walls lined the corners where the major avenues crossed the narrow street.

As Branch ambled farther away from the water, the colonial charm of the plaza and the waterfront faded, and then he was in old town, with its gas stations and junkyards, well out of the likely paths of the cruise ship passengers. The fresh ocean air gave way to an oily scent and the houses wedged in on either side of the narrow alleys were unpainted and crumbling.

After a couple of miles, he navigated back toward the waterfront boulevard, coming out just in front of Diamonds de la Caribe. He hadn't planned it this way, hadn't even thought about it, and it startled him, because he was not up for seeing Mel. He lowered his head and merged again with the tourist horde, now piling back onto the sidewalks for a final shopping spree before sailing time.

Then he was inside the cool foyer of Yvonne's Restaurant, where Morgan was working the front. The fat, bald man struck a wooden match against the host stand and lit a filterless Balkan cigarette.

"Mr. Branch Kilgore. You're late. Omar's still here, but he's presently engaged. Wait here with me." He took a hit off his cigarette then blew boiling blue smoke up toward the skylight as he gave Branch a critical look. "You're lucky that due to the casual nature of our clientele from the ships, Yvonne's Restaurant no longer enforces a dress code."

"Yeah," Branch said. "Lucky. And you, too. That Yvonne doesn't enforce the no-smoking code."

"We all have our vices."

Branch felt the tingling of the nitrogen bubbles burning his scalp. He tried to say something but the numbness in his lips seemed to glue them together.

The fat man laughed, his saggy jowls pulsating as he took another deep drag on his smoke.

"Stylistic differences aside, you and I are very much alike, young Branch. We both need a steady buzz to keep going. I smoke these little cigarettes and it's hazardous. But your buzz is far more intense and it comes from a much more hazardous activity. Many precarious hours underwater."

He took another huge hit from his cigarette then dropped the butt to the floor and stamped it out with his woven leather loafer. He lowered his voice. "I suspect you're here to report on some nasty occurrence on the mainland this morning. I think I'll stick to my little cigarettes."

Branch said nothing. He looked back through the window at the front of the restaurant foyer, over the seawall and out at the turquoise waters on the far side of Ocean Road. Suddenly a dolphin appeared on the surface of the water. It frolicked in the surf, dived down, then burst up through the waves and gave a mighty kick of its flukes. It was blue and massive and muscular in the afternoon light. Then the dolphin splashed back down into the water and disappeared.

"Look at him out there, Branch," Morgan said. "Experiencing so much bliss. You would like to know that feeling again, wouldn't you?"

"Again?" Branch asked. "When did I ever know it?"

"Surely there was a time," said Morgan. "But for now, a nasty occurrence to report on."

Dorian stepped into the foyer. He looked Branch over and shook his head.

"Hey, killer. How's life on the bottom?"

"Keep asking, you'll find out," Branch said blandly. The bubbles and the redhead were enough for him to worry about. "I have an appointment."

"He's in the back." Dorian moved aside and let Branch pass.

At his large round table at the rear of the restaurant courtyard, hidden behind a trestle of flowering bougainvillea vines, Omar sipped on sangria, slurped from a bowl of soup and looked at digital pictures on his phone.

"*This* is the Chinchamos the world will see," Omar said, showing Branch a picture of a large woman in hysterics as she straddled a dolphin. In the background of the shot Branch could see the chain-link fence that segregated the dolphin park from the open sea and behind that was the dark silhouette of a cruise ship anchored off Paradise Deep.

"People having the fun on a beautiful island. But the social media, everyone is a reporter now, no? Snap one picture, twist it around, shoot video with the smartphone, and the whole world is on my ass. Costs me money. You hungry? She don't like it but she make me the shark fin soup today."

"No, thanks. Not hungry."

"Then you drink the sangria with me. Waiter! Another glass."

Branch felt woozy as the nitrogen bubbles did their work on him. More alcohol wasn't going to help but it was best to sip sociably with Omar.

"Dark rum over ice."

"You bring me a picture? A nice portrait of the redhead, no?"

Branch pulled the camera from his pocket and slid it across the table. He watched as Omar powered it on and scanned its contents.

"Is beautiful," Omar said, smiling, his teeth a milky red from the sangria. He put the camera down and held up his glass as the waiter set a tumbler of Cuban rum in front of Branch. "Motherfucker making the coca unprofitable. Motherfucker coming to fuck with my pier today. *Salud*, Branch Kilgore."

As Branch held his glass up he saw a distorted reflection of the redhead's dead face from the camera's view screen. The decompression sickness merged with a wave of remorse and then he was nauseated. He rattled the ice around in his glass and took a big gulp.

"You'd said something about a bonus after this one."

Omar laughed, swilled more wine, then leaned over and snarfed a line of coke from the table. "Yvonne, she got your money." He wiped powder from his inflamed nose and lit a cigarette. "She cooking today. I make her fire one of the chefs. He no want to make the soup for me. I say kill him, but she say no. She coming out for you. She got your bonus. More lasagna. Big job. She tell you all about it."

"I don't know. This one was pretty rough. I appreciate the work, but I need a break."

"Fuck that. I say work and you work. Gonzago send you down here and you do good work. For me, for Gonzago. I got a big problem with the old bitch at the hotel. You keep your head, you do the work."

"Business is just business," Branch said, backing off at the sound of Gonzago's name, but he didn't like what Omar said about Pam. "It means nothing to me."

"I talk to Gonzago this morning," Omar said. "He back from his trip to Indonesia. Art buying. Fucking waste of time."

"You're not a collector?"

"Collect art?" Omar asked. He laughed, smoke spewing from his nose, then leaned over and snorted another line. "No. I *no* collect art. I collect money.

Spending too fucking much of it on the pier. Gonzago, he send a new guy to the island to help with the blasting. Len Kilgore. *Su padre, no?*"

"Yeah. *Mi padre*. But not really. It's been years."

"Gonzago tell me about it. You do your job. Len, he do his job. We all work. Here she come now. Get you some food. I got some girls coming. We talk later."

Branch turned and looked at Yvonne walking toward the table. She was a tall, full-figured woman with olive skin and liquid brown eyes. She waved at Branch then led him through the cool courtyard and into the steam and bustle of the kitchen. Chefs in their white coats and toques were busy searing, simmering and chopping, and there was the aroma of wood oven pizzas, and of olive oil, tomato sauce, and seafood dishes simmering in lemon and butter.

"Smells good, Yvonne. Must be good working in a fine kitchen like this."

"Good?" she asked. She led him into her office, took off her toque, and shook out her long black hair. "It's not good when you're cooking all day. When I go home I just smell like garlic. But since you like the food I'll wrap up something for you to take with you. More lasagna."

She shut the door and closed the blinds on the window that looked out onto the kitchen. "It's funny, but I've always thought it must be good working outside on the water. Like you do."

"Well, like you said. When you go home there's that smell on you."

Yvonne spun the combination on the wall safe, opened it, and took out a fat yellow envelope. "Did you get the pic?"

"Yeah. I gave him the camera already. Don't much like lugging evidence around with me. Not professional. What's the point?"

"You really don't know, do you?" She handed him the yellow envelope. "One side posts pictures of dead coral and imprisoned dolphins on the Internet. The other side threatens, tries to scare away the protestors. Ugly stuff."

"Yeah," Branch said as he appraised the weight of the yellow envelope in his hand. "I reckon so."

"What happened this morning?"

"I got in and out of the villa just fine. But then there were shots. I made it to the cave and I thought I was good. But they knew about it. They were waiting for me at my exit. At the Manhole."

"What did you do?"

"I took the back door. Had to go very deep, almost ran out of air. Had some lines laid there from cave dives I did last year. I ended up getting a little bent but I made it."

"No wonder you look so wretched. Maybe working out on the water's not so good. I *am* looking for a new chef. Can you cook?"

"No. But I love it here. The gourmet food. The wine. The courtyard. All of that."

"It was always my dream to have a place like this. The food, the wine, the courtyard. All of that. But I never could have done it without Gonzago's backing. I danced at his club in Monterrey. He put me through cooking school, set me up here, funded me. He put in a ton of cash. Well, Gonzago's a dear, and he has great taste. But now I have to put up with Omar and his thugs' club. Putting everything on a tab. I even had to make shark fin soup for him. So nothing's as pure as it seems. Is it all there?"

Branch scanned the contents of the envelope, stuffed some of the bills into his pocket, then gave the envelope back to Yvonne.

"Yeah. I'm taking out five for now. Incurred some expenses. Put the rest of it back in there with my stash."

"It's safe here." She put the envelope back in the safe, slammed it shut and spun the dial. "Nobody's going to hit a place owned by Gonzago and Omar."

Yvonne leaned toward him and took Bali's book from his shirt pocket. "What's this? *Life of the Hawksbill Turtle*, by Ed Imbricata. Doesn't seem like your genre."

She thumbed through it then read to him. "'Like other sea turtles, hawksbills are solitary for most of their lives; they meet only to mate.' Sound like anyone you know?" She laughed, flipped some more pages and continued.

"'Hawksbills can stay underwater for over seven hours when resting. However, a stressed turtle, for instance entangled in fishing nets, quickly uses up oxygen stored within its own body and may drown within minutes through panic.' Seven hours! You must be part turtle. Weren't you stressed? Having to go deep in that cave? Not being sure you had enough air to make it out?"

"You've got twenty minutes of air left. If you keep your head, keep your heart rate and your breathing down, you can find your way out in twenty. Like a cool turtle. But if you panic, even for a second, then you're not going to make it."

"I don't know. I think I need more backup than that. To me, the only way to fight off panic in that situation is not caring about dying to begin with. But even sea turtles care. This book says so, and they're reptiles. Could I stay cool in that situation? That's you, maybe, but not me. And what if it actually takes twenty-*one* minutes to get out?"

Branch smiled. "Well, at least you enjoyed your final twenty."

"Omar and Gonzago have got something lined up for you right away. It's in Cuba."

"Tough spot, Cuba."

"Seems like the mainland this morning was kind of a tough spot, too."

"What are they doing in Cuba?"

"I don't get access to that kind of information. I'm just the reluctant travel agent."

"Why not send big Morgan? He knows Cuba."

"He's retired. And he's gotten so fat. One more reason why you should shy away from working in a restaurant. You'll go in as a tourist. You can take your cute little friend. Good cover, traveling as a couple. She was in here for lunch today."

"Who?"

"Come on. You know who. Mel. Ate nothing but a tiny little salad, of course. She is *so* pretty. So feminine. She was wearing this pretty blue sundress."

"I'm sure it was something. I appreciate the lasagna. I need the money. But I don't know."

"Such a talented guy, but you're struggling with money."

"I got to say no."

"He's not going to like that. There's no one else. I'll just tell him you're thinking about it. You've got a little time. Until next weekend. You seem so different from the other guys in Gonzago's crew. How'd you ever find your way into this kind of work?"

"Been thinking about that a lot lately. But mostly I've been thinking about how to get out."

Chapter Ten

Reiner

After eighteen months in the fleet, Branch was accepted into BUDS, the Navy SEAL training program. He made it past the psychological evaluation, the indoctrination, and the conditioning and diving phases of the training with no problems. After all he'd experienced in his childhood with Len, on Grandpa's farm, and on his perilous projects for Gonzago, it was a breeze for him. Along with the adrenaline he was used to, he was finally getting the discipline he'd never known.

Branch endured the cold, the wet, and the sand. He abided the harassment and the underwater confinement exercises, and he found that, unlike many of his mates, he could easily turn away Panic's pitiful attempts to rattle him. He even tolerated the pointless humiliation the Navy SEAL training program at the Bucklew Naval Special Warfare Center was famous for. No matter what it took, he edged his training mate and rival Carlsbad in most of the exercises. At last, young Branch Kilgore knew his path.

Branch advanced to phase three—the weapons and tactics section of BUDS training—and right in the middle of that he was ordered by the training officer to undergo a more comprehensive psychological evaluation. Then he was abruptly cut from the program. Branch Kilgore was ordered back into ordinary fleet duty. The SEALs didn't want him.

Carlsbad was gleeful in the barracks when Branch returned from the commander's office with the bad news.

"You were good, Kilgore," Carlsbad had told him. "But you never understood this is a team. *Yummean*? Too much of an individual to make it."

Branch was devastated. He left Bucklew and checked into a seaside motel, a sleazy place close to a dive shop and close to the Deep Blue Saloon, where he could kill the pain for a few days before he had to rejoin the fleet as an ordinary Electronic Warfare Specialist.

The weight of his sorrow pulled him down into the depths, down below four hundred, and then the nitrogen did its trick. Hallucinations came as he descended, and the shadow of numbness crawled over him.

But afterward, lying on the beach, with empty air tanks piled up around him, with the sweet amnesia of the nitrogen evaporating, the sorrow would again surpass the elation. For two days, blowing through tank after tank, he mostly didn't know where he was or how much time had passed. Then the shore patrol arrived.

Branch was arrested and taken to the Naval Consolidated Brig, Miramar, where he was held while an investigation was carried out. The basic training officer had been murdered in his quarters the night after Branch had left Bucklew.

Branch was harassed and interrogated for several days, but he didn't tell the naval investigators anything. He couldn't. He was too narced to remember what had happened after he'd left the base.

After a week in the brig, Branch was visited by a briefcase-toting civilian—a tall Black man in an expensive suit, sporting mutton-chop sideburns and a goatee. The man identified himself as Reiner.

"You're trial defense services?" Branch asked in the interrogation room. "About time. You sure don't look military, though."

"Thank you very much for *that*," Reiner answered sharply, straightening the lapels on his suit jacket.

"So you're with the JAG? I already gave a statement. I don't know anything about the officer's death. They've been interrogating me for a week in this shithole. They've been pushing me to confess even though they got nothing. So you can fuck off, too."

"Your request for a military attorney is being processed as we speak," Reiner told him, and he sized up Branch as he twisted his goatee. "I'm not your lawyer and I'm not from the commander's office. But I *am* here to help you. You look terrible. They been torturing you?"

"No, but they haven't let me sleep, not one second. For the whole week."

"Would you be sleeping anyway?" Reiner asked, and then he tapped on the leather briefcase in front of him. "With these charges hanging over your head?"

"No. But not because I'm worried about the charges. I wasn't even on the base when it happened. I think. They got nothing."

"They found your cap next to the body. You call that nothing? I've read the file. No witnesses. Initial report is no forensic evidence other than some of your hair inside the damn cap. Too bad about that cap. Beyond that, if you did do it, you got in and out of the base like a ghost. Motive and the cap are all they have. But this is the navy and they don't need a damn thing more than that to hang your ass."

"Whatever," Branch said. He felt Panic lurking. He took a breath and then he was calm again.

"A decorated navy SEAL, a BUDS training officer, drowned. They found him face down in the john. Fascinating. Pretty awful, the way he went out. And pretty ironic, don't you think?"

"No," Branch said. "Not awful. Not ironic. Paints a pretty picture, though. Wish I could've seen it. But I didn't. Must have blown through ten or twelve tanks those two days. Super deep. All my gear was there on the beach. My cap, too, I guess, when I was down. I don't remember much. But if I'd gone back to the base, I think I'd remember."

"Sounds like a solid defense to me. But first, let me get this straight. You're not worried about the charges. Even with the evidence they got. So why wouldn't you be sleeping, even if they let you? Feeling sorrow about the death of your superior officer?"

"No. The training officer had him a good life, I suppose. A strong life, maybe. I got no feelings about him, alive or dead."

"Then what is it?"

"Because I've got no job, Mr. Reiner. This job, in the teams? I would've been the best there ever was at it. I was the best in my class, except maybe for this one other guy. But I guess they don't want me."

"I've been looking at your navy file. I think I already knew the answer. But I wanted to hear it from you. About always needing to have a job."

"So you're from the unemployment office."

"Just someone that wants to help because I think you can help me. You sign a confession, the old man gives you a DD, and then you go to work for me."

"Tell the old man to go fuck himself. I'm not taking a dishonorable. I'm innocent."

"They won't discharge you with honor. The murder of an experienced officer is no trivial matter."

"Mr. Reiner, if you can walk into Miramar and offer me a quick release then you must be working for somebody who can get whatever they want. So get me an honorable, or at least a bad conduct discharge, and then we'll talk."

"You're right. I'm a talented motherfucker and I can get anybody to do most anything. I can make a bulldog kiss a pussycat. But I can't get the old man to let you walk just like that. Not with that cap sitting in the evidence room.

"I've been studying your navy file," Reiner went on, and then he pulled a fat yellow folder out of his briefcase. "Your training scores are off the charts. And the psych evaluations—have you seen this shit? Of course you haven't. Very interesting reading, to say the least. It seems that the navy fails to appreciate your skills. They want mindless little robots they can control. Fucking SEALs. No way you were ever going to fit that mold. Not in your disposition. The marines, maybe, but never the navy. Sometimes it happens this way with exceptional individuals. But my outfit might have a place for such an individual."

"What outfit?"

"You don't need to know. I'm just a contractor. But what you *do* need to know is I got a job for you. Right up your alley. Plus, you'll get to work on your master's degree."

"How's that?"

"You'll take my deal. You'll plead guilty to a lesser charge—manslaughter—and you'll take the DD but no jail time. And then you'll work for me."

"A DD means a loss of all military benefits, Reiner. And a felony on my record means I can't ever rotate into any kind of decent straight life. So if I take your deal you'll have me by the balls."

"We've got our *own* file on you, too," Reiner said, pulling another folder from his case. "The JAG doesn't know about this one. And he doesn't need to. Says here your father is a convicted smuggler and commercial diver named Leonard Kilgore. Works for Gonzago Obeto. You were practically raised by Gonzago himself. Impressive. Quite a privileged upbringing in my book."

"That's what this is? If you want to use me to go after Gonzago, forget it. I'll sit here and rot."

"You insult me. Go after Gonzago? That would be DEA. What makes you think the DEA has a clue as to what's happening to you in here? You're not even on their radar. Does this suit look like something a scumbag DEA-type would wear?"

Branch admired the beautiful stitching on the suit. It looked like something Gonzago himself would wear. "You've got good taste. That counts for something."

"Got your GED at sixteen," Reiner said, scanning the file. "And an undergrad degree at eighteen. Now that's interesting to me. Raised by the South Texas mafia and you go off and get a degree in physics and math."

"Always liked math. Practical applications. And that's the way Gonzago wanted it. Education was real important to him."

"Isn't that the problem with the world today? Not enough people good at math. I need somebody good at math who's got no conscience and no religious bullshit morals. Now that would be a rare and useful individual."

"Never did me much good before."

"Now's your chance to do some good. Help your country. Give you a chance to work off this horrible thing you done to your training officer."

"I didn't do shit. But I'm listening."

"Good idea. I need someone to pose as a graduate student at a little college down in South Florida. Physics department. I need to get a better look at what's happening down there. So what do you say, Mr. Kilgore?"

"About working for you? I'd say it doesn't sound any better than that world I was in before I enlisted."

"I don't see the relevance of that. Because you're in a world of shit right here at Miramar. And I'd just hate it if the old man should get his hands on *our* file," Reiner said, thumping the folder. "Some of the stuff in here makes their circumstantial evidence look pretty solid."

"You're a sorry bastard, Reiner. With a felony conviction on my record you'd own me. I left the life with Gonzago and Len because I wanted something better. It's not too late for me to have that. I'll take my chances."

Reiner laughed. "Now listen to me, my reality-defiant friend. Some people just don't want to accept who they are. This is a good deal for you, Kilgore. Tell you what I'll do. The DD is nonnegotiable. The plea deal on the manslaughter charge, too. They both stick but I can guarantee you the file will remain sealed, hidden from your record and off the radar as long as you and I can remain on good terms."

If Reiner had the power to spring him, Branch knew he also had the power to keep him in the brig. That Gonzago file in the briefcase would ruin him. He had no choice. So the very next day, after signing a confession and a stack of plea papers for the judge advocate general, he said goodbye to the navy, walked out of the Naval Consolidated Brig at Miramar and stepped into Reiner's black sedan.

For a month Branch was briefed on Reiner's operation at a Los Angeles hotel. He was relieved to be out of the brig but pierced by disappointment he'd failed in his bid to become a SEAL. And then he was flying to South Florida, where he enrolled in graduate studies in the physics department at a small, exclusive private college near Miami.

He met with Reiner weekly at a Fort Lauderdale coffee shop, but other than that, he forgot about his real assignment and dived deep into his college studies, and deep into the aquamarine waters off Florida's Atlantic shore. As the weeks went by in that first semester he was spending less time in the Deep Blue Saloon and more time in the classroom.

Branch made good grades, and by the end of the school year he was nearing completion of his master's coursework. His infiltration of the college was wildly successful—he'd been hired after his first semester to teach entry-level undergraduate physics courses, to counsel students, and to maintain the research facilities on campus. Reiner couldn't be happier.

Branch was happy, too. He enjoyed teaching the theories of physics he'd witnessed during his extreme underwater activities, and he was passionate about presenting experiments to his freshman students.

The chairperson of the department, Dr. Huggins, admired Branch's enthusiasm for physics and his natural teaching abilities, and as a fellow scuba diver he joined Branch on weekend outings to dive sites up and down the coast. It became a Sunday ritual—picking tanks up at the shop, driving to the marina and taking the chairperson's big cabin cruiser out into the teal waters. But Branch never allowed Huggins, a novice diver, to follow him down into the super-deeps. He saved those sweet, reckless, and now infrequent couplings with that girl waiting down there for him, almost, for himself.

Dr. Huggins promised that once Branch finished up his master's degree, he'd be invited to get started on a doctoral program and take a full-time job as an associate professor with the school. Huggins became a mentor to Branch in the area of teaching, and Branch became a teacher to the chairperson in the area of underwater meditation. Dr. Huggins was everything that Len never could be, everything that Gonzago never would be, and for a time, Branch was very pleased with his little life and his little teaching job at the college. He tried hard to forget that the only reason he was at the college was to do a very different little job for Reiner.

The college's physics department faculty members were PhDs who also did consulting work for the Los Alamos National Laboratory. Using the hacking, lock picking, and electronic eavesdropping technologies that Reiner had trained him on, Branch extracted information from the computers and cell phones of the professors in the department. From that data, Reiner confirmed his suspicions: one of the professors was selling secrets.

Sitting in the coffee shop that day, near the end of the school year, Reiner finally gave Branch the assignment he'd been sent to Florida for.

"It's your buddy, Dr. Huggins," Reiner said blandly, sipping on his coffee. "Has to look like an accident. This thing is so damaging it can't ever go to trial. Can't ever get out on the Internet."

"Dr. Huggins?" Branch asked as he tried to mask the despair washing over him. "Can't be right. What'd he do?"

"It all revolves around this," Reiner said. He took a pen from his suit pocket and wrote an equation on a paper napkin:

$y = 1/x$

"Simple little calculus formula. What about it?"

"You don't know? Shit, Branch. I thought I was dealing with some kind of brilliant physicist here. This simple little formula is at the heart of the nuclear enrichment secrets he sold. Out in Los Alamos he'd figured out a way to use lasers to enrich spent fuel rods to super-high levels, and it all revolved somehow around this here formula. I did a little research on it myself and found out it's kind of a puzzle they been trying to solve for years. Called Torricelli's trumpet."

"Yeah. I vaguely recall reading about that."

"Shit, who's the physics instructor and who's the student now? This Torricelli's trumpet formula, pretty damn interesting. If you chart it out in three dimensions," Reiner said, drawing again on the napkin, "it makes a picture of a trumpet, a horn that gets infinitely long and infinitely narrow inside the pipe. But it keeps going forever."

Branch looked at the crude drawing of the ever-narrowing tube on the napkin.

"Which we all know is impossible," Reiner said. "This site I looked it up on? Said that this formula creates an object with *finite* surface area, but *infinite* volume inside the trumpet. Now that's some cool shit, if you ask me."

"Yeah. Pretty cool," Branch said, but he knew that being inside that tube—ever narrowing and never ending—was not cool. It was torturous. He'd been there.

"I want you to show your buddy Dr. Huggins *this* formula, on *your* dive slate, before you take him out. Down there in the salty blue, right before you drown his ass, I want him to know he's the one gonna have to squeeze forever, in hell, through that *infinite* narrow space. Traitorous fucking bastard."

Chapter Eleven

Which Way Forgiveness?

I t was the following Saturday night—the night before the weekly Sunday dive with Dr. Huggins—when Branch picked the lock on the dive shop's back door, entered and disabled the alarm just seconds before it zeroed out. Then he went outside and backed his truck up to the rear entrance of the shop, where the air compressor equipment was. He kept the engine running, got a long vacuum hose out of the bed, and slipped back into the shop. It was a crude way to poison a tank, but an effective one.

The next morning Branch drove back to the dive shop to meet the chairperson. Over the previous months it had become their happy Sunday ritual: pick up tanks at the shop, then stop for a bag of Cuban sandwiches on the way to the marina where Dr. Huggins kept his boat.

Branch grabbed the two tanks while Huggins chatted with the shop owner. The special tank—tank #180, tainted with an amount of car exhaust that would cause mere nausea when breathed at the surface but more serious results if taken deep enough—was right where Branch had left it. He grabbed it, along with one more from the rack and toted them out to the chairperson's Tahoe. The tanks felt heavy to him as he put them in the back.

"You're pretty quiet today, Branch," Huggins said to him as they cruised the ocean highway toward the marina.

"Yeah. Heavy load. These graduate courses and teaching, too."

"You've got the whole summer ahead of you. Got your whole life ahead of you. No mistakes in your past you can't get away from."

"I guess so. And you?"

"Pretty heavy, too, I guess. When you get older the mistakes are harder to shake. My wife moved out. Wants the house. Sometimes you do things. For money. To help you get over the pain. You see your time slipping away. Sometimes you do things that just don't make sense. Once done they can't be undone, either. But a young fellow like you? You wouldn't understand that."

"We all have to do things," Branch said, and he hesitated. "That we don't want to do."

They arrived at the marina and soon had the tanks, gear and ice chest loaded onto Dr. Huggins's fifty-foot cruiser.

So this is what you get for selling national secrets. An awesome boat, for sure. But it must feel like an anchor to him.

Half an hour later they were nearing their dive site, a reef that started in about sixty feet of water then dropped off quickly to more than three hundred.

This site will do just fine. But I don't want to do it. Want the fantasy to be real. A real job and a Sunday dive buddy. But it ain't real. It's vapor. Just like these morning clouds burning off as the sun comes up. It might as well be me that dies today. Fuck it. My life's been nothing but a spin on a roulette wheel, anyway.

Let him choose his own tank, Branch thought, and he closed his eyes. *Whatever tank I end up with is the tank I use. And I'll take it deep. Spend the time I have left down there. With her.*

He opened his eyes and looked up at Huggins, staring down at him from the wheelhouse, haggard and wrinkled from worry. He smiled at Branch.

"You going to let me go way down there with you today, buddy?"

"Absolutely," Branch said, and he smiled weakly back at him. "You ready to go on this deep one with me, or you gonna be a ...," he started to ask, but his voice trailed off before he could finish.

"Sure, I'm ready." Huggins grabbed a tank and started assembling his scuba gear.

Branch grabbed the other tank and set up his own rig without looking at the tank number.

"Nothing like a boat," Huggins said. "She never wanted to come out here with me. Nothing but lonely. I could go to Bimini in this thing. Could go all the way to Cuba. But what for?"

"How long would it take us? If we just went to Cuba?"

"I don't know. Every time I tried to get away I just felt trapped. But these last few months, diving out here with you? You're a good friend, Branch. It's the only real freedom I've ever known."

"Yeah," Branch said, nodding at the dark water. He cranked open the valve on his air tank, heard his hoses pressurizing, wondered what kind of air was waiting in there for him. "Freedom. Your experiences down there are a totally separate reality. Your problems up here don't matter. Down there. That's what's special about it to me."

"Too bad we have to come up at all."

"Yeah. Too bad. There's a sweet spot out off the wall. Way down deep. A place where we can forget about the mistakes."

Huggins laughed and shook his tanned, wrinkled head. "I'm ready for that."

Branch watched as Huggins placed his rig up on the bench. The digits 1–8–0 stenciled in black paint on the side of the chairperson's tank jumped out at him like a sea snake.

"Yeah, you're ready," Branch said. He felt no relief. "I hope you'll find the escape you're looking for. I really do."

There was no time for remorse. The roulette wheel had spun and it had come up black. Now there was only the job to do. Branch slung his gear on, spit into his mask, rinsed it, and then rolled back into the blue water. He quickly cleared his ears and kicked straight down. He heard his bubbles rumbling to the surface like the faraway banging of war drums.

Branch pressed his belly into the warm sand at about sixty feet and waited for the chairperson to join him. He looked up, saw Dr. Huggins eclipsing the sun and casting a long shadow as he struggled to clear and descend. In a moment they were together on the sand and then they dropped down onto a wall of coral. Sea whips and other gorgonians prayed in unison, bowing repeatedly to the east as they flapped in the swell.

At about ninety feet Huggins looked a little uneasy—the carbon monoxide levels were rising in his blood. *Got to get him deep, and quickly now. The poor bastard. Whatever evil thing he did, he's already suffered for it.*

At the bottom of the wall, at about one twenty, Branch finned silently, the mottled red and beige sand floor undisturbed beneath him. He looked back to see Huggins close behind, a sickly pallor overtaking his face. *Just a bit deeper and then he's done. Quick and easy. He deserves that much.*

At one eighty, the sandy slope was flattening out, the coral life sparser. A solitary devil's sea whip, a long, ropelike sprig of coral, sprang up from the slope, its spiraled end forming an abstract question mark. *Which way forgiveness?* the sea whip seemed to ask. The unsolvable riddle irritated Branch, so he kicked deeper to escape it. The light became softer, the glow of neon, and then Branch felt the depths working on him.

As the nitrogen's narcotic wonders overtook him, he enjoyed the delightful decorations. Butterfly fish hostesses seated him and he admired the wonderful lounge furniture made of barrel sponges, and the window shades crafted from deepwater sea fans. A soundtrack of distorted electric guitar music blasted in his ears—*Buddy Guy, isn't it?*—and he took a moment to drink it all in.

Branch knew that the same phenomenon of physics so pleasing to him was also causing massive amounts of carboxyhemoglobin to build up in the chairperson's bloodstream. He gritted his teeth. Surprised by the regulator clenched there, he was reminded there was work to be done.

At two hundred feet the sandy floor flattened out and the back rooms of his underwater nightclub became as dingy as any good opium den. The chairperson hesitated, hovering above him at one ninety.

Don't bail on me now, Mr. Chairperson, Branch thought, signaling for him to kick down. Branch pointed to the depths. *Isn't that a Maltese bikini fish down there?* He giggled that there was really nothing to look at, had to suppress the hilarity of it. In spite of the horrible task at hand it seemed to be the funniest thing ever. *There's really nothing there!*

Then Branch was in his classroom, lecturing his students. *Carbon monoxide at the surface will cause varying degrees of distress*, Branch told them, and he noticed that Dr. Huggins had slipped into the back of the room. Why is he wearing scuba gear in the classroom? *At fifteen hundred parts per million, it can cause headaches. At twelve thousand parts per million, it can kill you in two minutes. Breathing the same gas at depth intensifies the results exponentially, due to the increased number of molecules in each breath.*

Dr. Huggins raised his hand from the back of the watery classroom.

"A question, Branch. How much carbon monoxide is in tank 180? That's my tank, I believe."

"From a simple test I took on the tank valve," Branch lectured from the front of the room, "I can tell you that tank 180 has about two thousand parts per million in it. At two hundred feet, that's the equivalent of breathing carbon monoxide-infused air having twelve thousand parts per million at the surface."

Dr. Huggins lowered his hand. "And how long will that take to kill me, at, say, two hundred feet below the surface?"

"You're already dead," Branch heard himself say, dropping deeper, the classroom disintegrating away as the barrel sponges turned into barstools.

Huggins drifted down to him, his face a pallid green. Branch secured him by the straps, pinned his arms and dumped the remainder of the air from his vest.

Narcosis overpowered remorse and adrenaline defeated sympathy. He had a job to do, and Reiner was his real boss. Reiner had saved him from the brig. Branch put his underwater slate in front of Huggins's mask, as Reiner had requested, then watched with stoned fascination. Huggins read the writing on the slate, and Panic took him. Then the convulsions came: arms flapping, fins kicking.

The two divers tumbled round and round, their four arms and four legs creating a bizarre aquatic spider. Huge, jagged bursts of bubbles blasted away from the spider and roared to the surface.

Dr. Huggins's flailing fins pushed them into darker water and the spider dropped down deeper. Branch watched the needle on his depth gauge as it moved ... 300 ... 310 ... 320 ... and in his stupor he wondered: What exactly is this thing measuring? As the needle continued to move to the right, he thought he had it figured out.

The needle was measuring his own doom. It was measuring the unalterable, tragic course of his life. And then, a little deeper, and finally it was only measuring that underwater waitress's soothing caress.

And there she was, almost. Shot glasses crafted from seashells were bulging from her cute little sargasso vest as she poured him several rounds. *I'll have a few, then get back to business. Whatever that business may be.*

Strawberry sponge schnapps, she tells him, pushing the drinks on him. He slammed the shots—sweet, fancy, utterly intoxicating liqueur—and then he was taking the elevator down to the basement bar for more.

Dr. Huggins spit out his regulator, inhaled a huge gulp of sea water. Some people just can't hold their liquor, Branch thought, mildly irritated that the guy now sitting next to him at the bar was getting sick. Huggins raised his hand and knocked his own mask off. Branch watched in muted amusement while he gasped and burped his final few bubbles of air. Huggins's torso shook under the strain of cardiac arrest. Branch spoke to him as he spent the final few seconds of his life in convulsive, gagging bewilderment.

"I'm so fucking sorry," Branch droned drunkenly at him through his regulator. "But you chose that tank yourself. Anyway, you had you a good life. A strong life. Now it's over, you lucky bastard. To have someone like me take you out like this.

With a stiff martini and a coupla ciggies in a wonderful place like the Deep Blue Saloon."

Then he began a slow ascent back up the sandy slope. As Branch passed through, the enigmatic sea whips once again sprang their question at him: *Which way forgiveness?* And as Branch surfaced, holding Dr. Huggins's dead, saturated body, he knew, sadly, what the answer to their riddle was. *Down. Only down.*

Chapter Twelve

The Finer Things

"What do you mean you're quitting?" Reiner asked, sitting across the booth from him in the coffee shop in Lauderdale. "You don't get that option."

"I did the job for you," Branch replied calmly. He felt lousy about killing Huggins. But he also felt satisfied that the job was done and that the dean of the college had offered him a full-time teaching position. Now the anguish and the satisfaction were teetering dangerously back and forth in his mind but he couldn't let Reiner see it.

"And I did it well," Branch continued. "Stopped your little security leak, whatever the hell it was. Covered up the damage. The coroner ruled the death an accidental drowning."

"I know that. Due to cardiac arrest and exposure to carbon monoxide in the tank. You think there's a goddamn thing you do I don't know about? You might as well have a bracelet around your ankle I'm so on you. And it *was* outstanding fucking work. Very creative. That dive shop won't be in business much longer but *my* people are happy. Did you give him the message?"

"Yeah. I showed him my underwater slate. Before it was done."

"And he freaked?"

"I really don't remember. But it was the last thing he ever saw. Not professional, Reiner. You could've got me killed by messing around with a dramatic thing like that."

"Shit, Branch, you had him. I wasn't worried. The folks I work for been sniffing out this traitorous fuck for years. You should feel real good about the job you did. Got the data that proved it and then took the fucker out, too. You helped your country. Not that it makes up for the awful thing *you* did to your country back at Bucklew. But there's time for that. More work is stacking up. For your country. Back out on the coast."

"The only work I'm interested in now is teaching physics. Dr. Huggins had it all set up for me before—"

"Before what? Before you took him down and drowned his ass?"

"Before the accident, you mean? Yeah. I've got an associate professor gig, full-time, waiting for me at the college."

"You think you're going to keep teaching?" Reiner laughed and coffee dribbled down his goatee. "Huggins is dead and so is your teaching career. How's it feel, killer? Shit, I don't think you know a damn thing about physics, anyway."

"Now that Huggins is dead," Branch said, sipping his own coffee and ignoring Reiner, "that adds a little urgency for the college to fill the vacancy. I already talked to the dean about it. At the funeral. I'm going to take it, Reiner. I did my job for you. And now I'm done with you."

"You're done when I say you're done, Kilgore. Don't forget that sentence waiting for you back at the brig. Don't forget what's sitting in your fat yellow case file."

"You got your money's worth. I earned this. I think when you think about it, Reiner, you're going to be content to release me."

"I'm not content. Because you're my slave. And this was just your first god-damn job. You haven't earned shit. Maybe after four jobs, seven jobs, you might have earned some favor from me. Might let you buy your freedom from me then. But after your first job? You think just 'cause you're teaching equal and opposite reactions to a bunch of rich, pimply-faced Florida freshmen that you've done something? That ain't shit. Not with the debt you owe your country. I'll have you back in Miramar. Master's degree don't mean shit in that world."

74

"You don't have to worry about me, Reiner."

"I worry about everything, Branch. So forget all this nonsense. You're a talented dude. And your true talent *ain't* in teaching. Look, man, I know you got close to the target. Had feelings for him. You had to. That's what a pro does, am I right? He gets in close. You're not one of those robotic punks the navy trains back at Coronado. Remember? That outfit that didn't want you? That outfit that trains their little robots to kill from a distance? Using sniper rifles and drones? Am I right?"

"Yeah. You're right. But—"

"The chairperson," Reiner interrupted. "Dr. Huggins. I know you feel bad. He helped you out, mentored you and all that shit. The father you never had. But you're a professional. And he compromised our national security and cost our country millions of dollars. All so he could buy that boat you been spending your Sundays on and that fine-ass house of his on the beach and those thousand-dollar hookers in West Palm. So what you got to do now is give the college notice you won't be back in the fall, close out of your little shithole apartment, and then we move you on to the next job. So you'd best be here next week for coffee. Same place, same time, or else I'm going to give *you* something to worry about."

"I'm not some felon who's violated his parole, Reiner. I'm saying I want to stay here, live here. Teach school here. For the kids. Does that sound like I'm violating the terms of my release?"

"You are a fucking felon, motherfucker," Reiner said, and then his hollow, nasal laugh echoed again through the diner. "And teach school? You should have considered that career path before you made your first hit as a teenager back in Texas. You think the college might have a little issue hiring a professor who's got a manslaughter and a DD on his record? Who grew up under the wing of Gonzago Obeto? And what's the DA gonna have to say about Huggins's dive accident when they see that fat yellow file and read about how your training officer died back at Bucklew?"

75

Branch said nothing. He looked into Reiner's black, bottomless eyes and he saw his own imprisonment there.

"You got a real problem with authority, Branch," Reiner went on. "Killed your training officer back at the teams. You signed the paper. It's a matter of record. I'm not even going to mention that cop you killed on FM 182, back in Houston. You remember FM 182, right? And now you've killed your chairperson at the college. Ugly pattern."

"I don't know what you're talking about, in any of those cases. But if all that was true, I'm sure we'd both hate for that pattern to continue. Boss."

"Oh, you're a funny man. But I ain't worried about that," Reiner said. He smiled, brushed his jacket aside and showed Branch the blue semiautomatic holstered on his belt. "You're worth a lot to me. You're probably good for ten more jobs before you go completely insane."

"How much, exactly, Reiner, am I worth to you?"

"I'm not for sale, motherfucker. And I'm not worried about losing you. And the boys outside ain't worried, neither. We're watching you full-time. We know your every move. So you got two choices. You can make a graceful exit from this gig at the school and then we gear you up for the next job. Or you can stay here and face the consequences of what you've done."

"Those secrets Dr. Huggins was selling. Must have been some embarrassing stuff. Or else you would've prosecuted him. You bust me and all of that comes out. You're bluffing."

"No," Reiner said, and then he laughed again. "I'm not. *You're* bluffing. And even if you're not, you'll still be the one taking it up the ass from the leathernecks back in the brig. Not me. So shut the fuck up and let's have some breakfast."

Branch pushed the food around on his plate while Reiner gulped down his omelet. Later, out in the parking lot, Branch saw the two men in the tan Ford sedan parked next to Reiner's black Porsche.

"I see you spotted my two friends over there," Reiner said, as Branch climbed into his truck. "I called for some backup for this transition. You see, even though you did this job real nice you're still in what we like to call a settling-in phase. Kind of like your little freshmen students when they've just moved into the dorms. Those first couple of weeks and they've got a tendency to run back to mama when the classes get tough. That's why you have counselors and shit like that to help keep 'em calm. Those boys back there in the sedan. They're your counselors. To make sure you don't run back to mama."

"Like I told you, you don't have to worry about me," Branch said, starting up the truck. "Besides, my mama's been dead since I was a baby."

"I *know* that, idiot. I'm just being metaphorical. You do know what that means, don't you? But if I wasn't being metaphorical, who the hell would you have to run to, anyway? I'm all you got now. *I'm* your mama. Am I right?"

"Right," Branch said, waving to Reiner as he rolled off. "See you for breakfast next week. Mama."

As he drove away he looked into his rearview mirror. He saw the tarp in the back covering his dive bag and his other few possessions. And behind him, there was the tan Ford.

Branch had hoped to be on his way to sign a lease at a seaside apartment complex he'd scoped out. Then buy some furniture, settle in, maybe buy a few little things at Ikea, make the place homey, settle in, and dive all summer, knowing that in the fall, a real job—teaching at the college—awaited him. But those dreams had just been clouds, dematerializing in the morning sun.

So he pointed the truck toward the Fort Lauderdale Galleria instead. He pulled into the mall's underground parking garage and watched in his rearview as the tan Ford continued down Sunrise Boulevard. Parking quickly, he checked for the Ford again. Then he got out, crawled under his truck and detached the GPS tracking unit Reiner had hidden there months before. Pocketing the unit, he brushed himself off and went into the mall.

He walked through Neiman Marcus, unconsciously browsing through the furniture section. Nothing like the solid teak stuff in Gonzago's villa, but pretty nice all the same. He wished he could be buying a piece or two, for that seaside apartment. He walked on past, out of the store, and into the atrium, where he found the FedEx kiosk. He took the dive slate from under his shirt. Momentarily repulsed by the diagram of Torricelli's trumpet, he quickly packaged it up along with the GPS tracker. Then he shipped the box—via ground—to the Alyeska Ski Resort, care of the Ski Patrol, Anchorage, Alaska.

Branch went back to his truck, taking care to avoid the furniture department on the way, and drove through the parking garage and out the exit on the other side of the mall. The tan Ford was nowhere in sight. Then he hit the interstate.

Some weeks later he wandered into Houston, hoping that Reiner and his crew had chased the GPS tracker in the FedEx truck to the north. Branch had followed a beacon with a much stronger signal all the way back to Gonzago. The offices for Houston Antiquities Importers were still there, but closed for the weekend, so he drove out to the villa in River Oaks.

He scouted the estate carefully for any sign of Reiner's crew, then cruised up to the guardhouse and announced his arrival. The guard spoke on the phone and the huge gilded gates swung open. Then Branch was driving his old truck along the winding drive through the manicured, shaded grounds.

Gonzago had come out of the villa to greet him, tanned and trim in pleated Zanella shorts, a hemp blazer over a silk T-shirt, and woven sandals.

"Branch Kilgore, you son of a gun, you look like hell!" Gonzago exclaimed, smiling, looking him up and down. "What are you, trying to disguise yourself as an asshole? How many times have I told you that style matters?" Gonzago slipped out of the blazer and held it up for Branch to slip into.

"There. Now you're looking sharp. And your hair's this long? I like it, but I know the navy wouldn't let you grow it out. So, you must have been out for at least a year, huh? And you're just now coming to see me?"

"I've been out more than a year, Gonzago. It was a dishonorable."

"I know all about that. And I'm not surprised, Branch. I taught you to have good taste in things. Sleeping in a bunk and eating junk? Plus, all of that hurry up and wait nonsense? That's not your thing. You always liked to get the job done *now*, am I right? I've been asking Len about you. He said he hadn't heard from you in years. You don't keep in touch with your family? That's not right. But it's all good. We're still here for you."

Gonzago hesitated, looked down at the flagstone driveway, then put his hand on Branch's shoulder. "Len wasn't much of a father to you. I know that. I did my best to step in, show you some of the finer things. But you shouldn't blame Len for what you are, Branch."

"Oh, no?"

"No. Just consider that it could have been worse. You were born to be what you are. And I'm glad to see you. Anyway, Len's not around. I sent him to Monterrey to look into a problem I'm having with a new titty bar I bought down there. The manager is skimming like crazy. But what a place—you've got to see it! I'm building one in Veracruz, too. Got a Greek theme. Columns everywhere, looks like the Parthenon."

"The Parthenon Titty Bar, huh? Yeah, I remember from my Homer how much the Greeks loved a hundred-dollar table dance and a thirty-dollar shot of booze."

"You bet your ass they did," Gonzago said, laughing. "Come on in the house. Got a couple of dancers I'm taking care of by the pool. And let's get you something to eat. You look skinny."

Gonzago made him a plate of shrimp salad, cold roast beef, and new potatoes roasted in olive oil. Then they drank mojitos by the pool. Two bikini-clad girls were draped all over Gonzago. After a time, he sent them inside the house and he leaned close to Branch.

"So, Branch, you learned some stuff with the navy, huh? I heard you'd made it to special teams training. A sharp kid with balls bigger'n church bells like you, with all of that technical training? I bet you got *serious* skills now."

"Some exotic gas work, tri-mix and beyond. But you know me, I'm a nitrogen fiend. It's good to be diving with plain air again."

"Uh-huh. What else did you do in there?"

79

"Distance work. Mostly with the M4 and the Stoner. That's a rifle. Cowardly shit, you know."

"And what happened? Why'd you bail?"

Branch wanted to tell him more about the reasons behind his discharge but the words wouldn't come.

"No worries," Gonzago said. He motioned with his empty glass toward the house. "Teresa! Two more." Then he leaned over to Branch.

"Welcome back to the real world. You're safe here. But there was some Black guy, dressed real nice, beautiful Brioni suit, real polite, poking around the gallery last week. Asking about you."

"Reiner," Branch said, and he gulped his mojito.

"I think so. Yeah, Reiner. What is he? Navy cop?"

"I really don't know," Branch said, masking his disappointment that Reiner wasn't chasing him in Alaska. "NSA, something. I never knew. I'm sorry he bothered you. He got me out of a jam then I did some work for him. He's got a file on me. But I've got a file on him, too. So he shouldn't be a big problem."

"I made it clear to him that he'd better not be. In a nice way. I told him I hadn't seen you in years. The truth. He believed me. Left a card for you, in case you showed up. He said you've got thirty days to finish your vacation and give him a call."

"I won't be needing that card. I don't want to work for him anymore."

"Uh-huh. I'll hold on to it for you. They'll be looking for you here. You'll be needing cash. So you're a little bit desperate, I guess."

"Little bit, I guess."

"Desperation's a funny thing. It'll send a cowboy into a bank with a gun. If things go well, he can live high for a while. If things don't go well he goes to jail. Either way he's all set. But in our business, Branch, we can't act with desperation. No emotion. You remember?"

"I do."

"Then I'm glad to have you back." Gonzago lit a cigar and the thick smoke danced around his head. "So that's what you were doing for this Reiner? Working some cleanup?"

"Just one. A big one. Undercover. A complicated setup. I was teaching ..." Branch hesitated, the memory of that day on Dr. Huggins's boat haunting him. "Turns out I liked my cover a lot more than the real job."

"Teaching, huh? You always were an ace of a student. Maybe you should try to go straight. Get into that teaching thing for real."

"I would if I could, Gonzago. But Reiner ... he's got my record all messed up. For a while there I fooled myself. Told myself that teaching *was* the real job. Thought I was doing something to help the world."

"Teaching *is* an honest job. An important job. And like any job, you get paid for it. But helping the world? What have I always told you about the nonprofit work?"

"You were right, Gonzago. Too damn dangerous."

"That's right. Too much risk and no reward. Hell, you might as well join the Peace Corps and swat malaria mosquitoes all day long. That way you might do *some* good."

"Thought about it."

"That's not your thing. This," Gonzago said, spreading his hands and gesturing at the luxuriously appointed courtyard, "is your thing. You've got to work hard to have this. I taught you to appreciate the finer things." Then, in unbridled style, he shouted it out to the courtyard. "*The finer things!*"

The fresh mojitos arrived, and after they had taken a few sips Gonzago continued. "I may just have something for you, Branch. It'll get you out of the country, keep you out of sight until this Reiner thing simmers down. It'll pay better than teaching, too. I've been getting into more legal enterprises. Like this new breast emporium in Veracruz. I also financed an Italian restaurant in Chinchamos. You remember the place? The Mexican island, in the Caribbean? Lots of new tourism happening there. Cruise ships are bringing the suckers in by the boatload."

"Haven't been there in almost twenty years."

"I remember that trip with you and Len. Your first dive. You were just a boy. We were scouting out landing strips, remember? Anyway, the place is growing. They're pumping up the tourism. It's not just a hangout for smugglers and divers anymore. I have this lovely woman, Yvonne's her name, runs the restaurant for me there."

"What do you need me for? People walking the check?"

"No," Gonzago said, and he laughed and swilled his mojito. "I've got a partner down there. A Mexican hombre, Omar Rasgado. Most of my product that comes in from Colombia passes through there now. Typical business problems, you see?"

Gonzago paused to admire his cigar. "Omar handles the nastier end of the business. There'd be some contract work for you. But you'd be working for me, not him. You go down there, talk to Yvonne. She's my eyes and ears. The only person I can trust. All my communications for you will go through her. And the food at the restaurant is damn good. Real Italian. Fresh seafood."

"Talk to her and do what?"

"Settle in down there, get your nitrogen fix. Find yourself a nice girl. Just keep a low profile. Create a good cover for yourself. No cell phones, no Internet, social media bullshit, you hear me? *You know who*, they're always watching, always listening. There *will* be work for you from time to time. I've got a lot of cleaning up to do. I want to pull out enough cash from the coke business so I can quit all that and concentrate on the restaurants and clubs. I'll give you a little advance then you can work for me and Omar on a contract basis. Help me with the cleaning up."

"You're really getting out?" Branch asked, suppressing his envy. He'd tried a straight life, couldn't hack it, and now he would be stuck doing the work again.

"There's a lot of development opportunity down there in Chinchamos right now. Tourism dollars pouring in. Why should I continue to risk my ass when I can be some kind of restaurant or resort king? *The finer things!*"

Chapter Thirteen

Door Number Two

The sun was setting as Melanie made the short walk back to her bungalow. Her hair glowed golden in the waning light but the radiance in her face had been extinguished by the humiliation at the jewelry store.

Out in the channel another ship, the *Quantum of the Seas,* was coming in. There was a sudden blast from the ship's horn and then black smoke poured from her stack. Melanie didn't have the energy to descramble it, but the letters moved in her mind anyway. *Satan's Mouth Queef.*

That made her smile but the smiled faded when she remembered that Fernando was coming at six. She had to gain control of the situation, no matter what it took. The evidence that could get her killed was there on his cell phone.

She would go see Branch. He was strong enough, stoned enough, addicted to her enough to help her feel better. Later tonight she would go see him. Just as soon as she was done with Fernando.

Melanie's place was one of four bungalows in a compound several blocks from the oceanfront. Set back from the road and sheltered from the sun by a large grove of ceiba trees, the bungalows shared a shady courtyard of crushed coral providing a common entry point to the stuccoed residences.

The complex was owned by a dentist from the mainland who operated a practice out of one of the bungalows two days a week. As Melanie stepped into the courtyard, dead coral crunching loudly beneath her feet, Dr. Thompson hurried out from his door. Then she remembered that today was one of those two days.

"Mel, uh, Melanie, I need to t-t-t-talk to you." Dr. Thompson had been exposed to too much nitrous oxide over the course of his career and the result was a high degree of difficulty expressing himself verbally.

"Why, Dr. Tom, you're here today," Melanie said, instantly perking up her face. "Thought you'd be back home with that lovely wife of yours."

"Uh, had an emergency r-r-root canal to do. You know Eric, the t-t-tug captain at the m-m-marina? He broke a crown, had to stick around for him."

Melanie let her bag slip off her shoulder and moved toward him.

He backed away. She followed him to the doorway. "What was it you wanted to talk about, Dr. T?"

It took him a while to get it out but he told her what she already knew—her rent was two months overdue.

"Well, of course it is, Tommy." She commanded him gently back through the doorway with the tip of her index finger, took a wad of hundreds—the last of her cash—from her purse, unfolded the bills and straightened them out carefully. "And I've got the dough for you right here," she said, plopping the small heap of currency onto his instrument tray. "Or do you want to trade it for what's behind door number two?"

She let her bag fall to the floor, turned to the side and bumped him with her soft hip. Then she pushed him back a little harder with her finger toward his dental chair, closing the door behind her with her foot. Dr. Thompson looked at the stack of cash on his tray, swallowed nervously then looked back at Melanie.

"M-M-Mel, my wife expects me to come home on the f-f-ferry tonight with cash. And Mel, you know how s-s-sick I am."

"That's right, Thompson. The nitrous. I know all about it. I'm the only one who can make it all better now, aren't I? You've already got cash, from Eric the tugboat captain. So we can have our fun again."

Something about hearing the word "tugboat" seemed to push Thompson over the edge and he submitted as Melanie pushed him all the way back into the treatment chair.

He put his trembling hand on her ass, pulled her gently onto him, and then she felt him break.

"Yeah, but not for the cash. B-b-because you like me. As a f-friend."

"Of course, I like you, Dr. Tom," she said, pushing away from him while pulling a hose from the dentist chair's operatory package. She pointed its glistening silver tip at him. "But once you've crossed the line into a business relationship you can never be friends like *that*, ever. Rules of the trade, Doc. No matter how much I do like you. You've got to choose." She nodded back at the mound of bills on the tray. "What's it going to be, Tommy? The Benjamins or the bootie?"

"Y-y-yeah," he moaned as he pulled on the straps of her dress, placed his hands on her breasts and pulled her down on top of him on the chair.

"We have a deal, then," she said, poking the hose into his mouth. "For the past due and next month, too. Say it. Door number two."

"Yeah. Trade it for d-door number two."

"Always wanted to do this. What's this lever do?"

Melanie pulled the lever and water squirted into Dr. Thompson's mouth. He moaned again, gurgling. She dropped the hose and it snapped back into place. "But better enjoy it. I'm retiring soon."

"Then g-g-give me the g-g …" He couldn't get it out, but he cut his eyes to the tank valve on the wall.

"You want the gas, this time, Thompson? Is that it?" Melanie put the respirator over his nose, smacked the elastic band over his head and cracked open the tank valve. "So kinky."

"So I won't know what I'm d-d-doing," he said, taking a big snort as he pulled down his scrub bottoms. He convulsed, his eyes rolling back in his head as he reached for her. Melanie straddled him, leaned back and looked up at the ceiling, wishing she was somewhere else. The evil face of the dental light over the chair was looking down on her and seemed to be grinning.

Pelton-Crane said the writing below the evil face, and as Dr. Thompson convulsed below her she gladly let the letters move around in her mind. *"Rent-Econ Plan,"* she said, and gave a little laugh.

She leaned forward to get away from the light's grinning face and pushed Dr. Thompson's shoulders down against the vinyl of the dental chair. She moved her hips gently and looked now at the dental posters on the wall. Some dirty dentist talk might help speed things up, she thought.

"It's for the fast, efficient cementation of high-strength restorations, Thompson!"

Dr. Thompson only moaned. She sped up the action of her hips and continued to scan the posters on the wall. "It's a revolutionary treatment for incipient caries and white spot lesions, Thompson. Without drilling!"

Dr. Thompson was gasping behind the nitrous mask. She gyrated on him a little faster.

"Thompson, a premium non-foaming formula—now with xylitol!"

His entire body seemed to erupt into a burbling, stammering spasm. The job was over. She jumped up, straightened herself, took her cash and her purse and left him there in his chair, pants down, the respirator hissing on his face, the evil light above now only smirking at her.

A few minutes later, in her apartment, Melanie heard the crunching of dead coral. Slightly relieved that Dr. Thompson had survived the nitrous episode, she opened the door and watched him trudge across the courtyard, toward town and the last ferry to the mainland.

"That was fun, Tommy," she said, a little too loudly. The crunching stopped and Thompson turned to look at her. "Hope you enjoyed it. Because that was the last time."

"M-M-Mel—" was all she heard as she closed the door.

She looked up at the round retro wall clock, its second hand twitching slightly with each tick. It was still only half past five. Just enough time to rinse Dr. Thompson off of her and get ready for Fernando. She dropped the needle on the turntable vinyl, slipped out of her dress and ran a hot bath in the clawfoot tub. Easing into the bubbles, she sipped on a cup of chamomile and tried to clear her head, working in her sudoku book as the music played.

Miss Otis regrets she's unable to lunch today, madam ... When she woke up and found that her dream of love was gone, madam, she ran to the man who had led her so far astray ...

After bathing, she applied lotion to her pearly skin then looked at her naked shape in the steamy mirror on the wall. Natural, luscious, pink and porcelain, she observed, and no sun damage. Of that she was most proud. But she knew she was more than her body, and she didn't want to trade on it any longer.

Where had she gone wrong? She was smarter than any man she had ever met, yet here she was. She could have pointed to a hundred mistakes she'd made along the way. But feeling regret was a loser's game. There was only time to be in the moment, and at this moment she needed all of her skills to handle Fernando. She put on some baggy sweats and waited.

The knock came precisely at six. Leaving the chain on, she cracked the door and peered out at Fernando's warped, dingy smile.

"You know, my neighbor's a dentist," she said through the crack. Then she closed the door, removed the chain and let him in. "You should pay *him* a visit."

"I heard that *you* like to visit him," Fernando said, ambling into the living room. He took in a deep breath.

"Smells so good in here, Mel. Like lesbian angels been fucking in here."

"Just keep following your dick around, Fernando."

"A man *should* follow his dick. There's a real misconception about that, Mel. A man's dick is the one thing he's got that will never lie to him. Show me a man following his dick with true loyalty and I'll show you a happy man."

Fernando sat down on the tufted seats of the pink upholstered Chesterfield sofa.

"Anyway, you underestimate me if you think I'll settle for *that*," he said. "I'm not your landlord, you know? Sit."

"What do you want then, Fernando?" Melanie asked, sitting down across from him on the matching pink settee.

"It's a matter of what *you* want, Mel. Money's a problem for you. Omar's going to be an even bigger one," Fernando boasted, waving his smartphone at her then tossing it down on the French mirror top coffee table. "But you know the thing about Omar—he's really busy right now. All the problems he's having with the new cruise ship pier. He's *way* over budget on it, and if he did find out that someone had opened his safe—"

"If you're going to throw me to Omar, just give me a little warning, will you?"

"Omar's rich, I guess, but he's a cheap bastard. Probably wouldn't reward me if I did give you up. Don't get me wrong. I'll do it. But there's a better way. Stealing petty cash from the safe isn't a career with a good future for you, Mel. Time to think of the big picture."

"Of course it is, Fernando. And just what *is* the big picture?"

"You're stuck here in Chinchamos. Can't go back to the States. Omar holds the strings to your work permit. You lose that and you get kicked back across the border. And you go to jail, I'm guessing."

"No. Not jail. What's your point?"

"Omar goes to the mainland, on the ferry, with a satchel full of cash, once a month, always on the last Friday of the month. To buy diamonds."

"A robbery? Omar? On the boat? That's brilliant. He's got his own private army. Fibbi and all his deputies. He'll kill you. But for every downside there's an upside. I wouldn't have to walk in on you tossing off in the store bathroom."

Fernando laughed, pleased with his newfound indifference to her insults. "We all have our hobbies. Mine is masturbation. Yours is plastic surgery."

"No surgery, ever, you asshole. I'm natural."

Fernando picked his phone up from the coffee table and scrolled through his photo collection.

"You know what? Great pics. I think I believe you." He tossed the phone down again and nestled back into the sofa.

"Why not just rob the store?" Melanie asked.

"Fibbi and his deputies are watching the store all day long. When they're not out robbing and raping tourists, anyway. And there's really never that much cash there. And those rubies and diamonds? Pennies on the dollar if we could even fence them. But on the ferry he carries cold cash."

"But he's having cash flow problems. You said so."

"His coca revenues are down. No, he needs that diamond money. He's under pressure to make budget for the pier, so he goes to the mainland every month, with the cash in the case."

"You're serious." Melanie sat back on the settee, her feet on the edge of it, her hands clasped around her knees. "How much cash?"

"At least a million, US, every month."

"What about the bodyguards?"

"They see him to the municipal pier. He only brings one or two guys with him on the boat. Sometimes his nephew Dorian. Sometimes nobody. He feels safe on the ferry. Surrounded by tourists. No way to get on or off on the trip across. He likes to lounge around in the bar on the way across, too. Makes him feel important, drinking with the passengers like that."

"Nothing like a cocktail."

"He's been known to invite ladies from the bar into his berth. Likes to take a little nap before he buys his stones. His crew on the mainland meets him when he gets off. Then he buys diamonds from his wholesaler, he comes back across on the ferry, the briefcase full of diamonds, and his little Chinchamos army meets him here. But in between, in his private berth—"

"He's alone. Omar Rasgado, alone on the ferry with a million bucks, on his way to buy stones, taking a stone nap. I do love the man. But he's never hit on me. Never once."

"He's had his eye on you, but he's been busy. It's different for him on the ferry. I'll pick out something irresistible for you to wear. Maybe that Givenchy skirt suit? You just get him into his berth where the money is. I'll give you the stuff to drop in his drink and then you open the safe."

"That's not so easy."

"You'll handle it. That one in the store. Took you all of sixty seconds."

"Assuming he takes me into the berth and I open the safe—how do you plan on getting away?"

"I may be just the assistant manager of the store, but I do all kinds of errands for Omar, including making sure his speedboats get serviced. So, I have access to the fastest boats in the western Caribbean. We rob him, jump overboard, then we'll be away and hiding in one of those inlets on the mainland before they know what hit them. Gone!"

"And who'll be driving this magic speedboat?"

"Leave that to me."

"Uh-huh. You're going to use one of his own boats to rob him with. I like your creativity. Suicidal though it is. What if he doesn't want a drink?"

"I see you still have your little pink gun," Fernando said, nodding at Melanie's 4.25 mm Liliput pistol lying on the antique side table. "If he doesn't want a drink."

"My little peashooter?" Melanie answered, and she looked over at the tiny semiautomatic, all silvery, stainless steel with polished pink handgrips. She'd taken some risk bringing it to Chinchamos with her, had been tempted to pawn it once or twice, but she hadn't been able to part with it. It had been a gift from Vinnie, back in New York. A cherished memento from the good days. "What kind of safe is it?"

"It's like that one in the store, but smaller. But in case it goes bad we need help with the weapons. Your friend."

"My friend?" Melanie asked, then sat upright, curious again how Fernando knew about Branch.

"You don't know," Fernando said, and he laughed. "I *do* know. Things about him. He could help us. He has certain skills, certain tools. And right about now, certain motivations."

"You can't be serious. Branch is just a divemaster. He works at the dive shop."

Melanie paused, saw the serious expression on Fernando's face and wondered if it was possible she could have underestimated Branch. She leaned back into the settee and crossed her legs.

"You *are* serious. What do you know?"

"Branch is *not* just a divemaster. He really works for a restaurateur named Gonzago. Except he's not just a restaurateur. Well, he owns Yvonne's. You know the place."

"Yeah. I know it."

"That's where Branch was headed today. He had a meet with Omar. This Gonzago cat is a Texas mafioso, a famous guy. He's backing Omar on the mall. On the pier. I've heard some things about your boy. And my source tells me Omar was freaking out about some job he was on today."

"What kind of job?"

"He's a contract killer, Mel. Loves his work, hates it, too, I guess. But a real fiend for it. A hands-on kind of guy. The job went bad. He'll be feeling the need to leave Chinchamos soon. He might as well leave with a nice chunk of cash. You pay him out of your end."

Melanie was stunned and titillated at the same time. Branch—a professional? She'd been sleeping with a killer, had felt his secret strength. She'd felt the angst he protected at all costs.

"That sneaky little son of a bitch. He does always seem to have plenty of cash. Not a big spender but his pockets are never empty. I always felt something different with him. I don't know. A kind of hardness that seems so ... comforting to me."

"Hardness?" Fernando laughed. "You're fucking a dead man. Rigor mortis. Guys like that. They're in misery and they can't stop. They can't change." He paused, looked at Melanie's perfectly plump lips. "You never saw or heard anything when you're around him?"

"He's given up on ever being happy, I know that. And I guess the payoff is he's given up on ever being scared. On ever having anything to lose."

"That's the nature of his work. Military-trained guy. But I heard he got bounced out for being a little too enthusiastic."

A sudden surge of passion ran through her. The wires in him that had been cut long ago made him unique, made him the perfect man. A man without a conscience.

"How do I know it's true?"

Fernando chuckled. "You've been fucking him. You've watched him while he sleeps. No. You *know* it's true. He'd be perfect for this. I'm guessing he's got no real loyalty to anything, except you and that thing he does with you."

"Yeah, you're right about that," she said with a coy smile, but she wondered if Branch's loyalty to her was really that strong. "But even if it's true, what you say about Branch, what do you expect me to do?"

"You've got a hook in this guy. Talk to him. You've got one week. Last Friday of the month is coming up. Then I show my little photo collection to Omar."

Chapter Fourteen

The Blue Angel

B ranch lived at a hotel called the Blue Angel Inn, a name that might have
seemed odd, because the blue angel was a fish not found within a thousand
miles of Chinchamos. The original owners hadn't been fish experts, though, and
when the hotel, along with two hundred hectares of mangroves, was purchased
by seventy-year-old Pamela Linton and her husband, a retired admiral from Her
Majesty's navy, the name stayed. And in the following ten years, it seemed to fit,
because now there *was* a blue angel in the vicinity—Pamela herself.

The admiral hadn't survived his first year on the island, but Pamela lived on to
enforce her sense of civility and reason on the hotel's occupants. Her hair became
so bleached that it indeed looked blue, and in the Caribbean sun her once fair skin
became as wrinkled as a road map. But she was still bright-eyed and attractive and
her mind hadn't softened a bit. To the contrary, she watched over the lobby desk
and her part of the oceanfront with keen awareness.

The hotel was a five-story limestone affair, Moorish in design, sitting across
the street from the Caribbean Argonauts Dive Shop. It had taken the brunt of
several hurricanes with no more ill effect than a few broken windows. Steps led
up into a large stone archway and then into the cool lobby, with its high ceilings
and marbled floors. When the hotel was first built in the 1930s, the lobby featured
its own coffee shop and boutique. Now it had given way to shared space with La
Cucaracha Cigar Bar, a dimly lit saloon and whorehouse that had been spared
the effects of any modernization, and the Mean Bean, a café popular with the

local youth. It made for an interesting contrast, the Middle Eastern facade, the old fishermen, the whores, the tourists in the cigar bar, the young itinerants in the café, and there in the middle, stiffly English Pamela.

"Let me lay down the law of the Inn with you, Mr. Kilgore," she'd told Branch during the course of their initial meeting. "Drunkenness," she'd said, nodding toward La Cucaracha, "and disorder," she continued as she glanced at the Mean Bean, "seem to be surrounding me, as I no longer have control over either side of the lobby, due to some unfortunate lease arrangements I can't seem to get out of. But here in the middle, and in the rest of the building, they are not tolerated."

"I'm very interested in maintaining a clean lifestyle," Branch had told her, "and this location works well for me."

Pamela had beamed her wrinkled grin at him. "I'm not saying you can't have a life. I just don't want any of these tarts from the Cucaracha in my hotel. I like my tenants to err on the side of caution."

"Even if my tastes ran that way," he had told her honestly, "my budget won't allow it. I'm saving money so I can go back to the States and finish up my graduate work in physics. To make that happen I'll have to be careful with money."

So Branch had moved into a high-ceilinged room with a private bath on the top floor, and he *had* been cautious. Cautious with his cover job at the dive shop, cautious with the women he saw, and cautious as he worked the lasagna for Gonzago and Omar. But today caution hadn't been enough. And now he was bent and worried as hell as he approached the hotel.

Fighting off his numbness, he wobbled up the steps through the arch and into the cool confines of the Blue Angel lobby. The aroma of Cuban tobacco and the chatter of the whores drifted in from La Cucaracha as he approached the desk. He wanted to pick up his key and make it to the room without any questions, but a couple in front of the counter stood in his way.

"We don't rent rooms by the hour," Pamela bristled at them, a man in his forties and a Mexican girl about half his age.

"It looks like the kind of a place that might—," said the man, and then he quickly changed course. "I mean, they do at the cigar bar," he said, nodding across the lobby, then putting his arm around the young woman's waist. "They're all in use right now, the rooms over there. I'll pay for the whole night. But I have to be back to my ship in an hour."

"Oh yes, I see. And which one are you from?"

"The *Rising Soul Tangent*. I'm an actor for one of their shows."

"*Rising Soul Tangent*? The meditation and yoga at sea ship?"

"Yeah, but mostly they just eat. I'm in the cast of a drama on the life of Tibetan monks. I was supposed to be working on the *Poseidon's Aeria*. Shakespeare at sea, you know, lots of sexy girls in the cast? But my agent messed it all up."

The man chuckled nervously and squeezed the girl's waist a little tighter. "I was fortunate to run into Claudia here. I really need to have some time with her then get back out to the ship."

"Fortunate. It seems that fortune brings in some boats that are not steered."

"So how about the room?"

Pamela ignored him and turned her attention to the man's young companion. "You're from the Cucaracha? Claudia, is it? I haven't seen you around. You must be one of Elias's new arrivals. Perhaps no one told you. So I will, just once. You can't do business in here. Try the Marriott. Four blocks back toward town, on the water."

Pam watched them wander out to the street and then she looked Branch up and down.

"The nerve," Branch mumbled through puffy lips.

"Men are men. And the best of them sometimes forget it. Men like yourself. But you do look as though you've had a day."

"Rough day, Pam."

"For me, too. We were jostled about by the so-called police at the protest this morning. Then later Omar came by threatening me that I've got to sell the property. They were shooting guns into the water. Murdered one of my manatees. He and Fibbi."

"Fibbi? And Omar? They shot a manatee?" Branch felt his temperature rising but then he remembered what Omar had told him. "Maybe you should consider his offer."

"And let them kill the mangroves? Poor Dixie. And the other manatees. After what they've done already, capturing our dolphins from the sea and keeping them in that horrible pen across the street? No, I won't do it. This island is limestone and rose stone, and the witches in England knew that the limestone elemental is health, overall wellness and balance. And rose stone attacks nearby enemies by shooting brimstone fireballs at them. So, he's out of his element, do you see? He can't possibly succeed. We're meeting across the street tonight to talk about it all. Some environmental benefactor from the mainland is supposed to attend. But I suppose you don't want to get involved, do you? No. After those ugly oafs left I've been dealing with these tacky cruisers. And, oh yes, your young lady friend, lovely girl, I sent her away. Well, you look like you wouldn't be set for entertaining, anyway. She was here looking for you not half an hour ago."

"Ms. Lamy, was it?"

"Yes. Melanie Lamy. Seemed awfully anxious to see you. I do hate to turn away guests," she said, looking out at the street to make sure the couple had left the premises. "But without some kind of prior notice, I can't let just *anyone* into your room."

"I appreciate that. And you're right, I wasn't expecting her," Branch said, getting woozier with each second. "My key please, Pam, if you don't mind."

Pam looked in the box. "Don't you have it?"

Branch hesitated for a moment. He'd definitely left the key at the desk that morning before heading to the mainland in Victor's skiff. Someone else had grabbed it. Someone was waiting for him in his room. He prayed it wasn't someone from the mainland with red hair. But he couldn't let Pam know all that.

Tapping his empty pocket he told her, "You're right. I've got that key right here."

Chapter Fifteen

Glorified Glue-Sniffer

Branch stood at the door to his room and listened. He sniffed the air. He was getting numb from the nitrogen bubbles, but he was pretty sure it was the fragrance of cream and flowers he smelled. So after only a moment of indecision at the door he turned the knob and burst in. Melanie sat on the edge of his bed, dressed in a vintage pink knit suit, one leg tossed over the other in a display of gymnastic pliability. He wasn't sure if he was relieved or not.

"I've learned a thing or two from you, Kilgore," she said. "Your key's over there on the dresser."

"Funny, I don't remember seeing your name in my book today."

Melanie's laugh was like a songbird. "Of course you didn't, darling. I was just in the neighborhood and saw your truck across the street at the shop. I thought I'd give you a nice surprise when you got home. Hard day on the boat, I bet."

She sprang off the bed, moved the window blind and looked out at the water where the *Rising Soul Tangent* was preparing to put out. She closed her eyes for a moment and her mind did the automatic. *Insane Gluttons Rig.* She smiled, then walked over to Branch and put her soft hand on his shoulder.

"Day off today?" he asked her, and bent though he was, worried to death though he was, he looked down and couldn't help but admire her smooth, pale legs and her perfect pink toenails. He was aware of the pattern with her: overwhelmingly attracted to her, before, and equally repulsed by her, afterward. But in spite of that—even in his weakened state—he couldn't resist Mel Lamy.

"Might as well have been. Four ships in, but nothing."

"What ships?" Branch asked. He locked the door behind him and leaned back against it, away from Melanie, in exhaustion.

"Don't you know? I figured a divemaster would know which ships his divers are from. *Allure of the Seas*. And three others. Where do they get these names? It's always *Something Romance* or *Something Adventure of the Seas*. But then they storm down the ramp like a herd. It's bad enough to have to deal with them when they're *buying* jewelry. But they're *not* buying. Where's the *allure*, where's the *romance* in that?"

"Yeah. Where?"

"Fernando had one sale. Three weight ounce pure golden ring—no precious stone. A small commission for him. Nothing much for me, though. Tomorrow will be better, I suppose."

"I hope so, too," Branch said. He submitted to her embrace and enjoyed her buttery bouquet. "New outfit, Mel?"

"I got it at the thrift shop the other day. Isn't it divine? Gucci, 1960. Ten bucks."

She pulled away from him to show off her pink jacket then quickly opened it up to show off what was already unclad beneath it. "Anyway, after work today I was just so happy to be away from the rude cruisers I suddenly found myself in your room. In spite of being mistreated by that awful woman downstairs."

Branch felt the floor move beneath him. He staggered with her to the bed.

Melanie laughed. "Been at it again?"

"I'm sorry?"

"Oh, you're *sorry*. You think I don't know what you are?"

Branch let her go, sat on the edge of the bed, smiling, but worried. "I don't know. What am I?"

"You're nothing but a glorified glue-sniffer. With a tank on your back."

"Glorified glue-sniffer," Branch echoed. "Never heard that one before. That's a good one."

"Just love the deep dives, don't you, Kilgore?" She slipped off the pink jacket, straddled him and pushed her soft, bare paleness against him. "It's fine. I always had a soft spot for the junkies. You're my first nitrogen junkie."

The truth stung him, but he knew there was the one other thing he was addicted to, and his tingling and his numbness and his distress were pushed aside by a familiar, surging desire for her.

Each time with Melanie was like the first time: An overwhelming hunger, but there was only this sweet, delicate dessert, a dessert he'd never had before, a dessert he'd inhale ravenously. And, then, afterward, there was only regret for his overindulgence.

And afterward, as she lay with him, Branch was troubled. The tingling in his feet from the nitrogen bubbles had returned, had now caught fire. Melanie snuggled in tighter, her milky fragrance nauseating him. Intermolecular forces had pushed him to her. Now they ripped him away.

The rain in Spain, Branch thought, trying to prepare himself for the question he knew was coming. *Suspenders? No. Sheep? Maybe. Ski goggles? Come on, man, you can do better. Barbecue? Yeah, that's it*, he decided. *Barbecue.*

"What are you thinking about?" Melanie asked him.

"Barbecue," Branch answered decisively.

"Of course you are. Not too much of that here on the island. Not the right kind of wood here, I heard. But I love it. Good barbecue. The best I ever had was a restaurant in Manhattan. East Village, if you can believe that. They went broke paying for the permit to burn wood. But a girl's got to have more than barbecue to make a relationship work. Something more than buying beer at Takanaka's Liquor and feeding Taco Loco leftovers to the crocodiles in the swamp."

"Really? Who knew?"

"Yeah, really. Maybe now's not the time to discuss it, but you and I have got to set some goals. Work together toward them. Know what I mean?"

"No," Branch said. He pulled his arm from under her soft back and rolled over onto his side. "I don't."

"I liked it when you had your arm around me."

"I had my arm around you? But I hardly know you."

Melanie smiled and stood up. She remembered what Fernando had told her about Branch's true identity. It terrified her; it thrilled her. "Perhaps we'll talk about it another time. When you're feeling up to it."

"Yeah. Come back next week. I'll be up for it then."

"Of course you will," Melanie said, strutting back to the bed. "What we need is a getaway from Chinchamos for a couple of days. Some romance. A nice little weekend somewhere. You and me."

"Where?" he asked, even though he wanted to just say no. He rolled over in discomfort, trying to chase the nitrogen bubbles from his body. She lay down on top of him and for a moment he was comforted by her warmth and softness.

"How about the Bahamas?" she asked, pushing her body flat on top of his. "I could get massages while you dive. Then, later, at night, we could be naked on the beach."

"Don't know. Need to get away. Not sure. Cuba's a possibility, I guess."

"Cuba?" Melanie protested, but secretly she was pleased he was showing *some* kind of interest. "This time of year? Too darn hot."

Branch tried to say something to put her off but it came out as a grunt.

She got up again right away, dissatisfied with his response but satisfied that she *had* him now. Branch admired the tiny twin dimples set over her delicate bottom. As she put the silk thong and the pink skirt back on, Branch already felt his desire for her renewing. And suddenly the thought of having her for an entire weekend wasn't so bad.

He grabbed her around her waist, started to pull her back to the bed. He pressed into her skirt from behind, was at once fully recharged. Melanie only laughed at him.

"Get away from me," she said. "I'm done with you, Kilgore. For now. Save it for Cuba."

Hearing her mention Cuba swung his emotions the other way again, subdued him again, so he just watched her finish dressing.

"Anyway," she said, "your pal the Grouper is back on the island. I saw him heading into the Roach when I was in the lobby. So I expect you'll be wanting to get over there and get wasted."

Then as she was leaving, she looked at him and said, "You going to be OK, Kilgore?"

Branch paused, watched the door close behind her as she left.

"Of course I am."

Chapter Sixteen

It Don't Do No Good

"**Y**ou're bent, man," the Grouper said. "Can't fool me. I know you. I know that look. Lips swollen, eyes bulgin'. Can't talk right. We got to get you to the chamber."

Branch sipped his rum and looked at the Grouper, sitting next to him at the little front bar at La Cucaracha. He was a stout man with shoulder-length curly blond hair and a full beard. And like his underwater namesake, he was friendly and portly but stealthy and strong, too.

Melanie had been gone for more than an hour and Branch's decompression sickness symptoms had only gotten worse: feet burning, hands tingling, face swelling. But he couldn't go to the hyperbaric clinic. There was only the one chamber on the island and they might be looking for him there. So he'd gone to the Roach to try and ride it out.

"I'm fine," he said, with difficulty. "When d'you get in?"

"I went for a beer at my favorite go-go bar in Bangkok and the next thing I knew I was waking up here. I'm renting a forty-two-foot sailboat. Liveaboard."

"Which boat?"

"It's called the *Ogygia*. All teaked out, fully rigged for the open ocean, but I'll just be floating. Got her up off the north tip right now. She comes with a little dinghy."

"Yeah. I know *dat* boat. Chinchamos Outfitters."

"It's also for sale," the Grouper said, and he snorted and laughed. "But I'll never be able to come up with the cash to buy something like that. We should just steal it. Head for Honduras. Why not?"

Branch took a sip of his drink, closed his eyes and thought about the Grouper's question. "Because the *Ogygia's* pretty recognizable and because Chinchamos Outfitters is owned by Omar Rasgado. He'd have someone chase you down in one of his speedboats and shoot you."

Then he cringed at the thought of who that someone might be and took another drink. "If I had *dat* boat, I'd put an air compressor on it and never touch land again. How much?"

"Half mil is what they're asking." The Grouper twisted his beard then spat tobacco juice expertly into his empty beer bottle. "But I hear they'd take four fifty. Seems they actually need the cash. Why you care? Tips improving at the dive shop?"

"Not Honduras. Panama'd be better."

"Panama, huh? Who is it lives there? Is it Mezzicans?"

"No. I think it's Panamanians. What was going on in Thailand?"

"Went over there with a nice chunk. Spent a lot on booze, babes, smack. The rest I just squandered. Did some cave dives off Koh Tao. Big-breasted, ugly English college girls. Cute little Thai whores. Just trying to stay away from civilization."

"I admire that about you."

"You know me. Can't go home just yet so I'm here for a little peace and quiet. What's up with all the cranes and shit out on Paradise Reef?"

Branch tried to laugh but he was too short of breath to get it out. He swilled his beer, felt it pour into his hollowness without effect.

"Money. What's your stance?"

The Grouper tugged on his beard. "Ocean should provide. But these mother-fuckers take more than they need. Fucking cruise ships. Hell no, I'm not with the cruise ships. Worthless. I noticed there's a new KFC here and I like that, but it's diving *made* this island. Heaven just might be the sea. When I first come down here in '86 I thought it was cool they'd preserved the beaches on the south end. Where the deep reefs are."

"Preserved?" Branch managed a laugh this time but it came out shredded. "Not preserved. *Dey* just hadn't gotten around to fucking it up yet."

"Let's go in the back. I can't afford it but I want to see what kind of talent Elias has got in this year."

They left the little bar at the front of the Roach and headed in the direction of the saloon, passing through the cigar store and the walk-in humidor built of mahogany and cedar. Outside the humidor were a soft leather couch, a grand coffee table, and a glass display case full of smoking paraphernalia.

Elias, the owner of the bar and the cigar store and the saloon and the whore-house all known as La Cucaracha, was a big Cuban, a burly guy with graying hair hanging down over bright green eyes. He got his exercise from throwing out rowdy frat boys who didn't spend enough money in the bar, and when he was drunk, he was obnoxious, always trying to smack Branch in the balls.

As Branch and the Grouper wandered in, Elias was behind the front counter at the humidor, clinching a Romeo y Julieta Churchill in his teeth, and though the ever-present bottle of Chamucos was there beside him, Branch was relieved to see that Elias was sober.

"Branch focking Kilgore," Elias said, his voice gravelly from years of incessant tequila drinking and cigar smoking. "And the Grouper is back. Run out of chicken fried steak where you were? I heard you were renting the *Ogygia*. A *paleto* like you on that fine yacht? I'd have snagged it myself if I'd known. Sail it down to Cuba and smuggle a load of cigars back."

"Actually, Elias, I'm fucking back in Chinchamos to pay forty bucks for a cigar that only costs six in Cuba," the Grouper said. "And five for a beer. Like I said, KFC or not, this place is gettin' pretty fucked-up. See you in the back, Branch." Then he pushed through the swinging doors and into the saloon.

"How's life treating you, Branch?" Elias asked. "Haven't seen you in weeks."

"Full treatment, Elias. *Bidness* good?"

"Slow," Elias said, but Branch could see the wads of hundreds in his hand as he closed out the register. "The *Allure* left already. Couple of more ships just anchored but it's quiet, so I'm closing the humidor a little early tonight. My grandbaby's birthday party."

Branch nodded at the doors to the saloon. "Big crowd back *dere*?" His mouth seemed to be full of sand.

"Dutch skurfer boys in their pussy neon wetsuits. We're having birthday cake a little later. Come have some with us. Don't think we have enough to feed that fat Grouper, though." And then he was laughing as Branch made his way through the swinging doors.

Someone at the piano was tinkling out a Mexican folk melody and there was a gang of the old fishermen sitting at the tables, throwing down drinks and playing cards. The skurfers from Holland stood at one end of the bar drinking beer, and the bar girls buzzed about, talking, drinking, and texting as they waited for passengers from the cruise ships to come in.

Roomy leather booths lined the wall and black lights hidden in the recesses of the ceiling cast a psychedelic glow. At the back of the saloon, next to the booths, was a heavy, carved wooden door that led to four small rooms where Elias's girls did their work.

Branch joined the Grouper in one of the booths. There were beers and a bottle of rum and two coffee cups on the table.

"Fucking Elias." The Grouper twitched as he looked back at the crowded bar. "You know he don't care about us divers. Just makin' money off the *cruceros*. I love a good whorehouse, but at these prices? Thailand spoiled me. You're still diving for Victor, huh? I'm going out with you guys in the morning. Signed up to do the Pirati caverns in a couple of days, too. Those were some fucking great cave dives we did last summer. You still dating that girl? The one with the real sweet ass?"

"Who, Mel?" Her fragrance was still hovering all around him. "Yeah. Maybe taking her down to Cuba next weekend. What can you say about a girl *dat* just sneaks into your hotel room and is waiting for you?"

"I'm in favor of it, of course. Bring me some cigars when you go to Cuba. I can't afford Elias's prices." Then the Grouper pulled a plastic bag full of dried mushrooms from his pocket. "Look, man, I'm here in Chinchamos and I'm ready to celebrate. Do some of these with me. Brought 'em all the way from Samui."

He took a pinch of the dried buttons and pushed them into his mouth, his bearded cheek bulging and his stained teeth grinning as he thrust the bag at Branch.

"Even if it's not right, you've got to do it. You can't worry about what's right or wrong. You remember what Jesus said about worryin', don't you?"

"Not sure. What did he say?"

"He said it don't do no good."

"Don't do no good," Branch echoed.

"That's right, man. I know you. Kick out, go deep. Chew them, chew them."

Branch took a large helping of the dried mushroom caps, chewed them quickly, poured himself half a coffee cup of rum and washed it all down.

"Yeah, I know how it goes," the Grouper said, watching him drink. "Shit, I lived at elevations over ten thousand when I was on the ski patrol down in Argentina. Once you get acclimated to drinking at that elevation you can drink and drink at sea level and never feel it."

"Tragic. Got *da* same problem but opposite direction. Too much time at depth."

"Oh, yeah. Seductive is the deep. You always were a fiend for it. Noticed that right off when I started diving with Argonauts."

Branch nodded. He had something to say but the mushrooms were coming on and his mind wandered. The smoke in the saloon and the rambling Mexican piano music had all merged into one thing and it was taking him off in a cloud.

"So what is it?" the Grouper asked. "When you go down there past three hundred on regular air, like you were doing in those caves on the mainland last year? Get just far enough down, just close enough to death where you can see it?"

Branch sipped his beer. The bubbles were bouncing inside his tongue and stinging him. "See what?"

"You know. The afterlife."

"No afterlife. But like you and your drinking I got to go *fodder* down to get *da* juice."

"Yeah, well, better take care. She'll try to keep you there."

One of the bar girls pushed away from Janne and the Dutch skurfers and danced over to the booth. It was Claudia, the same girl Pam had turned away from the Blue Angel earlier. Now she was wearing a thong and lingerie top and she'd sprinkled glitter over her body. In the glow of the poster lights she sparkled at Branch like a dark sky full of shooting stars.

Claudia tousled the Grouper's curly locks, slipped the straps off her lingerie top, jumped into his lap, and pressed her breasts into his beard. Branch felt as if he was swirling around the room but then he was brought back down into the booth by their muffled conversation.

"I don't want to get married," Claudia was telling the Grouper. "I don't want more babies. I want to drink beer."

"We're in agreement on all of that," he heard the Grouper reply.

Branch was mesmerized by the sparkling glow from the girl's skin, but then the light was piercing him and inflaming his deco sickness.

"So, we'll have a beer," the Grouper said, laughing and then pushing the girl away playfully. "Later. And we won't get married and we won't make more babies."

The girl dismissed them both with a wave of her hand and twirled back to the bar. Branch looked at the Dutchmen. Their surfing attire was ablaze in flickering neon yellow and green.

"Somebody ought to talk to Elias about these girls, man. Like I said, damn cruise ships, ruinin' ever'thing."

"What kind of mushrooms did you say *dese* were?" Branch asked, oblivious, his skin itching all over and his lips almost swollen shut.

"Good, aren't they? Very exotic. They're indigenous to Cambodia. They only grow in cobra poop. Very dangerous to gather them. All kinds of healing and psychic properties, though, when you do 'em with proper ceremony."

"Healing," Branch said. But rather than healing him, the psychotropic chemicals seemed to be making it worse. He knew he had to do something about the bubbles. He had to make those bubbles smaller. "Proper ceremony. Gotta get in *da waddah*. *Lez* go for a night dive, *Grouper*."

"I don't know. Well, I would, man, but I'm going out with you guys in the morning. Don't have my gear with me. And I'm not crazy about night dives. The problem with night dives is you got to do 'em at night. Too damn dark."

"Got gear in *da* shop. What … would … Jesus … do?"

"Well, if you're bringing Jesus in on it, then fuck it, why not? Even if a tiger shark gets me, my last second will be a happy one. I'll just think of my ex-wives back in the States when they find out I've been eaten alive and it'll all seem just fine."

They headed through the swinging doors and into the cigar lobby. The lights had been dimmed and a birthday cake glowed with eight candles. The Grouper stopped to light a cigarette off one of the candles. "Happy fucking birthday," he said, sneering at Elias. Then they headed out into the street and over to the dive shop.

Chapter Seventeen

Dorian's Death

They lurched from La Cucaracha and crossed the street to the dive shop. Branch took out the key Victor had given him and put it in the lock. He wouldn't ever need to pick that lock again.

He swung the door open, surprised to see Pam and Victor sitting at the table. A small candle glowed and cast flickering shadows against the air tanks along the wall.

"Branch," Victor said. "You made it. Cool. Your friend is welcome, too."

"*Made it.*" Branch grinned at the kaleidoscopic ambience of the shop.

"The meeting. The pier problem? We were supposed to have some friends from the mainland but they didn't show."

"Didn't show, yeah. No. Just a night dive. You 'member *Grouper.*"

"A night dive? Sure. Not much to see out there anymore. But go ahead. Have fun. They're guarding the demolition platform. They think we're going to sabotage it. So make sure you don't drift into their zone."

While Victor and Pamela continued their quiet conversation, Branch and the Grouper tanked up. Branch assembled his double manifold—two tanks of enriched air, one having 32 percent oxygen, and the other 36 percent—while the Grouper strapped one of Victor's rental BCs to a single tank of plain air.

"Shit, Branch. Doubles? Nitrox? What kind of dive you goin' on?"

"Need *uh* outgas. Don't worry. You go up when it's time. I stay down."

"I ain't worried about you but I'm plenty worried about me. I didn't realize it in the club but I think I'm fucked-up, man."

"Get under some water. Get some nitrogen up in you."

"All of the lights on the beach are tripping me out," the Grouper said, nodding out the window at the construction crane. "We won't even need to use our underwater lights."

"Yeah, no lights." Branch could barely get a breath now. "Guards on *da* pier site. Slip in, stay dark, go around *da* ropes. Nice drift in *da* shallows."

"Yeah. Tell Victor to cancel my dive for the morning, though. After this, if I can come down a little bit, I'm going back to the Roach, find that Claudia girl and take her with me out to the *Ogygia*."

They carried their rigs and waded out from the shop's beach. Branch listened to the water as it lapped lightly on the sand behind him. His heart was pounding, from the mushrooms, he thought, and sweat beaded up on his brow. He turned back toward the shop. The palm trees behind Ocean Road seemed to be smiling and winking and waving at him as they shifted in the breeze.

They floated out in darkness through the shallows and rolled into their scuba units when they were waist-deep. The water was calm and it moved aside easily for Branch as he went under. He kicked hungrily for the deeper water, and then he felt the pressurized air hit his lungs.

He spun around on the descent and in the semidarkness the disorientation was pleasant. The Grouper had tied two luminescent glow sticks to his tank. Branch followed the bobbing fluorescent colors downward to sixty feet—three atmospheres—the approximate pressure he should've been treated at in a hyperbaric chamber.

He felt the nitrogen bubbles in his body compress to one-third the size they'd been at the surface. Boyle's law, he remembered, and then he thought about how Dr. Huggins would've appreciated such a practical example of it. And then he wanted to kick down, way down, to get away from the memory.

But he knew he couldn't. Like methadone for a heroin addict, all he could have was oxygen-enriched air at sixty feet. A hollow comfort, but at least he'd survive to hit the Deep Blue Saloon another day.

The sandy bottoms off the Caribbean Argonauts dock had once been studded with small coral heads, had been alive with swarms of dusky damselfish, wrasses, and Chromis. But now sand from the pier construction and nutrient runoff from the resorts had turned them into graying skeletons.

The shallow reef looked to Branch like an old, abandoned apartment building. A few tenants still hung around, he thought, remembering the good days when occupancy was full, when the walls were painted and when the neighbors were healthy and employed. But now, all that was left was the solitary green moray eel that slithered in and out of the dingy hallways, and the one-eyed parrotfish that followed Branch through the gray coral heads like a stray dog. A thin school of yellowtails sailed sluggishly about, and a pasty, spiritless balloonfish chugged along without direction.

An octopus hovered over the sand, scurrying from one craggy shelter to the next. Branch watched as the octopus's ink boiled within its translucent body, modulating from red to blue to purple to yellow, a colored roulette wheel spinning wildly until it landed on the proper shade of camouflage.

They drifted on, slowly to the north, leaving the area of the dead little coral heads and entering Paradise Shallows, now a forbidden area because of the new pier construction. Gnarls of debris, concrete pilings, and twisted orbs of rebar littered the sea floor. It looked like the site of a battle, with craters marking the spots where the coral had been blasted away.

Broken purple gorgonians and shredded nipples of baby sea anemones clung desperately to the sprawling stone footings of the new pier. Small dark openings gaped at Branch and the Grouper from the shoreline, marking the entry to the Garganta del Diablo, a tight, treacherous cave system that ran inland all the way to the island's freshwater lagoon.

They kicked quietly back to the sandy shallows. The Grouper signaled and started his ascent. Branch mindlessly watched the glowing light tubes drift up, then, remembering his decompression task, he settled down into the sand at sixty feet.

Tiny luminescent creatures buzzed around his bubbles, and then he was flying with them, chasing them through the galaxy like alien spacecraft. Each chase would end with the same result—Branch stunned to discover that he wasn't in outer space, but on Planet Earth, and even more staggering, that he was under-water.

As he breathed, as he waited, the gentle current of the Gulf Stream nudged him imperceptibly northward along the sea floor, the warmth of the sand pleasant against his belly. His eyes were closed and he was unaware of how far north he'd drifted until his head bumped into a chain-link fence. He'd accidentally meandered into another forbidden area—the no-dive zone of Omar's Swim With the Dolphins Park.

Divers were shooed away in the daytime when they got within fifty feet of the outer fence, and when Omar's security guards at the park spotted dive lights at night, they would come into the water with spearguns to enforce the zone.

He opened his eyes and peered into the darkness beyond the chain links. Suddenly there was a desperate burst of sonic squealing and the scarred snout of a bottlenose dolphin pressed through the fence. A large brown eye—warm, vivid, and worried—looked directly into Branch's mask.

The stare down between Branch and the dolphin was broken by another sonic squeal and then the dolphin shot up toward the surface. Branch heard a splash, watched as the dolphin jetted back to the bottom, nudging him once more through the fence with his snout. Then the dolphin disappeared into the shallows of the pen.

Unsure if he'd really seen it or not, Branch edged his way back across the sandy stretch toward the construction zone. He finished off the first tank, switched the manifold over to the tank with 36 percent oxygen, then carefully made his way up to thirty feet and closed his eyes.

In the darkness, he was inside the irrigation conduit at Grandpa's farm again. He moved forward in the pipe, ever-narrowing and never-ending. There was a light ahead of him. A flashing neon sign had flicked on. Branch kicked toward it. As the pipe got narrower, the sign became clearer, and then he saw it, flashing at him in bold red neon strokes:

$$y = 1/x$$

Torricelli's trumpet, he remembered, but now he had a new name for it: Reiner's formula. The never-ending tube, and he knew *he* was the one who'd have to kick forever into it.

He opened his eyes. The pipe had vanished and the flashing of the neon formula was replaced by the glare of a bright light, hurtling down at him from the surface. A free diver, an underwater light mounted on his mask, seemed to be coming at him.

Branch didn't react. Only hallucinating from the mushrooms, he thought. But the light got closer and Branch saw that the huge man in the tight wetsuit was holding a speargun as he kicked down. It was Dorian.

Dorian grabbed Branch by the straps of his vest and yanked him toward the surface. Branch instinctively pinned the big man's arms and knocked the snorkel out of his mouth. There was a blast of bubbles and then Branch wrapped Dorian's wetsuit zipper cord around his neck, yanking it as if he was starting the outboard motor on Victor's boat.

Three hundred pounds of fury thrashed at him. Dorian's fins flailed against the bottom and then everything was obscured by a sandy cloud. Branch yanked the zipper cord once more, hard, and the flailing stopped.

He let go of the cord. The body went limp and flopped to the bottom. He didn't want to believe it was real, but the glare from Dorian's mask light shining up through the murk confirmed that it was. When the sand cleared, he saw what had happened. Dorian, guarding the platform, had seen the glow of Branch's console and had free dived down to check it out. And then Branch had killed him.

He turned off the mask light, then drifted with Dorian's body through the dead coral heads by the dive shop's beach, looked up at the construction platform over his head, and worried who else might be up there. Then he looked at the footings and the concrete and the rebar that was invading Paradise Shallows.

It was well after four in the morning when his head broke the surface of the dark water. He'd been under for more than four hours and at least the one problem was solved. The dizziness and numbness from the deco sickness were gone, and his feet no longer burned. But now he had a three-hundred-pound dead guy floating along with him as he finned quietly on his back to the shore.

Chapter Eighteen

Strange Shadow on the Wall

B ranch brewed a pot of coffee, then sat down at the table in the dive shop office and waited for Victor to arrive. He checked the schedule book and saw the morning's dive reservation: six divers from the ships plus the Grouper. He scratched the Grouper's name out and poured himself a cup of coffee.

The DCS symptoms were gone—that was the good news—but any relief from the mushroom decompression dive had been interrupted by fretting over what to do with Dorian's three-hundred-pound body.

Branch sipped on the coffee as he thought about what had happened. In the adrenaline of the moment he'd reacted instinctively. Leaving the body in the water would've been disastrous, so in the dark he'd dragged it across the sand and into the shop, where he laid it on top of the pile of rental wetsuits and covered it with a blanket. And now there was no time to move it.

He thought about Mel. He knew she would be slumbering in her pink sheets in silky, milky splendor. He questioned why he was sitting here, all salty and tripping and recently bent, with no sleep for more than twenty-four hours, with the blood of two new murders on his hands, when he could be cuddled up with her. But he knew the reason. Intermolecular forces wouldn't allow it.

Victor arrived a few minutes after six.

"What the hell is this?" he asked, tripping over the burly bundle on the floor. He tugged on the blanket, saw Dorian's head twisted around the wrong way and then he had a sick look on his face. "What happened?"

"I was coming up. He came at me from the platform and we tangled. I guess he just drowned. It was almost daylight so I dragged him in here."

"You killed Dorian." Victor was calm and stunned at the same time. "Look, when I told you I wanted you on my team, I didn't think ... you know ... this? Anybody else on the platform last night?"

"Didn't see anyone. It's quiet out there. His replacement will show up by eight and then they'll be looking for him."

"Fucking bastard, this Dorian," Victor said. He rubbed at his chest, at the sore spot from the day before, then pulled the blanket down further, examining the small pendant and silver chain hanging from Dorian's thick, twisted neck. "Looks like some kind of key. There's a number on it. And some little design."

"Maybe." Branch took a close look at the pendant. "Just looks like evidence to me."

"What were you doing in the water so damn long?"

"I was just out there. Sort of drifting. The Grouper came up way earlier. He canceled for today."

"Just as well." Victor covered Dorian's face with the blanket. "We'll have to cancel the whole trip today."

"Nope. Business as usual would look a lot better. Can't call the police either."

"No shit. But if we don't call them, Omar'll catch us and kill us. This fucking Dorian."

"I didn't want to bring you in on this. But I couldn't leave the body in the water. And I didn't have time to do something else with it."

"Something else? Like what?" Victor shook his head and looked out into the channel. There was still no wind and the water was blue-gray in the early morning light. He saw another cruise ship smoking in from the north, and then he remembered how he'd been talking to Dorian right there in the office only the day before.

"All of our divers are from that ship," Victor said. "So we got an hour or two."

"I'll put him on the bottom when we go out. I'll captain today. Let Manny get a dive in with Bali and the divers on the first one. He said it with his own lips only yesterday. Now he gets to find out. Help me load him up. You don't know nothing."

Ten minutes later they had Dorian's blanket-wrapped body stuffed into the forward hold of the dive boat.

"I'm freaked about this," Victor said, breathing hard from the heavy chore. "But you've struck a great blow for us, Branch. You did something I wanted to do but never had the balls."

"It was an accident," Branch said, but he wondered if it was true. He felt the warmth of the morning sun streaming in behind him and he studied his own strange shadow on the wall. "And now we're going to cover this accident up. I can't afford to strike any great blows."

Chapter Nineteen

An Emerald in the Sun

T he name of the dive boat was *Argos I*, and it tore through the turquoise waters as it carried Branch, six divers and one dead body south along the leeward shoreline. Flat seas in front of the boat were ripped into a torrid white spray, dropping back into a clear calm only a few feet behind the craft. Branch was behind the wheel, looking for a dive site that had no other dive boats on it. He'd need a little privacy for dumping Dorian.

He killed the engine and the last ripples from the propeller faded into an endless, smooth skin of green and blue light. In spite of the Dorian problem, he was tripping along nicely again. The sea seemed to be solid, like an emerald in the sun, and it ran all the way into the eastern horizon without a flaw. There was nothing on the water in that direction that revealed its true nature, and for a moment Branch indulged in the hallucination that he might get out and walk on it all the way to Cuba. A line of thin pink clouds hung over the island to the east, and to the southwest Branch could just make out the Yucatán coast. The sun was directly overhead and as the rays hit the water they broke into tiny sizzling fireworks on the placid surface.

He suppressed a smile. *Focus on the job at hand*. Keep everyone away from the forward hold, get the divers in the water, and then while they drifted he would take care of it. Branch looked over the side and he could see the morning sun lighting up the white bottom sixty feet below. The sand was flat and still where it dropped off to the darker blue depths of the reef and he felt pretty good about the dive, knowing the current would be mild. The divers from the ship were out of shape and pathetic—all divers from the cruise ships were out of shape and pathetic—but maybe they wouldn't need assistance from the boat. Maybe he could be gone from the dive path for a while. Maybe it would work.

Branch positioned the boat up current from the site and let it drift back toward the reef as Manny got the gear ready. Then he watched Bali as she briefed the divers, her blue eyes and dark hair lighting up in the morning sunshine. Her wetsuit was pulled down around her waist, her golden bikini top in perfect creamy contrast to her black-coffee skin.

He heard the sincerity in her voice as she told them to respect the coral and the other animals they would see. She really loved her work. He knew it.

Branch had learned to be patient with the novice divers from the ships, but his motivation was different than Bali's. After what had happened at the college, when he'd confused his cover with his real job, he'd become cynical.

Now he was just playing a role, divemaster on a dive boat, so he could do his real job—killing for Omar. It was the real job that would give him enough money to buy a new start. But until then, he was what he was. Proof of that was in the forward hold.

Bali finished helping the customers. As she got into her own gear, Branch admired her streamlined, athletic physique. There was nothing voluptuous about her, nothing Mel about her. *Mel.* Just thinking of her, he was a little aroused, a little sickened. But Bali's simple, muscular beauty and her brown skin and dazzling smile snapped him back out of it.

He'd ignored her earlier while she was moving about the boat in only her bikini. The mushrooms and the bubbles had wiped away all physical desire. But as she zipped up her shorty wetsuit—chaste and insulated—he was intrigued by her.

"We're ready, Branch," she said, perching with the others on the edge of the boat. "Don't go yet," she said to the group as Branch fired the engine and wheeled the boat back to the drop spot.

Then the boat rocked as Bali, Manny and the divers from the cruise ship rolled back. Branch watched them descend on Wonderland Wall, huge belches of air blasting up from the cruisers, and tiny controlled bursts from Manny and Bali, all of them drifting northward with the stream.

He grabbed a cold beer from the ice chest, started the engine and pointed the boat toward the deep channel that lay between Chinchamos and mainland Mexico. From the size of the cruisers' bubbles he knew he'd have maybe thirty minutes to take care of business and get back to the northern tip of Wonderland to pick them up.

He drank the beer and pushed the boat full throttle to the west. The radio was squawking. It was Victor's voice, distorted and oscillating between English and Spanish. Branch didn't answer. After ten minutes he was far enough out in the deep channel, so he killed the motor, unlocked the forward hold and then scanned the horizon.

There were only two boats. One was several hundred yards away to the southeast, waiting for divers at Hammerhead Point. The other was a cigarette boat, buzzing due south in the shallows. Branch tossed the empty beer bottle into the hold, grabbed Dorian's bundled body, and tugged it out toward the wheelhouse.

When Branch scanned again, the cigarette boat was roaring back to the north along the shoreline, and the other boat was trolling to pick up one of its divers. After he rolled the green bundle up onto the stern deck, he took a length of line and quickly fitted a tight harness around the body's neck and knees. He tied ten feet of line to both ends of the package and then tied that to a weight belt loaded with all of the remaining lead on the boat—only about two hundred pounds. The pudgy cruisers had used even more weight than he'd figured. A body wouldn't stay down forever, even three hundred pounds of muscle, but maybe the tiger sharks would do their job.

Branch grunted as he rolled Dorian into the dark water, holding the line that connected it to the weights. He watched the green bundle float there for a moment and let it drift slightly away from the boat. Then he pushed the weight belt off the deck. Ten feet of line uncoiled furiously as the weights plummeted toward the bottom. Maybe only three hundred feet here, but deep enough.

The line snapped taut and Dorian's neck and knees banged together with an ugly crack. The bundle flapped, faded, and then disappeared into the depths. Branch tossed Dorian's speargun and mask in after him. He took a waypoint on the GPS, memorized the coordinates, and then cleared it.

Branch had killed in the ocean before, but he'd never dumped in it. The Deep Blue Saloon was the one thing he had—the only sure thing—and he didn't want to mess that up. Watching a final blast of Dorian's bubbles burst up from below, he wanted to dive in and retrieve the body.

But he couldn't. He lit one of Manny's cigarettes, leaned against the side of the boat, and let the sun take the chill away. He opened another cold Leon and drank, and then he motored back toward the north end of Wonderland Wall. He slowed the throttle to a crawl as he got close to the area where Bali and Manny and the divers would be surfacing.

Suddenly the cigarette boat roared toward him. It was a thirty-eight-foot Marauder, red with yellow stripes. The swell from the speedboat shook the *Argos I*, and as Branch steadied a tank that had popped loose he quickly spied the three men in the boat.

The man behind the wheel, with a cowboy hat hiding his face, throttled down the long boat. In the bow stood Omar, along with his other burly bodyguard, Dexter.

Branch waved then took a sip of his beer.

"I got divers down there," he yelled, firm but friendly. "You boys ought to be more careful ripping around like that. You might remove the head of some cruise ship passenger. Instead of just all their cash."

"You don't give a fuck about no cruise ship passenger," Omar shouted from the bow. He took a deep drag off his cigarette then flicked it, not yet half finished, into the sea.

"I don't care where they come from." Branch glanced down at the cigarette butt floating in the turquoise water. "If they're diving with me it's my job to protect them."

"Your job?" Omar asked, smoke billowing from his nostrils. "You work for Gonzago. You work for me, no? You *no* forget that."

The cowboy behind the wheel raised his head. The wrinkles were deeper and the nose was redder and more swollen but there was no mistaking him.

"That's right, Branch," Len said. "Don't you go gettin' confused 'bout what's real and what's not real. You always did have a problem with that. When was the last time? Musta been Cuba, six or seven years ago. Right before you went in."

"Hi, Len."

"We were checkin' out the pier site from the boat, Omar and me. We knew you must be out divin' today. Thought we'd come say howdy. I ain't seen Cap'n Manny for maybe twenty years. Why ain't *you* divin'? What were you doin' way out there in the channel?"

Branch tossed the empty beer bottle under the bench. "I was taking a piss. When did you get in?"

"Yesterday. Gonna be consulting for Gonzago and Omar on the underwater demolition work, hydraulic breakers, like that. We start blastin' for the big footers tomorrow afternoon. We're warnin' all divers to stay clear of Paradise Shallows."

"I'm planning on that, staying clear. Of everything. I'm letting Manny get under some water today."

"It's understandable you might not be feeling up for it today. After yesterday. When Gonzago told me you were down here in Chinchamos I was hopin' you might want to do some *real* dive work for us. On the pier."

"I *am* doing some real dive work. Got divers down on Wonderland right now. You zoomed right over their heads like a dickhead. Probably scared the shit out of them."

Omar looked down into the water. "I hunt the turtles out here when I was a kid. Hard to find now. What you see down there? Rocks and shit like that?"

"Yeah, rocks and shit," Branch said. "Coral, too."

"Oh," Omar said, his beard contorting and his dilated nostrils twitching as he pondered the distinction between rocks and coral. "We never make money on the island from the divers. When they come to see the rocks and shit. And the coral. Everybody poor. Now we bringing in fifteen cruise ships a week. More than fifteen when the pier is finished. You ready for the Cuba job?"

"I don't know."

"You'll go, no? Your real job. And your divers? I no think we hit nobody. If they turn up missing, you let me know."

"I'll be sure to do that."

"Speaking of missing persons, we looking for Dorian. He missing from the platform when we get there this morning. You see him?"

"Not an easy man to lose, that Dorian," Branch said, and then he could still feel the strain in his forearms from lugging the three-hundred-pound body. He looked at his gaunt reflection in Omar's mirrored sunglasses. "I haven't seen him," he watched the gaunt reflection say, and he almost believed what it was saying.

"Always somebody missing," Omar said. "Gonzago tell me about the *Negro Federale* in Florida that thinks *you* missing. You *no* need to worry about him. Not as long as you on my team. Know what I mean?"

"Yeah. I know what you mean," Branch said, fighting off rage that Omar knew about Reiner. He had enough to worry about.

"Well, it's good to see you," Len said, starting up the red boat's engine. "It's been too damn long." Then as he steered the craft away, Len shouted, "I'll catch you later, son. We got some catching up to do. Don't you be a pussy, now."

———

"They were looking for Dorian," Victor told Branch, standing inside the office at Caribbean Argonauts Dive Shop and watching through the window as Bali and Manny unloaded the boat. "How would I know where he is, right? And the other guy, the one with the cowboy hat? You didn't tell me your daddy was in town. I need to know you're with *me* on this thing."

Branch stepped to the window and watched Bali help the chubby cruisers off the dive boat.

"Omar has a new partner on the pier, a guy from Houston named Gonzago," Branch said. "Len works for Gonzago. He was never much of a father to me. I got no allegiance to him. I'm not on anybody's side. But I can't cross Gonzago."

Victor stepped up behind him. "You already crossed him, Branch. Maybe it *was* an accident, but you killed Dorian."

Branch cringed when he heard the words. "Please don't say that again."

"I was sick about it at first," Victor continued. "But now I don't feel so bad about it. Look what they've already done to Paradise Shallows. And it's only getting worse. They said they're doing some big blasting tomorrow afternoon. Omar warned me not to be near the site. I'm trying to make a living here with this dive shop. They're blowing up coral so they can bring in more ships."

Branch spun away from Victor and tried to shrug off the bad feeling coming over him.

"Where you going to run to, Branch? Don't you believe in anything?"

"I don't know, Victor. People that have seen the way the world works, who have seen too much, people like me. What's left to believe in?"

"You tell me. What's left?"

"Only the dark places," Branch said, closing his eyes. "The places where I can just kill the pain and pass the time. Pirati caverns in the morning, right? We'd best get an early start. Best be out of the water before there's any blasting."

"We'll get an early start. But we're way late on some things. Nobody wants to look at cruise ships as a problem. But it *is* the problem. They're bringing them in here to see the beauty. A fat American on a boat. All he can eat. All he can drink. All he can shit. And they kill the golden goose. If we lose the mangroves we lose the reef-building organisms. And then it's all gone."

"What time?"

"Shit," Victor said, disgusted with Branch's indifference. "Early."

"See you in the morning then. Early." Branch stepped outside, anxious to get to his room and get some rest but Bali stopped him on her way back into the shop.

"I'm driving to the other side tonight," she said. "Camp out, shoot video of the turtles. They're laying their eggs. Come with me."

Then she smiled. It was an honest, strong smile, and it startled Branch. It was a smile that had its origins in a good family, and it was a smile that beamed at some happy path ahead. It was a straight path those beautiful straight teeth smiled at, a path with heart. A smile of faith. And she smiled at all those things Branch had never been able to believe in.

"I can't make it," he told her. "But thanks for that book. I was reading it earlier. Good stuff about those turtles. Pretty cool."

"Yeah, it is. Come and watch." There was no hesitation or fear of rejection in her voice. "I'm heading home first. Then I'll take Ocean Road south. I'll stop off at the Bean for a little supper at nine. But it's no big thing. I can handle it on my own."

"Not tonight," Branch said, wanting to get away, but he took a quick glance at her anyway. Her nipples poked through her golden bikini top and her navel piercings glistened in the sun, the golden reflections shimmering on her flat, brown belly. "I got to get some rest. Be safe over there, Bali. The wild side's a wild place."

The summer twilight lingered and Branch was agitated as he flopped about in bed. He turned the light on and read from Bali's turtle book. It relaxed him a little, and after a while he turned the light off. But bad images flickered as soon as he closed his eyes. Len's swollen nose. The redhead's chalky-dead expression. Dorian's bulky bundle as it snapped and went under. There were too many loose ends from the mainland job and now he was edgy. Struggling to get free of the loose ends, he knew, could be fatal. Like a hawksbill turtle caught in a fishing net.

Branch got out of bed, went to his dresser, and from inside his top drawer he took out an old souvenir paperweight, a glass globe filled with water and sand and tiny golden fish. He shook the orb, the sand and the fish churning. He watched the sand settle while the golden fish swam, and then he sat back down on his bed and closed his eyes.

Chapter Twenty

Glassy Sweepers

Branch perched on the edge of the boat and looked down into the sea. Sunshine pierced the calm water, lighting it up like a turquoise prism. Leaning farther over the edge, he was startled by the dark shadow of the boat dancing on the white sand below.

He sat back up quickly on the bench, then gazed across the bay to the rugged beach skirting the shoreline. The beach was narrow and crowded by wild, low-growth jungle. A little river cut across the beach, spilling fresh water from an inland lagoon into the bay. Where the fresh water met the sea it turned brown, then orange, and then yellow, and then finally a very fine green by the time it got to where Branch watched it from the boat.

The water was so flat and still and clear that Branch doubted it was really liquid. He thought of the souvenir paperweight Len had just brought him from Acapulco, a tiny tropical globe filled with water and sand and fish, untouchable and teasing him behind its glass shell. He reached over the side of the boat, spread his little hand open and held it cautiously over the tranquil surface of the water. Then he pointed his finger down and dipped it into the ocean for the very first time. He was surprised by its warmth. Pressing in farther, he saw his finger distorted and magnified as he pointed down toward the dark spots and shadows on the sand, some sixty feet below.

"Daddy, are those dark places down there where the tigers are?"

Branch had heard Len talk to the boat captain earlier about twenty-foot tiger sharks in these waters.

"The tigers?" Len glanced at Manny, the boat captain, and grinned. "Maybe so. They come up in here to hunt at night. Don't see 'em much in the day. But maybe we'll see one."

Branch pulled his finger back in quickly. He moved away from the edge of the boat and stood up.

Len laughed. "Ain't like you to be scared, Branch. Daddy told me you wasn't scared of nothin' back on the farm. First time diving will do it, though, I guess. Them dark spots you see are just little coral heads. Nothin' down here below us but pretty little fish."

Branch edged again toward the side of the boat.

"But maybe we'll bag a grouper," Len said, and then he picked up his speargun and pointed it at Branch. "You going on this deep one with me? Or you gonna be a pussy and I'll have to tell ever'body?"

Len laughed again as Manny helped him into his tank and harness. Then Manny turned to Branch. "Put your little fins on first, amigo. Then we'll get you into your tank."

Branch sat back down on the hard bench and slipped his fins on, trying to remember everything Len had taught him about diving in the hotel pool the day before. Len had been in a hurry. He'd come back into the room with a bag full of bricks of heroin, and guns and dive gear, and then he'd hustled Branch out to the pool for a quick lesson.

Branch wasn't sure he could remember everything Len had told him, and he felt nervous. Back on Grandpa's farm there'd been plenty of adventure. But he didn't like being pressured by Len. Len had never wanted him around much. He was always too busy, doing the bad things for Gonzago, or doing the commercial diving out on the oil rigs. And now Branch was nervous about using his dive gear properly.

"Mas grande, si?" asked Manny, and he pointed out at the water. He sat the tank on the bench and Branch slipped his arms into the canvas straps. The straps felt tight and dry against his shoulders. Then Manny helped Branch up to the top of the gunwale and handed him a little black dive mask. *"Mas grande.* Bigger than the pool."

The boat shifted in the water as Manny moved to the wheelhouse to restart the outboard motor, and Branch struggled to stay on the edge. The practice in the pool seemed a long time ago, and he was suddenly angry that Len had called him a pussy. He had sparred with all kinds of wild animals back on the farm. But twenty-foot tigers swimming around in clear water? He didn't know if he was ready for that, and then he felt Panic poke him in the stomach.

"OK, Branch, put that mask on," said Len, examining the sharp, glistening points on his speargun. "Just like in the pool, remember? Just put the regulator in your mouth and roll back'ards."

The big man splashed wildly in, and again the boat rocked while Branch tried to control the weight of the heavy steel tank on his back. He looked down at the shadows in the water, saw them moving. They were big, dark, tiger-looking shadows and Branch felt Panic jabbing at him a little harder. The tank was tight against his back, and as the mask squeezed his face, he thought back to his time on Grandpa's farm, to that first day he'd met Panic.

"Let's go, Branch! Get in!" Len yelled from the surface of the water. Manny scolded him in rapid-fire Spanish, and then he spoke to Branch in English.

"Nice angelfish here," Manny said softly. "Blue angels. They watch over you. And I watch your bubbles, too. You remember the rule? The rule numero uno? Just keep breathing."

Manny helped Branch find the regulator and gently rolled him back into the water. Branch was upside down in the ocean and all he could see was the blue water and his bubbles roaring to the surface. Then his fins swung down and his head bobbed up. The boat drifted by and Branch saw Len's black fins kicking down into the sea.

"Go down," said Manny. "*Quedate con tu padre*. Stay with Len. Kick, kick. I watch."

Branch let all the air out of his lungs like they had practiced in the pool, and his little body slipped down below the surface. The tank no longer felt heavy; he finned down beside Len, equalizing his ears and his mask as he went. He looked up at the boat and for an instant he could see Manny's face looking over the side. The propellers spun, the engine droned, and the boat moved down current. Branch kicked hard to keep from bobbing back up, to get away from the propellers. His heart pounded and he was breathing hard, the bubbles cascading up and over his body like an upside-down waterfall of air.

Len signaled OK to him and Branch signaled OK back, but he just wanted to bolt to the surface. The old trick of ignoring Panic—waiting for it to go away—wasn't working. He couldn't let Len call him a pussy, though, so he stayed down and kicked on through the pain and the fear. Taking a big breath off the regulator, he looked up and watched his bubbles race to the surface. Manny, he knew, was in the boat, somewhere up above him, watching for his bubbles.

The current carried him past small coral heads, swarming with tiny blue Chromis and dusky damselfish. The water was so clear that Branch felt he was falling through air. Manny had said before the dive that the visibility in this place was two hundred feet. Branch gazed out to see what two hundred feet looked like underwater. The blue became a soft blackness at the edge of visibility, and he saw the shadows moving again just beyond that edge.

The air from the tank was cold and dry as he breathed in. The dryness ran all through his chest, and with each breath it moved higher into his throat. Then the dryness was up in his head, and when it reached his ears, it became a dull, unpleasant droning noise. All he could see and feel and hear was the dryness and the droning, getting louder with each breath. And then Panic was coming at him again.

Branch watched the blue-black periphery and wondered if that droning noise was an approaching tiger. Then there was a thump and a splash. He spun around to see a large spotted grouper impaled by one of Len's spears. The fish squirmed against the spear, and its blood was green in the water and streaming up toward the surface. Len let the speargun hang from its tether as he worked the reel. Then he ripped out the spear and placed the writhing, bleeding fish in his mesh catch bag.

Branch moved his fins and spun around once more, gazing at the purple vastness of the ocean's underside. The droning noise was louder now, constant and eternal. That noise had meant death for the grouper, and it seemed to Branch that the noise was nothing but the certainty of his own death. The source of the noise—the death—was impossible to pinpoint. It seemed to come dryly from everywhere. Panic kicked him in his chest and told him he'd better bolt to the surface.

But they'd told him in the pool to never bolt. That's how you get hurt, they'd told him. So, he stayed put, and again he was in that irrigation conduit with Panic, and Panic was thrashing him, Panic was killing him, and the awful noise Panic was making seemed to be right on top of him and far away at the same time.

Just keep breathing, he remembered, and with each breath he had to fight against Panic's bad advice to bolt up. He took a deep drag from his regulator, exhaled slowly, watched his bubbles rise up like silver umbrellas. The umbrellas merged with each other, broke apart into spheres of mercury, raced, halted, and then finally exploded as they crashed through the surface. With each breath the bubbles became more spherical, and then he found he could control his heart rate by changing the shape of those bubbles as he exhaled.

Branch looked up and saw the white underside of Manny's boat. The boat's propellers ground to a halt, and then Branch was stunned by sudden silence. The awful, droning noise of Panic—the sound from the boat's motor—had disappeared. Then there was only the sound of his own breathing, controlled, relaxed, and calm, and the sound of his bubbles as they danced upward.

Branch drifted with the current and kicked in toward the shallows, where colorful coral archways formed honeycombed caves. He hovered into one of the small caves and discovered that it split into several passageways, studded with yellow and orange spindles of coral.

Up above him, above the water and above the earth, clouds passed by and the sunlight flickered in the crevices, and the shadows danced with the gentle surge of the sea. Branch kicked farther into the little grottoes. Then there was a luminous golden shimmering under a coral ledge, a swarm of hundreds of tiny, mirrored, golden fish—glassy sweepers—dancing and darting in unison in their dark shelter, like underwater butterflies floating in a diamond cathedral.

Branch settled his belly down onto the warm sand and watched the golden dance. *Test and approve what God's will is*, he remembered. *A good life, a strong life*. Panic was long gone, and he was mesmerized by the simple and secret beauty he was witnessing.

Chapter Twenty-One

The Wild Side

Branch opened his eyes and looked again at the glass globe souvenir. The sand had settled to the bottom, and the tiny golden fish were fluttering happily. He got up from the bed and put the orb back in the drawer. Then he put on jeans and a sweatshirt and he grabbed his M9. The far side of the island was no place to be in the middle of the night without a weapon.

He strolled past the front desk at exactly nine o'clock. Pam was sipping a cup of tea and reading her daily copy of the *Chinchamos Times*. Her faded blue eyes were bloodshot.

"Anything interesting in the news today, Pam?"

She placed the paper on the desk, spun it around for Branch to see, and tapped it with bony fingers. Branch looked at the headline: Another new junk food joint was coming to the island. Then he smiled at her, admiring her fervor. He wondered if she'd be proud of him if she knew about Dorian. He realized that he *wanted* her to be proud of him. But it was something she could never know.

"I do declare," she said, her eyes shining again, her forehead cracking under her thick, silver coif. "We used to have a real newspaper here but then a few years back they found the editor with his head chopped off. Now all you can read about is development bringing money to the island. And nothing from the other side of the coin."

"Money," Branch said, quickly back to thinking how close he was to having enough of it. And how killing Dorian could ruin all of that.

"It's coming in but the locals don't benefit." She pushed the newspaper away from her on the desk and looked Branch square in his eyes. "These cruise ships. Everyone comes and goes, in at sunrise, gone by sunset. No one staying in the hotels, no more serious divers coming down anymore because the reefs have all gone gray."

"I'd hate to lose a good landlord, but why not sell and go someplace else? Someplace that's not already spoiled?"

She took a moment to size up Branch's fresh change of clothing then squinted at him suspiciously. "I thought you were going to get some rest tonight, Branch. Big cave dives tomorrow. The Pirati caverns."

"I'll be there." Branch walked toward the foyer then turned back to look at Pam. "Nice and deep. See you on the boat in the morning."

Out in the lobby he smelled the cigars and beer and heard the chatter coming from La Cucaracha as he walked to the café on the other side.

Bali was sitting at the counter, toying with a plate of quiche and nibbling on a brownie. "I knew you'd come," she said, wheeling around on her stool. "The hawksbill turtle fascinates you."

"An air-breathing reptile that can stay hours underwater on a single breath? Yeah. I could use that skill."

"I think you've already got it. Better eat something before we go. Help me finish this quiche."

Branch sat down next to her. He was hungry. He hadn't eaten much the previous two days other than the Grouper's mushrooms. They finished the food and then soon they were in Bali's Jeep, cruising south out of town along the leeward shoreline toward the lighthouse. Then they turned back north at the point into the darkness of the far side road.

The air was cool and the wild, pungent scent of sargasso drifted in from the open ocean. As they pushed farther from town, stars dilated above them and the grinding noise from the ships was gone.

The darkness was protecting him now, he hoped. He had no business being here, but he felt fine as they rambled north along the windward shore road. She told him about her dissertation project—filming and studying female hawksbill turtles laying eggs—and he started to forget his own turbulence.

They drove farther into the dark. Yellow road stripes flashed by, reeds swayed, and bonsai palms, bent by the ocean wind, reminded that hurricanes had hit this side of the island with full force, and would again.

Bali slowed and navigated a curve as the road curled back inland, then she turned the Jeep onto a dirt path leading into thick mangroves. They bumped along on the dirt for a few miles, rolling slowly through the low-growing palms and calabash bushes. She wheeled to the right and drove back toward the beach, mangroves lining either side of the narrow trail. Branch realized they were close to the spot where he'd come ashore after the mainland job, where the skiff and his unit were stashed.

They parked the Jeep and hiked in the vivid starlight through the jungle and toward the beach, where waves crashed in on the broad white shore. Bali briefly flashed her light across the sand.

"They're not here yet," she whispered.

"Who?"

"The turtles, moron. Set up the tent while I get the camera ready. We want to be out of their way when they start coming."

Half an hour later they lounged in the tent, the night-vision camera and tripod pointing out toward the sea.

"They come to this same spot every June to lay their clutch," she told him. "I'm trying to get a grant to do serious research on their mating and nesting behavior. Nobody knows their population size. They're seriously endangered from all the damage to the reefs."

"Right. Food sources. Sponges, crustaceans, mollusks. The book."

"Very good. If I'm going to preserve this spot I've got to be armed with data. You saw what happened on the other side of the island. Omar paid experts to say the pier wouldn't harm Paradise Reef. Now he's buying up all the land on this side, too. He wants to pave it and build resorts. I'm trying to get a head start. To stop him."

Their eyes adjusted to the darkness as they watched the waves roll in. Soon a large hawksbill rose up out of the surf and waded crookedly ashore. Bali knelt below the tripod and filmed the turtle as it trudged to a spot only ten feet away from them on the beach. The turtle dug its nest, laid its eggs, carefully covered the clutch with sand and then waddled back to the sea.

"Her job's done," Bali whispered, reading numbers from her GPS unit and then writing on a notepad. "We've got to do ours to make sure her babies have a world to live in."

Over the next couple of hours, three more turtles came ashore and laid eggs.

"I think that's it for tonight," she said, and then they exited the tent to relax on the warm sand. "I don't know why but you never see them come ashore in great numbers."

"How long before they hatch?" Branch asked, lying on his belly and gazing down the beach. Had he just arrived he never could have guessed such a multitude of life was brewing beneath the sand.

"A few weeks. Up to two hundred eggs in each clutch, but not many survive. Predators raid the nest. When they hatch the birds take their share. So do the fish. That's nature's way. Out of a huge pile of eggs maybe only one or two will go on to become one of those glorious old hawksbills you see on a dive. But the real problem comes from humans."

"That's what I heard."

"You give any thought to Victor's offer about being a partner in the shop?"

"No. I don't expect to be on the island that long."

"That's too bad," she said, pulling off her shirt and her baggy sweatpants. Underneath she still wore her golden bikini. "Could be a good scene for you here."

"Yeah. Could be. Just can't commit to anything right now."

"What about that woman you see in town. Mel Lamy? Where'd you two meet?"

"That taco place right by Takanaka's Liquor. Taco Loco."

"She *is* a taco loco. Seems to me she cares for nothing but herself."

"That's true enough. If you could count on everyone to be so predictable then things might work better. Pam sells her mangroves. Omar builds his pier. And Mel takes money off tourists and goes shopping."

"And Branch goes diving, way too deep."

"You got it."

"What is it you see when you drop way down there? You go way past the limits."

"See? More of a feeling, but what *do* I see? Neon lights. A bar. A waitress. A big tray of ... I think it's ... nitrogen martinis?"

"Getting stoned. As usual. What else?"

"In the Deep Blue Saloon, in the back rooms, in the dingy booths, down around two fifty and beyond, there's this angel of an underwater waitress down there."

"A saloon. Figures. But the angel part is interesting. What does this angel waitress do?"

"What underwater waitresses do. Serve up gorgonian gimlets. What angels do. Watch over you. And then forgive you for every bad thing you ever done."

"What bad things?" she asked, but when Branch said nothing she moved on. "It's that easy to find forgiveness?"

"Oh, yeah. Easy to find. Just one problem. The forgiveness fades away with every foot you rise up."

"You could serve a purpose here in the real world," Bali said. "Instead of killing yourself down there. You might miss out on some good things up here."

"Maybe so."

"These bad things you mention. Whatever it is you've done. There's bound to be a better way to put it behind you."

"What could be better?"

"Going that deep? Aren't you afraid of dying? Sorry, but if you browned out and started to sink I would *not* be coming after you. Not way down there. Not on plain air. Idiot."

"Plain air's the only way to go. It's a nitrogen thing, Bali. Nitrogen."

"Yeah, it's the way to go. Out. There wouldn't be any saving you."

"Guess not. You afraid of going out?"

"No," she said. "Not of dying. But wasting my life, yeah. Not reaching my potential and making a difference. Not knowing true love. That's why I wouldn't go past one thirty. Unless I was using tri-mix."

She reached across the sand and placed her soft, brown fingers on his hand.

Branch said nothing. It wouldn't be a casual thing, a Mel thing. He couldn't risk blowing his cover. He was so close to having enough, so close to being able to leave the life and make a fresh start. Besides all that, he knew he wasn't good enough for her.

"But when the moment comes," Bali continued, stroking his hand, "I do wonder."

"The moment?" Branch asked. He tried to distract himself but her hand was soft and smooth and she was talking about death and he found himself riotously ready for her.

"That moment. To make sure my life had meaning. That it counted for something."

Branch moved his head to get a better view of her firm physique plastered against the sand, still weighing the benefits of any involvement with her.

"Oh," he said. "*That* moment. You don't need to worry. You're young and smart. You'll have a good life. A strong life. It's a waste of time for you to worry about it. It'll do all the work for you. When it comes. You're not like me, Bali. I've been dancing with it too long. Anyway, that's a long way off for you."

She moved her hand away.

"You must jack off a lot. You and your imaginary barmaid."

Branch laughed. "Addicted, I guess."

"They say when you're trying to break an addiction you've got to believe in a higher power. What do you believe in?"

"I don't know. I believe in the laws of physics. I believe in evolution. I don't believe in Jesus, but I believe in *her*, in the Deep Blue Saloon. I guess that's it."

"Narcosis is real," Bali said. "But what you see when you're on it isn't. I'm into real stuff. Like love, family. Like protecting the reef and the turtles. And stopping Omar and the pier project. You should find *your* path. A real one."

"I had a real path. The path didn't want me. Then I found something I loved doing. But that wasn't real. And I just kind of fell into the cracks. Don't know how to get out."

Bali laughed. "That's a mighty deep crack you fell into. But you *can* get out. You've got a strength about you. We could use you. There's another protest planned soon. Next weekend. We're going to march from the pier to Omar's jewelry store. Walk the path with us."

For a moment Branch gave in to the notion he could be part of such a thing and he enjoyed that brief, warm feeling. But he couldn't cross Omar, and besides, he had to keep *that* weekend open for the Cuba job.

"Don't know if I'd really be helping y'all. You'd best do it without me."

"Come with us," she said. "A few people standing up against what's wrong can change the world."

"Yeah. I know that one. Saw the bumper sticker. But whenever I tried it, it only made things worse. From my experience, staying home is always safer and it yields better results. I advise you to just stay home."

"I won't stay home," Bali said. "I want to do great things with my life. When people google me, I want them to see real accomplishments. What do you want them to see—about you?"

Branch thought about how easy Reiner's job would be if he could just type the words "Branch Kilgore" on a keyboard and find him. "When they google me? Nothing. Absolutely nothing. My life is outside the tribe. That's the way I have to live, for now. Forever. No personal history."

"Lonely."

"It is. But there's always one more little thing to do to keep me busy," he said, rolling over on his back and watching a bright meteorite burn across the sky.

"We always think we've got time," she said. "It's like that last shooting star before dawn. You keep looking for one more. You don't want to admit that a beautiful night is over. And then it's getting light but you're not ready for morning. Time to stop running."

"What makes you think I'm running?"

Bali leaned forward on the sand toward him and then with a quick move she put her hand on his back. She lowered her hand and tapped the gun tucked into his pants.

"Why else would you need *that*? May I see it?"

"Sure," Branch said. He handed Bali the gun. "I'm not running, but like I told you, the wild side can be a wild place."

"That's a good gun. M9," she said, admiring its balance before handing it back to him. She unzipped her pack to show him the black, wooden-handled semiautomatic inside. "Almost as good as my Beretta. You get that piece in the navy?"

"Keep it," Branch said. He tossed the M9 down on the beach towel. "I hate guns. And you're going to need more than one if you plan on taking on Omar."

Then she quickly grabbed his sweatshirt and pulled him toward her.

"Let's forget about Omar for a little while," she said, and then she kissed him. They weren't like Mel's voluptuous kisses. They were searching, quick kisses, and for a moment he allowed himself to enjoy that difference.

She unsnapped her bikini top, let it fall to the sand, then took Branch's hand in her own, caressing her responsive, dark nipples.

He gave in for a moment but then he jerked his hand away.

"Why me? You've been on Chinchamos all this time, and everyone knows you've never done this. Not with a dozen guys who have asked. Victor talked you into this?"

"I do what I want. Victor's worried about you and he asked me to look after you tonight. But I'd never do this unless I wanted it."

"Victor has you believing I can somehow help your cause," Branch said, and then there was the lousy feeling again. "What did he tell you about me? It ain't true. I think I'd better take a walk."

He bolted down the beach. There was the vague sparkle from the lighthouse as he walked south, the half-moon rising over the water.

"Sure, go jack off with your fantasy waitress," he heard her say. "Keep running."

The beach glowed as the moon rose higher. Branch lurched to the south in hypnotic confusion. He snapped out of it when he realized he'd stumbled in front of the very mangrove channel where he'd stashed the skiff and his scuba unit.

The moon cast a yellow reflection off the sea, illuminating the interior of the channel. He approached the outlet quietly, crouching and watching. Then he waded twenty feet into the mangroves, finding the little boat still tied up where he'd left it. Farther in, the water was waist-deep and with each step he stopped and listened for any splashes, worried a little about crocodiles, and worried a lot about humans. And then there it was—the scuba unit, his favorite set of gear, right where he'd left it.

With this thing on my back I don't need anyone. Only her.

He grabbed the unit and turned to float back toward the beach. But before he could, he heard a splash and felt cold metal press against the back of his neck. He turned his head a tiny degree and saw the black barrel of a shotgun shining in the moonlight.

"*Afuera, a la playa,*" the shotgun told him. "To the beach."

Branch let go of the scuba unit and eased back out of the little channel. There was a heavy, sloppy splashing behind him.

"Stop," said the shotgun. "Turn around."

Branch turned around slowly and saw a young man, no more than twenty, his pale face and his red hair glowing in the moonlight, his right hand trembling as he fingered the trigger guard on the shotgun.

"Been in the reeds for a full day now, waiting for you, *Mr.* Cave Diver," the redhead said, in perfect English with an aristocratic Mexican accent. "I knew you'd come back for your gear. Someone as efficient as you would have to. Get your hands up."

"I'm no cave diver," Branch said, raising his hands. "I'm a turtle researcher. My camp is just up the beach. If you want the stuff, go ahead. You take it."

"I *saw* you, yesterday morning. Down under that clear water, looking up at me. I know it was you. What a fine job it *almost* was. But now you've been caught. By me."

He raised the shotgun and pressed the end of the barrel to Branch's chest. He looked just like the redhead in the villa but much younger.

Branch looked him in the eye, saw he was scared and fatigued. He'd probably been waiting in the swamp all day. The redhead pulled the hammer back on the shotgun and then suddenly he didn't look so fatigued.

"Will you feel better about things?" Branch asked. "When it's done?"

The young redhead lowered the shotgun slightly. "About the one thing, yes. About the other things, no, not until it stops. And anybody who works for Omar is guilty."

"Guilty? Of what?"

"Kidnapping dolphins. Killing coral. Finning sharks. Paving over mangroves."

"All I'm guilty of is filming turtles laying eggs. Just up the beach. The stuff you say—it's none of my business."

"It's *everybody's* business," the redhead said, lowering the shotgun a bit more. "I saw you. You killed him. Left that little plastic dolphin. You work for Omar."

Branch took a breath, then exhaled slowly. "I guess maybe so," he said. "But it was just a job. Nothing personal, me killing your *jefe*."

"You picked the wrong line of work."

"I *know* that. Maybe I'm trying to get out. Maybe that's why I'm here tonight."

"Too late now," the redhead said. "And that wasn't my boss you killed. That was *mi padre.*"

"*Su padre*. Yeah. I remember now. The photo in the den. Happy family. Sorry about that. If it'll make it up to you, you can kill mine."

"What?" the redhead demanded, and then the shotgun was up and poking Branch's chest again.

"*Mi padre. My* daddy. He's here on the island. Kill *him*. We'll be even, sort of. I won't get a damn thing. Bet you'll inherit a nice chunk. But you won't profit from shooting me."

"Interesting logic," the redhead said. "But my uncle's in charge now."

"What an asshole. Sending you solo to do a fucked-up thing like this."

"I'm alone. But he didn't send me. I do this on my own. And I've got a job to do."

"I respect that. The job. But you don't want to work like this. A wise man told me never work in anger. No profit in it. This is something I know about. It'll fuck everything up. Believe me. Don't fuck this job up."

"It would be really hard to fuck this one up."

"Maybe so," Branch said. "This is your first?"

"No."

"How many?"

"Plenty. You? Before Papa."

"I don't know. I stopped counting. But he's the last. What's your name?"

"You can call me Gusano. Gusano Verde. But not for long."

"Put the gun down and leave, Gusano Verde. Wait until you aren't mad. If you decide you'll profit from it, then come back and kill me later. It'll work out better then."

"Better?" Gusano Verde asked, and he raised the gun up to Branch's forehead. "Better than what?"

Then there was a blue-yellow flash and a loud bang that came from up the beach. Gusano Verde collapsed onto the sand and blood trickled from a gouge on his left shoulder. Branch snatched the shotgun and pressed it to his head.

"The wild side's a wild place," he heard Bali say. "You left without your gun. Thought I'd better bring it to you."

"I *had* him," Branch said. He turned his head away from Gusano Verde for a second to look at Bali, her Beretta smoking in her right hand and his own M9 dangling from the fingers of her left. "This bandito here. I had him. Get on back to turtle camp."

"Laws of physics and evolution and all of that," Bali said. "Personal history. Jackoff. You sure you're good?" Then she lowered the gun and trudged back toward the tent.

Once Bali was out of sight, Branch grabbed Gusano Verde by the hair with his left hand, still holding the shotgun with his right. He looked into his fair, youthful face.

"See what I mean, Verde? When you're angry it makes you hesitate. And he who hesitates is dead."

"Thought you said that was your last," Gusano Verde said, grimacing in pain from his wound. "You're really researching turtles?"

Branch backed away, tickled the trigger on the shotgun but then hesitated, violating his own advice. He'd killed two men since he last slept and now it was about to be three. And how good could sleep *ever* be after that? He knew what had to be done but then he thought of Bali, waiting for him. She'd hear the blast and she already knew too much. So it would have to be four. Gusano Verde tensed in his crouched position then relaxed a little as Branch continued talking.

"Yeah. Turtles."

"Then don't shoot me. Work for me. Remember what you said about not being emotional."

"It's only emotion that keeps me from *pulling* the trigger," Branch said. "I'll give you two options. The first is you can go back to Uncle—what's his name?"

"Carlos."

"Carlos Verde?"

"No. I'm *Gusano* Verde. That means 'Green Worm.'"

145

"I get it. You're a superhero. Option one, superhero. You can go back to Uncle Carlos and tell him you ran into the wrong guy."

Gusano Verde trembled on the sand, holding his wounded shoulder. "He doesn't even know I'm here. But what's the other option?"

"Two. I *will* pull the trigger, Green Worm, and you'll have the shortest super-hero career anyone ever heard of. And I'll let the little crocs in the mangroves dispense with your remains."

In the morning, the tide had washed all trace of their footprints away and the white sand was smooth and cool, running without end into the rosy sunrise. The dark water's nocturnal work had left a perfect finish on the beach. Branch stepped out of the tent and walked into the water for a morning swim. Bali lay naked inside, watching him as he kicked out.

Chapter Twenty-Two

Us and These Little Birds

O n the Caribbean Argonauts dock, Branch helped Manny load the dive boat with tanks, dive gear, and picnic lunches. He looked across the water to Paradise Shallows. The once tranquil cove was a bustling construction zone and the demolition barge anchored in its middle was surrounded by buoys and warning signs. Orange mesh fencing skirted the beach, and front-end loaders, cement mixers, boxes of explosives and technical gear were being ferried from shore out to the platform.

Once everyone was on board, Manny pointed the boat south toward the lagoon and the inland channel that would lead them to the Pirati caverns. They hit some chop from a cruise ship that had just anchored—ferries were already shuttling passengers to the municipal pier—and the *Trident's Parade de Caribe* cast a long shadow over them as they motored by. They pulled clear of the cruise ship and then Branch could see the silhouette of Len's broad frame on the demolition platform beyond. Then the boat was out of the chop, skimming over the smooth shallows and into the morning sunshine.

They neared the inlet to the lagoon and the sea was red and orange where the fresh water mingled with the salty Caribbean. Manny steered into a river that cut through the mangroves then drove the boat north into the stream toward the lagoon.

Manny made a sharp turn into a hidden channel that ran back toward the interior of the island. As the boat puttered along the tight passage, mangroves scraped along the bimini top, and tiny trogons darted in the snarl of branches. Then the narrow stream opened into a large cenote, a crystal teardrop of a pond in the middle of the thick jungles. It was less than a mile from the mangroves behind the Blue Angel, but was hidden away from tourists and locals by the labyrinth of swampy channels they'd navigated. Manny killed the motor and lowered a small anchor onto the pond floor.

A cloud passed, the sun emerged, and the shadows of the mangroves shifted and redrew themselves on the surface of the lime-colored water. The noise from the motor died away, the quiet of the oasis fell upon them, and the giddy conversation between Bali and the Grouper seemed to float off with the breeze. The divers started slipping into their scuba units.

"This place seems untouched, like when I first saw it," Branch said.

"It's still a magical spot," Bali replied. "But if they pave over the mangroves at Paradise, it'll stagnate and die. Your beloved saloon in the deeps ... gone, too. Maybe that'll get you to come to the protest next weekend."

"Branch can't make any protest next weekend," the Grouper said. "He's gonna be in Cuba with that fine piece of ass."

"Cuba?" Bali asked. "You're going to Cuba? With *her*?"

Branch said nothing. The Grouper gave him a kind of shrug and just turned away.

"What happened on the beach last night," Bali said quietly to Branch. "If you say it was a bandit holding that shotgun, I believe you. And later, in the tent. It doesn't have to mean anything. But please tell me you're not going to Cuba next weekend. With her. Something feels very wrong about it. Don't go, whatever the reason."

Branch remained silent and then Bali moved to the other side of the boat.

"Sorry, man," the Grouper said, turning back toward him. "I didn't know. My big mouth."

"It's alright, dude," Branch told him softly. "How could you know? But keep quiet about our beach dive the other night." As he said it the wind shifted and noises from the demo platform and the vague drone of dive boats on the open water drifted in over the cenote again.

"I heard you're renting the *Ogygia*," Pamela said to the Grouper. "A fan of the stock car races living on such a wonderful sailboat? Such a paradox."

"I only stay on that sailboat so I can spit tobacco in any direction and I'll hit water. Makes the cleaning up a lot easier. I love the ocean. But I love the races, too. When a car goes by you at two hundred? Totally surreal, like when you go *down* to two hundred on a dive."

"Everybody here's done this site before," Victor said, starting his briefing. "We're in an overhead environment. You know what the rules are. Follow the lines we've already laid down. We'll all stay up in the top level of passages."

Victor gave Branch a stern look, then continued.

"If we head north we end up in Garganta del Diablo, a really deep and dark cave system with tight restrictions that comes out right by the shop. But we can't go that way. All the pier construction is blocking the exit. So on this dive we go south. We'll hit a nice air dome then toward the end we get into a halocline. It comes out in the ocean on a sweet stretch of reef. Manny will be waiting for us there. Did I forget anything?"

"Yeah, watch out for the crocodiles," said the Grouper. He slapped his mask on and rolled back, splashing noisily into the water.

"Darling little animals," said Pamela. Her silver hair protruded wildly out of her mask strap and the wrinkles on her face bunched together like an intricate road map. "But they need to watch out for *him*."

Bali helped Pam over the side of the boat and into the pond and then Branch, Bali, and Victor slipped in. They descended together into the crystal clear depths of the cenote, with Victor leading the group down into a large cave opening.

They floated through liquid blue light for a time then came up in a large air pocket. Stalactites hung from the ceiling above them and the sun's rays drilled into the clear water through vine-covered apertures in the rock. Branch remained below, in the darkest depths he could find. It was his job to stay down and watch the divers, and he was glad for that. Only about one twenty at the very bottom of the trough, but it was enough for a quick nitrogen fix. His first real hit since he'd overdosed on the mainland. Not deep enough to see *her*, but a balance he could live with.

The sunlight made a prism of rainbow colors above him and there was a green glow from the jungle canopy invading through holes in the rock wall. He took a deep drag off his regulator, exhaled slowly, and watched his bubbles rise up like crystalline balloons.

And then he'd made his mind up. He'd tell Bali as soon as they were alone. He'd say no to the Cuba job and he'd join the protest. To hell with Omar. To hell with having enough.

He rose up slowly and joined the others in the air dome. A flock of swallows zoomed in and out through the various tiny skylights, skimming the smooth surface of the turquoise water.

"Fucking amazing, every time it amazes me," said the Grouper, his voice echoing in the dome. "You're not just in the water but deep inside the earth, too. This whole world is down here and nobody ever sees it."

"Just us and these little birds," Bali said.

The talking and laughter and the singing of the little birds inside the dome echoed against the rock ceiling and then was muted as it bounced off the soft water. To Branch it sounded like some faraway cocktail party. He closed his eyes and he heard strange, happy people talking and toasting, their champagne glasses clinking together. Happy people who wanted him to join them. And then, he was happy, too. The path.

After a few moments enjoying the air dome, they sank back down and finned into a passage adorned with brightly colored stalagmites. The group slowed up as Victor floated into a narrower section of the cave. A hundred feet behind the group, Branch was gazing at the fossilized conch shells that studded the walls. He put his hand to the wall to touch the fossils and then he felt a kind of electric vibration.

A sudden, sharp blast shattered the silence as an explosion ripped through the chamber. The roof above them cratered. The clear water churned with opaque silt and then everything went white in a milky cloud. A cave-in was pushing a subterranean tsunami through the tube. Branch dropped down and dug his fingers into the cavern floor, fighting the roaring current.

It was like thunder up above them. Silt rained down and the current surged. After a few seconds the rumbling stopped. The flow of murky water subsided and started to swirl about in the cavern.

Branch flapped his tank banger and listened as the metallic twang bounced off the stone walls. A tapping noise answered and then a different, higher-pitched tap came. The volley of taps went on for a while in the underwater fog. But he could only hear two divers tapping. Two weren't tapping back.

He looked at his console—now barely visible in the soup—and he saw the minutes and seconds counting down on his remaining air time. The double tank rig he wore would give him time to wait for the water to clear, but he worried about the others. He'd have to lead them through the muddle and back to the air dome.

Branch settled down onto the cavern floor, groped around, and felt nothing. He pointed his underwater light ahead into the muddy mess, and saw nothing. So he turned off his light and searched in darkness for the thick guideline he and Victor had laid down many months before.

This passage ran north-south, and Branch remembered that the line ran along the east wall. He inched along the slimy floor, holding his compass close to his face and hoping he hadn't strayed into one of the uncharted side passages. He bumped across the navigation line, gave his tank another series of taps, then followed the line back toward the dome.

The taps seemed to follow him, so he continued to the air dome and surfaced. Sunlight poured in from the vents above, bouncing and scattering off the silty white layer just below the surface.

Branch pushed his mask off and took a deep breath. Through the holes in the rock ceiling above, where the swallows were swooping and playing, he heard faraway clanging noises from the demolition platform, and somewhere out on the ocean a cruise ship's horn belched.

Bubbles broke the surface and then the Grouper's head popped up through the milky water.

"What the fuck?" He spit out his regulator. "Earthquake? I thought you were heading back out the main shaft. But it's totally blocked. So I kicked back here. Thought I was surfacing into solid rock. Sure was glad to find the air dome."

They looked at the next set of bubbles breaking the surface and in a moment Pam's silver head appeared.

"I followed the tapping," she gasped. "But Bali and Victor. They were ahead of me. And then they were just gone!"

The Grouper pushed his mask up and turned it around so the strap was on his forehead. "Can we make it out?"

"It was the blast," Pam said. "The work on the pier. They blasted early. They knew we were down here."

"Don't know," said Branch. "Could've been an earthquake."

"Yes," Pam said. "An earthquake, indeed. A natural disaster named Omar Rasgado. If I survive this I'll see that he never lands a ship at that pier."

"You sure the big chamber is blocked?" Branch asked.

"Solid wall of rubble," the Grouper answered.

"That spot we were at when it hit. That looked impassable to you, Pam?"

"There's no getting through there. I only hope Bali and Victor were on the other side of it."

"I doubt we can transmit from under these rocks," Branch said, "but it's worth a try."

He removed the radio from its waterproof housing and powered it on. There was no response to his repeated attempts to transmit a message, but a faint voice,

Len's voice, could be heard in the scratchy signal the radio was able to receive. *"... that one went good ... next charge in one hour."*

"We can't get up this rock," Branch said, hoping they hadn't heard, "and we can't stay in this water much longer or we'll go hypothermic. We go out the other way. The Garganta del Diablo. Either that or we'll have to fly out the cracks up there with these little birds."

They stared up at the dome ceiling some twenty feet over their heads and they watched as the swallows darted in and out of the tiny sunlit cracks.

"The Garganta?" the Grouper asked. "That comes out on Paradise Shallows. Right where they're blasting. If these tubes here collapsed, can you imagine what the Garganta tunnel must look like? You heard the radio. Another blast in an hour."

"We can make it," Branch said. "Let this silt settle. Then we'll drop down and have a look."

They waited on the surface until the billow below was a translucent haze. Branch took a length of line from his pocket and tied it off to his D-ring, a metal loop on his buoyancy jacket. He coiled ten feet of slack, tied it off to Pam's BC jacket then handed the end of the line to the Grouper.

They dropped into the pool and pushed back into the passage. The visibility had improved but it was like swimming through white smoke. Branch found the navigation line and followed it to the entry to the Garganta del Diablo. Shining his light inside the narrow opening he saw what looked like a passable mess of broken rock, and then there was the sign—*Prevent Your Death. Go No Farther*—and there was the grinning skull.

He kicked in.

Chapter Twenty-Three

Garganta del Diablo

They crawled and squeezed through the cold, dark passages of the Garganta del Diablo. It would lead them to the ocean at Paradise Shallows, if it wasn't blocked from the blast.

It was at Paradise Shallows, while diving from the Caribbean Argonauts dock, where Branch had first explored the small, shadowy openings under the shore. Over time he'd surveyed the system all the way to the lagoon. That was in good visibility, with stage tanks and reels, and he'd admired the brilliance in the darkness of the caves, and though the tunnels seemed to meander without pattern, he'd seen order in their imbroglio. But now it was murky, they were low on air, and the clock was ticking.

This part of the system was so tight that no divers, except the most hard-core cavers, dared to penetrate it. If they were to hit an impasse they'd have to crawl backward to the air dome. But for now they inched ahead.

Whenever the tight passage afforded him room to look over his shoulder, Branch shone his light behind to check on the others. Pam, shivering from the cold, was floating neatly behind him, conservative with her fins and her breathing.

The Grouper hovered behind her, his head down and his fins floating up toward the ceiling. Studying his console with his left hand, he used the fingers of his right to pull himself along the silty bottom.

Branch used hand signals to ask Pam about her air supply. She somberly placed two fingers of her right hand on her left wrist. Two *hundred* psi in her tank.

Plenty of air for outgassing in the shallows, but with a final stretch that would take them below one eighty, it was mere fumes. The Grouper shot him the OK sign and shrugged. Then the cavalcade of cramped divers continued onward and downward into the darkest and deepest portion of the Garganta.

They descended into the Lower Room, a prolifically decorated, spacious chamber that allowed them to leave their single-file positions and huddle up. Branch checked Pam's air again, now below one hundred and fifty psi, and he made sure both divers knew where his octopus—his extra regulator with the long hose—was located.

Branch looked at the scratches on the rock ceiling of the chamber above him, where two open-water divers had kicked in from the shallows the year before, had run out of air, thrashed, and drowned in the Lower Room. The scrape marks from their tanks looked to Branch like some kind of abstract art, a stone etching where the divers had fought and clawed for one more breath. He pushed the fright away and tried to feel the serenity of the deep galleries.

The three bottomed out at one ninety then began their climb toward the ocean. Branch felt a tug on his rig. He looked back and saw that Pam was breathing from his octopus. A few moments later the rhythm of the three-humped camel changed again and then Pam and the Grouper were sharing the spare regulator.

The air supply digits on his console clicked down fiercely with the two extra divers breathing from his tanks. As they finned around a sharp bend in the cave he startled a school of glassy sweepers. Old friends dancing in the dark, a dazzling, bejeweled drapery in a summer's breeze. They were close to the sea. His console indicated they were under a hundred psi and now he could hear the grinding, pinging noises of the demolition platform just ahead. They might have a chance to make a kick for it.

There was one last easy breath and then on the next, the hose chortled. Like sucking on a soda through a straw and then suddenly there was only crushed brown ice at the bottom of the glass. The tanks were almost empty. And there was still only darkness ahead in the cave.

The regulator squealed, fighting him as he inhaled again, and then it was like breathing through a tube the diameter of spaghetti. They were down to their final breaths.

Branch remembered the training instructor at Bucklew turning off his air supply while his hands and feet were tied. He'd loved it, but that had been a game. Someone was there to turn on the air and the surface was right above. And Panic had been easy to ignore.

But now, in the dark, with two souls clinging to life through his octopus and nothing but solid stone over his head, Panic was coming hard at him. He pulled for air, fending off the convulsions. The tiny breath that came didn't satisfy the urge. He closed his eyes, tightened his abs to fight off the gagging nausea and looked back at Pam and the Grouper. Their cheeks were sunken in, their eyes dark and pleading behind their masks. Three dope fiends, all of them fighting for one more hit from the hookah.

Branch kicked forward, trying to pull a breath, and almost nothing came. But he kept trying. As they ascended, as the surrounding pressure decreased, some good breaths might come. He could go without air for more than seven minutes if he was still, and kicking steady, maybe four. Even knowing there was nothing beyond that, he'd keep his composure and do the four. But dragging two dying divers along, what chance was there? There was only to kick into the darkness and wait for the end. A horrible, brackish, stinging flail it would be, and then there'd be a new work of art on the stone ceiling above.

A pinhole of light suddenly flicked on ahead of him. How far? And was it even real?

The Grouper and Pam swam furiously alongside him as the cave ascended and opened into a chamber the width of a subway tunnel. But the light ahead wasn't a train. It was the Garganta's mouth as it opened into the ocean at Paradise Shallows.

They kicked breathlessly and the pinhole expanded into a blue orb. There'd be no scrape marks on the ceiling from this dive. The glow of open water was just ahead.

A few final kicks and then a circle of gray light opened above them. Branch's console indicated no air and his watch told him the explosion at the pier was imminent. The chamber turned blue and they kicked up into the openness.

The three divers felt the salty warmth of Paradise Shallows as they burst through to the bright turquoise surface. Throwing their masks off, they gulped in breaths of smoky air. Small boats buzzed between the shore and the demolition platform, and warning buoys bobbed in their wake. Diesel exhaust swirled about them, radios squawked, and unintelligible garble blasted from a megaphone.

Gasping, they looked at the industrial complex sprawling over what used to be the most beautiful shallow dive site on the leeward side of Chinchamos. A hydraulic crane, perched on the demolition platform, towered over the reef like a mechanized bird and the orange mesh fencing on the shoreline was flanked by a dozen armed security guards.

The exhausted divers struggled on the surface and made their way onto the jagged coral shoreline. Branch flung off his double tank rig, laid his head down in the warm sand, and sucked in big breaths of the heavy, sweet air. Someone was trudging along the beach, and he saw the familiar pointy tips of reptilian cowboy boots. Then there was the metallic chambering twang of a .44 Automag, and then cold chrome pressed against his temple.

"I tell you what," he heard Len's voice say. "Looks like I caught me some sab-o-teurs."

Chapter Twenty-Four

Not What You Are Here For

"What's the charge?" Branch asked, sitting across the desk from Fibbi in the office of the Chinchamos jail. Fibbi's flak jacket bulged under his uniform and his brow furrowed as he squinted at his clipboard.

"Trespassing, it says here." Fibbi stood up. "And sabotage."

"Fuck off." Branch could see that the pockets of his black polyester pants were stuffed full, probably with US twenties he'd collected that morning from speeding tourists. "I got two divers missing in that cave back there. We got to get out there and rescue them."

"Shut the fuck up, bitch," Fibbi said, prodding Branch with a blackjack he produced from under the desk. "No divers missing. They surfaced south."

"They made it out? How do you know?"

Fibbi came over the desk with the blackjack and grazed Branch on the ear with it.

"Don't fuck with me. Omar wants you safe. But I'm still the law here, Kilgore. Don't forget that."

"No," Branch said. He touched his ear, and his hand came away with blood on it. "I won't forget."

"That's good, bitch. We got a good thing happening on the island. Jobs coming in now. Thanks to Omar, there are jobs for my kids when they grow up."

"Jobs? You'd better find yourself a new one. Taking twenty-dollar bribes from tourists ain't going to cut it."

"You're mistaken. I work for a paycheck. Stand him up."

The deputy behind Branch jerked him up, spun him around to face the wall, then unzipped his wetsuit and stripped it down to his knees.

"Getting in the way of progress, bitch, is not good for your health." Fibbi whipped Branch three times on his lower back with the blackjack. Branch moaned and slumped to the floor.

"Love taps," Fibbi said, gloating as he stood over him. "Omar's sending someone for you. So crawl on back to your cell. Tell those other two this is serious shit. I got more important things to do than waste my time with your bitch ass."

"Yeah," Branch said, his voice raspy with blood. He saw the zip ties hanging from Fibbi's belt, saw the deputy relax against the wall, and then his mind was made up.

"You're serving a real important purpose here on the island," Branch said, slamming his fist up hard into Fibbi's crotch. Fibbi fell to his knees and Branch grabbed the blackjack. He spun his legs around, kicked the deputy to the floor, and then he was on them, beating them both with the blackjack. He yanked the zip ties from Fibbi's belt, and seconds later he had them tied up, wrist to ankle.

Branch snatched the key ring off Fibbi's belt and turned for the hallway leading to the jail cells. But then he felt that familiar cold metal prodding the back of his head.

"That's my boy," Len's voice said. "I tell you what, that time you spent on Daddy's farm, back by the power lines, weren't wasted. Tied 'em up good. Now, before you make a big mistake, move over behind the desk."

Branch stepped over Fibbi and the deputy, both now groaning and struggling against their bonds. Then he turned around and looked at Len and the chrome Automag.

"I hate guns. You going to shoot me, Len? Just for roughing up law enforcement?"

"Hell, no. Won't have to. Not after I talk some sense into you. That big A-rab works for Omar is on his way here now to bail you out. Figured I'd better get over here and let you know before you got yourself in some real trouble. So whatever you might be thinking about doin', you can do it without killin' another officer of the law. Like that poor cop back on FM 182. Don't you agree with me, Sheriff Fibbi?"

Fibbi, prone on his belly, turned his head and spat out a string of obscenities in Spanish.

"Easy now, Sheriff," Len said, prodding Fibbi with the tip of his boot, the gun still pointed at Branch's chest. "You were likely 'bout to join the ranks of the missing here on the island. Before I untie you and your deputy, let me hear you say you won't press charges or even hold a grudge for Branch's little outburst today. *Sabe?*"

"Untie me," Fibbi said. "I don't want Omar or nobody else to know about this."

"Cut him loose," Len told Branch. "Then get on back to your cell with them other two. You'll be out in an hour. And then you'd best get on with your job. Your *real* job."

Branch cut the zip ties off and pulled his wetsuit back up around his waist, patting his bloody ear as he was jostled out of the office by the deputy.

"You're a real crime fighter, Fibbi," he said. "Best get back out there with your radar gun. I saw some sorority girls on mopeds doing thirty-five in a thirty. Bitch."

Then Branch was pushed back into the rancid cell with Pam and the Grouper.

"So, what's the deal?" the Grouper asked. His mask was still perched on his head and his thick hair bulged inquisitively from behind the strap. "They beat on you?"

"You got nothing they want," Branch told him, but he knew that didn't apply to Pam. "Don't worry."

"We used to have a real police force here," Pam said, dabbing at Branch's wounded ear with the blanket draped over her shoulders. "But one by one those poor officers went missing, and then Omar's private squad took complete control."

Another deputy approached the cell. "Senor Gruber?" the deputy barked through the bars. "Paul Gruber? Come with me." The Grouper was led away and then the steel door slammed shut again.

"Just wait until the British consulate catches wind of this," Pam said sharply to the slamming door, then turned her attention again to Branch's ear.

"Omar and I have a history on the island. When I first arrived, he was trying to buy the hotel. The Admiral and I had cash and Omar was scrambling around selling dime bags to kids. I'm afraid he'll use any technicality to turn the screws on me. Health inspectors, red tape, business permits under scrutiny. Now I suppose he'll charge me with something."

"It's my job to get you safely back to the dive shop, and that's just what I intend to do," Branch said. "After that, though—"

"Yes, I know, I really should think about taking the money. And do business with the man who just tried to murder us in the cave? No. 'Lawless are they that make their wills their law.' He probably *did* kill Victor and Bali. Poor things. You know bloody well Victor notified them we'd be in that cave system."

"Fibbi told me Bali and Victor were safe."

"Thank heavens! But I didn't make it through these eighty years by giving in to fascists. We survived the bombing in England when I was just a child. I suppose I had it drubbed into me then. You don't give in to thugs and fascists."

"I'm just an average dude. I'm afraid I don't know much about standing up to fascists."

"You're an average dude," Pam echoed. "You're also an extraordinary dude. You're the most extraordinary average dude I've ever seen."

"No. I'm just a divemaster. That's what I am here for."

Pam stopped dabbing Branch's ear and looked at him sternly. Her eyes were steely gray and blue. "There. The bleeding's stopped. But as for you being a simple divemaster? I know better. That is *not* what you are here for."

The Grouper was shoved back into the cell sometime later, and then Pam was taken away for her interrogation in Fibbi's office.

"Wanted to know about how well I knew old Pam," the Grouper told Branch. "I think Sheriff Fibbi finally realized I'm just a drunk tourist. But he won't even give us a damn phone call."

"No phone call will be required," boomed a voice from outside the cell.

Branch turned toward the door. "Morgan. Thought I smelled you. Can't put those ciggies down for even a second."

"These little cigarettes are all I have to protect me from the injustices of the world," the fat man said. He pressed his face through the bars of the door and exhaled roiling smoke into the cell. "What do *you* have, to protect *you*?"

"Nothing real. Omar send you down here for us?"

"No," he said quietly. "Just you. He seems to be worried about your upcoming project."

"And my divers?"

"I'm here only to facilitate *your* release. But I've been in Chinchamos since long before Omar owned it and I still have some favor with the *policía*." He moved aside as the deputy unlocked the door to the cell. "I feel certain that Mr. Gruber is of no consequence to anyone, so I can offer you his release as well. Provided you proceed with the job Omar has offered you."

"What about Pam?"

"Omar is content to let Mrs. Linton sit in jail. The trespassing charge onto the pier site seems to have some legal merit, so she could be in here for quite some time, enjoying the sheriff's hospitality."

"I won't leave without both of them."

"I'm only here as a messenger. But it's my understanding that Pam's release will coincide with the successful completion of the job."

"Let her go now," Branch said. "Guarantee her a safe passage off the island and then I'll do the job."

"Impossible. She stays. Until the successful completion of the job. Know thyself, young Branch. It's the job that's important to you. And whatever it may be, consider that you can do it better from *outside* the confines of this cell."

Branch thought for a moment then nodded his head. "Get us out of here."

"Very well. The contract is in play. You might be interested to know that your fellow divers, Ms. Bali and your Mr. Mendez, emerged from your dive unscathed and are already posting on various sites and organizing a new protest to the pier's completion. Omar cannot recommend too highly that you stay clear of such events."

"I don't get out much, Morgan. You know that."

The door swung open and Branch walked into the corridor.

"Thanks, buddy," the Grouper said as he followed Branch out of the cell. "Whoever you are."

"With pleasure," Morgan said, and he gave a little bow. "But you would both be advised to take into account that Omar has run out of patience with any interruption on either the pier construction or the acquisition of land needed for the mall. He has grown quite weary of these impediments. Do I make myself clear?"

Chapter Twenty-Five

Run Faster, You Vile Steed

"I'm surprised to see you here," Yvonne said to him, stirring marinara sauce in the kitchen. "We'll talk in my office."

Then later, behind the closed door, she said, "Thought you would be out of here, calling me to wire you your savings. Not that I have feelings about it one way or the other. But I guess I want to know ... after what happened to you in the cave, and then being thrown in jail ... why?"

"You mean why am I taking the job in Cuba?" Branch asked, feeling the dread, but also the relief that there was the job in front of him. "I wish I could tell you it was for Pam. But I guess it's not just that. It's for me. I can't commit to anything. For a second there I thought I could. But this work is all I know. And I need the money. If anything happens to me I want you to give what I've got in the safe to the girl who works at the dive shop. Bali. Tell her to split it up with Pam and Victor. My truck goes to Manny."

"Nothing's going to happen to you," Yvonne said. "That turtle shell on you is bulletproof. Are you taking your sexy little friend with you? It would be good cover, traveling as a couple."

Then Branch felt the usual thing: enticed and simultaneously sickened by the thought of it. But if he was going to turn his back on Bali, he figured, he might as well go all in.

"Use your phone?"

"Branch, darling, I thought you would never call back," Melanie told him on the phone at the jewelry store. "And we leave for Havana on Friday afternoon? Oh, it's perfect! I have the cutest new outfit to wear on the plane."

Melanie's mind had worked quickly. If Branch would make an appearance at the jewelry store it would buy her time with Fernando.

"You'll have to pick me up at work and we'll go straight to the airport for our flight," she'd said to him. "It's just that there's no place for me to store my bags here at the store, you see? Do be a dear and swing by my bungalow on your way and grab them. I'll leave you a key in the usual place."

She hung up the phone and looked at Fernando. "See? I've got the boy wrapped around my finger. He'll be here to pick me up Friday. And when we get back, I'll *have* him."

Branch parked on the road and walked through the cool shadows of the ceiba trees and into Melanie's compound. He found the key hidden under the birdbath and inserted it in the lock. But before he could turn it, a door behind him squeaked open. He turned and saw the dentist—the landlord, he thought—watching him from the porch, his blue scrubs smeared with blood.

"Hello, Doc," Branch said. "Just here to pick up Mel's bags. For a weekend trip."

"W-w-w, yeah," the dentist stammered. "S-sure. Go on in." He waved his hand toward Melanie's door then went back into his office.

Branch let himself in and glanced around. The place seemed messy and neat at the same time. Puzzle books were strewn on the red Formica kitchen table, its matching chrome chairs pushed out as if a poker game had suddenly ended. A cast-iron teapot hung from a hook, and the retro clock on the wall twitched and ticked the time by. Then he was hypnotized by the cream and sugar aroma that permeated the bungalow. Traveling as a couple wasn't just about cover. A whole weekend alone with her wouldn't be so bad.

Branch took Melanie's striped tweed suitcases from the closet and left the apartment. Still dazed by Melanie's fragrant bouquet, he failed to see the dentist-landlord waiting for him on the porch.

"C-c-can you help me?" Dr. Thompson asked, startling him, nodding back toward his lab. "It's the n-n-nitrous," he said.

"I'm sorry?" Branch asked, feeling awkward standing there on Melanie's front porch, holding her suitcases, trying to gauge just how deranged this dentist was.

"I need help, B-B-Branch."

"You know me?"

"Y-yeah. You're the nitrogen fiend. You see? We have the same p-problem."

Branch set the bags down on the porch. "What problem is that?"

"The g-g-gas, Branch. We both love the gas. N-n-n," Dr. Thompson said. He was determined to get it out, and Branch stood there and let him. "Nite. Nite. Nitrogen."

Branch glanced back toward Thompson's office door. "You got nitrous in there?"

"Y-yeah. You want to h-hit it?"

"No. I like the real stuff. Down deep. It's no good unless there's water all around me. It'd be like cheating."

"Y-yeah. Kind of like j-jacking off when you've got *her* to f-fuck."

"She does ruin you for that," Branch said, pausing, knowing he should just leave, but then asking anyway. "Did *you* fuck her?"

"N-not really. It was for money. She doesn't l-like me. The way she likes you."

"I guess everybody has. That's got the money."

"We all do things we don't w-want to do. For money. What will you do? For m-money?"

"I don't know," Branch said, and he got a bad feeling as he thought about what was coming up in Cuba.

"I kn-know a way," Dr. Thompson said. "And then you w-wouldn't have to do things anymore. For m-money."

They talked for a while there on the porch. It was some kind of a wild scheme Dr. Thompson laid out, and Branch could only tell him he'd need time to think about it. Then he loaded up the tweed cases in his truck and drove back to the waterfront, already swarming from the Friday morning arrivals. He walked from his truck along the palm-lined boulevard, slaloming and bumping through the crush of corpulent, colorful tourists, and he was nearly sweating as he entered the jewelry store. Melanie was behind the Rolex kiosk, petite and demure in a yellow blouse with matching short skirt and black wedge sandals.

"Help you with something, sir?" Fernando asked, creeping up on him as he admired Mel's smooth, bare legs. "Or are you only *looking*?"

"Yeah. Just looking. I'm here to pick up Mel. Tell her Branch is waiting."

"Certainly, Mr. Kilgore," Fernando said, holding out his hand. "I know we haven't been properly introduced, but we've both been living on this island for some time. Fernando Reyes."

Branch reluctantly shook Fernando's floppy hand.

"Mr. Reyes. Busy day?"

"Lots of just-lookers, Mr. Kilgore. If you'll excuse me, it's time for me to relieve Miss Melanie. I'll send her right up to you."

On the way to the airport, Melanie changed out of her yellow outfit and into the sleeveless pink pantsuit and matching beret Branch had brought from the bungalow. The panties came off, the pink thong went on, then the pants went on, up under the skirt. Then the skirt came off, and the process continued for the top. Bra, panties, everything changed out in the car without her being naked for even one second.

"Isn't this the most hideous thing you've ever seen?" she asked him, running her fingertips down the length of the blouse. "And I just love it."

"Me, too," he said, taking an admiring glance as he navigated to the Chinchamos airport. Ample, slender, comely. Outrageous. But already nauseating him. "Didn't Che Guevara wear a pink beret like that one?"

"Who's she?" Melanie asked, applying pink lipstick as she analyzed her face in the visor mirror. "Some girl you nailed?"

At the airport they waited in line to check Melanie's three bags but still had time for drinks before they boarded. The small jet took off into the late afternoon sunshine, circled the north end of the island then flew over the length of Chinchamos on its way northeast toward Cuba. Out his window Branch caught a glimpse of the small procession of protestors on the boulevard, marching from town to the new pier, their signs and banners held high. They would protest at the pier then march all the way to Fibbi's jail, Bali had told him, to protest Pam's arrest and the destruction of the reef.

Omar would be down there watching, Fibbi and his deputies would be watching, and somewhere down there, Len, too, was watching. All of them waiting for a chance to end it. Branch felt a twinge of regret, and for a half second he wondered why he was romping off with Mel.

This is a working trip, he reminded himself. And a man must concentrate on his work. And if it goes well, Pam will be released. Not because of what they're doing down there, with signs and smartphones, but because of some terrible thing he would do in Cuba. And then he'd get paid.

Melanie smiled at him as the jet climbed away from Chinchamos. *Life Vest Under Your Seat,* the sign in front of her advised, but the letters were already deciphering and reordering themselves.

"What are you grinning about?" Branch asked her.

"Nothing, darling." *Run faster, you vile steed.* "Just *so* looking forward to our romantic getaway."

Before he could finish his drink they were flying over Cuba, and Branch could see both coasts much of the way along the western tip of the island. Red skies glowed through the window as they circled to land at José Marti.

On the ground, the immigration booth door locked like a prison cell as he stepped in. The officer scrutinized his passport photo, compared it closely to Branch's face and looked sharply at the mirror behind Branch's head.

"Don't stamp my passport," he said. "I'm American." But the officer stamped his US passport vigorously and gleefully. It didn't matter. He wouldn't likely be using it to reenter the States anytime soon. Reiner would have made sure that wasn't a viable option for him.

Then the electronic lock on the other side of the booth clicked and Branch walked into Cuba.

Melanie was already waiting for him outside immigration, her pink, curvaceous figure a stark contrast to the boxy gunmetal gray of the baggage claim barn. They collected her bags and went through the screening area. After changing dollars for CUCs, they jumped in a private taxi, a red '57 Chevy, and then were on their way toward La Habana Vieja and their hotel.

The red Chevy came to a stop and the driver pointed up a narrow alleyway, blocked from motor traffic. They had to walk the rest of the way. Branch was sweating as he toted his own dive bag and Melanie's luggage to the arched entry, but soon they were in the cool, elegant lobby of the *Mesón Sol d'Habana*.

A brunette with light skin and bright blue eyes smiled at Branch from behind the front desk, then surveyed Melanie's smug face and vivid outfit.

"Checking in for the environmental summit?"

"I'm sorry?" Branch asked. "The what?"

"The Latin American Environmental Summit."

"No. We have a reservation. Branch Kilgore. And my wife."

"Yes. Your room is ready. And this package arrived for you a short time ago." She handed Branch a large envelope.

"Yes, that'll be our dive itinerary for tomorrow, darling," Branch said to Melanie, but as Branch slid the package into his pack he noted it was far too bulky to be just that.

"Don't you mean *your* dive itinerary?" Melanie said to Branch, suppressing a laugh as she finally got the puzzle of the hotel sign worked out. *Hold Some Bananas*. Then she looked back to the receptionist. "Is there a day spa itinerary back there for *Mrs.* Kilgore?"

"I'll be happy to make a reservation for you, madam. Just call the front desk any time."

"It is so *muggy* in this town," Melanie said once they were upstairs and in their suite. She peeled off her pink top and gave Branch a long kiss. He kissed her neck, worked his way down to her breasts and her pale belly, then knelt down and pulled the pink pants down around her ankles.

"I'm sweaty," she said, pushing him back. "And I can't just *give* myself to you until I know we're *really* going to be together. I'm going to take a bath in that wonderful big tub." She left him kneeling on the floor and walked to the bathroom. "Be a dear and order us something cold to drink."

The door closed and then Branch heard the sound of water filling the grand tub.

"Sure, Mel." He rose from the floor and walked to the closed bathroom door. "I'll just run down to the bar and get us a bottle of champagne," he said to the door, stuffing the envelope from Yvonne in his pants.

"Kilgore, darling," she said from the bath. "What's in the package? You know we've got to learn to share *everything* with each other."

She splashed, and then he heard the agreeable sound of her body slipping into the water.

"Just my itinerary. Enjoy your bath. I'll be back with something cold in a flash."

In the hotel bar, he ordered a double Havana Club over ice and took a peek in his package: a cell phone and a business card that read:

Morgan Dimitrino
9520316575

He downed the drink, threw down a wad of CUCs, and asked the barman to send up a bucket of champagne with two glasses to the suite. Then he walked out into the grimy Havana night.

Chapter Twenty-Six

Washed Up in Cuba

B ranch walked toward the Plaza de la Catedral. The decrepit streetlights flickered on and shadows danced across smooth, old cobblestones. He deciphered the digits on the card and punched them into the phone. The signal clicked through and then there was Morgan's sharp Turkish accent.

"We have a nice private supper arranged for you. Walk south along the Prado in an hour then take a tour of the Parque Central, to the statue of José Marti. You'll be picking up equipment, so be alone. Have the phone powered on at seven tomorrow morning. This is a moving target. We won't have more than one chance."

The phone went dead. Branch thrust it into his pack and walked back toward the hotel. He glanced down an alleyway that led into the heart of Habana Vieja: dark, steamy, unknown. He wanted to head down that alley, away from the perils of the job and away from Melanie's clutches. But he continued on to the hotel.

Branch rode up in the elevator with the barman and the bucket of champagne, tipped him at the door and slipped into the room just as Melanie, wrapped in a Turkish towel, emerged from the bath in a buttery burst of steam. He put the bucket down on the entry table and tugged at the towel then he felt her moist, fragrant body push into him as she reached behind him for the champagne. Her supple hands quickly worked their way on the neck of the bottle and then the cork shot vigorously across the room. She poured until the two glasses were full and then overflowing with champagne.

She dashed naked to an antique love seat along the wall. Branch checked his watch, downed his glass of champagne and followed her. She pulled him down on top of her on the settee.

"Delightful," Melanie said, then laughed, squeezed her legs together, sat up, and took another tiny sip of champagne. "And delicious. Branch, you know how I feel about you, but it's time we focus on the other aspects of our relationship. Like sharing. Now, do tell me all about your dive itinerary for tomorrow."

"I'll tell you all about it over dinner, *darling*." He smiled, knowing there'd be no wild shift from lust to disgust with her on this occasion. "Let's stroll down toward the park and see if we can't find a *paladar*."

"Sounds lovely." Melanie scooted her bottom to the edge of the settee, straightened her legs out and rested her dainty feet on Branch's chest. Her perfectly painted toenails stroked his chin. Then she pushed him back and hopped up.

"So I'd better get ready," she said, then kissed him. "Are we dressing for dinner?"

"We're walking for dinner," he said, letting her go, trying to also let go of the vulnerable feeling coming over him. "So keep it cool. Dark and casual. Something not too noticeable. But I don't think that's possible for you."

"I'm sure I can find something," she said, pulling out several outfits from her bags and spreading them out on the bed. Branch watched as she held various blouses up to her bare body and posed for him. Finally she settled on black stretch denims and a tight gray blouse.

Then they were strolling along side streets toward the Paseo de Marti. Wrought-iron balconies hung over narrow streets, the arched doorways below them carved, faded stone blocks. Yellow and blue paint and cracked masonry studded the walls, and windows were covered by rusted metal grates.

"Why don't they fix this place up some?" Melanie asked. She put her soft hand on his arm.

Branch laughed. He admired her delicate physique. In the streetlight it cast a curvaceous shadow against the textural collage of old buildings. But then he took a close look into her face and he could see she wasn't joking.

173

They meandered through the ancient alleys then dodged speeding taxis as they crossed the Prado. At the Parque Central they passed the statue of José Marti and strolled through the crowd toward the corner of the park.

A muscular man in a tank top was talking, and Branch easily filtered his Castilian Spanish. "*Félix Hernández era totalmente vale de la Cy Young!*"

His companion, a slender young man, glanced at Branch, quickly cast his eyes up and down Melanie's curves then replied to his friend in English. "I don't know. Hernandez only had thirteen wins. How can you win the Cy Young with only thirteen wins?"

"The game's different today," Branch said. "Luis Tiant won twenty or more three times. He never won it."

"That's true," Tank Top said. "Cuban pitchers never got any consideration in those days. The sports writers were against us."

"It's not about how many games," the slender one said. "Tiant was a team player. He wanted to win bad. '*If we lose today it'll be over my dead body,*' that's what he said. '*Fuck those guys who want to throw in the towel,*' he said. That's a team player."

"Dead body," Tank Top said. He took a long look at Branch. "Team player. Right?" Then he walked off into the park.

"Welcome to Havana," the first one said. He introduced himself as Javier and quietly offered Branch and Melanie a lobster dinner in his home for a modest price. Then they were following him along the Malecón and into the Vedado district.

They diverted off the Avenida de Maceo and trekked uphill toward a neighborhood of brightly plastered homes. Colorful window awnings smiled down on them and a dizzying network of telephone and electric lines crisscrossed overhead.

They went inside a four-story building and climbed a narrow stairwell to the top floor. Inside the small apartment there was the aroma of lobster grilled in butter, and also of black beans, white rice and fried plantains. Javier's wife, Ruth, diminutive and dark-skinned, came out of the little kitchen to greet them, and then they were all relaxing on an old sofa, drinking cold Bucanero beers.

"You can tell by the delicious smells we were ready for you," Javier said. "You're a baseball fan so maybe next time you can bring me a few packs of cards. I got a great collection in the bedroom. Come see. Mel, you too."

Ruth took Melanie's hand and led her toward the kitchen. "Please don't bother us with your cards, Javier," she said. "Mel and I are going to have a drink."

Inside the bedroom, Javier closed the door and laid out a sprawling portfolio of sports cards. Then he pulled out a cardboard box from under the bed. "These are for you," he said, shoving the box across the bed.

Branch peeked inside. A Beretta 9 and a long bundle wrapped in black canvas. He checked the Beretta: a full clip of fifteen, nothing in the chamber. He slipped the gun into his backpack's side pocket, then hesitantly unfurled the black canvas. What he saw there made his stomach turn: a modified CheyTac .408, a monstrous sniper rifle that had been hacked down with a folding shoulder stock and a reduced barrel, complete with scope and suppressor. The whole thing broke down into a package no longer than eighteen inches.

"What's this for?"

"I don't know."

"I won't be needing the CheyTac. You can keep it. Whoever gave it to you must know I don't use that kind of tool anymore."

"I don't know anything about that. It came in on a boat from Mexico yesterday. I picked it up myself. You got to take it."

Outside the bedroom there was an outburst of laughter from Ruth and Melanie and then the sound of their voices came closer. "You got to take it," Javier said again. "I'm not doing my job unless you do. This job gets me one step closer to being out of here. And I've got to be out of here. Do you understand?"

Branch hesitated, looked at the CheyTac as if it was a snake then bundled it all back up and placed it in his pack's large pocket. "Yeah. I understand."

"Take this, too, for luck," Javier said, handing him a red baseball cap with a white *H* emblem on the front. "That's a vintage Havana Leones cap."

Branch looked at the old cap. "My last cap wasn't so lucky."

"No? What happened?"

"It led me here."

The bedroom door swung open. Melanie and Ruth walked in just as Javier was flipping the card collection booklet closed.

"Very impressive, Javier," Branch said. "Mel, check it out. He's got José Tartabull, Cookie Rojas, Tito Fuentes. Some of the great players to come out of Cuba."

"Thanks," Melanie said, looking skeptically around the tiny, barren room. "Tito Fuentes? You must think I'm dumb. Isn't he a musician?"

"Tito *Puente*, you're talking about," Javier said. "Great drummer. I got all his vinyl. You want to see my collection? He played Latin music. Played with Santana, too. But he wasn't Cuban. From New York City."

"New York," Melanie said, and she sighed. "Of course he was." Then Javier ushered them all back into the kitchen for supper.

Later, back in the hotel room, Branch was sobered by Javier's optimism, in the face of so much limitation. His own life had been full of opportunities and he'd blown them all. And now Melanie seemed to be buoyed up by his insecurity. She pushed him down on the bed and was soon naked and on top of him.

The ceiling fan was spinning behind her head, and with each revolution it seemed to push her down harder on top of him. She was light as a feather, but it was the heaviest weight he'd ever known: airy and delicate but solid and unyielding. She gave herself to him now, and though he was physically present, in his mind he was still strolling the Malecón, looking at that crescent moon and thinking about Chinchamos.

Melanie's overwhelming feminine force made him feel insignificant. Wanting to break away from her, but helpless to, Branch wondered why he'd fretted about her earlier resistance. Intermolecular forces were once again demanding his participation. But they were also smashing any sense of his own identity right out of him.

After, he felt the lightness and openness of total physical satisfaction, but it was a place with no solid footing. He was depleted, nauseated, claustrophobic. The realization crept up on him again.

He would have to purge his desire for her, maintain the discipline, strip her out of his life. He'd be a monk now, leaving the guilty pleasures—like Melanie—for someone else.

The next morning, Melanie lay snuggled next to him in the plush, feathery bed, her botanical fragrance wafting up through the linens. There was no waking her for breakfast or for anything else.

"I'm just a lazy jellyfish," she mumbled. "Have a good day of diving." On his way through the lobby, he made arrangements at the desk for her spa visit.

Branch sat in the early morning sun at the Plaza Café. He wasn't hungry, still feeling the bloated sweetness of the hours in bed with Melanie, but he ordered a plate of food anyway. He didn't know what kind of day it would be and he'd need calories to get through it.

He sipped coffee, enjoyed the sunshine, and checked the time. A quarter to seven. He reluctantly reached into his pack and powered on the cell phone, then watched the shadows of the Catedral spirals as they etched across the cobblestone courtyard. At seven he took the backpack with him to the men's room, took out the phone and punched in the number.

"Your dive is on," Morgan told him. "Nine. Marina Hemingway. The boat's name is *Mantaraya*. Further instructions will be texted to you. There's a headset in your package if we need to speak again. The equipment reached you in good condition?"

"What's with the heavy hardware?"

"Enjoy your dives. Try to be a professional."

"What does that mean?"

"It means you do the job professionally."

"No. It means I'm doing something that I *will* get paid for."

"Well, yes. There has never been a problem, before, so—"

"Pam gets out."

"Another aspect of being professional means not letting personal issues get in the way."

"That's not personal. That's part of the deal."

"Understood. Do your job today and she'll be released. There was some pressure from the British consulate. Completely futile, but it will appear to be the reason for her release, when she's released. But the charges against her will remain. As will the pressure from Omar for her to surrender the mangroves."

"Any fallout from the protest yesterday?"

"What does *that* have to do with a job you're getting paid for? There were some arrests at the pier site, and then at the jail Fibbi's men got violent with the crowd. Omar has lost all patience for any further impediments on that project."

"And Bali? The Indian girl."

"Not arrested. But Victor's dive boat license has been mysteriously revoked, so sadly, she and Victor are out of work. You, too. So I recommend you focus on the job you have at hand. *This* job. Good luck. Wait for your text instructions."

Breakfast was waiting for him back at the table. He forced down the poached eggs and fried plantains, drank another cup of the oily, black coffee, and then worried with ferocity about the rifle in his bag.

A dark-skinned man in a grey overcoat approached the table. "*Recuerdo te,*" he said. The soft Cuban dialect was articulate and easy for Branch to understand. He saw in the man's light blue eyes that he was harmless but demented.

"*Tengo* Cuban license plates," the man said, opening his coat flap to reveal a collection of rusty orange plates. "*Buen regallo para llevar contigo. Buen suerte para ti.*"

"No, gracias," Branch said politely, scanning the plaza quickly, then scrutinizing the man's coat.

"*Hablas Espanol?*" the man growled. "*De donde eres? Estados Unidos?*"

Branch shook his head. "No."

"Canada?"

"No. I'm from Mexico, actually."

The man laughed. "You are no Mexican," he said brusquely, now in perfect English. "Where you coming from?"

Branch took a sip of his coffee and looked at his watch, hoping he could end this before the man went off on him. But the man did not move away, so he answered.

"I live in Mexico. I work there. I'm Mexican."

"No," the man laughed. "*Pero tu chica en Mexico sera muy feliz con un regallo. Veinte pesos.*"

"Very cool," said Branch, looking at the assortment of license plates the man had spread across the table. "But not what she wants, I'm damn sure of that."

"I remember you," the man said again, and his eyes went wild. "You got to fuck them all! It's your gift. It's because of the thing, the *regallo* he gave you."

"What thing?" Branch asked.

"When you were a boy. Your gift."

Branch was startled. The man was damaged by misfortune—like so many people who lived on the streets—but he was prophetic, and he had stirred a memory long forgotten.

"What was the gift?" Branch asked him, drawn in.

"He gave it to you, Mexican. You were so happy to have it. It chose you, nobody else. It gave you *your* gift. Don't let them get to you. You got to fuck them all."

"What was the gift?" Branch asked him again, but then the man began to rant.

"Back in '94," he said, "I was working all over Pinar del Rio, Matanzas too. I was rolling up and down the coast. Now, I go to sleep on the seawall. Once upon a time, there were so many fish flopping in the water all night that you couldn't sleep. Now, I sleep good. I get off the bus by the baseball field. The girl knows. She can help you to find the middle of a raindrop."

Branch looked around the plaza nervously, then back into the man's blue eyes. They were clear—too clear—and Branch could see his mind spinning uncontrollably.

"When the girl came into the neighborhood," the man growled, his eyes glowing, "we looked underneath the road! We didn't look *overneath*." And then he cackled furiously.

Branch shivered. He forgot the accidental prophecy and he now pitied the man's misery. He knew that it was only work that could keep him from a similar fate. And when there was no work, only the Deep Blue Saloon could keep him off of the streets. When his usefulness was gone, with no ability to commit to anything, what would be left for Branch Kilgore? And then he was grateful that for now, he had work.

"I'll take the plates. Those two," he said, pointing at a pair of rusty, dark orange Santiago de Cuba plates that read *UAB-180*. He slid a US twenty across the table and shoved the license plates into his pack. "For luck," he told the man.

Branch stood, slipped into his pack, turned away from the man and paid the bill. Then he quickly toted his dive bag to the corner and flagged down a car, this time a boxy little Soviet Lada. He was so preoccupied with the thought of having to use the rifle he didn't notice the vintage blue Mercury that followed.

At Marina Hemingway, the Lada made several laps through the labyrinth of channels before it found the *Mantaraya*, an aging but well-maintained thirty-foot cabin cruiser.

Branch paid the Lada driver and boarded the cruiser, still unaware of the Mercury, now parked nearby under the shade of some palm trees.

"So you are diving alone today, that's fine," said Martin, the tall, bearded divemaster, already wearing his full wetsuit and an overloaded weight belt. "You are from the States and you are in Cuba looking for some good dives and a good time, yes?"

"That's right. My girl's back at the hotel, getting a massage or a mud pack or something. She's not much into boats. So, yeah, let's go." He tried to sound enthused but it came out flat.

"We've got one other passenger to pick up, at the Hotel Comodoro pier, so we will get him now and then we will go out, yes? So we get ready."

The captain motored the cruiser slowly through the channel and out into the ocean, then throttled it to a roar along the coastline. Branch felt the phone vibrate. He peeked into the side pouch of his pack and checked the text message.

Stand by for pickup. What the hell else could he do? There had to be people on the ground involved, but who?

The boat captain? The burly Cuban was yakking into his radio as he casually motored the cruiser up the channel. Martin, the divemaster? The weight belt still strapped around his waist, he was chatting on his celly in rapid-burst, unintelligible Spanish. And where was Morgan? Probably sitting comfortably at Yvonne's, smoking and smiling at Branch's discomfort as information was relayed to him.

The cruiser bored through the chop then lurched to a standstill as the captain expertly reversed the throttles, threw them into neutral, reversed again, and backed the cruiser toward the Comodoro pier. Branch scanned the crowd standing there—about a dozen tourists waiting on fishing excursions. He looked up at the hotel: five stories with a central tower that rose up another thirty feet. As the cruiser rumbled back to the pier, Branch spotted a sixty-foot sloop putting lazily by out in the channel.

The phone buzzed, and the message told him *Toilet. Headset.*

While Martin and the captain were busy docking the craft, Branch slipped quietly into the head. There was no lock, so he leaned against the door, blocking it as he assembled the rifle and put the headset on. Then he took out the phone and hit redial.

"It's the green sloop, just to your south," Morgan told him. "You should be able to see them now out the port window. The red-haired man on the portside deck."

"That boat's hundreds of yards away," Branch whispered into the headset. "Did you say *red* hair?"

"We're a bit short on time. You're in position now for the equipment you've got."

"Not like this. Not a good loophole. They'll mark me. And it's windy. I got no wind meter, no range finder, no ballistics computer. No way to calculate a firing solution."

"You never use meters or computers. You're a cowboy. Totally unlicensed. Says so right on your business card. That's why you work so cheap. And you're *in* a loophole. They'll look at the high ground at the hotel, not the boat. If we had wanted such a level of technical proficiency we would have paid the extra money for your colleague Mr. Carlsbad. Do be a professional, Branch."

"Carlsbad?" He lowered the rifle and braced against the door of the head as the boat accelerated away from the pier. "You know Carlsbad?"

"Your boat's moving. Perhaps we should continue our little chat at a later time."

Branch backed against the door of the head, opened the aperture and raised the rifle again toward the window. Through the sight he saw the redheaded man relaxing bare-chested in a weathered teak lounge chair with orange cushions on the deck of the big sailboat. Too far away to be sure, but he was sure. The guy in the framed photo in the den of the villa, on the mainland. He looked innocent, vulnerable, and happy. Branch tickled the trigger. He felt a wave of nausea run through him and his heart pounded.

"Don't make me shoot him like this."

"Get on with it."

"I'll slip on board that yacht tonight, make it look like he drowned. Don't make me shoot him from a distance. This dive captain will be implicated. It'll be messy as hell."

"That yacht won't be there tonight," said Morgan, "and we want a certain effect. Shoot him now."

Branch made his best guess adjustment for the wind and sighted the redhead. He turned off his tension and turned off his pounding heart as if he was turning off a light switch. He squeezed off a single round, bearing the brunt of the terrible kick with his shoulder then checked his work through the scope. There was a crimson burst of blood on the orange cushions and the redheaded man had crumpled to the deck.

Morgan's agitated voice squelched through the headset. "Did we get him?"

Branch looked through the scope. "Yeah. We got him."

He disassembled the rifle in seconds and rolled it neatly back into the bundle. Then he picked up the shell casing and barely made it to the toilet before he heaved, the chunks of green plantain matter splattering the rim. The cabin cruiser roared away into the channel and Martin pushed opened the door of the head.

"You OK? Chop's a little rough today."

"No, it's all me, Martin. Ate some nasty lasagna." He glanced out the window and he could see at least ten men scurrying around the deck of the sloop. Then the cabin cruiser turned south and he lost sight of it. "I'll be fine."

"Our passenger's on board now. You should come out on deck before we really throttle up. You'll be good once you get in the water."

"Don't I know it."

Branch closed the door then pushed the rifle bundle and the shell casing out the window. He watched the bundle sink into the black wake then cleaned up the head and went out on deck.

The passenger from the Comodoro, a portly German man, was setting up his gear, oblivious to the melee playing out behind them on the sloop. Branch sat down next to him on the bench.

"So you work with Morgan, too?" Branch asked. He was buzzed from the kill, relieved and sickened. It all seemed unreal to him. He was on a dive boat. The target had been relaxing with a drink on a sailboat far away and he'd never get to finish that drink. And now Branch was going out to have one in that saloon down below.

"*Gibt es Haie in diesen Gewässern?*" said the German.

"No," said Branch. "No sharks in these waters. They're too scared. But you *must* be part of it. Just tell me."

"*Wo gehe ich hin, um junge Mädchen in dieser Stadt zu finden?*" the German protested.

"Girls? I'll tell you where to find girls. If you'll just tell me. These redheads. What's it all about?"

"He doesn't speak any English," said Martin. "What do you want to ask him? I speak a good German."

Branch looked up at the top floors of the Hotel Comodoro as the cabin cruiser zoomed south, back toward the marina. He knew that Morgan or somebody must be up there watching. He wondered how they'd managed to synchronize this thing.

"I just want to know one thing. Is he gonna go on this deep one with me or is he gonna be a pussy? And then I'll have to tell everybody."

"I'm sorry?" Martin asked. "What does it mean?"

Branch closed his eyes and rolled his head into the bright morning sunshine. He relaxed against the bench for a moment and watched the inside of his eyelids turn crimson with each beat of his heart.

"Never mind," he said. After a time he opened his eyes and glanced back at the sloop, now disappearing below the northern horizon.

Branch followed Martin and the German down into the cool waters of the Havana channel, down through the shallows and away from the chaos of the surface, but not yet into the numbness of the depths. Once more he ran his finger down that tattered list of blown opportunities in his life. What was the lowest common denominator among them? That one thing in him that caused his failure every time? Whatever that ultimate weakness was, it was the *only* thing that really scared him. And whatever it was, it would always vanish, at least for a while, in the Deep Blue Saloon. So he kicked down hard.

He drifted past the gray reef toward the drop-off. Algae grew out of a barrel sponge like an overflowing trash can, and a wizened old hawksbill turtle swam alongside him, flapping effortlessly into the current. He watched the hawksbill dive down, saw the jagged bite marks on its ancient shell.

Branch hovered, motionless, and allowed the divers to drift ahead of him. Then he let the depths of the channel take him down.

He looked up and saw the divers a hundred feet above. He pushed deeper, down past three hundred, and then he felt the anesthesia washing away the pain of what had happened on the boat.

The dim blue light reflected up from the sand and morphed into the gentle glow of footlights along some underwater dance floor, and then she was with him.

"You've been away so long," she said. "Have a drink." He closed his eyes and drank, pulling in long, briny, intoxicating snorts from his regulator. Yum—nitrogen and water, with a twist—then he was exhaling, listening to the drink bubbles bounce harmonically around him like chimes in the underwater wind.

"Where have you been?"

"I'm so sorry. I saved one, but I killed one. I'm so fucking sorry. I had to."

"You know that doesn't matter here. One more?"

He sucked in more tonic. He opened his eyes and then he was fine. A cylinder of silver barracudas was rotating all around him. Sunlight beamed through the cylinder, bounced off it like some spinning disco ball, and metallic reflections sparkled across his wetsuit.

"Drink deep of me," the girl said, "and then you will understand all." He looked up at her. Prisms of purple light reflected on her pale skin. Her hair was a school of dusky damselfish, pure black with golden highlights flowing over her white shoulders.

She caressed him, but as soon as the relief had come there was that something pulling him up out of the saloon. And then he heard her say goodbye.

Branch drifted slowly back above three hundred. Something was pressing hard into his ribcage. He reached for the unknown thing that pained him, was amused as he pulled the thing from his pouch. He wondered if the thing had stayed dry enough to work down there, and then he was equally delighted and terrified by the muffled bang and green flash that came from the end of the barrel.

He laughed through his regulator as he struggled to remember exactly what the thing was, but he knew he'd better get rid of it. *Totally* illegal to have the thing in the saloon. Hovering motionlessly in the grainy blue-gray light, he held it at his side. Then he opened his hand and felt the heavy thing drop away into the pitch.

The current in the shallows had carried Martin and the German much farther downstream, and when Branch surfaced, the boat, now just a tiny speck a half mile to the north, was trolling away from him. A hundred yards from shore, he could see huge waves crashing in on one of the seawalls that protected the marina. He relaxed for a few minutes and waited on the surface. The cruiser continued trolling away from him so he kicked in toward the waves.

When he made the shallows, Branch pulled his fins off and staggered through the swirling surge. With waves crashing against him, he tossed the fins over the six-foot-high seawall and scaled it, his scuba unit still on his back. Then he walked across the narrow road, put his fins back on, jumped into the channel and swam across it, finally walking the last few meters to the boat slip. The *Mantaraya* puttered up just as he got there.

Martin and the German were plenty steamed at him for ditching them, and in the commotion of being cursed at in two different languages, Branch again failed to notice the blue Mercury as it crept by the slip. Inside the vintage automobile, Melanie put her little binoculars back into her purse.

Chapter Twenty-Seven

What Happened at the Comodoro

A note was waiting for him on the pillow. *Meet me in the hotel bar for drinks!* it said in Melanie's curvaceous script, sealed with a plump pink lipstick kiss.

When he stepped into the bar he was freshly shaved, wearing tan slacks and a matching brown knit shirt. Relieved that the job was over, he was almost invigorated to have Melanie waiting for him. Sporting a retro striped romper, she sat in a booth along the wall, sipping from a frosty glass filled with something pink and frozen. The olive-skinned tourist who sat across from her drank beer.

"I was just admiring your beautiful wife," said the tourist in an Italian accent. "You are a very lucky man."

There he was, the very guy he'd wished for, ready to take Mel off his hands.

"Lucky? She didn't just fall into my lap, you know," Branch said. "I had to win her over, with poetry and all kinds of heroic deeds, too."

"Of that I have no doubt," said the Italian. "Please tell me some stories of these deeds. Or give us a poem."

Branch took a deep breath, smelled the man's strong cologne. "'For each thorn, there's a rosebud—'"

"Oh, he's much too modest for that," Melanie said, interrupting him and grabbing his arm. "And he needs a drink." She waved her pale hand at the waiter.

"But, Branch darling, do tell us about your dives today. Gino was just keeping me company until you arrived."

"Yes, actually, I'm afraid that I'm late for meeting my *paisanos* for drinks at the Inglaterra," Gino said, looking at his watch. "So the poetry will have to wait, eh? And, Miss Mel, it was a pleasure," he said, kissing her outstretched hand. "Mr. Branch, so nice to meet you."

Gino walked away from the table then he turned back and held his beer bottle up.

"To sweet memories, when sorrow is done," Gino said. "Don't give up on the heroic deeds, no matter what."

"Maybe so," said Branch, watching as Gino walked away. "Hard to know."

The narcosis from the deep dive had barely balanced out the adrenaline from the kill. Branch ordered a double Havana Club with ice to tip the scales back toward numbness.

"The diving was decent, but you didn't miss much, really," he said. "How was the spa? You look beautiful."

Melanie peeked around the bar, then whispered to him as she sipped her pink drink. "Thank you, darling, but I must still be glowing from last night. Hard to believe, but I skipped my spa time today."

"That's never happened before. Guess you wanted to focus on Gino all day."

"You know that I'm always true to *you*, darling. A guy like that? He doesn't do the trick for me."

The waiter set a glass full of icy dark rum on the table. Branch took a long slug.

"Trick. Yeah. What kind of guy *does* do the trick for you?"

"I need a man with spirit and guts, who's ruthless, cunning and charming at the same time." She shook her head and smiled at him. "Good-looking. With no conscience."

"Dang. All of that? So why you hang out with me?"

Melanie took another sip of her frozen. "All of that. You. My perfect man. I love you. I *saw* you today, Branch."

The words "I *saw you*" seemed to leap from her lips and slap him across the face.

"*Saw* you get on the ... *Mantaraya* ... I think it was? Followed the boat. It wasn't easy, but we followed it along the channel road to the Hotel Comodoro. *Saw* you go down below, then the most awful, amazing thing happened."

Branch took another sip of his rum, briefly set it down, then picked it up again and downed the whole thing. He moved to the other side of the booth so he could look into Melanie's eyes.

"You followed me? Why? You were welcome to come with me. Oh, and I wasted all that money on your massage."

She leaned forward on the table, idly scratching at the chipped wood with her perfect pink fingernails. She could survive in the wild with those claws, Branch thought, and in a way, he knew, that's what she did. He dreaded what was coming, hated her treachery, but looking at her smooth shoulders and her creamy cleavage, he was already mounting with anticipation for her. She was frail and vulnerable and completely rotten at the same time.

"Of course I was there, Branch. I know. *What happened at the Comodoro.*"

The five words seemed to thunder and echo and rain down on him but he stayed cool. "What *did* happen at the Comodoro? Yeah, we picked up some German dude at the Comodoro. So what?"

"Come on, Branch, I don't have to tell *you* what happened."

Branch crunched on his ice and scanned her face for any sign she was bluffing. There was nothing.

"Well, you'd better tell me anyway."

"After you picked up that *dude*, all hell broke loose on a fancy sailing yacht out in the harbor. Seems that some guy out on that boat—I think that's what my driver told me—had been shot. Dead! Nobody knew where the shot came from, but the police were closing off the hotel, searching for the shooter. An assassination, of some foreign diplomat, in Cuba, too! Can you imagine?"

Branch paused, chewed on his ice again and pondered the news. It was confirmation that the job was successful, but now he had *this* problem. It was bad enough he'd been on the dive boat, but now *she'd* been at the crime scene, too. Who could've guessed she'd actually turn down a facial?

"You kidding me? Wow. Lucky us divers got out of there when we did. Who was this guy that was driving you?"

"You don't have to worry about him. Just some *jinetero*. He didn't connect me with anything that happened there. He thought I was just tailing my adulterous husband. Happens here a lot. He won't talk to the police."

"If you think I don't need to worry then you don't know shit about Cuba. They'll put out an APB if you forget to pay your bar tab. Even though I had nothing to do with this thing you describe."

Melanie sipped on her frozen and smiled. "Of course you didn't. And as far as the driver goes, he doesn't even know who I am."

"Right. You get lost in the sea of fair-skinned blondes wearing pink berets around here. Anyway, I still don't know what you're talking about."

"Branch, don't be coy with me. I don't know *how* you did it, but I *know* you did it. I *know* what you are."

Branch signaled the barman for another drink.

"Sure you do. Like you said, I'm a glorified glue-sniffer. A divemaster on a budget. And I can't afford to buy facials you don't show up for."

She smiled at him, leaned back again into the plush booth, a smug grin on her face.

"It's fine, darling. You're perfect for me. We can talk later. What are you thinking for dinner?"

Branch couldn't tell her what he was thinking, because he was thinking he'd have Melanie find that driver and have him drive them to the beach. And then he'd kill both of them. But maybe he'd be all right if he just left it alone.

Later, they walked along the Malecón and had dinner at a waterfront restaurant. Branch stayed cool, but the uncertainty was working on him, and he continued to pour the rum down into that bottomless, empty place inside him. The narcosis had subsided and the rum had no effect. The rhythm of his longing and his hatred for Melanie was his only tonic now.

Back in the hotel room, the scent of cream and flowers drew him to her, but when it was over, it was just the scent of entrapment and again he hated the smell of it.

He poured himself a large shot from the bottle of dark rum he'd bought after dinner and drank it down. He watched Melanie slumbering, watched as she rolled over on her back, her oiled breasts swaying. There was nothing industrious about her. She was pure luxury, pure overhead. He poured himself another.

"Kilgore," she said. "That was wonderful. Come to me, darling. And what you did on the boat. Positively ectothermic. I think it's just divine!"

He sat on the edge of the bed, repelled by her, but he couldn't resist caressing her perfect curves. "What are you talking about?"

"I didn't believe it when I first heard it, but now I know."

"Know what?"

She sat up and pulled the satin sheets around her shoulders. "You're my perfect man. I know you're a killer, Kilgore."

The words stunned him again but he said nothing.

"Fernando knows," she continued, "from Omar, I guess."

"You should be scared to death. If what you say is true. I could kill you right now."

"I didn't say you were a psycho. Just a professional. I've hung out with a lot of mob types before. When I was in New York. I'm *not* scared. You don't profit one little bit by hurting me. Especially since I have the perfect job for you. Fernando's got it all lined up. A million bucks, cash. Maybe more. All we have to do is take it off the guy."

"Off *what* guy?"

Melanie tucked her knees up under her chin, and Branch admired her perfectly waxed skin as she rocked back and forth on the bed. In spite of the disaster playing

191

out in front of him, those intermolecular forces were pulling him down to her again, already.

"It's Omar. But it's perfect. And we need you to help us do it."

After she had told him all about it, he poured another drink then shook his head and laughed. It was a conflict of interest, in more ways than one.

"I'm just a divemaster," he said, doing his best to convince himself it was true. "I don't do this type of thing you're talking about."

She said nothing. She just laughed at him. There was no point in denying it. It was time to leave Chinchamos, anyway. Gusano Verde was on to him, and now Melanie. He had around fifty grand in Yvonne's safe. Not near enough to do what he wanted to do—erase his personal history, so he could just dive, so he could teach again. But at least it was enough to get him to the next hiding place.

"You must know that a lot of my work *comes* from Omar."

"Of course it does. I work for him, too. And I bet he doesn't pay you much better than he pays me. Risking so much for so little. Branch, darling, it's time to cash out."

Branch shook his head and stared down at the wild designs on the marble floor.

"I'm just a contractor. I execute my orders. Then I pick up my pay. It's the only way I know how to live."

"How do you get started in something like that?"

"How did you get started as a whore?"

"Asshole."

"I kept trying to do the right thing. But the right thing never worked. There was always somebody there to make sure it didn't work."

"Same for me."

"So I went back to doing the wrong thing."

"Same for me," Melanie said, grabbing his shoulders and pulling him down to her. The back of his head rested in her naked lap. She stroked his chest, ran her hands down to his belly. "Why not take this big chunk of cash? Then we can start over somewhere. Together."

Branch said nothing, and Melanie kept working on him with her hands and with her words.

"You gain nothing from this loyalty you give Omar. He's not worth it. What is it with you? Daddy didn't pay enough attention when you were a little boy?"

"Sure. What's *your* motivation? You can hustle up cash when you need it."

"I'm tired of hustling, Branch. There was a time I lived with this guy, an older gentleman in Italy for three years. We lived in his villa in Pisa. It was wonderful. Divine."

"Pisa, huh? That's just perfect. What happened?"

"He died. Left his wife and kids everything. After that, just like with you, the right thing never was right. This thing, though, darling, it's some real money."

Branch sat up, grabbed her legs, pulled her on top of him and looked into her face.

"Fernando must really have something on you. Otherwise you wouldn't be consorting with that reptile. You should stick with what you know. If you need money, what about your new friend, Gino? I'm sure he'd be good for a few thou'."

Melanie gave him a shove. "Asshole. I don't do that anymore."

Then he pulled her back close to him and kissed her softly. He had another day to go with her before the flight home, and this argument had gone too far already.

"I'll think about it, OK?"

The next day they ate breakfast at the hotel then took a taxi to a beach bar at Playa del Este. Branch sat in the shade of the patio, smoked cigars, drank cold Bucaneros and read from *Life of the Hawksbill Turtle* while Melanie strolled on the beach. Wearing a skimpy woven-twine bikini, her body glowed pearly and pink as she romped in the surf. Cuban police occasionally trudged by, gazing at her as they lugged their Uzis, but it was only business as usual in Cuba.

Branch was depleted from the weekend, but now he was stimulated from the cigars and from watching Melanie strut. He joined her in the surf. They ran down the beach and tumbled together into a little grove of palm trees. The turtle book fell out of Branch's back pocket as she pushed him down onto the soft sand.

She randomly flipped open a page of the turtle book and read to him. "'Copulation usually begins in shallow water near the shore.' Hmm. Have you been studying? 'Males lie and wait in the shallow water for the females to return. At times, males have been seen following the females on shore. However, this behavior is rarely observed.'"

She tossed the book aside, stripped away her bikini top and straddled him. "Don't worry," she said. "This kind of behavior *is* rarely observed."

Her pale, perfect body seemed contrary and improbable in the afternoon sun filtering through the palms. He felt passion but he was tempered by the truth. He could no longer explain it or try to formulize it. This would be the last time.

Back at the hotel they packed and checked out. As Branch toted Melanie's bags past the canons to the waiting taxi, he glanced toward the Plaza de la Catedral. A Black man in a dark suit strolled across the sunlit cobblestones and disappeared into the deep afternoon shadows on the plaza. Branch dropped the bags and squinted, and then the man came back out of the shadows. For an instant he could see the long sideburns and perfectly groomed goatee. He didn't want to believe it. He picked up the bags and ignored Melanie's objections as he hustled her into the taxi.

Branch glanced nervously out the window as the taxi wound its way to José Marti International Airport. Maybe Reiner had just happened to be there on a job. Maybe Omar had given him up after he heard the Comodoro job was done. Or, more likely, he knew, his name ended up in a database somewhere after they'd stamped his passport on the way in. His only comfort was in knowing that a US federal agent wouldn't try to take him, not in Cuba.

Branch fought off his paranoia at the airport and bought rum for Victor and cigars for the Grouper at the duty-free shop. After a nervous passage through immigration, they boarded the plane. Branch watched anxiously out the window while they waited to take off.

"Something out there that scares you," Melanie said. "And it's getting closer every day. Time to cash out and go, Kilgore."

Back in Chinchamos, they drove along the waterfront on the way from the airport to Melanie's bungalow. Anchored just offshore, the *Poseidons's Aeria* belched black soot into the soft twilight sky.

"You have to do it," she demanded as Branch wheeled into the crunchy coral gravel at the bungalows. *Poisoned Sea Air*. "You're done here, you know you are. Especially with what I know about you."

"What're you going to do? Run to the police? To Omar?"

Melanie looked out at the channel and saw another cruise ship, the *Anthem of the Seas*, smoking in. *Oh, she eats fat men*. She felt nauseated.

"Armed robbery," he said to her, once they were inside the kitchen in her apartment. The round retro wall clock ticked seconds away contemptuously at him. "And on a fucking boat, too. Pure rodeo. You must be out of your pretty little mind."

"I'm not out of my mind. But I can't make this scene anymore. This chance won't come along again. You're the only one who can help me." She put her arms around his neck and pulled him down into her soft, creamy aura. "And I'm the only one who can ease your pain."

Conflicted, he gently pushed her soft shoulders away, like concrete, like feathers. "You're wrong about that."

"You're deluded. A junkie. It's time to leave, Branch. With me, with money. The last Friday of the month. It can be the *best* Friday. Before you lose your grip completely. Before you lose your life. Down there. That place you go to." She pressed back into him.

He knew it wouldn't end—the cycle of hungering for her, having her, then purging himself of her, only to begin again.

"Yeah, Friday," he said, gently pushing her away again. "The last Friday. *My* last. I can't help you, Mel. What you're proposing is nothing but suicide. I can handle *that* without your help."

She grabbed him by his belt, caressed him.

"There's something better for you than this," he said, taking her hands in his own, kissing them, then letting them go and turning toward the door. "Than me," he said, looking back at her one final time. She looked more beautiful, more treacherous, than ever. "You're right about me needing to get away from here, Mel. But it can't be with you."

Her pleading was still stinging his ears as he trudged unsteadily to his truck, the dead coral gravel crunching under his boots. He drove along Ocean Road, unsure where he was going, the final glow of the sunset bathing the channel in orange light. The *Poseidon* was heading south toward the deep water, smoke billowing from its stack. The *Anthem*, anchoring in the shallows, gave a loud blast. He rolled down his window and took a breath.

Chapter Twenty-Eight

The Reunion at Yvonne's

"**B**ig pitcher of sangria for the table," Omar said, looking like a hungry wolf, his dark beard contorting and his hairy hands groping Yvonne as she wrote down the order.

Yvonne was smiling, but Branch saw the helplessness in her face as she submitted to Omar's mauling.

"Bring some prosciutto and melon, some garlic bread, and a couple of pepperoni pizzas, too," Gonzago added, looking elegant in his standard uniform, an impeccably tailored tan Italian suit. "We're expecting two more, so I'll order a special dinner for us all later. You fellows need anything else right now?"

"No wine for me," Branch said. "Double Havana Club, ice."

"You no share the *sangre* with us?" Omar asked. His black silk jacket contrasted with his starched white linen shirt, and he was fluorescent as he gazed uninhibitedly at Yvonne's statuesque shape moving back toward the kitchen. "I think you get enough rum in Cuba over the weekend, no?"

Yvonne returned with the tray of drinks and gave Branch a covert smile as she set his glass in front of him. She would've heard from Morgan that things had gone well enough in Havana, but she'd also be wondering what this sit-down was all about. He wondered, too. Was it to talk about the Cuba job? Could it be about Dorian? Or had they heard about Mel's rodeo robbery scheme?

After Yvonne left them with a pizza and a large pitcher of sangria, Omar raised his glass full of the milky-red wine. "To the job well done and to a new era on Chinchamos, no?"

Branch relaxed a little. He clinked his glass with Omar and sipped his cold rum.

"But before we get on to the business," Omar said. "About Dorian. He still missing. You seen him?"

"No. Like I told you on the boat last week. I haven't."

"Yes, like you told me," Omar said, mumbling and gulping sangria as he scrutinized Branch's face. "Well, if you see him, you tell me."

"Who's this that's missing?" Gonzago asked, already clinking the ice in his glass. "The big guy, Dorian? He was your nephew, kind of your protégé, Omar, so he's probably just off snorting coke and banging whores."

Branch knew Dorian wasn't snorting coke and banging whores, but he managed a smile as the others laughed. Then he listened to Gonzago ramble on about the trouble he was having with dancers and dishwashers at his new casino and titty bar in Veracruz.

"Everybody wants too much money. They see cash flowing in, they don't know about all the cash going out, to the security, to the police. They think I'm getting rich off the place. Really, I try to break even, to bring some beauty to the city, you know? The price I pay for beauty. Well, Branch knows. He remembers all those years I imported antiquities from Asia. By the time you pay everybody off and pay the bills, there's no profit. Only the beauty. But it's worth it. And that's why I'm here. For beauty. Played eighteen today at Omar's beautiful course on the north end and I had to get some of Yvonne's cooking."

Gonzago bit into a slice of pizza and kept talking. "Incredible. I met her at my first club in Monterrey, put her through cooking school, and now look at this place she's created for us."

Branch nodded. It was impossible to ignore the beauty of Yvonne's courtyard, with its flowering vines above, cobblestoned floors below, and classical music and appetizing scents wafting all around.

"I love this music," Gonzago said. "Mahler. Sixth symphony. Picked it out myself. You like it, Omar?"

"I no notice it. I like the rap. And the Lynyrd Skynyrd."

"Right," Gonzago said, laughing and pouring more sangria. "Skynyrd. I like that, too. What do you think, Branch? About the restaurant?"

"It's a fine place, Gonzago," Branch said. "And the food lives up to the atmosphere. You should be proud. But a long way to come for lasagna."

"It is. We have business to discuss. I asked you and Omar and some others to meet to discuss the special needs we have at the moment."

"The fucking protest, last Friday," said Omar. "Getting in the way of progress. And you see the story on the Facebook? About the bullshit collapse of the cave? The pier project getting the wrong kind of attention, no?"

"I was in that cave when it collapsed," Branch said. "It wasn't bullshit. It came down on us."

"Cave diving," Omar said, sucking the juice from an orange wedge he'd plucked from his wine. "Dangerous, no? Why not just play golf? At the protest, the crowd, they get violent. The police, they make some arrests. You make the right choice when you go to Havana."

"I heard it went well," Gonzago said. "Nice. Did you get a chance to go out and hear some Latin jazz? Do some salsa dancing?"

"Dancing? Yeah, as it turned out, I danced with a redhead. He was on one boat and I was on another."

Yvonne set another large platter of appetizers on the table. She turned to go back to the kitchen when Gonzago stopped her. "Yvonne, darling," he said. "Go ahead and bring that other thing out, for Branch."

"That was some kind of dancing," Gonzago said, after Yvonne had left the table. "And they said you were too cowboy for the navy, just because you didn't go in for the high-tech stuff. But a cold bore shot from a half mile away! On a boat, in the wind. Let those special ops guys try that!"

"That guy, he need the killing," Omar said. "He in a position of authority but he abuse it."

"And Branch loathes corrupt authority," Gonzago said. "Did I ever tell you about that cop on FM 182?"

"What's a FM 182?" Omar asked.

"Farm-to-market road. FM 182. A curvy little country road in Texas I used to drive on. Branch couldn't have been more than sixteen. I was in the Maserati, it was late, and this cop popped me with his radar gun. I was only joking when I told Branch what I thought should happen to that cop. But when I saw the videotape. It was really something."

"That's a good story, no? I like to see that tape."

"I burned it right away," Gonzago said. "Maybe that cop had it coming, abusing his charge like he was. But I tell you now what I told Branch back then. No nonprofit work. Too damn dangerous! I tried to help him channel his special talents the right way. Like the guy on the mainland. Like this cat in Cuba. We profit from that."

"Now we get on with our plans for Chinchamos, no?" Omar said. "I hope you with us, Branch. I hate for the *Negro Federale* to find you. To extradite you."

"I'd hate that, too," Branch said, masking his irritation. "But I'd like to know who these redheads are. Seems like my future might depend on it."

"Your future is good," Omar said. "You stay true. You take the girl from the store to Cuba. What's her name? With the rack like this and the ass and the legs? She fine. Mel Lamy, no? You take her with you to Cuba?"

The one with the ass and the legs, the one that wants me to rob you on the ferry next week. "Yeah, I thought it would make a nice touch. The couple on a romantic getaway."

"She get in the way of the work?"

"No. I sent her to the spa while I went out to work. And then we had some fun in the evenings."

"Yeah," Omar said. "Fun. As a favor to my friend in New York I help her with the work visa. I give her the job in the store. Vinnie say she know how to keep her mouth shut. You can trust her, no?"

"You don't have to worry about her," Branch told him. "She wanted something serious with me. So I ended it."

"Well, that's just fine," Gonzago said, and then he smiled. "Because I don't want to step on anybody's toes. And from your description, Omar, I'd like to meet this girl myself. Mel Lamy, is it?"

"I take you by the store and introduce you," Omar told him. "Then Branch, he find a *nice* girl, he have a family."

"Nice girl?" Branch asked. "You know one?"

"Hard to find one," Gonzago said. "Everybody uses the dating apps now. But I taught Branch better than that. Stay off the Internet."

"I'm still off it," Branch said, draining his glass and chewing on the darkened ice. "Not natural."

"You haven't changed," Gonzago said, stuffing an enormous slice of prosciutto into his mouth. "Do it the old-fashioned way, right? Find a woman, track her, follow her scent."

"Right. It's nature's way. I don't like long-distance things, like over a computer. Totally unnatural. Just like I don't want to work with the kind of tool I had to use in Cuba. Working from a distance. Leaves a bad taste."

Gonzago laughed. "OK, fine, Branch, no more long-distance work. And no Internet dating. But Omar's right. It's time to think about settling down, getting married. I'm too old now but maybe I can hook *you* up with somebody nice."

Branch had been on the fringes of some of Gonzago's orgies at the villa. He thought back to the many girls he'd known there. Beautiful, but if they weren't drugged out and unreliable they were gold-digging and greedy.

"A blind date with a Gonzago girl? Always fun, but not much of a long-term option."

"Hey, give me some credit. I fixed Len up. Ginger, your mother," Gonzago said, but then he lowered his tone. "God rest her soul, she was good-looking."

Branch looked at Gonzago and he let the awkward silence spread across the table. "Speaking of Len—"

"I know you wanted to maintain your separation from him," Gonzago said. "But it's been a long time. Len's on the team, supervising the construction of the pier, and that pier, along with the mall and the resort is going to make us all a lot of money. You, too. Time to get over past differences. And thanks to your good work we can get on with the resort plans. No more drug wars. This is a beautiful island, Branch. It can really be a paradise for us. Money just comes walking up the boulevard in the pockets of these cruise ship idiots."

Gonzago started to speak then looked toward the foyer and stood up. "Right on cue. Len, we were just talking about you!"

Branch looked down and saw Len's snakeskins on the cobblestone floor. He continued his gaze up the tight designer jeans, the oversized belt buckle, and the Western shirt and jacket, all topped off with an enormous cowboy hat. There was no doubting Len's authenticity as a bad man but you wouldn't know it to look at him. He was the caricature of a cowboy.

"We're inside a restaurant, Len. Take off the Stetson."

"Ain't a damn Stetson, Branch," Len said, leaving the hat on his head as he sat down. "It's a handmade Serratelli."

"Having my boys back with me for the first time in years," Gonzago said, and he laughed nervously. "Nice. I asked Len to meet with us tonight so we could talk a little business."

"Len and I caught up the other day," Branch said. "Put his pistol to my temple. Just like the old days."

Len smiled, pushed the hat up on his forehead and poured himself a glass of sangria from the pitcher.

"Gimme a break, Branch. I'm the same as you. Just a cowboy, drifting around for a paycheck. I coulda stayed out there on the rigs. But these fine fellows offered me a chance to come down here and work the pier. I tell you what, I'll take senoritas and margaritas over gettin' oiled up in the Gulf any day."

"Either way," Branch said, "you still get dirty."

"Y'all will have to forgive my son's manners." Len downed a big gulp of sangria and smiled at Gonzago and Omar with red teeth. "I love that sangria wine," he said, then turned back to Branch.

"They don't understand you the way I do, Branch. They just don't know what it is to be bent. Hell, you were *conceived* when I was bent. That very first night with Ginger. My sperm were bent, there ain't no doubt about that, son. And you came out bent. That's why you are what you are."

Omar and Gonzago laughed. Branch chewed his ice, shook his head and pretended to laugh with them.

"I'm glad you two will get a chance to talk," Gonzago said. "It's important for a family to stick together. And we need to stick together now. We got a lot of money on the line on this pier. And we can't put it into operation without the mangroves. The old English gal was ready to sell but then there were all these protests. These other interruptions."

"You see how wily she is, Branch," Omar said. "She get you to lead her into the restricted zone during the dive. The *policía*, they do the right thing to charge her with trespassing, no? Then Victor, the dive shop owner, he call the British consulate in Merida. We release her, but not because of the consulate. We release her because of what you do in Cuba. I'm a man of my word. But now Pamela, she in real danger."

"How's that?"

"The locals, they know how the pier, it bring money to the island. The old bitch get in the way. They no like it. We protect her when we keep her in the jail, no? But now, who knows what happens to her? And Victor. He the big problem for us."

"I only work for Victor. As my cover. Hardly know him. It's just a coincidence that I live in Pam's hotel. I got no influence with either of them."

"The time for influence," Omar said, "it is over, Branch. Pamela Linton, she old already. With the money we try to give her, she live in comfort back in Europe. But she no do it because of this motherfucker Victor Mendez."

"Victor's really worried about the reefs," Branch said. "His business depends on them staying healthy. He's a businessman, same as you."

"He need to adapt," Omar said. "Look at what they do down at Seahoss Dive Shop. They no always do the scuba diving, no? They take the people out tubing, they take them out on the dolphin-watching adventures. They take them out and tow them on the long inflated snake."

"Inflated snake, huh? That sounds pretty cool," Len said. "I tell you what, I might give that a try on my day off."

"The tourists, they hang on to the snake behind the speedboat, they bounce all over the waves," Omar said enthusiastically. "You see this thing? The tourists, they love it. It no matter to *them* if the coral down below, it alive or dead. Seahoss, he make big money on that. Victor, he do the same."

"A big snake?" Branch asked. "They ride a big snake?"

"They love the big snake," Omar answered. "Mendez, he make a lot of money when the golf course and the mall go in. But he stubborn. He talk bad to Pamela."

"Offer him some money."

"We offer him the money. We offer him the job where he boss of the fishing and the diving. But he say no. Now I got to pay the guards to watch the site."

"And the scientists have proved that the dang reef is already dead, ain't that right?" Len asked, nodding at Omar.

"All the reefs, they dead soon," Omar said. "All over the world. Any scientist, they tell you that. We lose money if we worry about something that can't be saved, no?"

"Branch, I know you're close to this thing," Gonzago said, putting down his glass of sangria and leaning toward him. "Ah, and here it is."

Yvonne set a small appetizer plate of lasagna down in front of Branch.

"Look at that," Gonzago said. "Looks delicious. Thanks, Yvonne. That'll be all for now. One more for you, Branch."

"We have to whack him," Omar said. "Got to look like an accident. A dive accident. You do this one and you no have to do the work again. This Victor must die."

Branch looked down at the lasagna.

"An accident. Very original. I'll need a little time to think about it. It's tougher than you might think. Victor's a professional diver. Trying to take him out underwater could be very dangerous."

Omar took a business card out of his shirt pocket then slid it across the table to Branch. It was the card Reiner had left with Gonzago in Houston. "If you *no* do it, then maybe I call the number, no? You take it. I got the number in my celly already."

Branch looked at the card on the table and at the small plate of lasagna. "I do appreciate the job offer, but I need some time to analyze the situation."

"I helped you out when you had no work, Branch," Gonzago said. "When you were running from Reiner. Your reluctance is coming at a bad time. You're in a unique position to help us out with this one. But it's all good. We've got somebody else that can handle it. He's an underwater specialist like you."

Gonzago punched on his cell phone, muttered into it briefly, then laid it back down on the table. "So it looks like we can finally order dinner. Our last guest is here. He's been waiting outside."

Branch turned toward the foyer, saw Morgan wave his hand then watched as a familiar, brawny shape approached the table.

"I believe you know Lieutenant Carlsbad," Gonzago said.

Branch looked at Carlsbad. His crew cut had grown out shoulder-length and grayish brown, shrouding his square head, but he was still in shape, his thick body poured into tight slacks and a golf shirt.

"You'll never believe where I found this guy," Gonzago said, laughing, then making room at the table and filling the last empty glass with sangria. "He'd been hired by the foreman of my ranch in Idaho to shoot coyotes from a helicopter. When I talked to him last month, it blew my mind that you guys knew each other. Trained in the service together, right? Quite a night for reunions."

Branch sipped his rum. Len was on one side of him, Carlsbad was on the other, Reiner's card was lying on the table, and there were Omar and Gonzago smiling at him with their red sangria lips.

"Carlsbad," he said. "Haven't seen you since Coronado. Didn't know you'd left the teams."

"Yeah, I'm out now. You fellows probably don't know much about it but Branch and I went through BUDS training together."

"That's the Navy SEAL training, right?" Gonzago asked, lighting a cigar.

"Yes, sir," Carlsbad answered. "That was tough training. As the old saying went, it separated the men from the boys."

"Yeah," said Branch. "The men had enough sense to quit. The boys stayed on."

"Hell, we were all just boys then," said Carlsbad. "*Yummean?* Plenty of them rang that bell. And we lost too many of those good boys who made it through and deployed. Iraq. Syria. Somalia. But Branch didn't quit. He was kicked out. Then he was DD'd from the navy altogether."

"You're really up on your history, Carlsbad," Branch said. "I figured you for a lifer. What happened?"

"Got caught carrying some goodies back from my second deployment in Syria. So I took the discharge, honorable, and went private sector. Like you. But unlike you, I'm grateful to have a job. The economy is tough right now."

"Private sector. Shooting coyotes in Idaho. That's pretty fucking private."

"It was. But now I'm down here, serving Mr. Gonzago and Mr. Omar while they complete their projects. And I won't have any hesitation about it, either."

"That was some extreme stuff they made you do," Gonzago said. "In that training. Right? All kinds of underwater harassment, making you swim with your hands and feet tied up. What was that like?"

"We did go through training together," Carlsbad said. "But, of course, I earned my Trident pin while Branch got sent back to the fleet. Then he ended up in the brig. And then he was mysteriously gone. He just vanished."

Gonzago thumped his cigar against the ashtray. "Branch was always a talented kid. But I knew he could never put up with that hoorah nonsense."

"Oh, yeah, Branch was something," Carlsbad continued. "A real individual. Nobody'd ever seen such fearlessness in the diving phase. And, yes, swimming while tied up was part of it. Branch just ate it up. He loved the confined stuff. He was a fiend for it."

"Branch is a fearless mother," Gonzago said. "We were just talking about that. So what happened to this guy in the navy? That got him kicked out? I always wondered."

Carlsbad smirked and sipped his sangria. "Well, we both made it into phase three. That's the weapons phase. I can't give you the exact details of what happened in those training segments. But I went on to graduation. To deployment. And Branch was sent in for more psychiatric evaluation. Then he was cut. He left the base, and then something really unusual happened. They still talk about it back at Bucklew."

"What was it?" Gonzago asked eagerly, buzzed from the sangria and the cigar.

"Branch became kind of a legend in the teams. I tried to keep track of him, but he just fell off the map after his DD."

The table was quiet and Carlsbad continued. "There isn't time to go into it all, but I *can* tell you that the worst tag you can put on a navy frogman is to call him an *individual*. To be on the teams you've got to be willing to put service above self. And Branch here, sounds like he hasn't changed at all. Not from what I'm hearing. In training, you live as a team. You suffer as a team. Now his team needs him again. But he's still what he was back then. An *individual*. Ain't that right, Kilgore?"

"I erased that part of my personal history a long time ago," Branch said. "Now I'm just a guy trying to do his job. Just not sure what that is anymore."

207

"Don't be so bashful," Carlsbad said. He took another drink. "They haven't heard the best part yet. Branch took a generous plea deal. Voluntary manslaughter and the discharge. Then he was gone. But they never could figure out how he'd done it. Sneaking into the training officer's quarters and drowning him the night after he'd been discharged. I mean, whoever heard of a Navy SEAL training officer drowning in his own toilet?"

"Branch always was talented," Gonzago said, sobered a bit by what he had heard. "And always into the damn nonprofit work."

"Indeed," Carlsbad said. "I saw it firsthand."

"Shit, I tried to stop him before he enlisted," Len said. "I tell you what, he always was a natural-born hell-raiser. Couldn't deal with authority."

"Yeah, well, we were *all* about to crack," Carlsbad said. "That training is designed to expose a man's moral deficits. What those bastards made us do out there at Bucklew? Rolling in the wet sand and the cold surf. Running all day. Pushing concrete all day. Practically drowning every day. We got a break between phases, got to let off some steam, but Branch didn't blow steam the normal way. No, he was always taking it down deep. Into that place he goes. That's what got him sent back to the shrink. What was that condition they said you got? That made you too unbalanced for the teams? That thing psycho killers got?"

Branch stared into his rum. "Shrunken ventromedial cortex," he said slowly.

"Yeah," Carlsbad said, grinning. "Shrunken ventromedial cortex. No conscience. Literally, a man without a conscience."

The Old Ways and the Old Days

B ranch grabbed a gas tank from the shop, hitched a ride to the windward shore and hiked to where the raft was stashed. He pulled the skiff out of the reeds and onto the beach then went back into the channel for the scuba unit. He was watching carefully for anybody with red hair, hoping Gusano Verde had heeded his advice about not taking things personally. But that was before the Cuba job. He couldn't count on anything now.

The outboard fired right up, and Branch was relieved as he throttled south along the windward shore, bouncing and flying off the big waves. All those days stashed in the mangroves and the boat still ran pretty smooth.

He shut down the outboard, rowed it in the last hundred yards then got the little boat tied off at the Caribbean Argonauts dock. He put his gear in the shop, crept around to the front and surveyed the street. A red Hummer was parked down the boulevard, right alongside the mangroves. He couldn't see the driver's face, but it had to be Carlsbad. They were already watching. Watching Pam, Victor, the shop. The mangroves. Branch, too.

After scoping the street for a while he slipped back into the shop, went out the back, and walked south along the seawall about a quarter mile until he came to the sushi bar. The restaurant had been closed for a couple of hours, and he could hear the yellowtails in the shallows feeding on fish scraps.

The sushi chef threw leftover sashimi out into the water after closing and the yellowtails would swarm to the surface. Then the lemon sharks would move into the shallows and feed on the yellowtails. He remembered the moonlit nights on the bottom, watching the show, his dive light turned off. He was sad he wouldn't be able to enjoy that show again. But there was an even better show where he was going.

He couldn't do the job they were asking, and there was no point in running, not with Reiner on his tail. There was only the one place left for him. And he'd be there soon. Just a few things left to take care of.

Branch went up the driveway by the side of the sushi bar, slipped through to the street and peeked north toward the dive shop. He was just under the crest of a little hill, and the red Hummer wasn't visible.

He crossed the street, slipped into the alley behind the Chinchamos Museum, jogged down to the back of the Blue Angel and eased into the lobby. It was all quiet, and it was dark, except for the glare from the high-intensity lights at the pier construction platform. There was the aroma of a burning Cuban cigar, and then across the atrium he saw Elias locking up the front door of the Roach.

"Branch," Elias said, all slurry and drunk. His bank deposit pouch was full of cash and his stainless steel .357 was stuffed under his belt. He staggered a little as he came across the atrium. "Are you up early or out late, *hermano*? Doesn't matter. Going out on my speedboat for the sunrise. Come with me. Drink some Chamucos."

He reached out and tried to pop Branch in the crotch with the back of his hand.

"I can't, Elias," Branch said, easily dodging the slap, grabbing the heavy gold Rolex on Elias's wrist, resisting the urge to give him a slap of his own. He let go of Elias's wrist. "Pam's taking a vacation. Do her a favor and keep an eye on the hotel for a few days."

"Pam hasn't been around much," Elias said. He stoked and twisted his cigar, and the construction lights shining through the windows reflected off the face of the shiny Rolex and momentarily blinded Branch. "I heard she was in jail. The maid's been working the front desk. What's focking happening?"

"Omar's happening. I'm just trying to find her a safe place to ride it out."

"And you?"

"Leaving."

Elias coughed, and a cloud of blue smoke filled the atrium.

"Look, Branch. I came here from Cuba when I was just a kid. My cigar business is doing great now with all the *cruceros*. The cigars, the girls, too. Tomorrow we got six focking ships."

"Yeah, six fucking ships," Branch said. "You're busy. Forget I said anything."

"You bet your ass I will." Elias leaned against his shoulder, and then Branch could smell the tequila on his rotten breath. "I don't want to cross Omar. You shouldn't either. The old ways are done. The island is a place for making money now. The old ways and the old days. They're done, Branch."

"Yeah, they're done, I guess," Branch said, looking out the window. Across the street the construction zone was ugly in the bright lights, and he could see small whitecaps foaming on the water. "Goodbye, Elias."

Branch got up to his room and stuffed the box of cigars for the Grouper and the bottle of rum for Victor into his pack. Then he made his way down to Pam's room. He could see she'd suffered plenty in Fibbi's jail. Not beat up at all, but looking much older. The wrinkles in her face were deeper, her blue eyes were pale and sunken, and her frail shoulders were slumped.

"I'm not leaving my hotel," she told him when she was fully awake, sitting on the edge of her bed in a worn cotton robe. "Omar won't bully me."

"Omar will do worse than bully you, Pam. He'll kill you, if he has to. You got to come with me. Right now."

"The British embassy," she said, her voice cracking. She pulled her robe in tightly. "They got me out of jail. They'll protect—"

"It wasn't the embassy. It was a bad thing I did for Omar, in Cuba, that got you out. I made a deal for you but now the deal's not good enough."

211

"What did you do?" she asked, and Branch could hear the crisp authority returning to her voice. "What happened in Cuba?"

"A man was killed, Pam. An innocent man, I'm sure. And now I can't have any more innocent people getting killed."

"*Who* killed him?" she asked. She stood up from the edge of the bed and looked directly into Branch's face.

He hesitated for a moment, noticing how her eyes were shining as silver as her hair, her shoulders now held back proudly. He didn't want to scare her. He just wanted to get her out of the hotel as quickly as possible.

"*I* killed him," Branch told her.

"Why?"

"I don't know anymore. But I won't be doing it again. Get dressed and pack a bag, Pam. Bring your wet weather gear. You're getting out of here for a while."

"I'll come with you," she said. "But you remember one thing. Sometimes you've got to do a little evil to do a lot of good."

On the way through the lobby it was all quiet—Elias had closed up and cleared out—and before it was 4:30 in the morning they were down the alley behind the museum and sneaking across the street to the sushi bar. Then they were behind the shop and on board the Zodiac. Branch pushed off, rowed for several minutes, then fired up the engine and took a reading on the GPS.

The sun was just starting to swell on the far side of the island and there was no movement on the banks. They cut through the choppy waters and as they curved around to the north side, Pam straightened up against the gunwale and stared off toward the shore. The stiff, silvery perm in her hair blew wild in the ocean gusts and she looked like some ancient, marauding pirate as she scanned the country club and Omar's golf course.

"Just look at that," she barked at Branch. "All green and manicured. And all that fertilizer seeping down into the limestone below and out into the sea. Now algae is choking the life out of the coral below us."

Branch looked at the golf course and noticed how the lush, groomed fairways stood out from the rocky, brushy landscape surrounding them. And underwater, when the current was strong, he remembered, the algae on those reefs looked like strands of Bermuda grass blowing in the wind.

They motored up past the northern tip and hit the swells where the open ocean water met the channel.

"Where in the blazes are you taking me?" Pam asked.

"The Grouper's got his boat anchored behind there," Branch told her, pointing at tall cedar trees sprouting up from a group of tiny, rocky islands. He navigated into the islets and then they could see the tall mast of the *Ogygia*.

As he tied the skiff to the *Ogygia's* rail, Branch could see the Grouper swabbing up a bit on deck. He started to wonder how this thing was going to work—a beer-drinking rowdy sharing a boat with an eighty-year-old hard case like Pam.

"I know you two don't share the same style," Branch said to the Grouper after Pam had gone down below to settle in. "But I figure it'll be the last place they'll think to look for her. She refuses to leave the island so we've got to keep her safe."

The Grouper spit over the side and then looked at Branch with wild, bloodshot eyes. He'd been tripping on the mushrooms and drinking beer, probably without a break, Branch could see, for days.

"I'll do my best for her," he said. "On that I give my word. Like I said, nobody knows I'm up here. Janne and his Dutch skurfer friends the only ones come up here."

"If things go bad you go talk to Yvonne. She's holding some money for me. Take half of it for you and Pam. Buy her a ticket out of here. Give the other half to Victor and Bali. Take care of her, Grouper. And take care of yourself, too."

"Where you going that *you* won't need that money?"

"I almost forgot," Branch said, and he pulled the box of cigars from his pack. "I brought these for you, from Cuba. The real deal. Trinidads."

"Less money in Elias's pocket," the Grouper said, watching Branch climb back down to the inflatable. "The greedy bastard. You don't want to burn one with me? Where can I find you?"

"You take care of Pam. Stay out of sight for a while."

He zoomed away in the Zodiac, thinking about how pissed Carlsbad would be when he found Pam had slipped out of the hotel. Carlsbad's first little job for Omar—keeping tabs on Pam—and he'd already blown it.

All that was left now was to say goodbye to Victor. Try to talk some sense into him about his future on the island and give him the bottle from Cuba. Then it would be infinite relief, down in the Deep Blue Saloon.

The sunrise was starting to glow red over the island as he gunned the skiff back toward the shop. He motored south on the leeward shore, saw a thousand tiny pink dots lining the mangroves where a flock of flamingoes had landed.

When he got to the dive shop, he tied up, let himself in, and made coffee. Not as rich or as sweet as the stuff he had drunk in Cuba, he noted, but it was good, and after being up all night, it invigorated him.

Branch looked at the dive schedule. There were a few names written in, along with the names of the ships they were coming from, but then he remembered what Morgan had told him: Victor had lost his dive operator's permit. There would be no dives. But Victor would still be coming to work. He noticed that the envy he usually felt over another man having real work was gone. And he knew then that his plan was good.

Victor walked in a little before six o'clock.

"Shit. Anytime you're here before me something *must* be wrong."

"Don't worry, Victor. I'm just up early. Actually, been up all night."

Victor rubbed his eyes, grunted and looked at him. "Again? How do you do that? Even when I was your age I couldn't do that and be worth a damn the next day."

"I'm *not* worth a damn. But at least I brought your boat back."

Victor looked out the window at the dock. "That's funny. Last I heard from you that thing was capsized."

"Like you suggested, I salvaged it. You diving today?"

"No." Victor peered out the window again just to make sure the Zodiac was really there. There was a little grit in his voice. "Not for money, anyway. We had some divers from the ships lined up, but after the protest, well, you were gone, how would you know? We got shut down. After we got Pam out of jail Bali went back to her turtles."

"Turtle beach," Branch said, and he smiled, thinking of that night with Bali. "I like that spot. She's OK?"

"She's pretty pissed, I guess. About the protest going so bad. About you taking off on your little vacation. So how was it?"

"Lousy. Sorry I missed out on all the action here but I'd been promising Mel a trip."

Branch could see the sour look on Victor's face. He'd abandoned him and his cause, just for a romp with Melanie, or so he thought. But he couldn't worry about it anymore. Just a few more minutes then he'd sling a tank on his back and there'd be no more worries.

"Do anything else other than roll with Taco Loco girl in Cuba?"

"Drank some rum. Brought you this." Branch pulled the bottle from his pack and handed it to Victor. "Did one dive. The reef was all browned out, just right off the marina. Terrible dive."

"Killing pain and passing time, huh?" Victor admired the bottle of rum. "I'm glad you had some fun. Because today we've got a job that's not so fun. Can you find the exact spot where you dumped him?"

"Why?"

"Remember the key he was wearing?"

"The pendant, yeah. Thought that was just jewelry."

"It's not. Dorian was the one who confiscated all our phones and cameras at the protests. At the pier. At the dolphin park. He was stockpiling videos, photos, and some other pretty good dirt. I need that key, Branch."

"Why?"

"Omar and the other developers get rich filtering all the money from the ships before it can get to the locals. The locals are poor. They've got nothing to lose. But they're too scared to come and occupy the waterfront."

"What scares them?"

Victor grabbed his laptop from the counter and typed on the keyboard. "*This* scares them," he said, spinning the computer around so Branch could see the site he'd brought up. "*This* is what Omar does to intimidate people who stand up against him."

Branch looked at the picture on the screen. The redhead's face was more bloated and chalky than he remembered. The little plastic dolphin hung from his neck, and his eyes were bulging, bloodshot, and terrorized. Gusano Verde's daddy. Branch almost heaved but fought it off, and then he was even more steeled toward his final plunge.

"This guy was Omar's enemy," Victor said. "A drug chief on the mainland. He was trying to stop Omar from building the pier, for business reasons, but he was also an environmentalist. Nobody wants to cross Omar when they see pictures like this."

"I get that," Branch said. He pushed the laptop away.

"He was supposed to come to that protest at the pier, week before last. He never showed."

"He sure didn't. What's with this key?"

"Back before the hurricane. There was no plan in place to evacuate the dolphins and the water was too rough to open the sea gates and let them go. The dolphins would've drowned in the pen, and after the destruction from the storm, Omar wouldn't be able to get in and cover up his negligence. He knew he could always go out and capture more dolphins later so he got proactive."

"How?"

"He sent the staff to the shelter when he saw we were getting a Category 5 hitting broadside. Then Omar and Dexter took care of the problem. They went to the park and shot all the dolphins. They trucked the corpses to the mangroves and slaughtered them for the *cocodrilos*. Dorian got video. Omar's done a lot of terrible things, but nobody cares. Small problem on a small island, they say. But when the world sees video of him shooting dolphins in a pen? It's stashed in a safe deposit box somewhere."

"So Dorian had some pretty good dirt on Uncle Omar," Branch said.

"He wanted to sell the videos to this drug lord from the mainland. We've been getting help on our protests from a secret benefactor for some time. Turns out it was *this* guy," Victor said, tapping his laptop. "This *dead* guy."

"Dorian was trying to help your redheaded benefactor. And now they're both dead."

"There's another one in the family," Victor told him. "He's more high-tech. He's been organizing the protests on Twitter. He calls himself Gusano Verde."

"Yeah. I heard of him."

"This Gusano Verde. He contacted me right before you got back from Cuba. We had just one phone conversation. Something happened last weekend, he said, that broke his resolve on the whole Chinchamos issue. Made him rethink his plans."

"What happened last weekend?" Branch asked. But he already knew.

Victor gazed at Branch through his deep, sun-drilled wrinkles and with that liquid clear look in his eyes. Those eyes that always looked dilated, that were always too open. Innocent eyes, Branch thought. Honest eyes. Eyes that made him hate what he'd done with his life.

Victor looked as if he was trying to peer into Branch's mind. Then he shrugged.

"I don't know, Branch. I thought perhaps *you* might know."

"No. I *don't*," he lied. He couldn't worry about it. It was much too late for that.

"I believe you," Victor said. "We got to try to get that key. I'll call Manny to come in and watch our backs while we're down. How deep is he?"

"Damn deep."

"Just the way you like it. Keep this bottle of rum handy. It's been too long since we cut loose like we used to. Like it was back before we knew the reef was doomed to die. Before I knew that I was doomed, too."

"Yeah," Branch said. "Before we knew."

"Remember that one day last year? Hanging out over at the Iguana Rio? That must have been the last time we had any fun."

"Yeah. That was a good time. Dived from the beach in the morning. Drank cold beer and ate grilled shrimp in the afternoon. Watched crazy tourists playing croquet in the sand."

"If we find that key I'll be ready to celebrate like that again. That video could sink Omar and his pier. I need you on this."

"I'm going out for a dive today, anyway," Branch told him. "My last on Chinchamos. I'll help you find that key, but promise me you'll get away from the island for a while, or at least hide out over there at the Iguana Rio if things don't turn out like you hope. Until things get sorted out."

"I promise," Victor said. "But things are *going* to work out, so get ready for that drink. And the good old days, again."

"I'm ready," Branch said. He smiled and nodded at the bottle, but he knew that Victor was going to have to drink from it alone. He had his own drink waiting for him, down below.

Chapter Thirty

The Sweet Smell of Success

B ranch watched the GPS and navigated the *Argos I* to the spot. He let the boat drift with the current then backed into the shallows and signaled for Manny to drop anchor.

It was a bright morning and the water was flat, but whitecaps were starting to kick on the southern point. To the north there was a gray plume of exhaust where a cruise ship had put out to sea.

On the bridge of that cruise ship, the *Grand Nautical Angel*, the captain watched the towboats as they tugged his vessel into the channel. Then he set course, southeast toward Honduras. The sewage bilge should've been pumped out while they were in port, in Chinchamos, but an encrypted message from corporate had told him to wait. The budget wouldn't allow the expense, the message had told him.

The captain held his hand on the lever that would release more than a hundred thousand gallons of blackwater into the turquoise seas. The cruise ship was sitting low in the water, so it would have to be done soon, but in a place where no one would see. From the helm he watched the dive boats buzzing like gnats in the shallows as he navigated the huge ship into deeper waters.

Onboard the *Argos I*, on the deep side of Hammerhead Point, all was calm and quiet.

"This is where he is?" Victor asked, kneeling on the bench and squinting into the clear water.

"No. He's out there." Branch pointed to where the turquoise shifted quickly to black. "Two fifty. Three hundred, maybe. Not much coral. It's on the outside of the current." Then he pointed to the dark fringe of reef that formed a horseshoe and circled toward the beach.

"Two fifty? Fucking deep. That's a bit of an obstacle."

"Someone once told me water is never an obstacle. It's a sanctuary."

"Right," Victor said. He strapped weight to two air tanks, tied a line and eased them over the side. Then he let go of the line and watched the tanks drop down to the sandy bottom. "We might need these stage tanks for some deco time on the way up from your sanctuary. It was a good deed you thought you were doing. The thing with Dorian."

"The same person also told me no good deed goes unpunished. Mostly I think it's true."

"I can't live that way," Victor said, gazing toward the dark spot on the horizon where the new pier was going in. "Just look at what they're doing to her. Drilling their piers into her, crushing her with anchors, choking her with sewage. You think she'll allow them to punish me for trying to protect her?"

"I don't know anymore," Branch said. He looked down at the water and shrugged. "Let's go get you that key. Then you come on up. I'm going deeper."

"Deeper? What for?"

"It's a project I'm doing. Research. Mating habits of the Maltese bikini fish."

"We'll see about that," Victor said, then he looked back to Manny. "Once we're down you motor back toward the reef. We're not supposed to be out here. No license. Make it look like you're just working on the boat."

They slipped into their double tank rigs and rolled back. Branch floated on the surface and looked at Chinchamos's leeward shore. New hotel construction in varying degrees of completion gouged the once unchecked tree line. He thought of Victor's dream for preserving what remained of the island's natural resources.

Manny shot him the OK sign. Branch didn't return it; he just waved goodbye. Then he gave his fins a flick, spun around so he was facing the channel and slipped under. At last he was going to where he almost belonged, and for a moment he was happy. There was only that one place where he could find relief from it all. So once more he dropped right down toward that place.

Branch kicked to the sandy floor at ninety feet and waited for Victor to join him. Then they dropped over the wall and hovered down a barren hillside toward blue oblivion. Only the devil's sea whips grew there, their curled, neon tips springing at Branch inquisitively, as they had on that last dive with Dr. Huggins so many months before. To the north, the cruise ship's propellers spun and he heard the grinding noises, like some faraway underwater factory.

He kicked through the nausea, down toward the numbness, Victor right beside him, and as the digits on his console clicked away, he felt it. The warm greeting—the bouncer at the door knew his name—and the pain from the surface was gone. *Get the key! Then find the girl!*

Branch glided up to Dorian's shredded bundle, snagged on a coral ledge at about two fifty. He grabbed the end of the bundle and spun it around to retrieve the chain. But Dorian's hulking head was gone, bitten clean off, and he could see from the bite marks that it had been a tiger shark. No head, no chain, no key.

He cut the burly bundle loose from the ledge and pushed it with the tip of his fin. As he watched it spiral down into the fathoms there was the sparkle of metal coming from a sandy plateau twenty feet below. He signaled for Victor to wait on the ledge then drifted down toward the reflection. Hanging perilously from the end of a devil's sea whip was Dorian's chain and pendant. He carefully lifted the chain, and the sea whip bounced, its curled end freed from the weight of the key.

He hovered back up to the ledge and placed the key in Victor's outstretched palm. Victor, smiling behind his regulator, closed his hand tightly around the key. Branch embraced Victor's fist with both hands. Then he stuck his thumb out, signaling for Victor to go up.

Without waiting for any argument, Branch gave his fins a kick and then he was taking the freight elevator down, the aquatic opiates coming on strong. Some invisible needle was attached to a tube and some medicine was dripping into his arm. Maybe, he thought, he was actually lying in a hospital bed somewhere, hallucinating it all.

Deeper still, into junkie twilight time he dropped, aware of the danger with but a grain of consciousness. A dark shadow hovered, and he did not mind. To kick out, go deep, his only friend.

He sank down headfirst, his bubbles cascading up and over his body like a waterfall of air. At four fifty, the muted glow from the surface was an aquamarine spotlight shining down from the balcony, down onto the stage of the underwater club, and it was shining on Branch. *Beautiful. A show tonight and I'm onstage!*

Then the girl was beside him, sexy in her little black coral dress as she introduced him to the crowd. *"Ladies and gentlemen, please give a warm welcome to the talented Branch Kilgore!"*

Branch smiled at the sound of his name, unsure if that was really him, and he squinted into the pleasant blue-green light. Someone up in the rafters was shining the spotlight on him but he'd forgotten his act.

He wrenched his mind and he pushed back his stage fright. It was some fantastic act but he couldn't remember the lines. He looked at his console for a cue.

He smiled and laughed with embarrassment, struggling to arrange the digits on the depth gauge into some meaning. But the symbols there spelled only ecstasy and bewilderment. The audience embraced his vulnerability and then he heard their thunderous ovation.

The clapping of the audience morphed into a kind of heckling, buzzing sound, and then the sound became something else. He looked again at his dive console.

The console said *5-0-8*. He looked down at the dark, sandy surface of the stage. The spotlight flickered and a jagged dark shadow passed over his head. Something was in the rafters up above the stage, screeching and screaming at him.

Take your mask off, he thought. *Always been a nuisance to me down here. That's the act! And spit out your regulator. The crowd will go wild!*

He pulled off his mask and spit out the reg, bubbles streaming slowly from his mouth. But then the girl was beside him on the stage, whispering in his ear.

"*No, Branch, no. This is not what you are here for. Remember?*"

"Lost my glasses. It's all blurry. But I remember. What's your name?"

"*Call me Calypso,*" the girl told him. Water swirled above his head, and then Victor drifted down beside him. He pushed the regulator back into Branch's mouth, tugged desperately at his jacket and flashed him a hand signal. Branch had seen the signal before but couldn't understand it.

Calypso stroked his outstretched arm, then gently took his hand and pressed his index finger to his thumb. Branch was pleased—he knew again what that signal meant. *Yes, I'm OK.* He crooned it into the microphone, *I'm OK!* Bubbles blasted from the mic and out into the dark audience. And the crowd went wild.

He shuddered at the loud ovation, then looked up and saw the dark shape of the *Grand Nautical Angel* passing overhead. It blacked out the spotlight. The show was over. Then Branch and Victor were crawling together up the sandy slope.

The grinding noise faded as they rose up. And then at two eighty Branch was again able to comprehend the digits on his console. The stage show was over but he was still totally baked.

The noise had faded to a buzz. He was clearer now. Something had happened to him down there. The angel of death—or was it just that ship?—had passed over him. And somehow, things were different.

Back on the sandy flat at ninety feet, Branch and Victor breathed off the stage tanks for an hour and looked up at a strange brown cloud that hung over them. As they surfaced they tried to find the edge of the cloud, but couldn't. So finally they ascended into the field of raw sewage the *Grand Nautical Angel* had released as she'd passed over. The stench of the blackwater was overwhelming as they waited on the surface for the dive boat.

Branch wiped the sewage from his face. He could see the cruise ship steaming southward, only a black plume visible on the horizon as she headed toward Honduras.

Manny motored up with the *Argos I* and the divers climbed back on board. Victor laughed as he slipped out of his gear. A white towel turned brown as he wiped his head with it.

"What the hell's so funny?" Branch asked. "We got cruise ship shit all over us."

"The sweet smell of success," Victor said, taking in a deep breath of the sewage. "We got the key, plus, I been trying to get proof for years the ships are dumping out here. This is great! In broad daylight, too. We got to get a sample."

Branch scanned the flats, saw the usual dive boats floating along the shallows. He didn't see any of Omar's boats, or any other vessel that Carlsbad might be lurking on. Probably still waiting in that Hummer for Pam to leave her room.

"No time for that, Victor. Get out of sight." His own voice seemed hollow and distant. "You got the key. But you'll have to hide now if you want to find whatever it unlocks. Lay down flat."

Victor argued with him for a moment, but if there was anyone watching the *Argos I* as Manny powered it out of the brown slick and back into the channel, they'd think it had one less diver on it than when it entered Hammerhead Point.

Branch's cell phone, the one Victor had given him, vibrated on the wheelhouse. Mel. Still trying to sell him on the ferry job. The last Friday of the month. She wanted his final answer each day, and each day he gave it to her. No way. But he moved to the stern and answered the phone anyway.

"I heard Victor lost his dive permit, and I was worried about you," she told him. "Was thinking you might have reconsidered things. About the job?"

"Sales still haven't picked up at the jewelry store?" Branch asked. "I was hoping you'd make a little money and come to your senses."

"No. Sales are horrible. And things are really tense right now. Omar was in the store today, pulling money out of the safe. Which I thought was kind of strange, because he doesn't take cash across to the mainland until *next* Friday. Oh, and I couldn't help but think of you. That wretched man, the cigar man that runs the dreadful bordello next to your hotel? What's his name? Yes, Elias, that's it. He came in, met with Omar briefly."

Something about that disturbed Branch but he was too narced to figure out what it was.

"And Branch, don't forget," Mel purred. "Next Friday—it's the last Friday of the month. If you're in, we need to scheme."

Chapter Thirty-One

Fish Food

"Half a million dollars is a lot of money, Elias," Omar said. "It would have to be some very useful information, no?"

"You mind if I smoke?"

Omar slid a heavy crystal ashtray across the mahogany desk.

"They've moved her," Elias said nervously, fumbling with his wooden matches as he lit a Bolivar Robusto. He looked through the open doorway of the office and into the jewelry showroom. He could get killed just for asking. Was a half mil too much? The diamonds, the rubies, and the watches, he'd heard, weren't selling like they used to.

Meanwhile, the cigars, the tequila and the blowjobs *were* selling, and La Cucaracha was doing all right. But he would have to sell a lot of cigars to put together *that* kind of cash. Omar needed this pier deal, and he needed it bad. It was worth the risk. Half a mil, Elias decided, should not be a problem.

"Hours ago," Elias continued. "He's hiding her."

"*No es posible,*" Omar said. He furiously punched numbers into his desk phone, spoke tersely, tapped his fingers on the desk and waited. Then he hung up and looked at Elias. "How you know about this?"

"He was at the hotel, before sunup. He said some things. I didn't think much about it, but later I was out on my speedboat. I saw where he took her, on that dinghy from the dive shop. A girl from my club, Claudia, she told me about the place. I knew he must be hiding her."

"Who's hiding her?" Omar asked. "Where is she?"

"I think you know who. But only I know where. Do we have a deal, Don Rasgado?"

"I only got fifty grand." Omar pulled a fat yellow envelope out of his jacket. "I drop by the restaurant earlier. I take this out of the safe," he said, showing Elias the cash inside. "It belong to Branch. But he won't be needing it no more, no?"

"Fifty grand will be just fine," Elias said. "Fifty grand *and* the *Ogygia*."

Three hours later, Omar pulled his white Land Rover into the four-car garage of one of the unsold villas at Chinchamos North Country Club. He entered the home into a large mudroom. Dexter, standing guard there, straightened his muscly body and nodded toward the kitchen.

Omar took a deep breath and inhaled the fragrance of twelve thousand square feet of opulent new construction. Marble, fruitwood, high-end appliances and electronics, and natural plasters and stonework. It used to entice him. It was the scent of money. Now, it smelled like poverty. And as he walked into the cavernous kitchen, that smell made him all the more anxious to get his share of the cruise ship cash. To get Pam to sign that deed over to him. And because of the bad publicity from the protests, it had to be a real signature, signed in front of a notary with a video camera.

She was strapped down motionless on the rose stone counter, her face covered with a wet towel. Carlsbad stood over her, and as he saw Omar walk into the room he jostled her frail shoulders. She started, woke up, and a muffled scream echoed through the empty kitchen.

"She's been drifting in and out," Carlsbad said to him, pushing the towel down over Pam's face. "No marks on her at all, but she's suffering plenty, Mr. Rasgado. The secret is to keep them alert, so the terror can really build, *yummean?* Buried

227

alive. You dig 'em up a few times just before they go out, after they've suffered so much, and then they'll do anything to keep from going back under."

"No problems on the yacht? And the other one? Just those two, no?"

"No problems, Mr. Rasgado," Carlsbad told him. "It was me, Dexter, and Len. A real nice operation. No shots fired. We got the other one tied up in the master bedroom."

"Leave him in there. Take the towel off. I talk to her now."

"She's not quite ready. She's got another minute or two in her. It's important to be real patient with this. I learned all about it at Gitmo."

"Maybe you go back to shoot the coyotes, no? Take it off."

Carlsbad uncovered Pam's ashen face, her body quaking as she sucked in deep breaths. Her eyes squinted to adjust to the light, and a small stream of blood ran from her nose.

Pam's contorted face unfolded slowly as she stirred from a breathless nightmare. Then her eyes were wide open.

"It's so beautiful," Carlsbad said. "*Yummean?* Each time you bring them out it's like they're reborn. A few more brain cells gone."

Pam's lips trembled and she struggled to speak. "What? Who's that?"

"*Hola, Pam-Ella,*" Omar said, leaning over her and stroking her silver hair. "You remember the current you tell me about? That current, it bring you to me at last."

"Where am I?"

Omar smiled approvingly at Carlsbad then glanced back at Pam.

"A safe place. Where we no be disturbed."

Pam blinked and her pale blue eyes scanned the ornate ceiling.

"Yes, Omar. I remember now. We're in one of your gaudy golf course homes. I shouldn't think you'd be getting any showings on this house anytime soon, so I suppose you're right. We won't be bothered. The current's not flowing *this* way, is it?"

Omar reached into his jacket pocket for the contract.

"We got a notary waiting. You sign this document, we take the photos. Then you walk away with two fucking million in cash."

"This is rose stone," Pamela said, straining her neck to view the countertop she was strapped down on. "My ancestors in England knew. Summons a friendly brimstone elemental to protect the innocent. Attacks nearby enemies by shooting brimstone fireballs."

"See what I mean?" Carlsbad asked, chuckling, still holding the wet towel over her head. "The brain cells."

"Brimstone fireballs," Omar muttered. "So you need more time to think about the things."

Pam cut her eyes toward the towel, then back to Omar.

"I had plenty of time to think when I was trapped inside that cave last week. And when I was in your jail all weekend. And every time I see some dead coral in the sea, or rubbish from the ships washed up on the beach, or a cruise passenger puking on the avenue. You can kill me. You'll never get what you want."

Omar's nostrils flared. He nodded. Carlsbad dropped the wet towel over Pam's face and poured water on her. She gasped and her body contorted. The towel puffed on her face but then she was resigned to it and her body became still.

Omar laid the unsigned deed on the counter. "You hear anything back from Branch? He finish the Victor job?"

"Len called in. He was watching. Victor and Branch went out on some dive earlier today. Looked like Branch maybe was going to kill him, like you wanted. But then Len spotted them coming back up. Together. Alive. He said Victor was lying down in the bottom of the dive boat as they headed toward the south point."

Carlsbad watched as the fury rose up over Omar's face. "You really didn't think Branch was going to kill that Victor, did you? Not after he tried to help this old lady get away."

"Branch do the good work for me, before," Omar said, lighting a cigarette and blowing smoke down at Pam's shrouded face. Her chest heaved and she groaned as the effects of the suffocation came over her. "He had a lot to gain. And a lot to lose, no? Yeah, I think he do it."

Carlsbad shrugged and looked down at Pam's writhing body.

"Well, he didn't. And that missing nephew of yours? That smells like Kilgore, too. Like I told you, he's nothing but an individual."

"And you?"

"Team player, sir."

"So you go do one for the team. Kill the Victor. Tell Fibbi to pick up the other people on the list. The girl, Bali. Put Len at the dive shop to watch for them."

"Len? But he's Branch's daddy."

"Not really. He does what he's paid to do."

"And Branch?"

"Bring him to me. Alive. I no can kill him yet. He belong to Gonzago."

"Yes, sir, Mr. Rasgado." Carlsbad checked his watch and took the towel from Pam's face. She sucked in air. He scanned her gray eyes for any sign that she was about to break, but she appeared calm. "Keep that towel good and wet. Pour water on her face when it looks like she's getting air. Let her go four, maybe five minutes without a breath, then give her a quick one. The old girl's tougher than you would think. I've had her in and out of that thing for an hour. Normally, they'd be caving in by now. Sign any damn thing to keep from going back under."

Omar smiled. "With proper motivation. Bring the fat one in. What's his name?"

"His passport says Gruber," Carlsbad told him. "Paul Gruber."

"Bring him here."

Carlsbad disappeared into the emptiness of the mansion then came back into the kitchen a moment later dragging the Grouper. Muffled curses emanated from the cloth sack that covered his head, and he struggled against the zip ties that bound his wrists and ankles.

"Tie him down to that chair in the corner," Omar said. "Tie the arms down good. Fancy torture tactics no working. I do it like I used to do it. Bring me my raincoat and my finger choppers from the car. Then you go."

After Carlsbad had gone, Omar moistened the towel in the sink, wrung it out, and squeezed a few drops of water onto Pam's forehead. "This is fun for me. But for you, not so fun, no? The bad way to go, for the scuba diver. Suffocation."

"You pave the mangroves," Pam gasped, "and you'll suffocate the reef. And everything that lives on it will die. Better me than the reef."

"I need that swamp, *Pam-Ella*. For the good of the island. Jobs for our children. For your own good. You sign and walk out rich."

"Poor and content is rich. And rich enough."

"Then you die today. I forge the document."

"If forging it was going to work you would've already done it. No, you need me to sign and walk away with that case full of money, waving goodbye as the cameras roll. You need me to tell everyone that it's all legit. But I won't do it. And then you're fish food, Rasgado."

"I fish food?" Omar asked. "*I* fish food?"

"Yes. Because without the mangroves you can't operate your pier. And your mob creditors will kill you. And then they'll dump *your* body—out there."

She nodded her matted, moistened silver head toward the window. "And I don't care what you do to me but I'm not signing that bloody thing."

Omar put on his raincoat and yanked the sack off the Grouper's head.

"Maybe you no care about yourself," he said to her, nudging the Grouper's belly with the chrome-plated medical scissors. "You old already. Maybe you looking for the easy way out now. But first you see the effect you have on the others. I start with him."

Omar opened the choppers and placed the razor-sharp edges around the Grouper's right thumb. "I hear about this big bear. I no think he really need the thumb, anyway."

"He's bluffin'," the Grouper said. "This motherfucker won't do anything. Sorry to curse, Pam, but he's a weak, worthless motherfucker. He's the one gonna have to change."

"Me change? *Lord know I can't change!*"

Omar jammed the choppers shut as he sang. Outside the home, golfers on the eighteenth fairway could hear the Grouper's screams but then went quickly back to their game.

"Fuck him, Pam," the Grouper screamed on. Blood streamed onto the floor. He looked down at his thumbless right hand and screamed again. It was the adrenaline-fueled, laughing scream of a thrill seeker, and it sounded like the Grouper had skied over a cliff and caught big air. Omar moved the shears to his left hand.

"What you say, Pam? Is no too late to save him. He still have the one good thumb. You open a *cerveza* with the one."

"Fuck him, Pam," the Grouper laugh-screamed again. "We should've died in that cave-in, anyway. If not for Branch we'd already be dead. So fuck this guy."

"Yes," Omar said. "I must thank Branch for that, no? Or else I no get this pleasure."

Pam grimaced and hesitated, and then the golfers on the eighteenth heard another scream.

"Untie me, Rasgado," she cried. "I'll sign the bloody thing. Just let him go."

Chapter Thirty-Two

The Final Redhead

I t was late in the afternoon when Branch made his way into the alley behind the Blue Angel. He was still stoned from the dive but he moved quickly as he entered the laundry room and headed up the rear stairwell.

Victor had interrupted his final escape into the Deep Blue Saloon and now it was time for him to find another way out of Chinchamos. He didn't have enough money, but he was content he'd done all he could to keep Pam and Victor safe.

After a few seconds of listening at the door, Branch inserted the key, and with one quick movement he was inside. He stuffed Bali's turtle book in his backpack, went to the kitchen and took a foil-wrapped bundle of cash from the freezer, then opened the door to the bathroom to get his gun. Gusano Verde sat there on the toilet, pointing the M9 at him with his right hand. His left arm was in a sling.

"Looking for this?" he asked, shaking the gun at Branch. He stood up.

"Verde. Yeah, I *am* looking for that. But you keep it. Don't need it no more."

"Interesting spot to keep your gun, taped under the toilet. I hope it's the only one you have, but that doesn't seem likely. You've been prolific at shooting people these last weeks. You have one on you?"

"No. I was on a dive. Don't like to take my piece with me on the boat. Bad things happen."

Gusano Verde laughed. "Indeed they do. The Hotel Comodoro pier, for example. And where's your little girlfriend in the sand? The one who shot me on the beach last week? With this very gun, I do believe."

"No. She used her Beretta. How's the arm?"

"It hurts," Gusano Verde said. He grimaced as he took his left arm out of the sling and straightened it, then wagged the M9 at Branch with his right. "Where is she?"

"Out with the turtles, I guess. Eggs will hatch soon."

"Quite a woman there. Before we get down to business, I want you to appreciate that I took your advice. I went home and thought things over. Now I'm back. With no emotion."

Gusano raised the gun and pointed it at Branch's face. "So, *bang!* You're dead."

"Fine with me. So pull the trigger or get away from the toilet. I have to take a piss."

Gusano sniffed at him. "You need a shower, too."

Branch had rinsed off at the dive shop but he still reeked from cruise ship sewage.

"It'll take more than a shower to get *this* stink off me."

"Agreed." Gusano pointed the M9 toward the living room. "We'll talk in there. Sit down. Then you can show me what's in that bundle."

Branch sat down on the couch. He stared at the bare white walls of his room then closed his eyes, his blood swimming with liquid nitrogen. The purple gorgonians and the orange hydrocorals from the deep dive filled the white space in his mind with vivid colors.

He opened his eyes and looked at Gusano, then looked down the barrel of his own gun.

"Just some traveling money." Branch tossed the foil package on the floor. "But it won't get me anywhere. It's not the method I'd hoped for but your timing is just fine. So go ahead and kill me."

"Couldn't be that easy. I may have the gun but surely you've got the advantage."

"Normally that might be true. But right now I'm all fucked-up on nitrogen negronis. And that's the way I plan to stay. I'm not even sure of my own name right now."

"Allow me to help. Your name is Branch Kilgore. You work for Omar Rasgado, and you've killed two of my clan the last couple of weeks. You could've killed me, too. And you did it all without getting so much as a scratch on you. Except for that nasty bruise on your ear."

"A fucking cop did that."

"Yes. The Chinchamos police have been roughing people up. But you weren't on the island during our recent and pointless attempts to occupy the waterfront. I'm quite sure of that. I'll show you in a minute."

He sat down on the couch across from Branch. "You got the better of me on the beach, and then you did something incredible. You let me go. It took me a couple of days after that to heal up and cogitate on it. I came to agree with your philosophy about not getting personally involved. But then, to test my resolve, this happened."

Gusano pulled a small computer tablet from his pocket and tossed it at Branch. ENVIRONMENTALIST ASSASSINATED, read the news headline on the UK Guardian website, and then below it: Havana Sniper Still at Large.

"Uncle Carlos?" Branch asked. He read the headline again then scrolled down the page on the tablet to make sure it was real.

"Uncle Carlos. He was shot on a sailboat while attending the Latin American Environmental Summit in Cuba. He was the delegate from Mexico, and his vote was to be a deciding one on some critical issues. Regarding climate change and ocean acidification. Now, the man who's taking his place as delegate, a cohort of Omar Rasgado's as it turns out, has decidedly different views."

"On what?"

"On what? On what. What's the biggest problem facing the world today?"

"Not enough people good at math," Branch said reflexively, remembering what Reiner had told him.

"So true," Gusano said, and he laughed. "I like that. The summit members were really close to being able to do good things, like making it illegal to blow up coral reefs. But they're so bad at math they think one more destroyed reef and one more stinking cruise ship doesn't affect the equation. And after the incident—well, nothing was accomplished. Nobody saw the shooter but it wasn't hard for me to learn you were indeed in Havana that weekend. And not here on the island for the protests. Are *you* good at math?"

Branch tossed the tablet aside, felt his narcosis begin to fade. "Yeah. Pretty good. Good enough to know that one protest is not greater than or equal to one guy like Omar. What are you, some kind of manatee-hugging drug lord?"

"We run the coca to fund our other endeavors. Eco-resorts around the world. Promoting ecological awareness. The pier project's an ecological catastrophe, of course, but if it succeeds, it would be a money machine for Omar. If it fails, that lovely patch of reef—Paradise Reef, they call it—would live, and Omar would be vulnerable. To slow him down, Uncle Carlos and Papa had established a relationship with Victor Mendez. They hoped the protests would do some good. They used Twitter to swell the crowds at those protests. A waste of time in the end, I think, all this social media, but it allowed them to support Victor without any direct involvement."

"It's a shame what happened to Paradise Reef."

"Indeed. Now that Papa and Uncle Carlos are dead, I'm free to change our tone. I intend to take a more aggressive stance toward these types of environmental injustices. Decimation of the reefs. The slaughter of dolphins in Japan. The killing of rhinos and elephants in Africa. Cruise ships polluting the sea while ugly Americans float drunkenly."

"A more aggressive stance?"

"Demonstrations, social media campaigns, all of that nonsense. It quickly dissolves before it can do any real good. It's the kind of work *you* do that could make a difference. If you were properly guided. I'm guessing you crave that kind of guidance."

"This job I did in Cuba." Branch glanced down at the headline on the tablet and his stomach heaved. "Instead of standing beside my friends at the dive shop I went to Cuba and took out one of the good guys."

"Ironic, isn't it?"

"I don't know. Why not just kill me now?"

"Some more math for you. Three variables in the equation. One, you broke into the estate a couple of weeks ago and you did only what your employer paid you to do. Kill the boss. You didn't steal any cash or valuables, though Papa had quite a bit lying around. You acted professionally. With honor."

"I guess maybe so."

"Two, the way you got in and out using the cenote. Very resourceful. I want you to know I appreciate that. More than Omar does."

"Yeah."

"Three. This Cuba business. Tragic though it was, it was impressive work, no matter how misguided you may have been. Now it's come to my attention you've moved Pam and Victor into hiding. I'm sure that goes against Omar's plans. Your shift in attitude is most encouraging. I was hoping you might want to work for me."

"I already got a job for one drug dealer. Don't much like it. And he wouldn't take kindly to me changing teams."

"Your work for me wouldn't have anything to do with drugs."

"Saving the rhinos, then?"

"A kilo of powdered rhino horn sells for more than a kilo of coke. There are people in the world who will murder a rhino just to cut off its horn. They do that horrible thing to fund their terror. Those people have to die, and right away. Coke can be produced without harming the environment, if it's done right. I plan to take my coke profits and kill the poachers. Now. And I plan to kill those who would kill the coral reef. Now. And the Omar types in the world who would destroy the habitat of the orangutan. Kill them all. Along with the—"

"Yeah, I get it. Nonprofit work."

"With Omar out of the way, the coca would make me huge profits. Profits I could use to help fund my new organization. A totally underground organization. No websites. No social media. Just killing those who have it coming. To make sure that these types of things," he said, nodding toward the window and the new pier, "don't ever happen again."

"I do love the reefs here. You can save Chinchamos?"

"Chinchamos has become like one of those restaurants you find on the interstate highways in your own country. No quality. No character. The customers won't likely be coming back, so there's no profit in worrying about a little thing like quality. And there are plenty more customers driving down the pike, so what's the point? With these cruise ships pulling in here, Chinchamos has become just another highway joint. Environmentally, it's a lost cause, but if the new pier fails, if Omar fails, it could be a rallying cry for those places on earth that are not yet lost."

"Not yet lost," Branch echoed.

"It's still a big world. It can still be saved, but not with UN resolutions, or with Twitter. That's all a bunch of talk. And while they're talking, men like Omar, to make money, abandon the precautionary principle."

"The what?"

"You don't harm the earth that you live on. You don't pollute the water you drink, or the air you breathe. Omar's done that, and he's beyond corrupt. Blowing up a coral reef so he can park a boatload of numbnuts and take their money? He's a predatory capitalist and he has to die. You'll work for me. To start, you'll take out Omar. I'll pay you well."

"What good would it do?"

"The people need a precipitant before they'll rise up. Here in Chinchamos, if Omar should be killed, for example. Then, Africa." Gusano took a photo of a long-haired, bearded man from his pocket and held it up for Branch to see. "This violator kills elephants and rhinos to fund his jihad. He cuts down protected forests and makes charcoal for money to make bombs. He's next. Your next job."

"Slow down. Regarding Omar, you're asking me to whack my own boss."

"He's not your boss anymore. You crossed him. You hid Pamela. You got soft on whacking Victor. Omar will be looking for *you* now."

"I already did my part. For Pam. As much as she's willing to be helped, anyway. She should take the money and leave. But she won't."

"I know something about Pamela. I come from a privileged family. I've traveled. I studied at a school in England. When I was there, I saw these types, like Pamela. Very rare to find these types in the world anymore."

"What type is that?"

"Have you ever seen the incredible old forest estates and gardens in England? Certain people considered it their charge to create beautiful gardens, to preserve the forests, though they made no money from the endeavor. They did it, no matter how many decades and how much money it took. They would never violate the precautionary principle. Because they knew those forests and gardens would be appreciated by others for centuries to come. These certain types of people, I believe the English word for it is the *nobility*, gladly gave everything they had to create beauty. The *true* nobility. But all of these noble types have one thing in common. They're an endangered species. Like the rhinos and the orangutans and the coral reefs. They can't survive in the world anymore. I was hoping you might want to use your particular set of talents to help them. But I guess I was wrong."

Branch paused. The high from the dive had almost completely evaporated out of him.

"Yeah. You were wrong."

"A man without a job. What will you do now? Where will you go?"

"Someplace they don't dump in the ocean. Someplace where I can just kill the pain and pass the time."

"Good luck finding that place." Gusano Verde spun Branch's gun around on his finger and handed it back to him. "Take your money and go. I hope you find what you're looking for. Be careful as you're on your way there. If we hurry we can catch the next ferry to the mainland."

"You came on the ferry?" Branch peeked out the blinds and saw the flash of a red Hummer rumbling by. "You must be crazy. What happened to your helicopter?"

"Filthy thing. Got rid of it. I rode my bicycle to the marina, took the ferry across. Who would look for me on Omar's own ferry? It's the safest way in and out of Chinchamos."

"At least hide your red head." Branch handed Gusano the old Havana Leones cap Javier had given him in Cuba. "The survival rate for redheads is not so good right now. I'm told it's a lucky cap."

"Did you get this on your recent Cuba trip?" Gusano ran his finger over the big white *H* on the front. "It wasn't so lucky for poor Uncle Carlos. A very unusual souvenir for me to have, but I'll take it anyway. For luck."

"You'll need it. We've waited too long already."

Branch popped the clip back into his gun, chambered a round and slid it into the back of his trousers, safety off. He pocketed the bundle of hundreds and the extra clip, slipped into the straps of his backpack, but then hesitated. He went back to his dresser and grabbed the souvenir glass globe from the top drawer. He took a moment to admire the globe, its sand and golden fish churning wildly. Then he stuffed it into the pack and led Gusano Verde downstairs to the Blue Angel's rear exit, scanning both directions before easing into the alley.

They stepped around the trash cans and passed the narrow driveway that led down to the waterfront. The Hummer had turned around and pulled up in front of the hotel, and before Branch could react, there was the familiar blast of a Stoner SR-25 round as it screamed past his head.

Chapter Thirty-Three

Swamp Tacos

T he Havana Leones ball cap was knocked off his head, a hole in the bill where the bullet had ripped through it, but Gusano Verde was unharmed, crawling past the drive and toward the trash cans that littered the rear of the Roach. Branch pulled his pistol and fired in the direction of the Hummer, then dived to the other side of the driveway. The heavy door of the SUV slammed shut and then Carlsbad and Dexter were sprinting across the street and up the driveway.

Branch pushed Gusano Verde down the alley behind Taco Loco and then into a tiny corridor that led to a loading dock for Takanaka's Liquor store.

"I told you that hat was lucky. When we get in there," Branch said, nodding toward the store as he pushed the fresh clip into his gun, "get to the front door, then you head north up Second and don't stop until you get to the ferry boat."

Then he stepped onto the loading dock and fired several shots toward the trash cans in the alley. Carlsbad stepped around the corner and answered back with his .45.

Branch pushed Gusano into the storage room of the liquor store. They tumbled past crates and cardboard and piles of broken bottles and into the front of the shop. Takanaka was already coming from behind the counter with his shotgun.

"Takanaka, don't shoot!" Branch yelled at him. "They're coming. Get down!"

Takanaka chambered a round with a fierce pump then stepped back. "Branch, you smell bad. Really bad! And I already told you—don't use my back door no more."

Branch could hear Dexter and Carlsbad crashing into the storage room.

"Get down, Takanaka," Branch said, pleading with him. "This doesn't concern you." Then he pushed Gusano Verde with him out the front door. They tumbled out to the sidewalk and onto Second Avenue.

"Get going," Branch told Gusano. "They want *me*. They don't know you're on the island. They couldn't possibly think you're this dumb. Go save those rhinos, and the reefs, too. I'll take them into the swamp."

Branch darted to his right and ran toward the mangroves that lay behind the hotel, the mangroves that were the source of all his problems. He took a quick glance behind him. Gusano Verde was jogging to the north, looking back at him indecisively.

The front door of the liquor store kicked open. Dexter ran out, turned and followed the redhead. Then Takanaka fell onto the sidewalk, his shotgun spinning away to the curb. Carlsbad stepped out, aiming his .45 down at the diminutive shop owner's head.

"Throw your gun down on the dirt, Kilgore, or I'll shoot this motherfucker right here."

Branch looked up the boulevard. Gusano and Dexter had disappeared, but there was Takanaka crouching on the sidewalk. Branch laid down his piece.

"Good. Drop that backpack and lie down on your belly."

Branch dropped the pack and stretched out on the ground.

"Get back in your shop and stay there," Carlsbad said, shoving Takanaka into the liquor store. Then he kicked the shotgun out into the street and walked slowly toward Branch. "If you were gonna run, you shoulda run right after our little party at the restaurant. *Yummean?* But you stuck around. Can't figure that."

"Had some things to take care of," Branch said from the ground.

"Musta been some damned important things. Put your hands behind you." Carlsbad knelt down to zip-tie Branch's wrists together. "What *is* that fucking smell?"

"What this whole damn thing's about. It's the stink of the cruise ships."

"Nobody ever said money had to smell good," Carlsbad said, gasping. He took another tie from his pocket and firmly bound Branch's ankles. "Now you're all trussed up like your fat buddy."

"Who? What buddy?"

Before Carlsbad could answer, Branch vaulted to his feet and thrust the back of his head into Carlsbad's face. There was an ugly cracking sound. Carlsbad screamed and fell back onto the dirt, blood streaming from his nose.

"How's it smell now?" Branch taunted. Then he vaulted into the murky shallows and dived down into the gray water of the mangroves, his wrists and ankles still tied tight.

A shot from Carlsbad's .45 tolled through the water and past his shoulder. He stretched his body out and kicked like a dolphin down to the silt of the bottom.

Branch came up for air just inside the line of red mangroves. He hovered, gently moving his bound feet. He looked back and saw the splash and then the stream of bubbles where Carlsbad had dived in after him. He took a breath and plunged down into the soot of the bottom, using his head to feel his way back toward the sea among the mangal roots.

Swimming through the brown water, Branch navigated the labyrinth of tubers toward a patch of light. Fighting the breathlessness and the panic, he wedged his shoulders into the thick roots, forced his belly down into the muck and waited. He tested the zip ties that secured his wrists and ankles. They weren't budging. He figured he had two more minutes in him, and again he remembered Bali's book. He had to be one cool turtle.

He heard more shots from the .45 pierce the water but they weren't close. So he waited until the convulsions came, then he kicked toward the patch of light and surfaced in a tidal pool, separated from Ocean Road by thirty feet of thick manzanillas. He gulped in a huge breath then spun around to scan the surface for crocs. The barrel of Carlsbad's .45 banged into his forehead.

"You had to surface sooner or later, Kilgore," Carlsbad said, prodding him with the blue steel. His nose was bleeding and his body was muddy and scratched where he'd flailed through the sharp branches. "As much as you just want to stay down there forever."

"That's been my plan all along," Branch said, pulling in deep breaths. "Stay down there, forever. But nobody will let me." He looked around the tidal pool, surrounded by mangrove trees on all sides.

"You coulda helped your team," Carlsbad said, waist-deep in the muck. "But you just had to be an individual. Even the old Brit had something you don't got, Branch. As the Mexicans say, she had *elemento principal*. Backbone. But not you. You didn't follow your orders. Didn't take care of the dive shop owner."

"I don't want to do the work anymore, Carlsbad."

"Just as well then, that it ends this way. A man's worthless when he can't do his job. Omar wanted you alive. But I can't march you back through this shit. Not with you smelling like you do. I'll just bring him your head. I expect he'll understand. I'm not without mercy, Branch."

"Yeah."

Carlsbad stroked Branch's temple with the .45.

"Nothing personal. Even though you are an insubordinate fuck and a quitter, I don't feel the least bit good about taking out a former mate. So long, Kilgore."

"So long, Carlsbad." Branch stared down into the shallow brown water then closed his eyes. He smelled the rich mud of the mangroves and heard the wind coming off the sea, from the deep waters, as it gusted and swirled through the thorny trees. He knew he'd done his best for Pam and Victor. His only disappointment was that he wouldn't get to see *her* again, the glassy sweepers again, down in the Deep Blue Saloon.

The blast came, but it wasn't from Carlsbad's gun. It came from a shotgun that was poking through the mangroves. Carlsbad's body skimmed like a stone across the surface of the pool and then it was impaled on the sharp branches.

Gusano Verde splashed into the pool holding Takanaka's smoking shotgun. His shirt was ripped, his sling hung tattered from his shoulder, and he was bleeding.

"We should try to stay out of the mangroves in the future," he said, chambering the next round with enthusiasm. "Somebody's always getting shot."

"I had him, Verde. But thanks. There's a blade in my pocket."

After Gusano Verde cut off the zip ties, Branch swam across the pond and pulled Carlsbad's head out of the murky water. There were a thousand little holes in his chest and his neck and every time he took a breath bloody bubbles oozed out.

"Carlsbad. Can you hear me? What buddy were you talking about? That's trussed up?"

"Brimstone fireballs," Carlsbad gurgled as he looked down at his shredded torso. "The old lady. She wasn't kidding. But Omar got the signature from her. And your bearded buddy. They got him. Killed 'em both."

"They're not dead. They're on the *Ogygia*, anchored way up at Cedral. Omar couldn't have possibly found them."

"Cigar man sold you out," Carlsbad wheezed, and he gave a little laugh. "For a damn sailboat."

Carlsbad coughed, and then blood was pouring from his nose. "He dumped the bodies. Made it look like a dive accident. Just your style. Something else. The training officer at Bucklew. Your hat. Some Black guy. Paid me to steal it from your duffel. Before you left."

"Reiner paid you?"

"That shrunken ventromedial cortex of yours. Guess it's growing. In that place you go, down there." Carlsbad gasped and then his final breath was raspy with blood.

Gusano Verde splashed over and prodded Carlsbad's body with the shotgun.

"What do we do with him?"

"Leave him here for the crocs. It's what he would want. An honorable burial. In the water. You were right, Verde. What you told me that night, on the beach. About the mangroves. It *is* my business. You get going. Run your dope. Save the planet."

"You're going to kill Omar now, aren't you?"

"Brimstone fireballs," Branch told him. "But first I'm going to get the hell out of this swamp. This shallow water is too damn dangerous."

Chapter Thirty-Four

Ride the Snake

B ranch crouched on the wild side beach, studded with driftwood and littered with trash from the cruise ships. Victor waited behind him in the thick *manzanilla de la muerte* trees that lined the craggy shoreline. The *Ogygia* was anchored two hundred yards out, and on the horizon, Janne and his friends were skurfing through the waves on their boards, their neon wetsuits flashing as they slalomed around the *Ogygia's* hull, their red and orange kites racing across the cloudy, gray sky.

"Dutch *pendejos*!" Elias screamed at them from the aft deck. "Get away from the yacht!"

When he saw Elias go belowdecks, Branch, wearing one of Janne's wetsuits, grabbed a surfboard and launched out into the water. He paddled furiously out to a tiny sandbar, left the board there, then put his mask on and dived deep into the hazy blue water.

By the time he came up under the *Ogygia's* bow, the kitesurfers had scattered, streaking out to sea, their bright suits still luminous on the stormy horizon. Branch peered around the curve of the hull and saw the short barrel of Elias's stainless steel .357 resting on the railing.

Elias was gazing out to the east, still hurling insults at the kitesurfers. "*Pendejos*," he said again, waving his revolver at the horizon as he strutted back toward the stern. "Wooden-shoed *pendejos*."

Grabbing the yacht's anchor line, Branch pulled himself up to the pulpit and onto the forward deck, then crawled toward the cabin. The teak deck of the *Ogygia* was warm and comforting against his belly. Through the hatch, Branch watched as Elias went below again, watched as he tucked the .357 into the back of his pants and sat down at the console, staring at a chart laid out in front of him.

Branch stepped into the companionway.

"Time to set a course and go, Elias."

Elias almost fell off his chair as he spun around from the chart table to face him.

"Branch? What the hell! You'll get killed doing this shit."

He smirked at Branch's orange wetsuit then took a breath to compose himself.

"You're about as colorful as the beer aisle in a Mexican liquor store. Just like your Dutch boyfriends out there. What you doing sneaking on board my yacht?"

"*Your* yacht? When did this become *your* yacht? I just dropped by to see how the Grouper and Pam were getting along. Where are they?"

Elias swilled from an open bottle of Chamucos, then bit the end off a cigar and lit it. He carried the bottle and climbed past Branch onto the deck, laughing as he blew out a huge cloud of smoke.

"You don't smell so good."

"Lot of people been telling me that," Branch said, turning to face him on the deck.

"You know about Pam. You know why she's not here."

"I do. You sold her. For this boat. And now Omar's looking for me, too."

"I'm a businessman. Some months I make money at the Roach. Some months I don't. Can you blame me? I never could have had *this*." He tapped the *Ogygia's* mast with the bottle and it rang like a bell. "But now I am ready to set course. For Cuba. And you're on my focking boat."

"Prevent your death," Branch said. "Go no farther."

"What now?"

"If you're fortunate enough to sail off in this thing you won't be coming back."

"You're just jealous, Branch. She's mine. And all for the price of one little meeting with Omar."

"He killed her. The Grouper, too."

"Yeah?" Elias sat down on the bench and took another gulp of Chamucos. "I didn't know *that*. But that's not my problem. I got my family to think of. You don't know what it is to take care of a family, do you?"

"Never really had one. Pam was the closest thing. And she really cared about this place. About the mangroves. About the coral."

"Uh-huh," Elias said casually. He lifted his leg off the teak bench and farted loudly. "She did. Too bad. So what?"

"Omar's not going to let you keep this boat. He won't let you live. You know too much."

"Omar don't care about me."

"He's busy right now. But he's going to get back around to you. So take my advice, Elias. Swim to shore and take the first ferry to the mainland. Then run."

"You're confused, Branch. I'm not leaving Chinchamos. *You* are. This is my boat. Now you'd best get off it and swim your ass back to shore."

"The old ways and the old days, Elias. Remember what you said? You still think they're done?"

"Yeah. Chinchamos is for making money now."

"You got even less style than I gave you credit for. And with no style, how can you appreciate this boat?" Branch asked, looking down at the *Ogygia's* smart lines and teak trim. "Why do you need it? Why not just ride some inflated plastic snake that's towed behind a motorboat? Is that what you want, Elias? You want to ride the snake?"

"Don't spill your blood for this place." Elias stood up, and there was that wild, drunk look in his eyes, like when he was about to slap Branch in the balls. "And I don't know what the hell you're talking about but I'm not riding any snake."

"Do you want to ride the *fucking* snake?" Branch screamed at him, unrestrained. Elias took another swig, grunted and fidgeted nervously, then set the bottle down on the bench.

Nervous with his tool, Elias pulled the .357 and pointed it toward Branch.

A thousand yards out in the Caribbean, Janne streaked on his board and skimmed his hand on the surface of the water as the red kite pulled him along. He was exhilarated by the speed. The kite filled with wind and he hit a small wave and launched from the sea and into the air. As he landed and turned for another run, he heard a gunshot ring out. Was it from shore, or was it from that yacht that Branch had been interested in?

Janne lowered the handle and let the kite zoom down near the water for a moment. He chugged along lazily on his board as he surveyed the boat. He couldn't see anything. Best leave well enough alone, he thought. Branch had always been a square guy. Branch knew what he was doing. Janne spun his board around and sped southward as the kite gusted high in the sky.

Chapter Thirty-Five

Elemento Principal

Sometime in the middle of the night Branch heard a pod of dolphins moving close to the *Ogygia*. He took a mask and some fins, plunged into the waves and free-dived down to the sandy bottom at fifty feet. He kicked down over the wall and into the depths and the darkness, the luminescent particles sparkling and spinning from his fins. He kicked on deeper—it felt like about one twenty to his ears—then he righted himself and hovered there weightlessly, holding the full breath in the dark water. He felt the pressure behind his mask and in his ears, so he breathed out a few bubbles and started to sink. He kicked gently, his sinuses squealing, and slowly he rose up.

Then the ocean spit him up through the darkness. The silence of the sea was broken only by the sonic yipping and clicking of the dolphin pod, somewhere above him, free and frolicking in the nighttime shallows. Completely breathless, Branch floated upward. He waited for the surface to come to him, if it would. He didn't kick. He wondered if he would make it there before his lungs involuntarily gasped for air. But something up there was pulling him back.

He bobbed to the surface, drifted for a moment in the dark surge then heaved himself back on board. The cell phone was buzzing at him—not yet five o'clock and Mel was already calling. He dried off with a towel and enjoyed the cool wind coming from the open ocean. The phone went off one more time—this time it was Dr. Thompson—and again he didn't answer. He had to figure out his plan before he talked to anybody.

Branch spent the rest of the early morning on deck, watching the last of the stars that sparkled through breaks in the clouds. He monitored the shore road for headlights, but everything was dark and quiet. At daybreak, he sat on the wheelhouse bench and drank coffee. Storm clouds were hanging gray and ominous on the eastern horizon, and he watched them illuminate with a pink tint as the dawn swelled.

There was some banging around in the galley, and then from down below Victor grumbled. "Nothing good to eat on this boat?"

"There's food," Branch told him. "And beer. The Grouper was stocked up pretty good. Fix yourself some breakfast. Stay away from the dried mushrooms."

"You call this food?" Victor asked, poking his head through the galley hatch. His face was a distorted road map of wrinkles. "Twinkies and canned chili? Budweiser?"

"The Grouper was a good guy but he didn't have good taste. It'll have to do."

Victor came out on the deck. "It's so beautiful," he said, looking out at the mounting sunrise. "I see the color. But I can't feel it. I'm numb. About the Grouper. And Pam. She stood up for what she knew was right. She had something special."

"Somebody told me yesterday that the word you seek," Branch said, "is nobility. Or maybe there's a better way to say it in Spanish. *Elemento principal.*"

"How do you know for sure?"

"I called Morgan last night, before I brought you out here from the Iguana Rio. Fishermen found them. The bodies are at the morgue."

"Can't believe Elias gave them up," Victor said, and he glanced nervously at the swath of blood on the deck that led to the forward hold.

Just point the thing toward Honduras and don't look back. That's what the Grouper said, and that's what I'll do. For him. For Pam. Just as soon as the job is done. But I've got to do it in a way that doesn't betray Gonzago.

"It's what most people do," he told Victor. "For money. Elias had him a good life. A strong life. I did him a favor, because it wouldn't have been good much longer. Not when you crawl into bed with Omar. Chinchamos Outfitters puts one of these on all of their boats," Branch said, showing Victor the GPS transmitter he'd removed from the mast. "They would've killed him for sure. To get the boat back. To make sure he didn't talk."

Branch opened up the forward hold and grabbed Elias's head by the hair. He put the GPS transmitter in Elias's dead, gaping mouth and strapped it shut with a piece of duct tape.

"He won't be talking now. I'll float him to the mangroves later and leave him for the crocs. Too damn good for him. When they track him they'll find he didn't get very far from home. Now Omar's trying to track me, too."

Branch went below and took a closer look at the provisions the Grouper had stashed in the galley. There were cases of cookies, canned food, beef jerky, beer. Then he sat down in the cabin and organized the chart table. He checked the engine room and saw he had half a tank of diesel for the inboard motor and a full tank of fresh water.

Then he went back up top and drank a beer and chewed on some jerky.

"I want to know why you think Omar's tracking *you*," Victor asked, taking a drink from the bottle of Cuban rum Branch had given him. "You weren't at the protests."

"I did some work for him. Surely you know that by now."

"What kind of work?"

"I betrayed him. When I helped Pam hide. When I didn't finish a job he gave me to do. Yesterday."

"Yesterday. You were with me on that deep dive yesterday. What job?"

Branch was relieved when his cell phone buzzed. But then he saw it was Mel. He didn't answer.

"The job was me," Victor said. "And you didn't do the job. That's why Omar's after you. You never wanted to be involved with this fight before. Whatever it was that changed you, I'm glad you're on our side now."

"I'm not on your side. Just got some business to settle. I have a meeting with Dr. Thompson today. Then I'm gone."

"Dentist appointment? Today? With Omar on your ass?"

"Yeah, today," Branch said. "I'd best get on up to Bali's campsite, too. Warn her that things have gone to shit. She doesn't carry a cell phone."

"I know. She doesn't use them. I tried to give her one, same as you, but she hates the cell towers. She's pretty well hidden at that turtle beach, so she's safe. You're the only one she ever took there. Anybody else know how to get there?"

Branch looked at the shore road and saw Fibbi's squad car speeding away from the lighthouse, toward the wild side's northern beaches and swamps. Toward Bali's turtle beach.

Chapter Thirty-Six

A Roll in the Sand

"There's this spot I know up north," Fibbi said into his cell phone, his foot heavy on the accelerator, his squad car speeding past the dunes and the reeds of the wild side shore road. "We dug there for turtle eggs when I was a kid. I don't know. It might be the place."

"Pretty fucking great," Omar said sarcastically into the phone. He lit a cigarette, inhaled it furiously then pounded the desk in the jewelry store office. "A place you know as a kid. Great."

"What about the old woman?"

Omar unfolded the deed on his desk, ran his finger down the length of it and smiled.

"Just bring me the Bali girl. You do this, you get nice and fat sitting in the air-conditioning, no? I need a security director for the new mall."

Fibbi hung up the phone and stepped on the gas. A rented car zoomed by, heading the other way, and his radar unit beeped. *Eighty in a forty*, he noted, staring at the red digits lighting up on his dashboard and flashing across the interior of the squad car. He lifted his foot, reached for the switch to light up the roof and started to turn around, but then he hesitated.

"Security director," he said to himself. "Air-conditioning." He hated to pass up on an easy hundred bucks, but he drove on, barely slowing to navigate the curve as the road turned back inland. Then he veered onto the dirt road that led into the swamps and rugged beaches of the island's northern tip.

He bumped along for more than a mile, looking for tire tracks in the rain-washed sandy road. Then he turned the squad car around, looping through the trails and winding past the clusters of twisted palms.

After meandering for an hour, he stopped, got out and lit a cigarette. He could smell the rich sargasso drifting in from the wild shore, less than a hundred meters to the east. He heard the waves crashing and the squawking of frigate birds scavenging the beach. He threw his cigarette down and ventured into the scratchy mangroves, following the sound of the birds. The birds that were circling high above, waiting for turtle eggs to hatch.

Fibbi almost bumped into Bali's Jeep, hidden under low-hanging calabash branches. He peered past the jungle onto the beach and saw the tent, camouflaged at the edge of the mangroves. Bali, wearing only her golden bikini bottoms and a scuba mask, was coming back toward the tent, her hair wet and slicked back from a swim in the ocean.

Her sinewy shoulders gleamed in the sun and her abs rippled as she walked across the sand. And her breasts, Fibbi observed, were soft and feminine and muscular at the same time. She wasn't armed. He stumbled out onto the beach, his thick rubber-soled boots plowing through the wet sand. Bali stood her ground and watched him come at her.

"Bali Mukherjee?" Fibbi asked, out of breath from his rumble across the sand.

"You know who I am." Bali glanced toward her tent, where she'd left the Beretta. "From the protest at the jail. What do you want?"

Fibbi gawked at her dark body as he caught his breath.

"Security director," he muttered. "Air-conditioning." He knew he just should take her straight to Omar. But instead he took another look at her toned figure and at her brown, erect nipples, then looked up and down the beach. They were totally alone.

"You need to come with me. There's a problem. The old woman at the hotel needs you."

Bali started toward the tent but Fibbi blocked her path.

"What kind of problem?" she asked.

He looked at her breasts again and then his breath was jagged.

"Eggs are hatching. That's why you were out there. Helping them get away."

"What do you want?"

"Who's going to help *you*? Get away? When I was a boy I used to come up here to harvest eggs. You get them right before they hatch and they're crunchy. Like a deviled egg but with a nice baby turtle inside. Delicious."

Bali looked down the beach where baby turtles were escaping the clutch and crawling toward the water.

"Nutritious," Fibbi said. "Makes me hard." He stroked Bali's toned shoulder with one hand. "Used to bring my girl over here. We'd soft boil those crunchy eggs and then roll on the beach all night long."

"Is that all you want?" Bali asked. She didn't back away from him. "A roll on the beach?"

Fibbi put his other hand between Bali's thighs, cool from the ocean, sliding it up until he felt the warmth from her bikini bottoms.

Bali grabbed his wrist, stepped back in the sand, then pivoted as she delivered a quick, twisting sidekick to his groin. Fibbi hunched forward and Bali kicked again, landing her heel to his throat. He fell back, grabbing her leg and taking her down with him.

Fibbi slapped at Bali but hit only sand as they rolled and tumbled along the beach. When they stopped, his face was in the wet sand. Bali sat on his back and twisted his arm behind him. She raked the gun out of the holster on his leg and pressed it to the back of his neck.

"There's the roll in the sand you wanted, Sheriff."

Fibbi spat sand. The frigates were squawking all around him, and then he looked out toward the water. He could see the crooked tracks where the baby turtles had been crawling down to the sea. Their tumble across the sand had landed them directly on top of the clutch of turtle eggs.

"Yeah," he said, and he laughed. "The eggs should be nice and crunchy. Let's take a look."

He clawed down into the sand with his free hand until he felt the slime of the eggs, warm and wet and ready to burst with turtle life. Then he pushed his face down into the clutch and began thrashing and breaking the eggs.

"Give me the gun or I'll break all these motherfuckers," Fibbi yelled, banging down on the clutch with his forehead and clawing at the eggs with his hand.

Bali drew back the hammer on Fibbi's gun and pressed the barrel down harder against his oily flat-topped scalp. "Roll over."

He turned over in the wet sand, his face covered with broken egg matter, a turtle hatchling clenched in his teeth. He gulped it down and smiled at her.

"Now I'm ready for you."

He swung wildly, missing, and then she bashed him hard with the butt of the gun. Fibbi screamed again in pain, cowering away from her on the beach. Bali jumped to her feet, hurled the gun into the surf and ran for her Jeep.

She fired it up and roared away on the sandy, bumpy road. In her rearview mirror she could see Fibbi limping into his squad car, coming after her.

Chapter Thirty-Seven

FM 182

Gonzago arrived home at the villa that night, enraged. A county sheriff's deputy, lurking with his radar gun in the dark curves of FM 182, had pulled the Maserati over as Gonzago was driving home from the club. "And it's not just that he doesn't know who I am," Gonzago complained. Len was away on the rigs, so he talked to whoever would listen—young Branch.

"I had the scanner on, he never even called me in," Gonzago fumed, pouring himself a rum over ice in an amber tumbler. He plopped down on one of the courtyard's poolside teak chaise lounges and reclined into the four-inch-thick cushions covered in colorful Afghan Kazak wool.

"He wanted money. Marquette, I think was his name, the son of a bitch, his shirt pockets looked like they were stuffed. I gave him what I had on me, just a couple hundred. It's just that he's being so damn tricky and so unsafe, hiding in the trees like that, you know? Shooting radar at me in the dark, his lights all turned off then lighting up the roof and giving me a heart attack. He's going to get somebody hurt. You want to do something for me?" he asked Branch absentmindedly. "Go kill that motherfucker. Or at least convince him to change professions. He's not serving a purpose except to make his trailer payments, probably kicks some back to the county judge. And I already pay him plenty."

Branch knew he wasn't serious, but it sounded like an opportunity to practice his tactical surveillance skills, so he grabbed up the gear he would need—Tantal with scope, police scanner, celly jammer, binoculars, tactical helmet with night vision goggles—and drove his truck out into the county to the red clay roads that ran parallel to FM 182. He parked, strapped on the helmet, fired up the infrared and hiked up the ridge through a grove of loblolly pines to the hillside overlooking the Houston highwayman's haunt. With the goggles on, in total darkness, lying low on a soft carpet of pine needles, he could see the front bumper of the squad car lurking on the far side shoulder of the blacktop as if it were broad daylight.

After about five minutes a car came speeding toward him through the curve. The cruiser's lightbar strobed and invaded the darkness, illuminating the yellow stripes and the tall pines as an old El Camino—gray with primer, a dent in the rear quarter panel, chrome Cragars with baby moons—pulled off. The scanner squawked in Branch's earpiece as the officer called in the vehicle plates.

"El Camino, looks like 1973, Texas, one eight zero, uh, Romeo Foxtrot Alpha."

Branch flipped up his night vision goggles in the red flashing glare and went to his binoculars to watch the transaction. The radio conversation squall continued in his ear, then the pudgy deputy rolled out and strutted up to the driver's side window. The license and insurance were handed out by the El Camino's young male driver, the officer went back to the cruiser, the scanner screeched again, and a few minutes later he emerged with his clipboard. Undoubtedly ruining the dude's evening, Branch noted, but the deputy never seemed to put the pinch on for cash, like he had with Gonzago, and it all seemed pretty normal.

The El Camino rolled slowly away. *This ticket is a hit on his budget, but it's gonna be a sweet ride when he gets the dent out and puts the paint on*, Branch thought. The squad car turned around and resumed its position in hiding in the darkness of the trees. The next car through, after a pause of about ten minutes, was a shiny new Jeep Grand Wagoneer. For variety Branch watched the scene through the infrared sights of the Tantal rifle, but this time the deputy stayed off the radio. Branch understood why when he saw the driver handing a wad of cash out the window.

Over the next hour there were two more pullovers—an old Honda Civic, cop on the radio and a ticket written; later a new model Dodge Challenger repro, radio silence and another cash bribe paid. Through it all, Branch had the deputy in the crosshairs, one in the chamber with the safety off, and tickling at the trigger he had to remind himself that Gonzago had only been joking. After the Challenger drove away and all was black in the piney woods again, Branch put the rifle down and went back to his goggles.

It was almost an hour before the next car, a '96 Toyota Camry, came dashing around the curve. Again, the deputy lit up the roof, destroying the darkness and irradiating the loblollies in red and blue flashing fright. The Camry quickly pulled over to the gravel shoulder and the officer, staying off the air once more, rolled out and swaggered up to the driver's side window.

Branch switched again from the night vision goggles to his binoculars to study the interaction. "License and insurance," he could read on the deputy's lips, and after documents had been handed out and then back in, he could clearly see the fuzzy, pink steering wheel and the driver through the windshield—attractive, female, curly red hair, and about twenty—pleading her case.

"Perhaps we could handle this another way?" Branch read on the officer's lips. After more conversation, the door opened, the young driver slid over to the passenger side and the deputy got in, the Camry heaving under his weight. He shifted around in the seat, grabbed the curly red hair with his right hand, and then the girl's head disappeared below the dash.

To hell with Gonzago, Branch thought, and he went back to the Tantal. He zeroed in with the scope on the deputy's face, writhing, smiling, laughing behind the Camry's windshield as he pushed down forcefully on the back of the girl's curly red coif. No clear shot, so he lowered the rifle down to the officer's chest. He took a quick, shallow breath, trembled slightly with excitement, remembered to flip that switch inside of him. And then—as he prepared to squeeze off—there was only calm and quiet.

But he hesitated. He fidgeted with the scope, recalibrating the crosshairs again to the middle of the deputy's starched shirt. He thought back to the buck he'd killed with Grandpa. That killing had served a purpose, but he remembered how unsatisfying it had been, and he recalled the two Mexicans. *Just isn't right. I'm no better than him with his radar gun if I do the job like this. From a distance.* Anyway, he couldn't tell if the officer was wearing a vest or not. And the girl. There would be a witness. And what a mess it would make of her car, and her life. Besides, it was totally unauthorized.

So he lowered the Tantal and packed away his binoculars and scanner and goggles. He took a final look down at the Camry, now wobbling flagrantly from side to side, then turned his back on FM 182 and reluctantly scurried through the loblollies down to his truck, parked on the red clay below.

Branch drove slowly back into Houston, telling himself that ignoring it all was the best move, the only move. As he neared the villa, he thought again of Camry girl and her fuzzy, pink steering wheel. He remembered how Grandpa had taught him to turn the other cheek. But it didn't ring true. It would stay with her forever.

But what could he have done? As traumatic as it must have been for her, a dead cop and a bloody car would have made it even worse. She'd have been victimized, she'd have been blamed for the killing. There was nothing he could have done. He slowed down to turn right into the villa.

Impulsively he pushed down on the pedal and veered left instead. If she could read about it in the news, he thought, she might feel better about it. She *would* feel better about it. Still traumatized, but she would feel better. So he accelerated away from the villa and drove back into the city, pondering his options.

He parked the truck near downtown, shoved latex gloves, toboggan, scanner, jammer, and his programmable immobilizer into his pack, and walked to a used car lot a few blocks away. After checking for security cameras, he crept onto the lot and used the immobilizer to open and fire up a shiny red Mustang—*Low Miles, Leather, Built-In Radar!*—and then he was following the same path the Camry and its young driver had taken, speeding back into the wooded curves of FM 182. As he neared the spot, Branch shifted into fifth and pushed in on the pedal, the Mustang rumbling nervously. The radar detector issued a series of *blaps* and *bleeps* and then there was the squad car's obnoxious red beacon blazing behind him. Branch looked inquisitively, hopefully down at the police scanner on the seat beside him as he pulled over. There was nothing but quiet static.

"License and insurance, please," the officer said robotically as Branch punched the power window button down.

"Evening, Officer ... Marquette," Branch said, noting the name on the tag and the Kevlar vest clearly bulging under the stiff blue shirt. "Had to get in close. Yep, I can see that now."

Marquette twitched and shined his flashlight anxiously about the interior of the Mustang. Branch's face was lit up by the flashlight, and though it was the middle of summer, a black toboggan was perched on top of his blond locks.

"Do you know why I've pulled you over?"

"You didn't call this one in, so, yeah, I think I do. But I'm not into that. You got a stain on your trousers, Marquette."

"I'll warn you just once to be friendly, now."

"Friendly. A lawman in the state of Texas. You even know what Texas means? I mean how it's derived?"

Marquette twitched again. "What now? I need to see your license and insurance."

"It's from the Indian word *Tejas*," Branch said, ignoring him. It was one of the first things Grandpa had taught him. "Means 'friendly.' And you *ain't* friendly."

"You talk a lot. Seemed like you was in a hurry to get somewhere."

"Somewhere? I'm there."

"You like to talk, we can talk," Marquette said, and with his pudgy palm he nudged his holstered service revolver. "You can talk to the judge if you want."

"No, I won't be talking to the judge. It was a judge sent me here to talk to *you*. To tell you it's time to find a new occupation. Even if it's flippin' burgers, he said, it'll give your life more purpose than this. But now, after seeing how unfriendly you are, a talkin'-to won't do. You got no purpose. And you never will."

"Purpose?" Marquette smacked his suddenly dry lips, swallowed and laughed nervously. "I got you doin' ninety in a fifty-five. But ..."

"But what?" Branch asked. He tingled with anticipation, delighted with Marquette's edginess. Panic whispered to him—telling him to forget about Camry girl, to forget about the whole thing, to take the ticket and be gone—so he blew Panic a little kiss and continued.

"Your life, Marquette. Not good. Not strong. You got to find a new path and make reparations to the girl."

"What girl?" Marquette demanded, clumsily pulling at his revolver. "Step out of the car, motherfucker! Now."

Branch pulled the toboggan down over his face and threw open the car door. Then he was out and was on him. He grappled the .38 away, bashed the deputy on the forehead with it, pushed him down on the blacktop and sat on his chest. He bashed him again, frightened by his own flickering silhouette against the trees in the red light. Then he put the revolver to Marquette's temple and clicked back the hammer.

"What girl? What girl. The girl in the Camry. And I'm here to kill you for what you did to her."

Branch eased off the hammer. "But not the easy way," he said, and he tossed the .38 into the woods. Then he stood and dragged the cowering Marquette by his collar to the squad car and hoisted him inside. He climbed in after him, pushed him down in the front seat. He closed the door, turned off the lightbar, then took a moment to enjoy the sudden blackness.

He wrapped the coiled cord of the radar gun around the deputy's neck. Marquette whimpered and thrashed his thick black boots against the windshield.

"All cops *ain't* bad. But, Marquette, you're bad," Branch said, and then he yanked hard on the cord like he was firing up the chainsaw back at the farm. He held the cord tight, strangling him slowly with it.

"By the way," Branch said, tugging the cord a bit tighter. "That was a '72 El Camino, not a '73. They changed the trim package in '73. But '72, now that was a good year. Idiot."

Marquette looked at Branch in confusion through bloodshot, bulging eyes. The kicking continued for a brief moment, then the whimpering stopped and the officer's legs flopped limply down onto the dash. The windshield was smashed like some poisonous glass spider's web, and the soft red light from the radar console—"*9-0*" it strobed in the darkness of the squad car—flickered across Marquette's bloated, burnished face, chalky white from asphyxiation, his body a heap in the passenger seat.

Branch got out, took the video unit from the trunk and walked slowly to the Mustang. He looked back, saw the glow from the radar unit still flashing its fractal semaphore through the cracked glass. Then he got in and pushed the button. The Mustang growled at him fearfully as he wheeled around and drove away, and then it was only purring in relief as he eased it back down through the wooded curves of FM 182, back down toward the city lights of Houston. He returned the car to the auto lot, wiped it down, took his tools and things and walked back to the truck. *Gonzago does not need to know about this.*

He drove carefully back to the villa and slept well that night, but in the morning, it was all over the papers. Branch denied it, but Gonzago knew. He railed on about it the entire weekend. Finally, during their weekly Sunday night barbecue in the courtyard, Branch relented and admitted it. Deep inside he *wanted* Gonzago to know. He even showed Gonzago the video, but only the final few minutes of it. Gonzago didn't need to know about Camry girl. No one did. She had suffered enough. But she would be feeling a lot better about things.

"That cop may have been asking for it," Gonzago ranted, a snifter of brandy in his hand, a platter of barbecued ribs in front of him as he watched the video of the red Mustang and the beating and the bashing and the strangulation in utter amazement. "But somebody else will just step in and take his job, you see? At least you wore gloves. You got the tape. That was all perfect. Perfect job. Amazing! He wasn't on the air? You had the jammer on? No body cam. That fucking Marquette. But there could be heat from this thing. Killing a cop is no small matter! Somebody in *your* family gets killed, they don't have the manpower to deal with it. But when they lose one of their own, they send hundreds of cops out into the streets. To look for you! And we didn't profit from it, not one fucking bit. Nonprofit. This served no purpose. Bad karma!"

But Branch knew differently.

Chapter Thirty-Eight

A Little Evil, a Lot of Good

Branch floated Elias into the mangroves. Then he sprinted north, sloshing through the ravine along the wild side shore road. When he finally got to the point where the road turned back inland, he ran straight up the beach toward turtle camp.

It was another two miles through wet sand, and Branch's heart was pumping furiously as he passed the inlet where he'd hidden the skiff, the same inlet where Bali had shot Gusano Verde. He'd been careless to betray Omar without planning for the fallout, and now innocent people were dead.

Branch saw the frigate birds swarming over the beach, and then he saw Bali's tent under the low-hanging palms. He wished she could be waiting for him in that tent. But when he saw the mess of footprints on the beach—Bali's own barefoot prints and Fibbi's heavy rubber boot tracks, and then the roughed-up patch of sand where the two had tumbled—he knew she wasn't waiting for him in the tent.

Then he heard the Jeep firing up, the tires peeling off, followed by the sound of the squad car bouncing on the dirt road. Branch ran across the beach and onto the narrow path, like a tunnel through the palm branches, and then he came to where Fibbi had spun out in the mud.

The red lights of the squad car pulsated through the ragged branches of the wind-torn palms. Branch pulled his M9 and crawled around to the cruiser's passenger side door. Rising up on his knees, he tapped on the window with the barrel of his gun and then fired one shot through the glass. Fibbi's left ear disappeared and pressurized blood and glass sprayed the interior of the squad car.

Branch scrambled to the driver's side of the squad car while Fibbi rolled out screaming, blood pouring from the side of his face. There was only a hole where his left ear had been.

"What you doing up here, Sheriff?" Branch asked, straddling him and pinning him down on the dirt road. "Looking for manatees to shoot? Turtle eggs to eat? Or you just come up here to rape Bali?"

Fibbi jammed the left side of his face down onto his shoulder and squealed in pain. "You're with *her*?"

Branch heard the sound of Bali's Jeep bumping along the dirt road, escaping to the blacktop. But he knew she wouldn't be safe for long.

"No, I'm not with her. But I should've been."

"You're on the list, too, bitch."

"I warned you before. To find a new job. I'm doing it. Going to help the world. There was something Pam told me, before Omar murdered her. It's OK to do a little bit of evil if it does a lot of good."

Fibbi lifted his head away from his shoulder. He looked at his bloody sleeve, then into Branch's face. He took a breath and trembled.

"Thought I'd have to leave the island without saying bye to you," Branch said, poking at Fibbi's bloody ear hole. "Told you I wouldn't forget about that love tap you gave me back at the jail."

"You'd better fucking leave," Fibbi said, struggling feebly against Branch's firm hold. "Omar wants you alive. But now I'll kill you myself."

"Yeah," Branch said. He looked inside the squad car and saw Fibbi's radar unit flashing its red hieroglyphics—"*8-0*"—across the interior. "Out working the radar so early? Eighty in a forty. Pick up a quick hundred for that? Or maybe a hand job from some teenage tourist girl?"

"Fuck off, bitch."

"Yeah. That's what I thought. You *weren't* looking for a new line of work."

"Air-conditioning," Fibbi begged. "Security director."

"Uh-huh. I was thinking I couldn't perform *my* particular line of work anymore. Thought I'd lost my taste for it. But I guess what Gusano Verde told me the other day is true. I just need to be more selective about it."

Then Branch reached for the coiled cord of the radar gun. "A little bit of evil."

Chapter Thirty-Nine

Now You Goin' on this Deep One with Me?

Bali stepped on the gas, tires smoking and squealing as she roared away from the beach and onto the blacktop. She slipped into her sweatshirt and accelerated the old Jeep as fast as it could go past the mudflats and dunes. Then she downshifted and ground the gears through the hairpin curve at the lighthouse, punching it again and speeding north toward Caribbean Argonauts.

Fibbi's crew had removed all of the speed bumps on the road months before—they were too effective at slowing down the speeding tourists—so Bali flew unencumbered past the southern resorts and the sea salt plant on her way to the shop.

Victor's bicycle was chained up in front, Branch's truck was across the street at the hotel, and behind the truck was a red Hummer she'd never seen before. On the beach, in front of the pier construction zone, six armed men in dark fatigues loitered with assault rifles. Bali parked, ran into the Blue Angel, and seeing no one behind the desk, she dashed across the street to the dive shop.

The door was unlocked. She pushed it open, relieved to see through the ocean-front window that the *Argos I* was still tied up at the dock, but worried that Victor and Branch weren't in the shop.

The stone floor felt cool and smooth to her bare feet. After so many days camping on the wild side, in the hot sand, in the tent, the little dive shop with its glass windows and air-conditioning felt luxurious.

270

Len slipped out of the bathroom and came up behind her.

"Can I help you with something, miss?"

Bali spun around and cringed at the sight of him: the sun damage, the cowboy costume, the skinny legs, the blackened hands, and the chromed semiautomatic pistol stuffed in his pants.

She'd never seen him before, but still, she knew who he was. Behind his brown-green eyes there was something very much the same.

"You must be Branch's father. Is he OK?"

Len smiled and tilted his hat back, exposing the deep lines in his forehead.

"I was hoping you could tell *me* that. I *am* Branch's daddy. Len Kilgore. Awful worried about the boy."

Len held out his crusty paw. She reluctantly offered her own soft hand. Then he grabbed her and pulled her to him, choking her with his forearm.

"I tell you what. You gonna tell me where he is. Him and that Victor."

Bali clawed at his arm, and her smooth, dark feet scraped against his starched jeans. She stomped down on his scaly boots, but there was no escaping Len's industrial grasp. She stopped kicking and then he loosened his hold on her.

"I came here looking for them. I don't know where they are."

"You're that Bali girl. Why'd you come back here when you know they're on the run?"

"I didn't know that. I've been camping all week. Watching the turtles hatch."

"Turtles. Why'd you come back here, then?"

"I heard that Pam was in trouble."

"The old lady? Yeah, you might say she's in a bit of a jam," Len said, biting and ripping at a roll of duct tape and pulling off a length of it while he dragged her across the shop floor. He wrapped the heavy tape effortlessly around her with one hand as he pushed her down into the chair with the other. The roll of tape crackled tightly around her, and despite her struggling she was quickly bound to the chair. "You gonna sit tight right here and tell me what you know about the whereabouts of those two."

"You're the demolitions man," Bali said. She stopped her kicking and nodded out the window toward the unfinished pilings sticking out of the turquoise water. "You work for Omar. You did that ugliness out there."

Len looked out at the abutments and the shreds of rebar protruding like metal claws from the cement cylinders.

"Yes, ma'am. That concrete set up real nice. Mighty proud of it, alright. I do indeed work for Omar. And Omar'll be wanting to talk to you. And all them others you been scheming with. See them armed guards? That's expensive. All because of you cowardly lawbreakers. Tryin' to stop a lawful project."

Bali looked out the window. "If you're going to blow up more coral you'd better hire more guards."

"Removal of marine infrastructure, actually, is what it's called. We can talk about that if you like. I tell you what, we'll get a blanket and a picnic basket and debate that bullshit all day long. But first I need you to tell me where Branch and that dive boss of his can be found."

"You knew we were in those caves. You tried to kill us, setting off those charges. You killed reefs that day. You almost got us, too."

"You're wrong about that. I didn't know you divers would be in them caves. I just did what Omar told me. But sometimes a nice dive accident does solve a problem. That would be Branch's little specialty."

"Is that why you're looking for him? So he can perform his specialty?"

"No. That ain't why." He drew his .44 Automag, tossed it nervously from hand to hand, then slammed it down on the counter. "My son has become confused the last couple of days. He forgot what his real job is. As for me, I'm just doin' *my* job."

"Some father you are. Some family."

"He *had* family," Len said. "Hell of a family. Got to travel, learn about the world. The real world. Got to learn to dive when he was just a boy. But Branch always thought he was too good for his family. Got him a diploma and he was too good. And when he was older, the family business didn't please him too much.

The business that paid all the bills. He could have been anything he wanted. How many boys get a family like that? A family who provides for 'em and is willing to leave 'em alone? Not try to control 'em? Hell, my daddy pushed me out in the fields when I was only five, and if I come in before sundown he beat me with an old rope. *That's* family. I never treated Branch that way. Never laid a hand on him. Like family. He is what he is because of me. I let him become who he was born to be."

"And what's that?"

"The rarest of all things, honey pie. A man without a conscience."

"There's nothing rare about that. And Branch does have a conscience."

"You just don't know him like I do. You stay still. I ain't gonna hurt no woman." He picked up his gun from the counter and stuffed it back in his pants, then swilled from a bottle sitting there and smacked his chapped lips.

"I know him well enough. Branch has changed. I've seen it in him. He knows the difference between right and wrong now."

"Right and wrong?" Len leaned against the counter, pressing his hat back down over his eyes, a wrinkled grin cracking over his face. "Branch lacks the capacity to distinguish between those two things. That's his greatest asset."

Then there was the sound of a car lurching to a stop in front of the shop.

"There's Fibbi now," Len said, peeking out through the blinds. "We'll see what he knows. You stay put." He grinned and patted Bali's tightly taped torso. "Too bad you didn't cooperate when you had your chance. I can't help you now."

Len opened the front door of the shop and looked at the squad car, the driver's side window smudged with brownish-red matter.

"What the hell *is* that stuff?" Len asked as he walked across the sidewalk toward the car. "You need to clean your windows, Sheriff. I can't even see you."

Then the heavy door flew open and slammed into his legs. Len moaned and dropped to his knees. Branch jumped out of the car, took the Automag from Len's waistband and pressed it against his temple.

"Branch. Shit. You know how arthritic my knees are. All those years of commercial diving. You had to hit me in the knees?"

"How's it feel, Len?"

"Well, it hurts."

"No. This cold steel up against *your* head."

"Oh, that. Hardly noticed. All in a day's work, ain't it?"

"Get back inside. Stay low. So the guards on the platform can't see."

Inside the shop, at Branch's direction, Len took out his blade, cut the tape away from Bali, and helped her up. Then he slumped down in the same chair and threw the knife to the floor.

"Family," he said to Bali. "Just like we was talkin'."

Bali looked at Branch, pointing the gun at Len.

"I came to find out about Pam," she said, gently pulling at the tape that stuck to her brown arms. "Fibbi told me something. Is it true, Branch? That Omar took her?"

"Yeah," Branch told her, but then he hesitated. She didn't know. It wasn't going to be easy. He'd gone to Cuba to help Pam. Then he'd hid her on the *Ogygia*. But none of it had been enough.

"It's worse than that. He killed her, Bali. Got her to sign the deed somehow, then he killed her. The Grouper, too."

Bali's tears exploded down her face and she crumpled against Branch's chest.

"You get going," he said. "Get back to your turtles. You won't have to worry about Sheriff Fibbi anymore. I'll know where to find you when it's done."

Bali wiped her tears away. "When what's done? Pam was my friend, too. I'll stay and help you."

"Just get going. Chinchamos is going to need you. You and Victor. Take care of those turtles."

Bali pressed in closer to him and shook her head. "I shot at a man on the beach last week. I may have missed him, but my aim will be better next time. I'll kill him."

"Don't do it. You won't feel any better."

"What should I do?"

"Let *me* do it."

"Remember what I said? A few people standing together against what's wrong can change the world."

"Indeed," Branch said, and he smiled at her. "It's the only thing that ever has. We can stand together, then. There's a Hummer parked down the street. Big, ugly thing. There's something in there I can use." Branch handed her the keys he'd taken from Carlsbad. "You'll need these."

Bali parted the blinds and peeked south toward the Blue Angel. "I see it. What's in there?"

"Carlsbad's rifle. Wrap it in one of these wetsuits and bring it back here to me."

"Won't this Carlsbad have a problem with that?"

"No," Branch said flatly, and he casually tossed Len's Automag from one hand to the other. "He won't. Just make it quick."

"It ain't right," Len said, after Bali had gone to retrieve the rifle. "Omar killing the old woman. I can't condone that. I tell you what, I didn't know about that. But Carlsbad? If you got his car keys you must have killed him. Because he was trying to kill you. Am I right? A fair duel. How'd it go down?"

Branch said nothing.

"I can tell you don't feel too good about it." Len nodded toward the bottle on the counter. "Have a drink."

Branch just looked at the bottle.

"We all have our own ways of killing the pain," Len said. "You got your own way. Look, son, we can't change what happened to Pamela. Our job now's to protect Gonzago's investment. You come back with me to Omar now and I'll do my best to see he forgives you going rogue."

"I don't work for Omar anymore. Time for you to rethink your position with him, too."

"Don't try it on your own, Branch. You need guys like Gonzago. Like Omar. You're just a tool. You got no conscience and you don't appreciate what a gift that is. Don't try to make decisions for yourself."

"You made quite a mess out there, Len," Branch said, pacing the floor in front of the windows that overlooked the channel. "I think you got a choice to make. I'm giving you a chance to clean up that mess."

"Clean it up? Why?"

"That pier's not going in. The footings have to come down. The rubble will be a good foothold for the reef to start growing back."

Bali came back in the shop holding the long wetsuit bundle. Branch laid Len's Automag down on the counter and unwrapped the bundle. He looked at the gray and black rifle, menacing with its scope and suppressor, and shook his head.

"You can make a real mess of a man with a thing like this. All without ever having to look him in the eye. Stoner SR-25. Good to get this off the streets. What a beautiful piece. What an ugly piece. They would've given me one of these if I'd made it through."

He pulled back the bolt on the rifle and checked the chamber. "Still got one chambered, Len. From when Carlsbad was trying to make a mess of *me* the other day."

Len looked at the rifle and nodded. "Well, it all comes out in the wash, then, don't it? It's yours now."

"I don't want it anymore. Might have one more use for it, I guess. Might have use for you, too. You've got access to the platform. To the explosives. The fuses and the timers. We'll do a little dive together, tonight. Something you never had much time for, back in the day."

"A dive? Where?"

"Through the Garganta del Diablo. I've become quite fond of that little cave dive. Comes out right there in Paradise Shallows. Right out on the pier site."

"I'll be coming along for that dive, too," Bali said.

"But it's deep. Way below one thirty."

"I can put aside the rules for this one dive, I think."

"Fine. How about you, Len? You coming with us?"

Len cleared his throat, crossing his arms as he slumped down further in the chair. "What exactly are you suggesting here, son?"

Branch looked out toward the water, then poked the barrel of the Stoner against Len's chest. "Well, I suppose another way to say it is this, Len. *You goin' on this deep one with me, or you gonna be a pussy and I'll have to tell ever'body?*"

Chapter Forty

Swim with the Dolphins

It was almost dark. They lugged the double tank rigs down to the dock, pushed off in the Zodiac and rowed away silently. When they were clear of the demolition platform and the guards, Branch fired up the outboard and then they were skimming south over the smooth twilight waters toward the lagoon entrance.

Branch steered the inflatable into the little freshwater river that flowed from the lagoon, and in a few minutes they were anchoring in the crystal teardrop cenote.

"You'd never know this place is back up in here," Len said, gawking at the mangroves in amazement. "Seems like we're all alone up in here."

The silence was broken by a flock of swallows whizzing by, making a final pass hunting flies before the darkness came down.

"Yeah," Bali said. "All alone up in here. Just us and these little birds. Seems like yesterday I was sitting right here, getting ready to do a dive with Pam. The Grouper, too."

"You made it out alive from that dive," Len said. "All of you. For a while anyway, I reckon. That blast on Paradise Shallows, I can see now it was a little reckless, if you was down below here when it went off. And I can see why you wouldn't want to lose a place like this. But I tell you what. I was just earnin' my pay when I set those charges."

"That blast started a really bad chain of events, Len," Branch told him. "Just like Victor said it would. We're going back down there now, through the deep caves to Paradise Shallows. What we're going to do there, it won't bring back Pam or the Grouper. But we're going to try and set things right."

They eased into their rigs then slipped out of the skiff and into the tranquil waters. The glow of the twilight faded fast upon their descent. All three divers switched on their lights and then the cenote illuminated like a blue lantern. Branch led them out of the cavern zone and into the ominous, dark shaft that plummeted straight down.

At two hundred Branch felt the sweet numbness come over him, and he remembered the girl's name. *Calypso*. He shrugged off the thought of her—there would be time for that later—and he continued to navigate the tight, deep passages that led them down into the Lower Room. He took a moment to shine his light at the scrape marks on the ceiling. Then they continued into that stretch of tunnel that would lead them straight into Paradise Shallows.

When Branch felt the warm, salty water surging in from the ocean he turned off his light. Len and Bali did the same, and then they kicked silently and imperceptibly out of the cave and into Paradise Shallows.

The construction lights glared and glowered above them on the surface, and the divers finned softly along the bottom, raising no sand, until they were in the shadow of the demolition platform. Len took a breath off his regulator, slipped out of his rig and glided up to the surface wearing only his mask and fins. Moments later a large crate, lowered from a rope, appeared next to Branch and Bali, and then Len was free diving back down to the bottom, quiet, smooth and strong like a dolphin. He expertly swung back into his scuba rig, took a breath and cleared his regulator. He shot Branch the OK sign, smiled, and winked at him through his mask. Branch smiled, nodded, and signaled back.

All three divers looked up at the surface to see if the momentary blast of bubbles had been seen by the guards on the beach. But all was quiet. Len signaled that he was ready to do his work on the pier's footings, so Bali and Branch kicked north, out of the construction zone and into darkness, leaving their lights turned off.

When they came to the outer fence of Omar's Swim With the Dolphins Park, Branch took the bolt cutters from his tool pouch and cut through the thick chain links. It was hard work, but within a few minutes he'd sheared away a hole in the fence big enough for even the largest of the captive dolphins to swim through.

And swim through they did, clicking and squealing in delight at Branch and Bali as they waggled their powerful tails toward the depths and the freedom of the open sea.

"See you down there," Branch said to them through his regulator. "See you down *there*."

Chapter Forty-One

Stone Nap Murder

The boat was docking right in front of her. Melanie tried not to look as she waited on the municipal pier, a ticket in her hand. She couldn't let her busy little mind run away from her. Not with the job that was at hand.

She stole a glance at the boat. One hundred twenty feet of high-speed transport, it was custom-built to move tourists back and forth across the Chinchamos channel, and optimized for pumping cash into Omar's pockets. Melanie spotted the wooden blinds that covered the windows of his private berth. A teak-trimmed deck wrapped around from the port side of the berth and extended high over the stern.

This was it, her boat ride to freedom. Or, her ride to the bottom of the Chinchamos trench. Unhappy with her lack of options, she gave in to distraction and looked at the words on the side of the boat.

Neptunos Dreamer was the name it bore boldly on its hull. For a moment Melanie was relieved. Her brain had taken a break from its usual pastime and hadn't deciphered the letters into some prophetic rearrangement. But then it came, and she gasped.

Stone Nap Murder.

It was only nine in the morning but it was already hot, and the coconut scent of cheap suntan lotion drifted in the breeze as tourists from the mainland swarmed down the gangplank. They milled about the pier, considering offers for snorkel excursions and horseback rides on the beach, the crowd slowly churning toward the storefronts along the avenue.

Omar's got it all figured out, Melanie mused. They flock off the cruise ships and the ferry, and they're funneled right into his traps. Everything from T-shirts and tequila to furs and diamonds, and they can't get enough of the stuff. Then he takes their money back across to the mainland and buys smuggled blood diamonds for pennies on the dollar.

She wondered why Omar had never hit on her in the jewelry store, and she fretted over the fact that, for the first time in her life, a straight man had found a way to resist her.

She was too seductive for him, too feminine for him, she told herself. And Fernando had assured her that Omar had simply been too busy. On the ferry, he promised, Omar wouldn't be able to resist.

Waiting now for her chance to be irresistible but needing to avoid attention until the time came, Melanie backed out of the sunlight and into the shadows of the waiting area. She glanced at her watch. Five minutes until departure, but still no sign of Omar's entourage. She felt a wave of relief. Maybe the crazy thing wouldn't happen. But then the wave surged the other way and she felt the panic. What could she do, if not this? Where could she go without money? And there was that video on Fernando's phone.

A white Land Rover pulled up to the curb, followed closely by one of Fibbi's squad cars. Dexter stepped out, scanned the avenue, and waited while the deputy stopped traffic.

Omar, wearing all black and carrying a large crocodile-skin duffel, stepped onto the sidewalk. Then a suave, silver-haired man wearing a tan suit stepped out of the Land Rover. Omar was *supposed* to be alone, but there was no turning back. One way or the other, the *Neptunos Dreamer*—the *Stone Nap Murder*—was her way out.

Dexter climbed back in, the Land Rover followed the deputy's cruiser into the burgeoning morning traffic, and then Omar and Gonzago walked past her, engrossed in conversation.

"Once the deed is filed," she heard Omar say. "The banks are happy." Gonzago was smiling and nodding. "The construction on the pier can resume."

They walked on past the ticket office and boarded the *Neptunos Dreamer* on a ramp that had been lowered for them. They disappeared into Omar's private berth and the ramp was pulled back in quickly.

Disembarking tourists filtered out of the ferry and then passengers bound for the mainland stormed up the main ramp. Six uniformed deputies milled about the pier, scanning the crowd.

She waited in the shade until she saw Fernando make his way on board with his backpack. The throng subsided, so she slipped off her jacket, left it on the bench, and walked toward the ramp. She eyed her reflection in the window of the ticket office and confirmed that what Fernando had told her was true: in her little black minidress, she was lithe, adorable, totally irresistible.

Before she could finish admiring herself, she was nearly knocked down by a man rushing toward the ramp. She didn't see his face, but from the blue scrubs and the antiseptic scent she knew it was Dr. Tommy Thompson bounding past her to board the ferry. *Of course.* It was Friday, and Dr. Thompson would be in a hurry to get home to his wife on the mainland.

Melanie worried for a moment. But Dr. Thompson had always been a pushover. He shouldn't be a problem at all. Not today. And after today, she wouldn't be making trades with the landlord for the rent, not ever again.

"You sure this is safe?" Gonzago asked, peering out through the blinds and scanning the crowd. He glanced down at Omar's huge reptilian satchel. "I mean, you are carrying a million bucks in there."

"Absolutely," Omar said, dropping ice cubes into a glass and pouring vodka over them. He smiled as he remembered that it was actually *two* million in the large case. Two hundred lovely little sandwiches. One mil for his diamond purchases, plus an extra million left over when he never had to pay Pam for the mangroves. Gonzago didn't need to know about his little budget surplus, he thought, and then he could indulge in some extra goodies on this buying trip. Right after he filed the deed with the bank on the mainland. And then his life would be all good again.

"I love riding the ferry," he said, handing Gonzago the drink. He poured another one and sat down on the leather couch next to him. "Incognito. I walk through the crowd, they have no clue who I am. Like having a private yacht, but making me thousands of dollars each trip, no? Instead of *costing* me money. All the overhead on the yachts and the planes, eating me up. No, *this* is the way to go. Everything makes money. Anything, anybody, that don't make the money is gone. *Gone*! Any problem with the boat, we call the Mexican Navy. The government, they pick up the tab."

"Low overhead. Profit, even. I like that."

"The ferry ride, it sells out every trip, no? We squeeze another hundred passenger seats in here next month. Code violation, but I got that taken care of already."

"A real cash machine," Gonzago said, but he looked nervously through the window at the passengers boarding the *Neptunos Dreamer*. He didn't want to be part of an overcrowded ferry disaster like he was always reading about.

"A cash machine, like the new pier will be," Omar assured, immediately thinking of ways to push Gonzago out of the picture when he was no longer needed. "A cash machine that maintain itself. The cruise ships, they bring the suckers in. They swim with the dolphins. They buy the T-shirt. They see the *paraíso*. We gross a hundred mil a year on it, no? Five mil a year to fund the corporation, and we show a loss on the paper. All of the maintenance on the pier, it come out of the corporation. The rest of the cash? In the pocket."

"Right. How did you finally get Mrs. Linton to come to terms?"

"Business acumen, you might say," Omar told him, tapping his suit coat's inside pocket to feel the deed.

"Yes, I can see that," Gonzago said skeptically. "It's a shame she drowned just one day after becoming a rich woman."

"You hear about that already?" Omar reached out and clinked his glass against Gonzago's. "Some people, they no can handle the prosperity."

He laughed heartily but Gonzago remained silent.

Omar got up to pour two more drinks and glanced out the window toward the crowd.

"Here come something, Gonzago," he said enthusiastically. "She coming on board now. Check her out!"

Gonzago squinted out the blinds and saw Melanie prancing up the ramp.

"Umm-hmm. Now that *is* a work of art. You know her?"

"That her! That her! Mel Lamy! The piece of tail you want to meet. Branch's little *chula* he take to Cuba?"

"You weren't kidding. The ass and the legs and all of that. Is Branch with her?"

"No. You no need to worry about Branch," Omar said, peering over Gonzago's shoulder. "He leaving the island, one way or the other. Your new boy Carlsbad, he got a better attitude. Anyway, you hear what Branch say at the restaurant. They break up. I introduce you."

Gonzago nodded, but he didn't like what Omar had said about Branch. Branch belonged to *him*. And that thing with Pamela.

"You only have this one private room?" Gonzago asked. "What is it? About an hour trip across?"

Omar smiled back. It would be a small price to pay—a few hundred for Melanie—to keep Gonzago and his ten-million-dollar investment happy.

"Yeah, just the one. I like to spend time out there in the cantina. Keep an eye on the cash flow, no? I bring her back here for the lunch. With you."

He spun open the safe underneath the bar, pushed the bulging satchel in, and slammed it shut. "I be back. The good times, they just beginning for us, Senor Obeto. Lock the door behind me."

In the darkest corner booth of the *Neptunos Dreamer's* cantina, Dr. Thompson nervously sipped on a Bloody Mary and muttered uninhibitedly to himself. "C-can't do it anymore. C-can't stand her anymore." He was distracted momentarily as he saw Melanie strut by and take a seat at the bar, but then he laughed to himself and continued his rambling. "Yeah. No. C-can't d-do it anymore."

In another dark corner of the cantina, Fernando also watched Melanie as she found her perch on a barstool. He scrutinized her carefully as she adjusted her black minidress and quickly touched up her lipstick. She was good for this, he knew. And then he pushed the button on his cell phone, smiling as he scanned the shots of her on the office floor at the jewelry store.

Out in the middle of the Chinchamos channel, Branch lay with his belly down on the warm teak deck of the *Ogygia*. Through high-powered binoculars he scanned the horizon to the west. Seeing the first plume of exhaust from the *Neptunos Dreamer*, he smiled, then patted Carlsbad's rifle, lying beside him on the deck.

Back on board the ferry, Omar left the private berth, pushed his way through the swarm of passengers milling about the main cabin and glided into the cantina. He quickly spotted Melanie, sitting at the bar and stirring her drink, her solid black dress and perfect pale skin a lovely contrast to the tourists' bright outfits and splotchy sunburns.

"*Hola,* Mel Lamy," Omar said, pushing in next to her and signaling the barman for a drink. "Vodka, rocks. You go to *la playa* on the mainland today? Why is it we never spend the time together? Since Vinnie, he send you down here, I stay too busy, no?"

Melanie smiled, relieved by Omar's attention but repulsed by him at the same time. She forced herself to subtly press against him as she sipped her cocktail.

"Why, of course you have, Senor Rasgado," Melanie said, drinking her drink in immeasurably small sips. "Been *too* busy."

"You call me Omar."

"What a delight to see you, Omar, and what a surprise. And on the ferry boat, of all places."

"*Sí*. I own this ferry. Business on the mainland today. I have an important associate, he waiting in my stateroom right now. He want to meet you, no? A private lunch."

His associate, thought Melanie. *The man in the tan suit. He was cute.* And then she was relieved she wouldn't have to be alone with Omar. But it was Omar's million she was after.

Melanie quickly glanced down the length of Omar's black-clad torso to confirm he didn't have the satchel with him. "Your stateroom? Yes, lunch would be nice."

"Seven, *sí*?" Omar asked. He took a wad of folded bills from his front pants pocket and slid it across the bar. "Vinnie, he tell me you get seven for the hour. New York prices, they higher. But I feeling generous today."

"Seven hundred is a *wonderful* gift," Melanie said, slipping the wad into her purse, and thinking that a million would make an even more wonderful tip.

Then Melanie was alone in the private berth with Gonzago. He poured her a drink, took her hand, and kissed her delicately on the neck. In spite of her nerves, she was attracted to him, and she felt the anxiety of the job mingling with a rising desire for him. The guy obviously had manners, had class. It had been such a *long* time since New York.

She set her drink down and pulled the straps of the minidress off her shoulders. Then she led his lips down to her breasts while unbuckling his belt and tugging at his silk trousers. She caressed him with one hand, reaching for her purse with the other.

He brought his hand up between her thighs. "What have you got on?" he asked. "You're wearing a swimsuit? I guess you're heading for the beaches on the mainland, huh?"

Then quickly she had her metallic-pink Liliput pistol pointed into his crotch. "I'm heading for a beach, somewhere, but not on the mainland, I'm afraid, darling."

"What about lunch?"

"I regret I'm unable to lunch today. I really do. Where's the satchel?"

"Oh, the satchel," Gonzago said, and he shook his head as he shifted his gaze from her bare breasts down to the little pink gun in her hand. "That's what this is about? Too bad. That damn satchel. Bad karma. He put it in the safe. Behind the bar."

She kept her gun pointed at him as she moved behind the bar and looked at the safe.

"It's a Pierce and Hamilton," she said. "A goddamn P & H! Goddamn that Fernando. It'll take me an hour. Open it."

"I surely would, if I only could. But I assure you, Mel, I don't have the combination. And I'd like to know where you think you're going after you get in there."

Melanie wondered about that herself. It looked like a long jump off the private deck, and the ferry's wake churned the water below into a frightening froth. She'd worn a tight pair of swim shorts under her dress, but the water looked cold and black. What if Dexter was late in the speedboat? What if he never showed up at all?

"Get your pants back up," she commanded, pushing her fright away while pulling the straps of her minidress back over her shoulders. "We're going to the bar. Tell Omar we want him to join the party."

"Damn. You, me *and* Omar? Not so fun for me. Can we bring another woman in, too?"

"Of course we can. Right after I shoot your cock off."

"Oh my God," said Gonzago. "Sexy *and* desperate. I do believe I love you. Even your gun is cute. And look at me. Still ready to go. Even though you're pointing it right at me. Mel Lamy, if we both come through this alive, perhaps you'd consider working for me? Or marrying me?"

She blushed, flattered by the tiny amount of truth she could detect in Gonzago's proposal. But she quickly recovered and tapped the gun against him again.

"Of course I will. Let's do it. Let's fall in love. But later. Right now, *this*," she said, pushing the gun in a little harder, "is the extent of my love for you." Gonzago carefully lowered his hands, zipped up his Italian slacks and fastened the button.

Then there was a knock at the door. Melanie checked the peephole as she pressed the Liliput into Gonzago's ribcage.

"Looks like we won't have to go to the bar after all," she whispered. "It's Omar."

The thing might work out anyway, she thought. The gun felt good in her hand as she pressed it into Gonzago's belly. It actually worked; you pointed it at someone and told them what to do, and they did it. Wonderful. And how beautiful it was, too, all pink and shiny and powerful.

"We'll try to arrange a proper *ménage à trois* for you soon, darling," she said quietly, "but for now, let him in. And do be cool. I'm far more desperate than you think."

"I think I will," Gonzago whispered back. "I have a theory about desperate people. They genuinely scare me. You're obviously not working just for profit. Darling. I take that very seriously. Since it's not *my* money you're after, I'm inclined to follow your advice. But please, do be careful with *that*."

Gonzago looked down at the gun and admired her ivory hands and flawless red fingernails. He shook his head, grinned, then twisted the deadbolt and opened the door.

Omar fell forward into the berth. Dr. Thompson stormed in after him, holding a silenced silver Ruger semiautomatic.

"Nobody b-b-better f-f-fucking move!"

Melanie pointed her little pink gun at him, then at Omar, and then shifted it back to Gonzago. Dr. Thompson kept his own gun pointed at Omar's head.

"Thompson?" Melanie was furious. "What are you doing here? This is *my* thing. You're going to fuck this thing up!"

Dr. Thompson ignored her. "Open the safe, Omar! M-Mel, be c-cool."

"You two are working together?" Gonzago asked. Melanie and Dr. Thompson pointed their guns briefly at each other then quickly pointed them back at Gonzago and Omar.

"No," Gonzago said, answering his own question. "I guess not. I picked one hell of a day to take my first ride on your ferry boat, Omar. You're being robbed. Twice."

"Open that m-m-motherfucker," Dr. Thompson said. He fired a silenced round next to Omar's ear and mahogany splinters burst from the thick wood wall. Omar quickly moved behind the bar and dialed the combination.

"That a lot of money in there," Omar said. He flung the safe door open and then backed away. "You no walk off this boat with it. Put the gun down on the bar, now, and we work something out, no?"

Dr. Thompson pulled the satchel out of the safe, appraised its weight, and tossed it to the floor. Then he pointed his Ruger at Omar's head again.

"N-now the d-deed, Omar."

Omar reluctantly took the deed from the pocket of his blazer and laid it on the bar. Thompson unzipped the satchel, scanned its contents, stuffed the deed inside then zipped it back up. He pulled a satellite phone from his pocket, slipped the headset over his ear, and quickly dialed a number.

"Stand by for the G-G-PS coordinates. I'm going nuh-now. Start the count duh-down." Then he put the phone back in his pocket and motioned Melanie, Gonzago and Omar toward the glass door that led to the berth's private balcony.

Melanie kept her eyes on the satchel and her gun on Gonzago, but she was scared of the crazy look on Dr. Thompson's face. So she followed the others out through the slider and onto the teak deck.

"Om-Om-Omar," Dr. Thompson said, pointing the gun at Omar's forehead. "Look b-back at the island."

Omar and Gonzago both turned and looked to the east toward Chinchamos's leeward shore.

290

"Three. T-two. One," Dr. Thompson counted into the headset, with great difficulty. There were three huge flashes of light, and then a series of explosions ripped along the southern shoreline.

"There goes your new p-pier," Dr. Thompson said. "A g-gift from P-Pam. Coral will be g-growing there again soon."

Omar and Gonzago stood at the rail and gazed in disbelief at the thin columns of white dust that billowed up from the former site of the new cruise ship pier at Paradise Shallows.

"Son of a bitch," Gonzago said.

"Brimstone fucking fireballs," said Omar.

"And this is from the G-Grouper." He stepped away from Omar. "See the y-yacht to the south?"

As soon as he'd said it there was a thump and a bloody little burst as the bullet from the Stoner SR-25 pierced Omar's forehead. Before he could fall to the deck, Dr. Thompson gave him a push and flipped him over the rail and out into the ferry's wake. His body flopped briefly in the turbulence, and then Omar Rasgado was gone.

Gonzago watched the water in disbelief for a moment, gazed out at the *Ogygia*—a tiny point to the south—and then eased carefully away from the rail. Melanie pointed her gun alternately between him and Dr. Thompson.

"Take it easy," Gonzago said calmly to both of them. "Thompson, is it? It's going to be fine. The three of us can work this thing out."

"I'm, um, s-s-sorry, M-M-Mel," Thompson said, again rotating his gun between her and Gonzago. "I t-told you I was sick. So sick. B-but I have a message for you."

Dr. Thompson was suddenly lucid, his eyes were clear, and for the first time in many years he spoke without stammering.

"He did it for you, Mel. He doesn't want you to live on the run. He says there's something better for you."

Then he spoke into the headset. "Mark my coordinates now. Send the boat." And then Dr. Thompson jumped from the ferry with the satchel.

The door to the berth splintered open and Fernando crashed in. He fired a shot through the open slider, missing everyone. Gonzago stripped Melanie's pink gun away from her and shot Fernando with it, exactly between the eyes. As he fell, dead, his cell phone slipped out of his pocket and tumbled onto the floor.

Melanie and Gonzago looked at each other. One of the porters from coach class peered into the berth, alerted by the loud retort of the Liliput, and Gonzago pointed down at Fernando's dead body.

"Get on the radio and call the police, or the coastguard, or the navy, or whatever you do way out here in the middle of the channel," he said. "This guy on the floor here killed Omar Rasgado. Was trying to rob us. Poor bastard. Killed by a little pink gun."

Then he looked at Melanie and he smiled.

Chapter Forty-Two

Deep Into the Diamond

Branch carried his satchel past the Greek-style columns and onto the marbled portico of the biggest and most lavish gentlemen's club in all of Veracruz, Mexico. Two men on a hydraulic boom lift were in the process of taking down the huge sign overhead that read *Obeto's Parthenon* in stone and neon letters, and were preparing to replace it with another, covered by a tarp.

In the lobby, Branch paid the fifty-dollar cover charge and then he was escorted through a stainless-steel door that led to the club floor. The quiet, well-lit foyer gave way to neon darkness and wildly thumping subwoofers. Ten naked women danced on ten different stages, and black lights glowed purple, illuminating glitter and strobing stardust across the toned bodies of the dancers.

Branch sat down at a table near a small round stage, ordered rum over ice, and admired the dark, psychedelic atmosphere of the club. Not as good as *his* club, but very good all the same.

Generously tipping the dancers with hundreds as they rotated by, he sipped the cold rum, and tried to relax.

"*Uno más ron, guapo?*" the waitress asked, before he was halfway finished with the first. Gonzago had trained them right. Thirty bucks a pour and they kept coming at you.

"Maybe later," Branch told her. He'd gotten the feel of the place, he'd loosened up a bit, and now it was time to get down to business. "But first I need to see

Senor Gonzago. Is he here?" But Branch already knew Gonzago was there—the red Maserati with the *GONZO* plates was parked prominently by the entrance.

Ten minutes later a security guard led Branch through a courtyard behind the club, past the casino, and into the saloon's private complex. A long hallway split the VIP area into several luxurious suites, available for rent to the high rollers who could afford to pay for extra privacy with the dancers. After another checkpoint they continued into a series of offices with a heavily armored counting room.

Branch waited in the cedar-paneled reception area. The young Mexican woman behind the desk typed furiously on her computer, despite her long fingernails. She occasionally looked up at Branch, curious as to what his business with Gonzago might be. She hadn't seen him before, and he wasn't in the book, but Gonzago had told her to let him wait. He would get to him when he got to him.

Finally, Branch was led into the spacious office. Festooned with wooden wall carvings and Persian rugs, it was pleasantly lit and tastefully decorated. Buddhas, bronzes, pillars, and architectural pieces occupied every inch, and the fragrance of burning champa incense filled the air.

Gonzago spun around in his office chair, snapped off his cell phone and lit a cigar.

"Fucking Branch," he said ferociously, blowing smoke toward the ceiling and eyeballing the briefcase. "You got a lot of nerve coming in here."

"Just wanted to see where I stood with you. You've got everything, Gonzago. Look at this place. Cash machine in front. Ancient Tibetan bronzes in the back. Rajasthan antique artwork on the walls. You're rolling in it. Some small losses on the Chinchamos pier? That's not going to keep *you* down."

Gonzago stoked his cigar for a moment while he pondered his reply. "You like the Rajasthan, huh? I just put it up. It's good you waited a while. I was plenty mad. What've you been doing these past months, since everything went to hell down there?"

"Turtle research. Diving."

"Turtles, diving. And now you just stroll into the club?"

"I happened to be sailing by the port of Veracruz. Thought I'd stop in for a hundred-dollar table dance and a thirty-dollar shot. Hope I brought enough cash with me," Branch said, tapping the satchel.

"Sailing?" Gonzago worked the cigar, twisted it between his lips and blew more smoke into the room. "Let me guess. In Omar's old yacht. The *Ogygia*."

Branch nodded.

"It's in a man's nature to take what he wants," Gonzago said. "You whacked that cigar impresario, didn't you? Killed him and took the boat."

"I know all about *man's* nature," Branch said. "Now it's *real* nature I'm interested in. But if I did kill him, it wasn't just for the boat."

"Want a drink?"

"Yeah. What you're having."

"Pour yourself one, will you, Branch? Behind you there. And give me another while you're up."

Branch poured out two glasses of rum then took a seat on the couch, covered with brightly colored Afghan Kazak wool.

"Let me guess, then. You took him out because he gave your landlady over to Omar."

Branch took a drink, looked into Gonzago's eyes, said nothing. He knew he was taking a chance just showing up here, but he had to know where he stood.

"You always were sentimental," Gonzago continued. "That old lady caused me so much trouble. All those millions I invested in Chinchamos. Who knows what's going to happen down there now? The journalists got their story. All those videos Dorian had stashed? Your pal Victor used them to his advantage. Environmentalists got their foot in the door. And you killed Cuban cigar man just to avenge the old lady."

"No, Gonzago. It wasn't just to avenge her, or the Grouper, either. The truth is I just got tired of Elias slapping me in the balls all the time."

"Self-defense, then, was it? That's justifiable. You came out of it with a sailboat, too. So it's not nonprofit. But those redheads on the mainland. That war cost us all too much. What's the name of that last one you didn't get to?"

"Gusano Verde. He offered me a job."

"Job offer?" Gonzago asked. He looked around the office with a pained expression. "You belong to *me*. You come in here to my own club and disrespect me like this?"

"I didn't say I was taking his offer. But he wanted me to tell you he plans to stay out of your way. With the coca."

Gonzago shrugged and blew more smoke. "Things *have* been smooth lately in that area. But that ferry robbery? A cold bore shot on the water like that. Picking off a target on a moving boat. And you said you weren't going to do the long-distance work anymore. Of course it was you."

Branch said nothing.

"That was a sorry thing Omar did," Gonzago said. "Bad karma. He had it coming to him. But that deed. And the pier. I lost a lot of money that day."

"Pam never would have signed that deed willingly," Branch said. "But she did, because she thought it would save the Grouper's life. And she thought it would save mine, too."

"That was messed up. She was wrong about it saving the Grouper. Truly tragic. And I'm wondering if she wasn't wrong about it saving you. You know I can't stand disloyalty. *Can't stand it*! And Len, too. He disappeared right after the pier got blown up."

"Len's gone back to the farm."

"And you? What's this Gusano Verde job all about?"

"Saving the planet. Nonprofit work."

"Nonprofit?" Gonzago laughed. "There you go again. What about Chinchamos?"

"Verde's funding Victor, helping him set up a proper marine park to protect the southern reefs, the mangroves, too. No pier. Clamping down on the cruise ship pollution. And those Dorian videos made it easy to get the captive dolphin facility shut down."

"Yeah, I know. Saw it on YouTube." Gonzago puffed his cigar and shook his head as he clinked the ice around in his glass. "And where would you fit in with all of that? You wouldn't be working for him in the coca trade?"

"No. He wants me to protect the ocean. Anywhere it's threatened. Anyone who violates it, like Omar was doing, and Gusano Verde will intervene. Anyone, anywhere, anytime. That's the job."

"And you're taking it?"

"No. Because I still work for you, Gonzago. Even though it sure looked like you were firing me when you brought in Carlsbad."

"Carlsbad. Another bastard that disappeared. Coyotes are overrunning my ranch now, too. Guess you wouldn't know anything about his whereabouts, would you?"

"Seems like the coyotes on your ranch are going to be safe for a while."

"You turned out just like they said you would. So, what do you want from me? A release so you can go off and do green hits for this Gusano Verde?"

"It's not my top choice. I still think there's a straight life for me somewhere. Teaching school again. But there's that mess with the navy."

"Yeah, Reiner. The feds can be very tough to deal with."

"Right. So for now, I'm just floating on the *Ogygia*. Watching, waiting. And diving. Got an air compressor installed and a desalinator, too."

Gonzago looked sternly at Branch, stroked his chin thoughtfully for a moment then broke into his roaring laugh. "You son of a gun. Take the Gusano Verde job if it makes you happy. Defender of the reefs they'll call you. But you're going to learn someday that it's money makes the world go round. Just ask that stammering fool. The one who jumped off the ferry with my million bucks."

"Dr. Thompson was desperate. Really very ill. Like you told me back in Houston, desperation can drive a man to do anything."

297

"Desperation? No. That was pure luck on top of stupidity. Do you know what I'll do to that Dr. Thompson when I find him?"

"It was really *two* million in Omar's case," Branch told him. "This case right here. The million you gave him to buy the mangroves from Pam? He kept that. Dr. Thompson asked me to bring it to you."

Branch slid the satchel across Gonzago's desk. "He was hoping you might consider it as settlement on the whole matter."

Gonzago poked his finger uncertainly at the satchel. "Really ill, is he? What's he got? Anything contagious?"

"Something bad. Conventional medicine wasn't working. But now he's going to try some alternative therapy. Deep diving therapy. In my opinion it'll cure anything. Take a look. There's something extra on top that I brought you from Cuba."

Gonzago peeked into the satchel and laughed as he pulled out the rusty, dark orange license plates sitting on top of the cash. "What the hell. Cuban license plates. They'll look good on the wall. Maybe you're right. Maybe I do have everything now."

"So we're cool?"

Gonzago tapped the side of the satchel with the Cuban plates while he pondered. He twisted his cigar and blew out another cloud of blue smoke.

"Yeah. Sure. We're cool. Yvonne's Restaurant is doing fine. My titty bars are making money. The coca money is flowing again. And maybe in the name of good karma I'll make a million dollar donation to turtle research. But none of that would've been enough. You got really lucky, Branch. You caught me at a time when I'm feeling good. Because I'm in love. Getting married, too."

"Married? I believe congratulations are in order." Branch held up his glass.

"Yeah," Gonzago said, raising his own glass. "Can't you see I'm all mellow now?"

"Who's the lucky girl?"

"Sexiest thing you've ever seen. She needed a job, so I brought her here to dance. But the first time she went onstage I could see she was too high quality for that. Turns out she's a genius with numbers. She straightened the books out. You should see last month's P&L statement. Profit! Putting the place in her name, you know, tax purposes? Changing the sign out front today. But I really am in love with her. She's on her way up here now. We're going shopping at some resale store. Then lunch. Probably just a salad."

"Healthy. That's great."

"And if it weren't for you, I guess I never would've found her. Ah, here she is now."

Branch heard the heavy wooden door open behind him, and then he saw the curious grin on Gonzago's face. He didn't need to turn around. The essence of cream and flowers enveloped him, and he felt the intermolecular forces drawing him to her then simultaneously pushing him away.

"Mel, come on in here, darling," Gonzago said. "You remember Branch. You two know each other, right?"

Later, after they had toasted the engagement—Branch with rum, and Gonzago and Melanie with champagne—they headed out to the parking lot. Branch walked with the happy couple to Gonzago's Maserati.

"I wish you would join us for lunch, Branch," Gonzago said. "Not any good Italian food here, but I guess you've had enough of that. For a while, anyway. Come and visit us anytime. I'll fix you up with a dancer. We'll go to the opera. The four of us. Show him the ring, baby."

Mel held out her pale, perfect hand. "Light is pulled deep into the diamond," she said, "creating a spiral effect, like a small stone tossed into the center of a glassy pool."

"Deep into the diamond. Yes, I can definitely see that," Branch said. He let go of her hand. "Goodbye, Mel." He kissed her on the cheek, hugged her lightly then lingered for a moment to drink her in, one final time.

"Goodbye, darling Branch. I'll think of you night and day."

"I'm happy for you, Mel. Do you have any idea how special you are?"

Melanie smiled, pushed him back gently with the tip of her index finger then pointed up toward the club's gigantic marquee, where the old sign—*Obeto's Parthenon*—was being removed and replaced with a new, bigger sign, the tarp now removed. She closed her eyes; her mind did its trick.

"I do. And they're both right. But especially the new one. You were right, Branch. There was something better for me. I'll always love you for knowing that."

Mel climbed in, the Maserati rumbled away, and then she was gone with Gonzago.

Branch looked up at the huge stone and neon letters of the new sign that hung on the facade above the Greek columns. *Mel Lamy's Parthenon*, the sign read. He admired the sign and wondered what she had meant. But then there were so many things about Melanie Lamy that he would never understand.

Later, back on board the *Ogygia* with Bali and Dr. Thompson, Branch set his sails with the tide then pointed the craft toward the open sea. They rode the westerly winds out into the Gulf and tacked south into turquoise waters. The *Ogygia* was running fast and strong in a staunch breeze, and they sailed aimlessly for two days before the winds calmed.

They anchored over unmapped shoals near a patch of dark, deep water, and then without a word, the three tanked up and perched on the edge of the boat. But before they could roll back, the satellite phone buzzed. Bali picked it up off the teak bench and peered at the screen.

"Verde again?" Branch asked her. "The guy just won't give up. I appreciate him giving us the phone to use. But tell him I need more time to think about the job. Namibia's a rough place."

"I don't know who it is," Bali answered, handing the phone to Branch. "But it's not Gusano Verde."

"Bet you thought I'd given up on finding your ass," the nasal voice droned. "That Alaska trick? Pretty good. Sent my crew up there to look for you. I wasted time in Houston looking for you, too. Just missed you in Cuba. Should have known you'd turn up as a dive bum in the Caribbean."

"How'd you get this number, Reiner?" Branch asked, barking bravely, but inside he was getting that claustrophobic feeling again. "What's up, mama?"

"I still own your ass, Branch," Reiner said. "Now that I've got a location on you, I'll be coming. You'd best sail on back—"

Branch clicked off the phone and handed it back to Bali. "Power it down. You were right all along about cell phones being harmful."

"Right," Bali said. "Maybe it would make a good artificial reef? But maybe you'd better call Gusano Verde back before we toss it. There's still the job waiting for you."

Branch nodded his head and smiled. He didn't want to do the work anymore. Not for Gonzago, not for Gusano Verde, not for Reiner. And now it looked as if the *Ogygia* wasn't the refuge he'd hoped it would be. There was only that one place that was.

"Let's just do this dive," he told her. He looked down on the teak bench at the souvenir globe sitting there, its sand calm on the bottom, its golden fish fluttering happily. "There is surely nothing more than the single purpose of the present moment."

And then all three rolled back into the warm water and kicked down. Bali leveled off at one thirty while Branch Kilgore and Dr. Thompson finned on into the fathoms. And then Calypso was throwing open the grand doors of the Deep Blue Saloon for him. Her hair was billowing purple-tip sea anemones and she wore a low-cut opera dress made of swarming dusky damselfish.

"*Conform no longer to the patterns of this world,*" she told him, a halo of glassy sweepers shimmering all around her. "*Drink deep of me. Then you can test and approve what your own destiny is. Is it really so terrible?*"

Branch had to make a decision, but for now, he knew, there were more dives to be done, more weightless, carefree drifts for him along the sandy seagrass of his narcoses.

Calypso put her arm inside his and hoisted a magnum of the finest bubbly champagne to his lips. Branch sipped it—cold, amber and analgesic—and he knew she was right. Then he raised his hands and the music started. He conducted the subaquatic orchestra, and the hawksbill turtle beside him soared and sang the majestic strains of "Nessun dorma." Schools of blue Chromis darted all around him, resonating the violin parts. The turtle stroked ever deeper into the blue, singing the aria with abandonment, with certainty, and Branch dropped down, deep down, with her.

Dr. Thompson guzzled nitrogen from his own champagne glass, nodded at Branch, his eyes rolling back with appreciation for the music. *Maybe he is sick*, thought Branch, *but maybe this is his cure. He's left his dentistry practice. Gave his family the million bucks and left. Said it was all making him sick.* And up above them, staying cautiously at one thirty, Bali looked down on the opera from her seat in the balcony box.

Branch drifted on. Slowly the music of the aria faded out, and there was only the sound of his own bubbles, and then the perfect silence of his mind. No grinding noises. A scrawny devil's sea whip sprang up from the ocean floor, its neon tip forming a question mark, again offering Branch its perpetual riddle. *Which way forgiveness?* This time Branch was sure he knew the answer. *Up. Only up.*

About the Author

Thomas Courtney Click is a writer and ocean conservationist. His earlier works have appeared in Cobalt Review, Literary Juice, Rathalla Review, and The Westerner, and focus on the human struggle to balance short-term desire with long-term vision.

Deep Blue Saloon, the author's first full-length novel, is inspired by his own nature immersion experiences, and centers on the intrigue and conflict that spark between economy and environment.

For more information on the author and his work, please visit ThomasClick.com.

You can follow "Deep Blue Saloon" on Tik Tok, Instagram, X, and Facebook.

www.ingramcontent.com/pod-product-compliance
Lightning Source LLC
Chambersburg PA
CBHW071251170626
46809CB00001B/168